Pearl
in the Mist

Pearl
in the Mist

V.C. Andrews ®

G.K. Hall & Co.
Thorndike, Maine

This Large Print edition is published by G.K. Hall & Co., USA and by Chivers Press, England.

Published in 1995 in the U.S. by arrangement with Pocket Books, a division of Simon & Schuster, Inc.

Published in 1995 in the U.K. by arrangement with Simon and Schuster Limited.

U.S. Hardcover 0-7838-1164-0 (Core Collection Edition)
U.S. Softcover   0-7838-1165-9
U.K. Hardcover 0-7451-7815-4 (Windsor Large Print)

Following the death of Virginia Andrews, the Andrews family worked with a carefully selected writer to organize and complete Virginia Andrews' stories and to create additional novels, of which this is one, inspired by her storytelling genius.

This book is a work of fiction. Names, characters, places and incidents are products of the author's imagination or are used fictitiously. Any resemblance to actual events or locales or persons, living or dead, is entirely coincidental.

The text of this Large Print edition is unabridged.
Other aspects of the book may vary from the original edition.

Set in 16 pt. News Plantin by Juanita Macdonald.

Printed in the United States on permanent paper.

British Library Cataloguing in Publication Data available

Library of Congress Cataloging in Publication Data
Andrews, V. C. (Virginia C.)
    Pearl in the mist / V.C. Andrews
      p.   cm.
    ISBN 0-7838-1164-0 (lg. print : hc)
    ISBN 0-7838-1165-9 (lg. print : sc)
    1. Large type books. I. Title.
[PS3551.N454P35   1995]
813'.54—dc20   94-40716

Dear Virginia Andrews Readers:

Those of us who knew and loved Virginia Andrews know that the most important things in her life were her novels. Her proudest moment came when she held in her hand the first printed copy of *Flowers in the Attic*. Virginia was a unique and gifted storyteller who wrote feverishly each and every day. She was constantly developing ideas for new stories that would eventually become novels. Second only to the pride she took in her writing was the joy she took in reading the letters from readers who were so touched by her books.

Since her death many of you have written to us wondering whether there would continue to be new Virginia Andrews novels. Just before she died we promised ourselves that we would find a way of creating additional stories based on her vision.

Beginning with the final books in the Casteel series we have been working closely with a carefully selected writer to expand upon her genius by creating additional novels, like *Pearl in the Mist*, *Ruby*, and the Cutler series, all inspired by her wonderful storytelling talent.

Pearl in the Mist is the second book in the Landry family series. We believe it would have given Virginia Andrews great joy to know that it will be entertaining so many of you. Other novels, including some based on stories Virginia was able to complete before her death, will be published in the coming years and we hope they continue to mean as much to you as ever.

Sincerely,
THE ANDREWS FAMILY

Prologue

Dear Paul,

I waited until the last minute to write this letter to you, mainly because I wasn't sure until now that I would do what my father asked and, with my twin sister, Gisselle, attend a private school for girls in Baton Rouge. Despite the promises I made to him, I have been having nightmares about it. I've seen the brochures of the school, which is called Greenwood. It does look beautiful, consisting of a grand structure containing the classrooms, an auditorium, a gym, and even an indoor pool; as well as three dormitory buildings, each with sprawling willow and oak trees in front; its own lake filled with lavender hyacinths; beautiful wooded grounds of red oak and hickory; clay tennis courts and ballfields; in short, everything anyone could want. I'm sure it has far better facilities and opportunities than I would have at our public school in New Orleans.

But it is a school attended by only the wealthiest, upper-class young women from the finest Creole families in Louisiana. I'm not prejudiced against wealthy people who come from highly respectable backgrounds, but I know I'll be surrounded by dozens and dozens of girls who have been brought up the way Gisselle has. They will think like her, dress like her, act like her, and they will make me feel like an outsider.

My father has great confidence in me. He thinks I can overcome any obstacles and I would be more than a match for any and all snobby girls I might encounter. He's so confident in my artistic talent that he believes the school will immediately recognize it and want to see me develop and succeed so they can get credit for it. I know he's just trying to help me shake off my doubts and fears.

But no matter how I feel about going to this school, I guess it's the best thing I could do at the moment, for it will at least get me away from my stepmother, Daphne.

When you came to visit us and you asked me if things had gotten better, I told you yes, but I wasn't telling you the whole truth. The truth was, I had almost been put away and forgotten in the mental institution my poor Uncle Jean, my father's brother, is in. My stepmother had conspired with the administrator to have me committed. With the help of a very nice but deeply disturbed young man named Lyle, I escaped and returned home. I told my father what had occurred and he and Daphne had a horrible argument. After things settled down, he came to me with the proposal to send me and Gisselle to Greenwood, the private school. I saw how important it was to him that we get away from Daphne, and I saw how happy she was that we were leaving.

So I am being pulled in two directions. On the one hand I am very nervous about attending Greenwood, but on the other I am glad to get away from what has become a very dark and dreary home. I feel bad about leaving my father. He seems to have grown years older in just a few months. Strands of gray have popped up here and there in his chestnut hair, and he doesn't stand as straight nor move as energetically as he did when I first arrived. I feel almost as if I'm deserting him, but he wants Gisselle and me to attend this private school and I want to make him happy and ease his burdens and tensions.

Gisselle hasn't once stopped complaining and whining. She is constantly threatening not to go to Greenwood. She moans and groans about having to be in a wheelchair and has everyone in the house running this way and that getting her things and satisfying her every whim. Not once did I ever hear her say the automobile accident was her and Martin's fault because of their smoking pot. Instead, she wants to blame the unfair world. I know the real reason she complains about going to Greenwood is that she's afraid she won't get what she wants whenever she wants it. If she was spoiled before, it was nothing compared to the way she is now. It makes it hard for me to feel sorry for her.

I have told her everything I know about our

backgrounds, although she still won't accept the fact that our mother was a Cajun woman. Of course, she readily accepts all I tell her about Grandpere Jack, how he took advantage of our mother's pregnancy to make a bargain with Grandpere Dumas to sell Gisselle to the Dumases. He didn't know our mother was pregnant with twins, and Grandmere Catherine kept that fact from him until the day we were born, refusing to sell me too. I told Gisselle she could have easily been the one left in the bayou and I could have been the one brought up in New Orleans. That possibility puts the shudders into her and gets her to stop complaining for a while; but nevertheless, she has a way of getting under my skin and making me wish I had never left the bayou.

Of course, I often think of the bayou and the beautiful days we had together when Grandmere Catherine was still alive and you and I didn't know the truth about ourselves. Whoever said ignorance is bliss was saying the truth, especially when it comes to you and me. I know it's been harder for you to face up to it. You, perhaps more than I, have had to live with lies and deceit, but if I've learned anything, it's that we must forgive and forget if we are to go on enjoying anything in this world.

Yes, I wish we weren't half brother and half sister, and yes, I would come running home to you and we would build our lives together in the bayou, which is where my heart really is; but this isn't the course Destiny has laid out for us. I want us to be forever friends as well as brother and sister, and now that Gisselle has met you, she wants the same. Every time I get a letter from you she insists on my reading it aloud, and whenever you make a reference to her or tell her hello, she brightens with interest. Although with Gisselle you can never tell if it's just a momentary whim.

I love your letters, but I can't help feeling a bit sad whenever I get them. I close my eyes and hear the symphony of cicadas or the owl calling. Sometimes I imagine I can actually smell Grandmere Catherine's cooking. Yesterday Nina made us a crawfish etouffee for lunch, just the way Grandmere Catherine used to make it, with a roux glazed with butter and sprinkled with chopped green onions. Of course, as soon as Gisselle heard it was a Cajun recipe, she hated it. Nina winked at me and we had a private laugh, for we both knew Gisselle had eaten it heartily before.

Anyway, I promise I will write to you as soon as we are settled in Greenwood and maybe shortly, if you are able, you will come to visit us. At least you will know where to write.

I'd like to hear about the bayou and the people there, especially Grandmere Catherine's old friends. Most of all I'd like to hear about you. I suppose a part of me wants to hear about Grandpere Jack too. Although it is hard for me to think of him and not think of the terrible things he has done. I imagine he's a pathetic old creature by now.

So many sad things have happened to us so soon

in our lives. Maybe . . . maybe we've already had our share of hardships and misfortune and maybe the rest of our lives will be full of good and happy things. Am I a fool to think so?

I can just see you smiling at me with those darling blue eyes of yours twinkling.

It's a very warm night here tonight. The evening breeze carries the scent of the green bamboo, gardenias, and camellias up to me. It's one of those nights when every sound can be heard seemingly for miles and miles. Sitting by my window, I can hear the streetcar rattling along St. Charles Avenue, and somewhere in another house someone is playing a trumpet. It sounds so sad, and yet it sounds so beautiful.

Now there's a mourning dove on the upper galerie railing, moaning its sad cry. Grandmere Catherine used to say I must wish for something good for someone the first time I hear the dove at night and wish it quickly, otherwise the dove's sad note will bring hard luck to someone I love. It's a night for dreaming and for making wishes. I'll make one for you.

Go out and call to the marsh hawk for me. And then make a wish for me.

As always,
Love, Ruby

1

First Day

The rap, rap, rapping of a woodpecker woke me out of a restless sleep. I had been awake for most of the night, tossing and turning with worry about what the next day would bring. Finally the weight of fatigue shut my eyes, and I felt myself falling into the world of twisted dreams, until once again I had a familiar nightmare. In it I was drifting in a pirogue through the swamp. The water was the color of dark tea. I had no pole; the current was taking me mysteriously along into the darkness draped with Spanish moss, ghostlike as it undulated in the slight breeze. Over the surface of the water, green snakes slithered, following my canoe. The luminous eyes of an owl peered at me with suspicion through the darkness as I drifted deeper and deeper into the swamp.

In this nightmare there was usually the sound of a baby crying. It was too young to form words, but the cry sounded very much like a call for "Mommy, Mommy." It drew me on, but usually I woke up from this terrible nightmare before I went much farther into the darkness. Last night, however, I passed my furthermost point and continued into the murky, black world.

The pirogue made a turn and moved a little faster until I could see the luminous bone-white outline of a skeleton pointing its long, thin forefinger ahead, urging me to look into the darkness, until finally I saw the baby all alone, left in a hammock on the front galerie of Grandpere Jack's shack.

The pirogue started to slow down and then, right before my eyes, Grandpere Jack's shack began to sink into the swamp. The baby's cries grew louder. I reached over the side of the pirogue to row myself along faster, but my hand became entangled in green snakes. The shack continued to sink.

"NO!" I screamed. Deeper and deeper into the murky, muddy water it sunk, until only the galerie and the baby in the hammock remained. She had a small face, the color of a pearl. I reached out as I drew closer, but just as I could finally take hold of the hammock, the galerie sunk too.

It was then that I heard the rapping of the woodpecker, and my eyes snapped open to see the morning sunlight seeping in around the curtains to light up the pearl-colored silk canopy above my dark pine queen-size bed. As if they were blooming, all the colors in the floral wallpaper brightened under the warm illumination as well. Even though I had barely slept, I was happy to wake up to so much sunshine, especially after my nightmare.

I sat up and scrubbed my face with my palms until I had wiped the Sandman's traces out of my eyes and cheeks, and then I took a deep breath and told myself to be strong and be ready and be hopeful. I turned toward the window when I heard the voices of the grounds staff as they fanned out to clip the hedges, weed the gardens, and sweep the banana leaves off the pool patio and tennis courts. My stepmother, Daphne, insisted that they always make the grounds and buildings look as if nothing had happened the night before, no matter how gusty the wind or hard the rain.

The night before I had chosen and laid out my clothing for traveling to our new school. Expecting my stepmother would scrutinize how I was dressed, I chose one of my longer skirts and matching blouses. Gisselle finally relented and permitted me to set out her things as well, although she went to sleep vowing never to get up. I could still hear her threats and vows echoing in my ears.

"I'd rather die in this bed," she whined, "than make this dreadful trip to Greenwood tomorrow. Whatever you choose for me will be what I will wear when I take my last breath. And it will be all your fault, too!" she declared, falling back histrionically in her bed.

No matter how long I might have lived with my twin sister, I never got used to how unlike we were despite our virtually duplicated faces and figures, eye and hair color. And it isn't only because of the differences in our upbringing, either. I am sure that even in our mother's womb

15

we didn't get along.

"My fault? Why would it be my fault?"

She propped herself up on her elbows quickly.

"Because you've agreed to all this, and Daddy does whatever you agree to do. You should have argued and cried. You should have thrown a tantrum. You'd think you would know how to throw a tantrum by now. Haven't you learned anything from me since you ran away from the swamps?" she demanded.

Learn how to throw a tantrum? Learn how to be a spoiled brat is what she really meant, and that was one lesson I could do without, even though she thought she had been doing me a favor by teaching me to be more like her. I swallowed back my laughter, knowing it would just enrage her more.

"I'm doing what I think is best for everyone, Gisselle. I thought you understood. Daddy wants us to be away. He thinks it will make life easier here for Daphne and him and for us too. Especially after all that has happened!" I emphasized, my eyes as big as hers could be.

She sank back in her bed and pouted.

"I shouldn't have to do anything for anyone else. Not after what's happened to me. Everyone should be thinking of me first and my suffering," she moaned.

"It seems to me everyone does."

"Who does? Who?" she snapped, with sudden energy and strength. "Nina cooks what you like, not what I like. Daddy asks your opinions before he asks mine. Beau comes around to see you, not me! Why . . . why . . . even our half brother, Paul, writes only to you, never to me."

"He always sends his regards to you."

"But not a separate letter," she emphasized.

"You've never written one to him," I pointed out.

She considered this a moment. "Boys should write first."

"Boyfriends, maybe, but not a brother. With a brother, it doesn't matter who writes first."

"Then why doesn't he write to me?" she wailed.

"I'll tell him to," I promised.

"No you won't. If he won't do it on his own . . . then . . . he won't. I'll just lay here forever, left to stare at the ceiling as usual and wonder what everyone else is doing, what sort of fun they're having . . . you're having," she added sharply.

"You don't lay here wondering about anything, Gisselle," I said, finally unable to stave off a smile. "You go wherever you want, whenever you want. You merely have to snap your fingers and everyone jumps. Didn't Daddy buy the van just so you could be taken everywhere in your wheelchair?"

"I hate that van. And I hate being taken in the wheelchair. I look like something being delivered, like breads or . . . or . . . boxes of bananas. I won't go in it," she insisted.

Daddy had wanted to drive to Greenwood in Gisselle's van, but she vowed she wouldn't set foot in it. He wanted to use it because of all the things she had insisted on taking with her. She had had Wendy Williams, our maid, in her room for hours and hours packing everything, deliberately demanding the most insignificant things just to make it all that much more difficult. My pointing out to her that we had limited space in the dormitory and we had to wear uniforms didn't dissuade her.

"They'll make space for me. Daddy said they would do all that they could to accommodate me," she insisted. "And as for wearing uniforms . . . we'll see about that."

She wanted her stuffed animals — each and every one — her books and magazines, her photograph albums, almost her entire wardrobe, including all her shoes, and she even had Wendy pack every last thing from her vanity table!

"You'll be sorry when you come home for vacations," I warned her. "You won't have the things you want here, and then —"

"And then I'll just send someone out to buy them for me," she replied smugly. Suddenly, she smiled. "If you would insist on more, Daddy would see how horrible this move is and maybe then he would change his mind."

Gisselle's conniving never ceased to amaze me. I told her that if she put half as much energy toward doing the things she had to do instead of working on getting out of her responsibilities, she would be a success at anything.

"I'm a success when I want to be, when I have to be," she replied, so I gave up on another sisterly conversation.

Now it was the morning of our trip to the school and I just dreaded going into her room. I didn't need one of Nina's crystals to predict how I would be greeted and what to expect. I dressed and brushed out my hair before going in to see how far along she was. I met Wendy in the hallway hurrying away, practically in tears and muttering to herself.

"What is it, Wendy?"

"Monsieur Dumas sent me up to help her get started, but she won't listen to a word I say," she complained. "I plead with her and plead with her to get her body movin' and she lay there like a zombie, her eyes sewn shut, pretending she's asleep. What am I supposed to do?" she wailed. "Madame Dumas will yell at me, not her."

"No one's going to yell at you, Wendy. I'll get her up," I said. "Just give me a few moments."

She smiled through her tears and wiped them off her plump cheeks. Wendy wasn't much older than Gisselle and me, but she had stopped going to school when she was only in the eighth grade and become a maid for the Dumas family. Ever since Gisselle's car accident, Wendy was more like Gisselle's whipping boy, bearing the brunt of her rages and tantrums. Daddy had hired a private duty nurse to look after Gisselle, but she couldn't tolerate Gisselle's tantrums. Neither could the second and third nurse, so the responsibility of looking to Gisselle's needs was unfortunately added to Wendy's chores.

"Don't know why you even care about her,"

Wendy said, her dark eyes as furious and bright as two shiny discs of black onyx.

I knocked on Gisselle's door, waited, and then entered when she didn't respond. She was as Wendy had described: still under the blanket, her eyes shut. I went to her window and looked out. Gisselle's room had a view of the street. The morning sunlight glittered off the cobblestone walk, and there was light traffic. Along our cornstalk fence, the azaleas, yellow and red roses, and hibiscus had all bloomed in a burst of breathtaking color. No matter how long I lived in this mansion, this estate in New Orleans's famed Garden District, I remained in awe of the homes and landscaping.

"What a beautiful day," I said. "Think of all the nice things we're going to see on the trip."

"It's a boring trip. I've been to Baton Rouge before," she said. "We'll see ugly oil refineries belching smoke."

"Oh my, she is alive!" I declared, slapping my hands together. "Thank heaven. We all thought you had passed on during the night."

"You all *wished*, you mean," she said angrily. She didn't pull herself to a sitting position. Instead, she turned and left her head sunk in the big, fluffy pillow, her arms at her sides, and sulked.

"I thought you finally agreed to go and not to make a fuss, as long as you could take everything you wanted along, Gisselle," I said with controlled patience.

"I just said I give up. I didn't say I agreed to go."

"You and I looked over the brochures. You admitted it looked like a beautiful place," I reminded her. She focused her gaze on me, her eyes small.

"How can you be so . . . so . . . agreeable? You'll have to leave Beau behind, you know," she reminded me. "And when the cat's away, the mice will play."

Beau had taken my going to Greenwood very hard when I first told him. We had been having a hard enough time as it was, continuing to see each other. Ever since Daphne had discovered my secret painting of Beau, we'd had to keep our romance quiet. He had posed nude for me and she had found the picture and told his parents. He was severely punished and we were forbidden to see each other. But time passed, and slowly his parents eased up, as long as Beau promised to see other girls as well. He really didn't, and even if he came to a school dance with someone else or took someone else for a ride in his sports car, he ended up with me.

"Beau's promised to visit as often as he can."

"But he didn't promise to become a monk," she stabbed back quickly. "I know half a dozen girls just waiting to sink their nails into him: Claudine and Antoinette for starters," she happily pointed out.

Beau was one of the most sought-after boys in our school, as handsome as a soap opera star. He merely had to turn his blue eyes on a girl and smile to make her heart pitter-patter so fast she

21

lost her breath and said or did something foolish. He was tall and well built, one of our school's football stars. I had given myself to him and he had pledged his deep love for me.

Before I'd arrived in New Orleans, he was Gisselle's boyfriend, but she loved to tease and torment him by flirting and seeing other boys as well. She never realized how sensitive and serious he could be. All boys were the same to her anyway. She still saw them as playthings, not to be trusted and not worthy of loyalty. Her accident hadn't slowed her down, either. She still couldn't be in the company of young men and not torment them with a twist of her shoulder or a whispered promise to do something outrageous when and if she and the young man were ever alone.

"I don't have a collar around Beau," I told her. "He can do what he wants when he wants," I said with such nonchalance it made her eyes widen. Disappointment flooded her face.

"You don't mean that," she insisted.

"And he doesn't have a collar around me, either. If being apart for a while causes him to find another girlfriend, someone he likes better, than it was probably meant to be anyway," I said.

"Oh you and your damned faith in Destiny. I suppose you'll tell me Destiny meant for me to be a cripple for the rest of my life, won't you?"

"No."

"What, then?" she demanded.

"I don't want to speak badly about the dead," I said, "but you and I know what you and Martin

22

were doing the day of the accident. You can't blame Destiny."

She folded her arms under her breasts and fumed.

"We promised Daddy we would go and give the school a chance. You know how things are here now," I reminded her.

"Daphne doesn't hate me as much as she hates you," she retorted, her eyes flaming.

"Don't be so sure of that. She's eager to get both of us out of her life. You know why she resents us: We know she really isn't our mother and that Daddy was more in love with our mother than he could ever be with her. As long as we're around, she can't escape the truth."

"Well, she didn't resent me until you arrived," Gisselle flared. "After that my whole life went downhill, and now I'm being carted off to some girls' school. Who wants to go to a school where there are no boys?" she cried.

"It says in the brochure that the school arranges dances with a boys' school from time to time," I said. The moment the words left my lips, I regretted them. She was always eager to pounce on any opportunity to point up her paralysis.

"Dances! Can I dance?"

"I'm sure there are many other things for you to do with a boy at Greenwood on the days they're permitted to visit."

"Permitted to visit? It sounds dreadful, like a prison." She started to cry. "I do wish I was dead. I do, I do."

"Come on, Gisselle," I pleaded. I sat on her bed and took her hand in mine. "I promised you I would do everything I could to make it easier for you, help you with your homework, whatever you need, didn't I?"

She pulled her hand back and ground her eyes dry with her small fists before peering over them at me.

"Everything I want?"

"Everything you need," I corrected.

"And if the school is terrible, you will side with me against Daddy and insist we come home?" I nodded. "Promise."

"I promise, but it has to be really terrible and not just hard with rules you hate."

"Promise on . . . on Paul's life."

"Oh, Gisselle."

"Go on or I won't believe you," she insisted.

"All right, I promise on Paul's life. You're absolutely dreadful sometimes, you know."

"I know," she said, smiling. "Go tell Wendy I'm ready to get up and get washed and dressed for breakfast."

"I'm right here," Wendy said, coming around the door jamb. "I was here waitin'."

"You mean you were spying on us," Gisselle accused. "Listening in."

"No I wasn't." Wendy looked at me, horrified. "I don't spy on you."

"Of course she doesn't spy on us, Gisselle."

"Of course she does, you mean. She likes listening in and living a romantic life through us,"

Gisselle teased. "It's that and your romance magazines, isn't it, Wendy? Or are you meeting Eric Daniels behind the cabana every night?"

Wendy nearly burst with embarrassment. Her mouth dropped and she shook her head.

"Maybe we are better off going to a private school and not being watched and spied upon all the time," Gisselle said, and sighed. "All right, all right," she snapped. "Help me wash and get my hair brushed and don't stand there looking like you were just caught with your panties down."

Wendy gasped. I turned away to hide my laughter and hurried down to tell Daddy all would be fine: Gisselle would be dressed and ready for the trip.

Ever since Daphne had tried to have me locked away in the institution and my subsequent escape, life at the House of Dumas had been difficult. Our meals together, whenever we were all available to eat together, were usually very quiet, formal affairs. Daddy no longer joked with Gisselle and me, and if Daphne had anything to say, it was usually abrupt and to the point. Most of the time was spent sympathizing with Gisselle or promising things to her.

Although something of a truce had supposedly been declared between us, Daphne never stopped complaining or looking for things to criticize about me. I think it was her constant badgering of my father that finally convinced him that shipping us off to a private school and getting us out of the house would be the wisest thing to do. Now Daphne behaved as if the idea had been hers and that it was all so wonderful for the family. My guess was she was afraid we would refuse to go at the last minute.

Daddy was alone in the dining room reading the morning paper and sipping his coffee when I arrived. A croissant with butter and some jam was on a small plate beside his cup. He hadn't heard me enter, and for a moment I was able to observe him without his being aware.

Our daddy was a strikingly handsome man. He had the same soft green eyes Gisselle and I had, but his face was leaner, his cheekbones more pronounced. Lately he seemed to have gained a little weight around his waist, but he still had a firm upper body with gracefully sloped shoulders. He was proud of his rich, chestnut-brown hair and still kept a small pompadour, but the gray strands that had invaded at his temples were beginning to appear in the back and top as well. Most of the time these days he looked tired or in deeply meditative thought. He spent less time outdoors, hardly ever went fishing or hunting, and consequently had lost the dark tan he used to always have.

"Good morning, Daddy," I said, and took my seat. He lowered his paper quickly and smiled, but I could see from the hesitation in his eyes that there had been some trouble between him and Daphne already this morning.

"Good morning. Excited?"

"And frightened," I admitted.

"Don't be. The last thing I want to do is send you someplace where you won't be happy. Believe me."

"I do," I said. Edgar appeared in the doorway with a silver tray carrying my orange juice.

"I won't have anymore than coffee and a croissant either this morning, Edgar."

"Nina won't like that, mademoiselle," he warned. His dark eyes looked darker this morning, his face glum. My gaze followed him out of the dining room and then I turned to Daddy, who smiled.

"Edgar is very fond of you and sorry to see you leaving. Like me, he knows that the brightness and the happy sound of your voice will be dearly missed."

"Perhaps we shouldn't go then. Perhaps this is a mistake," I said softly. "Gisselle is still complaining."

"Gisselle will always be complaining, I'm afraid," he said with a sigh. "No, no, regretful as it is, I think this is the best thing for you. And for Gisselle," he added quickly. "She spends too much time alone, feeling sorry for herself. I'm sure you won't let her do that at Greenwood."

"I'll look after her, Daddy."

He smiled. "I know. She has no idea how lucky she is to have a sister like you," he said, a warm smile around his tired eyes.

"Isn't Daphne coming to breakfast?" I asked.

27

"No, she's having breakfast in the bedroom this morning," he replied quickly. "Nina's just taken it up."

It didn't surprise me that Daphne would ignore us as much as possible on the day of our departure, but I half had expected to see her gloat about it too. After all, she was getting what she wanted: She was getting rid of me.

"I'll be visiting Jean on Wednesday," Daddy said. "I'm sure he'll be interested to hear all about you. And Gisselle, of course."

"Tell him I'll write to him," I said. "I will, too. I'll write long letters describing everything. Will you tell him?"

"Of course. I will visit you too," Daddy promised. I knew he felt guilty about sending Gisselle and me off to this private school because he had made that promise to visit at least a dozen times during the last week.

Edgar returned with my croissant and coffee. Daddy began reading his paper again. I started to sip my coffee and nibble on my croissant, but my stomach felt as if it had a sac au lait fish swimming in it, tickling my insides with its tail. A few moments later, we heard the whir of the electric chair that brought Gisselle down the stairs. As usual, she moaned and groaned as she descended.

"It moves so slowly. Why doesn't Edgar just come up and carry me down? Or Daddy? Someone should be hired just for that. I feel so stupid. Wendy, did you hear what I said? Stop pretending you didn't hear."

Daddy lowered his paper and gazed at me as he shook his head.

"I'd better go help her," Daddy said. He got up and went to help Wendy shift Gisselle from the stairway chair to the wheelchair on the bottom floor.

Nina came bursting out of the kitchen and stood in the doorway with her hands on her hips, glaring at me.

"Good morning, Nina," I said.

"What kind of 'good morning' is it? You don't eat what Nina has prepared. It be a trip to Baton Rouge and you need your strength, hear? I got hot grits. I got eggs beat just the way you like."

"I guess I'm too nervous, Nina. Please don't be angry," I said.

She lowered her hands from her hips and pressed her lips together as she shook her bead. "Nina don't get angry at you." She thought a moment and then approached, taking something out of her pocket. "I be giving you this before I forget," she said, and handed me a dime with a hole and a string through the hole.

"What's this?"

"You wear this around your left ankle, you hear, and no bad spirits come after you. Go on, put it around your ankle," she ordered. I glanced back at the doorway to be sure no one was looking and quickly did as she commanded. She looked relieved.

"Thank you, Nina."

"Bad spirits always hovering around this house.

Got to be vigilant," she said, and went back into the kitchen. I wasn't one to doubt charms and talismans, superstitions and rituals. My Grandmere Catherine had been one of the bayou's most respected *traiteurs,* a treater who could drive away evil spirits and cure people of various ailments. She had even helped wives unable to get pregnant to get pregnant. Everyone in the bayou, including our priest, had deep respect for Grandmere. In the Cajun world from which I had come, various voodoo and other religious beliefs were often married to produce a view of the world that was more reassuring.

"I don't like this skirt," I heard Gisselle complain as Daddy wheeled her into the dining room. "It's too long and it feels like I have a sheet over my legs. You picked it out just because you think my legs are ugly now, didn't you?" she accused.

"It's the one you agreed to wear when we picked out your clothes last night," I reminded her.

"Last night I just wanted to get it over with and get you out of my face," she retorted.

"What would you like for breakfast, honey?" Daddy asked her.

"A glass of arsenic," she replied.

He smirked. "Gisselle, why make things harder than they have to be?"

"Because I hate being a cripple and I hate the idea of being carted up to this school where I don't know a soul," she said. Daddy sighed and looked at me.

"Gisselle, just eat something so we can get

started. Please," I begged.

"I'm not hungry." She pouted a moment and then wheeled herself up to the table.

"What are you having? I'll have that too," she told Edgar. He lifted his eyes to the ceiling and then went to the kitchen.

As soon as we'd had our breakfast, Daddy went to see about all the luggage. It took Edgar and one of the grounds workers four trips to bring down everything, Gisselle had three trunks, two cartons, three bags, and her record player. I had one suitcase. Because Gisselle insisted on taking so much, Daddy had to hire someone to follow us in the van.

As I was wheeling Gisselle out to the galerie, where we could watch the loading of the vehicles, Daphne appeared at the top of the stairway. She called to us and took a few steps down. She had her pale reddish blond hair pinned up, and she wore a red Chinese robe and slippers.

"Before you go," she said, "I want to warn the both of you to be on your best behavior. Just because you're going a considerable distance away, it doesn't mean you're free to act and say whatever you like. You must remember you are Dumases and what you do always reflects on the family name and reputation."

"What are we going to do?" Gisselle moaned. "It's just a dumb girls' school."

"Don't be insolent, Gisselle. You two could bring disrespect to this family no matter where you go. I just want you both to know we have

31

friends sending their children there, so we will be well informed as to your behavior, I'm sure," she threatened.

"If you're so afraid of how we'll behave away from home, don't send us," Gisselle retorted. Sometimes I enjoyed my spoiled twin sister — especially when she annoyed our stepmother.

Daphne pulled herself up abruptly and glared down at us with her blue eyes turning icy.

"If anything," she said slowly, "you both need this school, need the discipline. You've both been horribly spoiled by your father. The best thing that could happen is for you to be away from him."

"No," I said. "The best thing is for us to be away from you, Mother." I turned and pushed Gisselle toward the door.

"Remember my warnings!" she cried, but I didn't turn back. I felt my heart pounding, the tears of rage burning just under the lids of my eyes.

"Did you hear what she said?" Gisselle muttered. "*Discipline.* They're sending us to a reform school. There will probably be bars on the windows and ugly matronly women slapping our hands with rulers."

"Oh Gisselle, stop," I said. She rattled on and on about how terrible this was all going to be, but I didn't listen. My eyes kept sweeping the street and my ears kept listening for the sound of a sports car instead. Beau had promised to be here before we left. He knew we were planning to be on our way by ten o'clock and it was already nine forty-five and he hadn't appeared.

"He's probably not going to come say goodbye to you," Gisselle teased when she caught me looking at my watch. "I'm sure he's decided not to waste his time. He probably already made a date to meet someone new today. You know it's what his parents want him to do anyway."

Despite my brave facade, I couldn't help but worry that she was right. I was afraid his parents had stopped him from coming to say goodbye to me this morning.

But suddenly, his sports car came careening around a turn. The engine roared and the brakes squealed as he came to a stop in front of our house and hopped out of the car. He raced up to the galerie. Gisselle looked very disappointed. I left her and hurried down the steps to greet him. We hugged.

"Hi, Gisselle," he said, waving to her, and then he turned me away so we could walk off and be alone for a few moments. He looked back at the luggage being loaded into the van and shook his head.

"You're really going," he said sadly.

"Yes."

"It's going to be impossible for me here now," he predicted. "Without you, my life has a gaping hole in it. The halls at school will seem empty. To lift my eyes while I'm on the playing field and not see you watching from the stands . . . Don't go," he pleaded. "Refuse."

"I have to go, Beau. It's what my father wants. I'll write you and call you and . . ."

"And I'll come see you as much as I can," he promised. "But it won't be the same for me as knowing every morning when I get up that I'm going to see you soon."

"Please don't make this any harder than it is for me, Beau."

He nodded, and we continued walking through the gardens. Two gray squirrels scurried along on our right, watching us with interest. Humming-birds flitted around the purple bugle vine while a bluejay that had settled on a low branch in a magnolia tree jerked its wings nervously above us. In the distance, a train of narrow clouds rode the crest of a sea breeze east toward the Florida Gulf Coast. Otherwise, the sky remained a soft blue.

"I'm sorry I'm being so difficult. I'm being self-ish. But I can't help it," he added. Then he sighed with resignation and wiped the strands of golden hair from his forehead. "So," he said, "you're going off to a ritzy school. I bet you'll meet a lot of rich young men, sons of oil barons who will charm you."

I laughed.

"What's so funny?"

"Gisselle threatened me this morning with you falling in love with another girl here, and now you're telling me it's going to be me who falls in love with someone else."

"I have no room in my heart for anyone else," Beau said. "You take up too much of it."

We paused, facing the old stable. Daddy told me there hadn't been a horse in it for more than twenty years. Off to the right, one of the grounds staff was completing the clipping of a banana tree, the fonds piling up beside him. Beau's words hung in the air between us. My heart ached, and tears mixed with happiness and sadness flooded my eyes.

"I mean it," Beau said softly. "I don't think a night passes when I don't think about us in your art studio."

"Don't, Beau," I said, and put my forefinger on his lips. He kissed it quickly and held my hand against his cheek.

"They can do anything they want; they can say anything they want. They can send you away, send me away, threaten, whatever, but they can't take you out of here," he said, pressing my hand to his temple, "and here," he added, bringing my hand to his heart. I felt the quickened beat and looked back to be sure no one was watching us as he pulled me closer and closer to him so he could press his lips to mine.

It was a long but soft kiss, one that sent a tingle down the back of my neck and brought a warmth to my bosom. His kisses were like little electric reminders of the passion we shared now. They awakened the memory of his touch, his fingers on my arms, my shoulders, and finally my breasts. His warm breath on my eyes brought back the image of his naked body that day he forced me to draw him. How my fingers had trembled; how they trembled now. The stirring in me was so great it frightened me, for I felt as if I could just turn and run away with him, run, run, run until we were alone in some dark, soft place, holding each other more tightly than ever. Beau aroused feelings in me that I never knew existed, feelings that were stronger than any warnings, any sensible thoughts could ever be. If they were set loose, there would be no way to rein them in again.

I pulled back.

"I've got to get going," I said.

He nodded, but as I started back, he pulled my hand.

"Wait," he said. "I want to give you this without a dozen eyes watching," He dug into his pocket and produced a small white box tied with a tiny pink ribbon.

"What is it?"

"Open it," he said, putting it into my palm. I did so slowly and plucked out a gold locket on a gold chain. The locket had a tiny ruby in the center circled with diamond chips.

"Oh, Beau, it's beautiful! But it must be very expensive."

He shrugged but smiled, indicating I was right.

"Now open the locket," he said, and I did so. Inside was a picture of him, and across from it was a picture of me. I laughed and kissed him on the cheek quickly.

"Thank you, Beau. It's a wonderful gift. I'll put it on immediately," I said. "Help me with the clasp." I handed it to him and turned around. He draped the locket between my breasts and fastened the chain. Then he kissed me on the neck.

"Now if any other boy gets close to you, he'll have to get through me to reach your heart," he whispered.

"No one else will get that close, Beau," I promised.

"Ruby," we heard daddy call. "It's time, honey."

"Coming, Daddy.

Beau and I started back. Daddy and Edgar were taking Gisselle off the galerie and transporting her to the rear seat of the Rolls-Royce. The wheelchair was folded and placed in the van.

"Beau, good morning," Daddy said.

"Morning, monsieur."

"How's everyone at home?"

"Fine," he said. Despite the passage of time and the healing of wounds, it was still hard for Daddy and Beau to speak to each other. Daphne had done so much to sensationalize and escalate the situation.

"Ready, Ruby?" Daddy asked, looking from Beau to me. Daddy knew what it meant to leave someone you love behind. His eyes were full of sympathy.

"Yes, Daddy."

Daddy got into the car, and I turned to Beau for our goodbye kiss. Gisselle had her face in the window.

"Come on, already. I can't stand sitting in here when we're not moving."

37

Beau smiled at her and then kissed me.

"I'll call as soon as I can," I whispered.

"And I'll come as soon as I can. I love you."

"Me too," I said quickly, and ran around the other side to get into the car.

"You could kiss me goodbye too, Beau Andreas. It wasn't so long ago that you couldn't wait to kiss me every chance you got," Gisselle said.

"I will never forget those kisses," Beau teased, and he leaned inside to kiss her quickly.

"That wasn't a kiss," she said. "Maybe you forgot how. Maybe you need an expert to teach you again." She flashed a look at me then and added, "Maybe you'll practice while we're away." She laughed and sat back.

Daddy conferred with the driver of the van, reviewing the route to Baton Rouge and the school just in case we got separated.

"What's that?" Gisselle asked when she saw the locket lying between my breasts.

"A gift from Beau."

"Let me see it," she said, leaning forward to take the locket in her fingers. I had to lean over so she wouldn't snap the chain off my neck.

"Be careful," I said.

She opened it and saw our pictures. Her mouth dropped open and she looked back through the window at Beau, who stood talking with Edgar.

"He never gave me anything like that. In fact," she said angrily, "he never gave me anything."

"Maybe he thought you had everything you wanted," I said.

She dropped the locket back on my chest and flopped back in the seat to pout. Daddy got into the car and looked at us.

"All set?" he asked.

"No," Gisselle said. "I'll never be set for this."

"We're all set, Daddy," I said. I looked through the window at Beau and mouthed, "Goodbye. I love you." He nodded. Daddy started the engine and we began to pull away.

I looked back through the rearview mirror and saw Nina and Wendy on the galerie, waving. I waved to them and to Edgar and to Beau. Gisselle refused to turn around and wave goodbye to anyone. She sat with her eyes forward, hatefully.

When we reached the gate, I lifted my gaze slowly up the front of the great house until my eyes focused on a window in which the curtains had been drawn back. I studied it, and as the shadows moved away, I saw Daphne standing there gazing down at us.

She was wearing a smile of deep satisfaction.

2

Further from the Bayou

As we drove out of the Garden District and headed for the highway that would take us to Baton Rouge, Gisselle grew unexpectedly quiet. She pressed her face to the window and gazed out at the olive-green streetcar that rattled down the esplanade, and she looked hungrily at the people who were sitting out in the sidewalk cafés as if she could smell the coffee and the freshly baked breads. New Orleans always seemed busy with tourists, men and women with cameras around their necks and guidebooks in their hands, gazing up at the mansions or at the statues. Some parts of the city had a quiet, lazy rhythm, and other parts were bustling and busy. But the city had character, a life of its own, and it was impossible to live here and not become part of it or stop it from becoming part of you.

When we passed under the long canopy of spreading oaks and passed the great homes and yards filled with camellias and magnolia trees, I too suddenly felt melancholy. The feeling surprised me. I hadn't realized that I had grown to think of this as home. Perhaps because of Daddy, because of Nina and Edgar and Wendy, and certainly because of Beau, I felt a sense of belonging now. I realized I would miss this part of the world that I had come to claim as mine almost a year ago.

I would miss Nina's good cooking and her superstitions and rituals to ward off evil. I would miss the chatter I overheard between her and Edgar when they argued about the power of an herb or the evil eye. I would miss Wendy's singing to herself as she worked, and I would miss Daddy's bright, warm smile when he greeted me every morning.

Despite the clouds of tension Daphne had kept hovering over us from the moment I arrived in New Orleans, I knew I would miss the great house with its enormous entryway, its impressive paintings and statues, its rich, antique furniture. What a thrill it was for me during my early days to leave my room and descend that grand stairway like a princess in a castle. Would I ever forget that first night when Daddy brought me to what would be my room and he opened the door on that enormous bed with the fluffy pillows and linen all in chintz? I would miss the painting above my bed, the picture of the beautiful young woman in a garden setting feeding a parrot. I would miss my large closets and my large bathroom with a tub I could soak in for hours and hours.

I had become so comfortable in our mansion,

and yes, I had to confess, somewhat spoiled. Having grown up in a Cajun toothpick house built out of cypress with a tin roof, a home where the rooms were no bigger than some of the closets in the House of Dumas, I was bound to fall into awe when I confronted what was rightly *my* home too. I would surely miss the evenings when I sat out on the patio and read while the bluejays and mockingbirds flitted around me and settled on the railings of the gazebo to stare. I would miss smelling the ocean in a breeze and occasionally hearing a foghorn in the distance.

And yet I had no right to be unhappy, I thought. Daddy was spending a great deal of money to send us to this private school, and he was doing it so we wouldn't have gray, sad days, so that we would enjoy our teenage years unmolested by the dark burdens of past sins, sins we had yet to understand or even discover. Maybe in time, some joy would return to Daddy's life. Perhaps then we could all be together again.

There I was, believing in blue skies when there were only clouds on the horizon, believing in forgiveness where there was only anger, jealousy, and selfishness. If only Nina really had a magical ritual, a chant, an herb, an old bone we could wave over the house and its inhabitants and turn out the dark shadows that lived in our hearts.

We made a turn and had to come to a stop to wait for a funeral procession to go by, something that accented my sudden mood of despair.

"Oh great," Gisselle complained.

"Just be a moment," Daddy said.

Half a dozen black men in black suits played brass instruments and swayed to their music. The mourners who followed carried furled umbrellas, most swaying to the same rhythm. I knew that if Nina were with us, she'd see this as a bad omen and cast one of her magical powders in the air. Later, she'd burn a blue candle, just to be sure. Instinctively I reached down and fingered the charmed dime she had given me.

"What's that?" Gisselle asked.

"Just something Nina gave me as a good luck charm," I said.

Gisselle smirked. "You still believe in that stupid stuff? It embarrasses me. Take it off. I don't want my new friends knowing you're so backward and you're my sister," she ordered.

"You believe in what you want to believe in, Gisselle, and I'll believe in what I want."

"Daddy, will you tell her she can't bring those silly charms and things to Greenwood. She'll embarrass the family." She turned back to me. "It's going to be hard enough keeping your background a secret," she claimed.

"I'm not asking you to keep anything about me secret, Gisselle. I'm not ashamed of my past."

"Well you should be," she said in a humph, glaring at the train of the funeral procession as if annoyed that someone had the audacity to die and have his or her funeral just when she wanted to pass.

As soon as the procession did go by, Daddy con-

43

tinued and we turned toward the exit that would take us to the interstate and Baton Rouge. It was then that the reality of what was happening pinched Gisselle again.

"I'm leaving all my friends. It takes years to make good friends, and now they're gone."

"If they were such good friends, how come not one came by to say goodbye to you?" I asked.

"They're just angry about it," she replied.

"Too angry to say goodbye?"

"Yes," she snapped. "Besides, I spoke to everyone on the telephone last night."

"Since your accident, Gisselle, most of them hardly have anything to do with you. There's no sense in pretending. They're what are known as fair-weather friends."

"Ruby's right, honey," Daddy said.

"Ruby's right," Gisselle mimicked. "Ruby's always right," she muttered under her breath.

When Lake Pontchartrain came into view, I gazed out at the sailboats that seemed painted on the water and thought about Uncle Jean and Daddy's confession that what was thought to have been a horrible boating accident was really something Daddy had done deliberately in a moment of jealous rage. He had spent every day since and would continue to spend every day hereafter regretting his action and suffering under the weight of the guilt. But now that I had lived with Daddy and Daphne for months, I felt certain that what had happened between him and Uncle Jean was primarily Daphne's fault and not Daddy's. Perhaps that was another reason why she wanted me out of sight. She knew that whenever I looked at her, I saw her for what she was: deceitful and cunning.

"You two are going to enjoy attending school in Baton Rouge," Daddy said, flicking a gaze at us in his rearview mirror.

"I hate Baton Rouge," Gisselle replied quickly.

"You were really there only once, honey," Daddy told her. "When I took you and Daphne there for my meeting with the government officials. I'm surprised you remember any of it. You were only about six or seven."

"I remember. I remember I couldn't wait to go home."

"Well now you'll learn more about our capital city and appreciate what's there for you. I'm sure the school will have excursions to the government buildings, the museums, the zoo. You know what the name 'Baton Rouge' means, don't you?" he asked.

"In French it means 'red stick,' " I said.

Gisselle glared. "I knew that too. I just didn't say it as quickly as she did," she told Daddy.

"*Oui*, but do you know why it's called that?" I didn't and Gisselle certainly had no idea, nor did she care. "The name refers to a tall cypress tree stripped of its bark and draped with freshly killed animals that marked the boundary between the hunting grounds of the two Indian tribes at the time," he explained.

"Peachy," Gisselle said. "Freshly killed animals, ugh."

"It's our second-largest city and one of the country's largest ports."

"Full of oil smoke," Gisselle said.

"Well, the hundred miles or so of coastline to New Orleans is known as the Petrochemical Gold Coast, but it's not just oil up here. There are great sugar plantations too. It's also called the Sugar Bowl of America."

"Now we don't have to attend history class," Gisselle said.

Daddy frowned. It seemed he could do nothing to cheer her up. He looked at me and I winked, which made him smile.

"How did you find this school anyway?" she suddenly inquired. "Why couldn't you find one closer to New Orleans?"

"Daphne is the one who found it, actually. She keeps up on this sort of thing. It's a highly respected school and it's been around for a long time, with a long tradition of excellence. It's financed through donations and tuition from wealthy Louisianans, but mainly from an endowment granted to it from the Clairborne family through its sole surviving member, Edith Dilliard Clairborne."

"I bet she's a dried-up hundred-year-old relic," Gisselle said.

"She's about seventy. Her niece Martha Ironwood is the chief administrator. What you would call the principal. So you see, you're right in what we call the rich old Southern tradition," Daddy said proudly.

"It's a school without boys," Gisselle said. "We

46

might as well check into a nunnery."

Daddy roared with laughter. "I'm sure it's nothing like that, honey. You'll see."

"I can't wait. This is such a long, boring ride. Put on the radio at least," Gisselle demanded. "And not one of those stations that play that Cajun music. Get the top forties," she ordered.

Daddy did so, but instead of brightening her outlook it lulled her to sleep, and for the remainder of the trip, Daddy and I had some quiet conversations. I loved it when he was willing to tell me about his trips to the bayou and his romance with my mother.

"I made a lot of promises to her that I couldn't keep," he said regretfully, "but one promise I will keep: I will see that you and Gisselle have the best of everything, especially the best opportunities. Of course," he added, smiling, "I didn't know you existed. I've always thought your arrival in New Orleans was a miracle I didn't deserve. No matter what's happened since," he added pointedly.

How I had come to love him, I thought as my eyes watered with happy tears. It was something Gisselle couldn't understand. More than once she had tried to get me to hate our father. I thought it was because she was jealous of the relationship that had quickly developed between us. But she was forever reminding me that he had deserted my mother in the bayou after he had made her pregnant while he was married to Daphne. Then he compounded his sins by agreeing to let his father

47

purchase the baby.

"What kind of a man does such a thing?" she would ask, stabbing at me with her questions and accusations.

"People make mistakes when they're young, Gisselle."

"Don't believe it. Men know what they're doing and what they want from us," she'd said with her eyes small, the look cynical.

"He's been sorry about it ever since," I had said. "And he's trying to do what he can to make up for it. If you love him, you will do whatever you can to make his suffering less."

"I am," she'd said joyfully. "I help him by getting him to buy me whatever I want whenever I want it."

She's incorrigible, I thought. Not even Nina and one of her voodoo queens could recite a chant or find a powder to change her. But someday, something would. I felt sure of that; I just didn't know what it would be or when.

"There's Baton Rouge ahead," Daddy announced some time later. The spires of the capitol building loomed above the trees in the downtown area. I saw the huge oil refineries and aluminum plants along the east bank of the Mississippi. "The school is higher up, so you'll have a great view."

Gisselle woke up when he turned off the Interstate and took the side roads, passing a number of impressive-looking antebellum homes that had been restored: two-story mansions with columns. We passed one beautiful home that had Tiffany glass windows and a bench swing on the lower galerie. Two little girls were on it, both with golden brown pigtails and dressed in identical pink dresses and black leather saddle shoes. I imagined they were sisters, and my mind started to create a fantasy in which I saw myself and Gisselle growing up together in such a home with Daddy and our real mother. How different it all could have been.

"Just a little farther," Daddy said and nodded toward a hill. When he made another turn, the school came into view. First we saw the large iron letters spelling out the word GREENWOOD over the main entrance, which consisted of two square stone columns. A wrought-iron fence ran for what looked like acres to the right and to the left. I saw some buttonbush along the foot of the fence, its dark green leaves gleaming around the little white balls of white. Along a good deal of the fence were vines of trumpet creepers with orange blossoms.

From both sides of our car we could see rolling green lawns and tall red oak, hickory, and magnolia trees. Gray squirrels leapt gracefully from branch to branch as if they could fly. I saw a red woodpecker pause on a branch to look our way. There were stone walkways with short hedges and fountains everywhere, some with little stone statues of squirrels, rabbits, and birds.

An enormous garden led to the main building — rows and rows of flowers, tulips, geraniums, irises, golden trumpet roses, and tons of white, pink, and red impatiens. Everything looked trimmed and manicured. The grass was so perfect it looked cut by an army of grounds workers armed with scissors. Not a branch, not a leaf, nothing appeared out of place. It was as if we had ventured into a painting.

Above us the main building loomed. It was a two-story structure of antique brick and gray-painted wood. Dark green ivy vines worked their way up around the brick to frame the large panel windows. A wide stone stairway led up to the large portico and great front doors. There was a parking lot to the right with signs that read RESERVED FOR FACULTY and RESERVED FOR VISITORS. Right now the lot was nearly full of cars. There were parents and young girls meeting and greeting each other, old friends obviously renewing friendships. It was an explosion of excitement. The air was full of laughter, the faces full of smiles. Girls hugged and kissed each other, and all began talking at once.

Daddy found a spot for us and the van, but Gisselle was ready to pounce with a complaint.

"We're too far from the front, and how am I supposed to get up that stairway every day? This is horrible."

"Just hold on," Daddy said. "They told me there is an approach built for people in wheelchairs."

"Great. I'm probably the only one. Everyone will watch me being wheeled up every morning."

"There must be other handicapped girls here, Gisselle. They wouldn't build an entryway just for you," I assured her, but she just sat there scowling at the scene unfolding before us.

"Look. Everyone knows everyone else. We're probably the only strangers at the school."

"Nonsense," Daddy said. "There's a freshman class, isn't there?"

"We're not freshmen. We're seniors," she reminded him curtly.

"Let me go find out how to proceed first," Daddy said, opening his door.

"Proceed home, that's how," Gisselle quipped. Daddy waved to our van driver, who pulled up alongside our car. Then he went to speak to a woman in a green skirt and jacket who was holding a clipboard.

"All right," Daddy said, returning. "This is going to be easy. The gangway is off right there. First you go to registration, which is being held in the main lobby, and then we'll go to the dormitory."

"Why don't we go to the dormitory first?" Gisselle demanded. "I'm tired."

"I was told to bring you here first, honey, so you can get your information packet about your classes, a map of the grounds, that sort of thing."

"I don't need a map of the grounds. I'll be in my room all the time, I'm sure," Gisselle said.

"Oh, I'm sure you won't," Daddy replied. "I'll get your chair out, Gisselle."

She pressed her lips together and sat back with her arms folded tightly under her bosom. I got out. The sky was crystalline blue and the clouds were puffy and full, looking like cotton candy.

There was a magnificent view of the city below and beyond, a view of the Mississippi River with its barges and boats moving up and down. I felt like we were on top of the world.

Daddy helped Gisselle into her chair. She was stiff and uncooperative, forcing him to literally lift her. When she was situated in it, he started to wheel her toward the gangway. Gisselle kept her gaze ahead, her face twisted in a smirk of disapproval. Girls smiled at us and some said hello, but Gisselle pretended not to see or hear.

The gangway took us through a side entrance into the wide main lobby. It had marble floors and a high ceiling, with great chandeliers and a large tapestry depicting a sugar plantation on the far-right wall. The lobby was so large the voices of the girls echoed in it. They were all standing in three long lines, which line they were in depending on the first initial of their last names. The moment Gisselle set eyes on the crowd, she moaned.

"I can't sit here like this and wait," she complained loudly enough for a number of girls nearby to overhear. "We don't have to do this at our school in New Orleans! I thought you said they knew about me and would take my problems into consideration."

"Just a minute," Daddy said softly. Then he went to speak to a tall thin man in a suit and tie who was directing the girls into the proper lines and helping them to fill out some forms. He looked our way after Daddy spoke to him, and a moment later he and Daddy went to the desk upon which was the sign A–H. Daddy spoke to the teacher behind our desk, and she then gave him two packets. He thanked her and the tall man and quickly returned to our side.

"Okay," Daddy said, "I've got your registration folders. You're both assigned to the Louella Clairborne House."

"What kind of name for a dorm is that?" Gisselle said.

"It was named after Mr. Clairborne's mother. There are three dorms, and Daphne assured me that you two are in the best of the three."

"Great."

"Thank you, Daddy," I said, taking my packet from him. I felt guilty getting the preferential treatment along with Gisselle and avoided the jealous gazes of the other girls who were still waiting in line.

"Here's your packet," Daddy said. He put it into Gisselle's lap when she didn't reach for it. Then he turned her around and wheeled her out of the building.

"They told me there's an elevator to get you up and down in the main building. The bathrooms all have facilities for handicapped people, and your classes are all pretty much on the same floors so you won't have great difficulty getting from one to the other in time," Daddy said.

Reluctantly, Gisselle opened the packet as we descended the gangway. On the first page was a letter of welcome from Mrs. Ironwood, strongly advising that we read each and every page of the orientation materials and concern ourselves especially with the rules.

Two of the dormitories were located in the rear and to the right and the third dorm, our dorm, was located in the rear to the left. As we drove slowly around the main building toward our dorm, I gazed down the slope and saw the boathouse and the lake. A solid layer of water hyacinth stretched from bank to bank, their lavender blossoms pale with a dab of yellow on the center petals, surrounded by light green leaves. The water of the lake shone like a polished coin.

To our left, directly behind the building, were the playing fields.

"What beautiful grounds," Daddy said. "And so well looked after."

"This is like being in a prison," Gisselle retorted. "You have to go miles to find civilization. We're trapped."

"Oh, nonsense. There will be plenty for you to do. You won't be bored, I assure you," Daddy insisted.

Gisselle fell into her sulk as our dorm came into view. Structured like an old plantation house, the Louella Clairborne dorm was almost hidden from view by the large oaks and willow trees that spread their branches freely in front. It was a building constructed out of cypress, and it had upper and lower galeries enclosed with balustrades and supported by square columns that reached to the gabled roof. As we drove up, the gangway, built on the side of the front galerie, came into view. I didn't want to say it, but it did look like it had been especially made for Gisselle.

"Okay," Daddy said. "Let's get you two settled in. I'll go tell the dorm mother we're here. Her name's Mrs. Penny."

"That's all she's worth, probably," Gisselle quipped, laughing at her own sarcasm. Daddy went up the front steps quickly and disappeared within.

"You're going to have to push me all the way from this place every day to the classes, you know," Gisselle threatened.

"You can roll yourself along easily, Gisselle. The walkway looks smooth."

"It's too far!" she cried. "I'd be exhausted by the time I arrived."

"If you need to be pushed, I'll push you," I assured her with a sigh.

"This is so stupid," she said, folding her arms tightly under her breasts and glaring at the front of the dorm. Moments later Daddy appeared with Mrs. Penny, a short, plump woman with gray hair woven around her head in thick braids. She wore a bright blue and white dress over her stout body. When she drew closer, I saw she had innocent blue eyes, a jolly, wide smile with thick lips, and cheeks that ballooned to swallow up her small nose. She clapped her hands together as I stepped out of the car.

"Welcome, dear. Welcome to Greenwood. I'm Mrs. Penny." She extended her small hand with its thick, stubby fingers, and I shook it.

"Thank you," I said.

"You're Gisselle?"

"No, I'm Ruby. That's my sister, Gisselle."

"Great, she doesn't even know which is which," Gisselle muttered from within. If Mrs. Penny heard her, she didn't let on.

"This is so wonderful. You two are my first set of twins ever, and I've been dorm mother at the Louella Clairborne House for over twenty years. Hello, dear," she said, leaning over to look into the car at Gisselle.

"I hope we have a room on the ground floor," Gisselle snapped.

"Oh, of course you do, dear. You're in the first quad, the A quad."

"Quad?"

"Our rooms are designed around a central study area. Four bedrooms share two bathrooms and the sitting room," Mrs. Penny explained. "All of the other girls, except one new girl," she added, her smile flicking off and then on again, "are already here. They're all seniors like you two. They can't wait to meet you."

"And we're just dying to meet them," Gisselle sang sarcastically as Daddy brought her chair around again. He helped her into it and we headed for the house.

The dorm had a large front parlor with two large sofas and four high-backed cushion chairs around a pair of long, dark wood tables. There were standing lamps beside the sofas and chairs and standing lamps, chairs, and smaller tables in the corners. In one corner a small settee and another high-backed chair faced a television set. All the windows in the room had white cotton curtains and light blue drapes, and the hardwood floor had a large blue oval rug under and around the sofas. An enormous portrait of an elegant-looking older woman adorned the rear wall. It was the only painting in the room.

"That's a picture of Mrs. Edith Dilliard Clairborne," Mrs. Penny said in a reverent voice and nodded. "When she was a lot younger, of course," she added.

"She looks old there," Gisselle said. "What does she look like now?"

Mrs. Penny didn't respond. She continued her description of the house instead.

"The kitchen is at the rear," she said. "We have set times for breakfast and dinner, but you can always get a snack when you want. I try to run the house as if we're one big happy family," she told Daddy. Then she looked down at Gisselle. "I'll take you for a tour once you're settled in. Your quad is right this way," she added, indicating the corridor on our right. "First we'll show you where you're at, and then we'll get your things in. How was your ride from New Orleans?"

"Nice," Daddy said.

"Boring," Gisselle added, but Mrs. Penny ignored her and never changed her smile. It was as if she couldn't hear or see anything unpleasant.

Along the walls of the short corridor were hung

oil paintings of New Orleans street scenes interspersed with portraits of people I imagined to be descendants of the Clairbornes. The hall was lit by two hanging chandeliers. At the end of it was the sitting room Mrs. Penny had described: a small room crowded with two pairs of cushioned chairs like the ones in the main lobby, an oval dark pine wood table, four desks at the rear, and standing lamps.

The sound of someone laughing drew our attention to the first door on the right.

"Well, we might as well start our introductions here," Mrs. Penny said. "Jacqueline . . . Kathleen."

A girl at least five foot eleven, if not six feet tall, stepped out first. I saw by the way she slouched when she walked that she was conscious of her height. She had a narrow face with a long, pinched nose above a small mouth with thin lips that became pale rubber bands, especially when she smirked. I was soon to learn that smirking was her favorite expression. Her bitterness was centered in her disapproving brown eyes that more than not were merely slits. She looked like someone spying on the world, an uninvited guest who attended a party for people much happier than herself.

"This is Jacqueline Gidot. Jacqueline, meet Gisselle and Ruby Dumas and their father."

"Hello," Jacqueline said, looking quickly from me to Gisselle. I imagined that the girls in our quad had been warned that Gisselle was in a wheelchair, but of course, actually confronting her in it was more impressive.

"Hi," I replied. Gisselle just nodded, but she looked up with new interest when Jacqueline's roommate stepped up beside her.

"And this is Kathleen Norton."

Kathleen had a warmer smile. She was a dirty blonde about our height, but much wider in the hips and shoulders.

"Everybody calls me Kate," she told us quickly and followed that with a quick giggle.

"Or Chubs," Jacqueline inserted dryly. Kate just laughed. It looked to me like she laughed after most everything she said or everything and anything said about her. It was more of a nervous reaction. Her blue eyes were wide as if in awe when she looked at Gisselle, and I knew Gisselle wasn't going to like that.

"Chubs?" Gisselle snorted.

"She eats everything in sight and hoards candy all over our room like a gray-tail squirrel," Jacqueline added disdainfully. Kate laughed. Like a sponge she absorbed Jacqueline's sarcasm, smiled, and went on as if nothing had been said.

"Welcome to Greenwood."

"Thank you," I said.

"Which room is ours?" Gisselle demanded impatiently.

"Right across the way," Mrs. Penny said. When we turned, we confronted an adorable doll-like strawberry blonde with a face full of dimples standing in the doorway of the room adjacent to ours.

"This is Samantha," Mrs. Penny announced.

"Hi," Samantha said. She looked years younger than us.

"You're a senior?" Gisselle asked. The tiny Samantha nodded.

"Samantha's actually from Mississippi," Mrs. Penny explained, as if Mississippi wasn't just the adjacent state but another country too. "Samantha, this is Gisselle and Ruby Dumas and their father."

"Hi," she said.

The sound of someone coming down the hallway behind us returned our attention to the corridor. A studious-looking girl hurriedly entered the quad. She wore her dark brown hair just below her ears and a pair of thick-lensed black-frame glasses, which made her brown eyes seem so much larger. She had large, hard features and was pale to the point of looking sickly but she had a large bosom, almost as large as Mrs. Penny's, and a figure Jacqueline would tell us later was wasted on that horsey face.

"Victoria. Just in time to meet the new residents, Ruby and Gisselle Dumas," Mrs. Penny said. "This is Samantha's roommate," she explained to us.

"Hi," I said. "I'm Ruby."

Victoria took off her glasses before extending her long-fingered hand. I shook it.

"I just came from the library," she said in a quick breath. "Mr. Warden posted his outside reading assignments for European history already."

"Vicki is determined to be the class valedictorian," Jacqueline declared from her doorway. "Or else she'll commit suicide."

"I will not," Vicki retorted. "It's just smart to get a head start," she told me. And then she looked down at Gisselle, who wore a smirk almost as disdainful as the one on Jacqueline's face. "Welcome."

"Thank you."

"Which is our room already?" Giaselle moaned.

"Right this way, dear," Mrs. Penny said and directed us to the open doorway. The moment Daddy wheeled Gisselle in she wailed.

Two single beds were side by side separated by a night table. There was a closet on the right and a closet on the left. Adjacent to the beds, with just enough room between the bed and them for Gisselle's wheelchair, were two dark wood dressers, the wood matching the bed frames and headboards. At the right of the doorway was a small vanity table with a mirror a quarter of the size of the one we had in our rooms in New Orleans. The windows were above the headboard and had the same plain cotton curtains. The walls were covered with a simple flower-pattern wallpaper and otherwise unadorned. The floors were uncovered hardwood.

"This is too small! How are we going to share this? There's not enough room in here for my things, let alone Ruby's too."

"I'm glad someone else thinks so," Jacqueline chorused from behind us.

"Now don't you fret, dear," Mrs. Penny said. "I have storage space you can have."

"I didn't bring my things to put them into storage. I brought them to use."

"Oh dear," Mrs. Penny said, turning to Daddy.

"It'll be all right," he assured her. "We'll bring in what is most necessary first, and then —"

"Everything is most necessary," Gisselle declared unrelentingly.

"Maybe she can put some of her things in Abby's room too," Mrs. Penny suggested. "Abby's by herself," she added.

"Who's Abby? Where is she?" Gisselle demanded.

"She hasn't arrived yet. She's our other new girl," Mrs. Penny said, directing herself to Daddy, who nodded. "Whatever, don't you worry your little heart, dear. Mrs. Penny is here to make things work and keep her girls happy. I have been doing it for a long time," she said, smiling. Gisselle turned away and pouted.

"Let me start bringing their things in," Daddy said.

"Do you want me to help, Daddy?" I asked.

"No. Stay with your sister," he said, raising his eyebrows. I nodded, and he left with Mrs. Penny.

Jacqueline, Kate, Samantha, and Vicki gathered in our doorway.

"Why did you bring so much?" Vicki asked. "Didn't you know you don't need a big wardrobe? We wear uniforms."

"I will not wear a uniform!" Gisselle screamed.

"You have to," Kate said and followed it with a short laugh.

"I don't have to. I can't. I have special problems," Gisselle declared "I'm sure my father will arrange for my wearing my own clothing, and there just isn't enough closet space in here for all my things. They'll have to remain in the trunks taking up the little space we have."

Vicki shrugged. "You don't spend all that much time in your room anyway," she pointed out. "Most of the time we're out here doing our work."

"Most of the time *you* are," Jacqueline said. "Not us. So what part of Louisiana are you girls from?"

"New Orleans," I said. "The Garden District."

"That's beautiful," the doll-like Samantha said. "My daddy took me there last year when we visited New Orleans. Maybe I walked right past your house."

Gisselle turned her wheelchair so she could look more directly at the girls.

"And where are you all from?"

"I'm from Shreveport," Jacqueline said. "Chubs is from Pineville, and Vicki is from Lafayette."

"My father and I live in Natchez," Samantha said

"What happened to your mother?" Gisselle asked.

"She was killed two years ago in a car accident," she replied and bit down on her lower lip quickly, all of her dimples evaporating.

"That's how I got crippled," Gisselle said angrily. It was as if she believed all the accidents were the fault of cars and not people. "If you're from Mississippi, how come you're going to school here?" Gisselle asked.

"My father's family is from Baton Rouge."

"Everyone's room is this small?" Gisselle asked, looking around.

"Yes," Jacqueline said.

"How come this Abby gets her own room?" Gisselle demanded.

"It's the way it worked out," Kate said and laughed. "The luck of the draw, maybe."

"Or maybe no one wants to room with her. We haven't met her yet either," Jacqueline said.

"You don't think she's . . ." Kate began.

"No," Jacqueline said. "They don't let them into Greenwood, no matter who protests. This is a private school," she added with some pride.

"Well, she'd better get here soon," Vicki said. "We've got to go to the orientation assembly in an hour."

"What orientation assembly?" Gisselle asked quickly.

"Didn't you read the first page in your packet? The Iron Lady always has a getting-to-know-you and getting-to-know-her assembly."

"Where she reads us the riot act," Jacqueline added. "Fire and brimstone."

"Iron Lady?" I said.

"When you hear and see her, you'll know why we call her that," Jacqueline replied.

"They're not serious about all these stupid rules listed in here, are they?" Gisselle asked, holding up the packet.

"She is, and you had better pay attention to the demerits. Chubs can tell you about that," Jacqueline said, nodding at Kate.

"Why?" I asked.

"I got ten last year and had to wash out the bathrooms for a whole month," she complained. "And don't let anyone tell you girls are neater than boys. They leave the bathrooms disgusting," she said.

"You won't ever see me washing any bathrooms," Gisselle said.

"I doubt she would punish you that way," Vicki said.

"Why?" Gisselle demanded sharply. "Because I'm in a wheelchair?"

"Of course," Vicki said, undaunted. Gisselle considered a moment and then smiled. "Maybe this isn't so bad then. Maybe I can get away with a lot more than the rest of you."

"I wouldn't count on it," Jacqueline said.

"Why?"

"After you meet the Iron Lady, you'll see yourself."

"It's not all bad," Samantha said. "This is a good school. And we have fun."

"What about boys?" Gisselle inquired. Samantha blushed. She seemed frozen at the border separating childhood and adolescence, someone shocked and confused by her own sexuality. Later,

I would discover that she was overly protected and spoiled by her father.

"What about them?" Vicki asked.

"Do you ever get to meet any?" Gisselle spelled it out.

"Of course. At the socials. Boys from proper boys' schools are invited. We have a dance once a month."

"How peachy! Once a month, just like a period," Gisselle quipped.

"What?" Samantha said, her little heart-shaped face in shock. Kate giggled and Jacqueline smirked.

"A period," Gisselle repeated. "You know what that is, or haven't you gotten yours yet?"

"Gisselle," I cried, but not before Samantha's face had turned bright crimson as the other girls laughed.

"Oh, how nice," Mrs. Penny said, following Daddy and our driver in with some of our things, "the girls are already getting along. I told you everything would be all right," she said to Daddy.

3

Getting Along

A half-hour before we all had to leave for the main building to attend Mrs. Ironwood's assembly, Abby Tyler and her parents arrived. I thought she was the prettiest of us all. About my height, but slim with dainty features like Audrey Hepburn, Abby had turquoise eyes and thick ebony hair, the strands brushed straight to her shoulders. Her rich, dark complexion was almost mocha, suggesting she had spent a great deal more time than the rest of us at the beach.

She spoke with a soft, melodic voice, her accent clipped and different, with some French intonation, obviously influenced by her mother's side. When she smiled at me, I felt there was something sincere about her. Like us, she was tentative and unsure of herself, being a Greenwood student for the first time.

After she was introduced to all the girls, Mrs. Penny asked her if she minded having some of Gisselle's things in her room. I knew that Gisselle didn't want to appear that she was asking anyone for anything, but Abby was very cooperative.

"Oh, no," she said, smiling at Gisselle. "Come in and use whatever space you want."

"I hate the idea of having to go from room to room to get my own things," Gisselle whined.

"You just tell me what you want when you want it and I'll fetch it for you," I said quickly.

"Or I'll be glad to bring it to you," Abby offered. She glanced at me with an understanding and sympathetic look in her eyes, and I felt an immediate kinship with this soft-spoken, dark-haired girl.

"Sure, I have to go around and beg people to get me my own things," Gisselle continued, her voice shrill. I was afraid that at any moment she would burst into one of her tantrums and embarrass Daddy.

"You don't have to beg. That's a ridiculous thing to say. Asking for something isn't begging," I said.

"I don't mind getting things for you," Abby said. "Really, I don't."

"Why not?" Gisselle snapped back instead of being grateful. "Are you practicing to become somebody's maid?"

The blood drained from Abby's face.

"Gisselle! Why can't you be gracious and accept someone's kindness?"

"Because I don't want to be dependent on the kindness of others," she cried back at me. "I want to depend on my own legs."

"Oh dear," Mrs. Penny said, pressing her palms to her plump cheeks. "I just want everyone to be happy."

"It's all right, Mrs. Penny. If Abby is willing to share the space in her room with my sister, my sister will be happy," I said, glaring down at Gisselle.

Frustrated, she turned on Daddy after all our things had been brought in, and she started to complain to him about having to wear a uniform, especially when she set eyes on it: a drab gray skirt and a drab gray blouse with thick-heeled black shoes. The dress code on the second page of our booklet also specified that makeup, even lipstick, was forbidden, as was any ostentatious show of jewelry.

"I'm trapped in this horrible wheelchair all day," Gisselle protested, "and now I have to wear those horrible, uncomfortable clothes too. I felt the material. It's too rough for my skin. And those ugly shoes will hurt my feet. They're too heavy."

"I'll go speak to someone about it," Daddy said and rushed out. Fifteen minutes later, he returned to tell Gisselle that, under the circumstances, she had been given permission to wear whatever made her comfortable.

Gisselle sank into her wheelchair and sulked. Despite every effort she made to complicate things and make our arrival at Greenwood difficult, someone figured out a way to placate her and make things smooth.

Daddy was ready to say his goodbyes.

"I know you two are going to do well here. All I ask," he said, gazing down at Gisselle, "is that you give it a fair chance."

"I hate it already," she fired back. "The room's too small. I have to go too far to class. What do I do when it rains?"

"What anyone else does, Gisselle. Open an umbrella," he replied. "You're not a piece of fragile china and you won't melt," he said.

"We'll be all right, Daddy," I promised.

"*You* will," Gisselle snapped. "I won't."

"We both will," I insisted.

"I've got to go and you two have things to do now," Daddy said. He leaned over to give Gisselle a kiss and a hug. She turned away and wouldn't return his kiss, not even a quick peck on the cheek. I saw how sad and unhappy that made him feel, so I gave him a bigger-than-usual kiss and hug.

"Don't worry," I whispered, my arms still clinging around his neck. "I'll watch over her and make sure she doesn't drop the potato too fast," I added, which Daddy knew was an old Cajun expression for giving up. He laughed.

"I'll call you two in a day or so," he promised. He said goodbye to the other girls and left with Abby's parents, who had spent most of their time talking with Mrs. Penny. As soon as they were gone, Vicki declared that we had to leave for the main building and the assembly. That started Gisselle on her tirade about the distance she had to travel from the dorm to the main building.

"They should provide a car for me and drive me to and from the school," she declared.

"It's really not that far, Gisselle."

"Easy for you to say," she countered. "You can

70

run if you want to."

"I'll be glad to push you along," Samantha volunteered.

Gisselle glared at her. "Ruby pushes me," she said sharply.

"Well, if there's ever a time when Ruby can't, I will," Samantha volunteered happily.

"Why? Does it amuse you?" Gisselle fired.

"No," Samantha said, taken aback. She looked quickly from one of us to the other. "I only meant . . ."

"We'd better get going," Vicki said, looking nervously at her watch. "No one comes late to one of Mrs. Ironwood's assemblies. If you do, she screams at you in front of the whole school and gives you two demerits."

We started out, Abby walking alongside me and behind Gisselle.

"What brought you to Greenwood for your senior year?" I asked her.

"My parents moved and they didn't like the school I was supposed to attend," she explained quickly, but she shifted her eyes away too, and for the first time I felt she wasn't being completely honest. I thought that whatever her real reasons were, they were probably painful ones like ours, and I didn't pursue it.

"That's a very pretty locket," she said when she turned back to me.

"Thank you. My boyfriend gave it to me this morning before we left for Greenwood. His picture and mine are in it. Take a look," I said, pausing and leaning over.

"Why are you stopping?" Gisselle demanded, even though she had been listening in on our conversation and knew very well why.

"Just a moment. I want to show Abby Beau's picture."

"What for?"

I snapped open the locket, and Abby glanced quickly at the pictures.

"Very handsome," she remarked.

"Which is why he's probably with someone else by now," Gisselle said. "I told her to expect it."

"Did you leave any boyfriends behind too?" I asked, ignoring Gisselle but pushing her forward.

"Yes," Abby said sadly.

"Well, maybe he'll come to visit you and write you and even call," I suggested.

She shook her head. "No, he won't."

"Why not?"

"He just won't," she said. I paused, but she quickened her pace to catch up with the other girls.

"What's with her?" Gisselle asked.

"Homesick, I suppose," I said.

"I can't blame her. Even an orphan could get homesick here," she added and laughed at her clever exaggeration. I didn't laugh. I had come here thinking I was the one who would have the most mysterious background and the most secrets to keep hidden, but in less than an hour I had discovered that that was not to be so. It seemed like there might be more doors locked in Abby's past than in mine. I wondered why, and I wondered if I would ever be permitted to find out.

"Catch up with the others," Gisselle ordered. "You push me like an old lady."

We caught up, and as we continued on our way to the main building, our conversation turned to what we did during our summer, the movies we had seen, the places we had been, and the singers and actors we thought were dreamboats. Gisselle dominated each topic, forcefully expressing her opinions, opinions that Samantha especially clung to, basking in her words and looks like a small flower hungry for the warmth and light of the sun. But I noticed that Abby remained very quiet, listening with a gentle smile on her lips.

When we arrived at the main building, everyone decided to accompany Gisselle up the gangway and into the building, which was something that, I saw, pleased her. She was being treated as if she were someone special, not just someone handicapped.

Two male teachers, Mr. Foster and Mr. Norman, were at the two entrances to the auditorium, quickly ushering the girls inside.

"We go to the left," Vicki directed.

"Why?" Gisselle demanded. Now that she had to accept the fact that she would be here at Greenwood, she would demand to know why something couldn't be white if it was black. As Grandmere Catherine would say if she were here, "Gisselle is determined to be the pebble in everyone's shoe."

"It's where our assigned seats are located," Vicki replied. "It's explained in your packet. Didn't you read any of it yet?"

"No, I didn't read any of it yet," Gisselle said, imitating Vicki's condescending tone. "Anyway, I can't have an assigned seat. I'm in a wheelchair, or haven't you noticed?"

"Of course I noticed. Even so, you should remain with us," Vicki continued patiently. "It's the way Mrs. Ironwood has organized assemblies. We are seated according to our dorm and quad."

"And what else is in this precious packet? When we should go to the bathroom?"

Vicki blanched and turned to lead the way. When we reached our row, everyone filed in. Gisselle remained in the aisle in her wheelchair, and I took the outside seat so I could sit next to her. Abby sat beside me. All around us, the girls laughed and chatted, many gazing our way with interest and curiosity. But no matter who smiled at Gisselle, she refused to smile back. When the girl on the aisle seat across from us kept turning toward her, Gisselle nearly snapped her head off.

"What are you staring at? Didn't you ever see anyone in a wheelchair before?"

"I wasn't staring."

"Gisselle," I said softly, putting my hand on her arm, "don't make a scene."

"Why not? What difference will it make?" she retorted.

Jacqueline waved to some friends, as did Vicki and Kate and Samantha. Then Jacqueline began pointing out other girls and giving us abbreviated opinions.

"That's Deborah Stewart. She's so stuck up, she gets a nosebleed every day. And that's Susan Peck. Her brother goes to Rosedown, and he's so good-looking everyone plays up to Susan in the hope she will introduce them to her brother when his school attends one of our socials. Oh, there's Camille Ripley. She looks like she got her parents to give her that nose job, doesn't she, Vicki?"

"I forgot what she looked like," Vicki said dryly.

Suddenly a ripple of silence began to pass through the assembly of girls. It started toward the rear and made its way toward the front, accompanying the arrival of Mrs. Ironwood, who marched down the aisle.

"There's the Iron Lady," Jacqueline said in a loud whisper and nodded in her direction. Abby, I, and Gisselle turned to see her start up the short stairway to the stage at the front of the auditorium.

Mrs. Ironwood looked no more than five-six or -seven. She was stout, with gray hair pulled severely back and tied in a thick bun. She had a pair of pearl-framed glasses on a silver chain around her neck, the glasses resting on her bosom. Dressed in a dark blue vest with a white blouse beneath it and an ankle-length skirt, she walked firmly in her thick-heeled black shoes, her shoulders back, her head high, until she reached the podium at the center of the stage. When she turned to face the assembly, not a sound was heard. Someone coughed but quickly choked it to an end.

"How come she doesn't have to wear that ugly uniform too?" Gisselle muttered.

"Shh," Vicki said.

"Good afternoon, girls, and welcome back to Greenwood for what I expect will be another successful year for all of you." She paused, put on her glasses, and opened her folder. Then she looked up, seemingly turning our way and gazing directly at us. Even from this distance, I could see how steely cold her eyes were. She had thick eyebrows and a firm mouth set in a jaw that seemed made of granite.

"I would like to begin by first welcoming all of the girls who are with us for the first time. I know that the rest of you will do whatever you can to make their arrival and familiarity with our school smooth and easy. Remember, once all of you were new girls.

"Next, I would like to introduce three new faculty members. Teaching freshman English, Mr. Risel," she said and gazed to her right, where some of the faculty were seated. A tall, lean, blond-haired man of about forty rose and nodded at the assembly.

"Teaching advanced French, Monsieur Marabeau," she said in a perfect French accent. A short, stout, dark-haired man with a dark mustache stood up and bowed to the assembly.

"And finally, our new art instructor, Miss Stevens," she said with a little more sternness in her voice than I had detected when she'd introduced the previous two.

An attractive brunette who couldn't be much more than twenty-eight or twenty-nine stood up. She had a warm, friendly smile, but she looked uncomfortable in her tweed suit and high-heeled shoes.

"Wait until she hears about your paintings and finds out how talented you are," Gisselle quipped. All of the girls in our row turned toward her, but Mrs. Ironwood shifted her gaze our way too. I could feel the sting of her reproach.

"Shh," Vicki warned.

"Now to review our rules of behavior," Mrs. Ironwood continued, her eyes still fixed in our direction. My heart was pounding, but Gisselle just glared back.

"As you know, we expect everyone to be serious about her work. Consequently, a grade-point average of less than C-plus will not be tolerated. If any one of you should fall beneath that acceptable threshold, you will lose all of your social privileges until you bring your average up."

"What social privileges?" Gisselle asked, again a little too loud. Mrs. Ironwood raised her gaze from her folder and glared our way. "I expect you to remain quiet while I am speaking. At Greenwood respect for teacher and staff is required. We do not have time for, nor will we tolerate, insubordination in class or in any classroom situation. Is that perfectly clear?"

Her words echoed in the deathly quiet hall. No one moved, not even Gisselle. Even though Mrs. Ironwood continued in a lower voice, her consonants were so sharp I thought she could slice the air between us with her words.

"I would advise you all to turn to page ten in your orientation booklets and memorize the rules set down. You will note when you read the list that the possession of any alcoholic beverage or any drug on campus will result in your immediate expulsion. Your parents know that means they forfeit the tuition. Loud music, smoking, or any act of vandalism carries severe punishments and high numbers of demerits.

"Last year I was a little more lenient than I should have been when it came to our dress codes. Unless you have prior approval, you are to wear our uniform, keep it clean and well pressed, and abstain from using cosmetics. Looking attractive at Greenwood means being clean and neat, not painting your face."

She paused and smiled coolly.

"I am pleased to announce that we will have as many dances this year as we had last. There were only one or two instances of inappropriate behavior, and those offenders were dealt with quickly before they ruined things for everyone else. We expect you to behave in a proper manner when you have guests visiting on visiting days. And remember: While your guests are on this campus, they are to obey our rules and regulations the same as if they were students here. That goes for the male guests as well as the female," she emphasized.

"I remind you," she said slowly, pulling her

shoulders back and looking toward the ceiling at the rear of the auditorium, "you are all Greenwood girls now, and Greenwood girls are special. To the newcomers, I recommend that you memorize our slogan: A Greenwood girl is a girl who considers her body and her mind to be holy, and a girl who knows that what she does reflects upon us all. Be proud you are Greenwood girls and make us proud you are one of us.

"Those who have to be issued uniforms and shoes, proceed directly to the commissary in the basement. Everyone, study your schedule, note your times to be at class. Remember, one lateness is a single demerit. The second lateness is four, and the third is six."

"I can't get demerits for being late," Gisselle muttered. "Not moving around in this wheelchair."

Some of the girls who overheard her glanced her way and then looked quickly at Mrs. Ironwood, who once again seemed to be fixed on us coldly, as a butcher bird in the bayou. The long pause caused a ripple of discomfort to pass through the assembly. I felt like I was sitting on a hill of ants and couldn't wait for Mrs. Ironwood to look in a different direction. Finally, she did.

"Our enrollment has gone up, but our classes are still small enough for all of you to get the individualized instruction you need to be successful, if you work up to your full capacity. Good luck to you all," she concluded, then took off her glasses and closed her folder. She glared our way

79

one more time and then marched off the stage. No one moved until she had left the auditorium. Then the girls, many of whom who had held their breaths, broke out in loud chatter as they got up to leave.

"Thanks a lot," Gisselle said, spinning around on me, her eyes full of fire.

"For what?"

"For bringing me to this little hellhole." She spun herself around in her chair, pushing other girls out of her way. Then she looked back. "Samantha," she called.

"What?"

"Push me back to the dorm while my sister goes for her pretty new outfit," she ordered and laughed. Samantha jumped to do her bidding and we all left the auditorium, following behind her as if she had just been appointed queen.

After Abby and I had been issued our uniforms and shoes, we returned to the dorm. On the way I told her the story of Gisselle's car accident and subsequent paralysis. She listened attentively, her dark eyes watering when I described Martin's funeral and Daddy's deep depression during the days immediately following.

"So you can't say the accident made her this way," Abby said.

"No. Unfortunately, Gisselle was Gisselle long before, and I'm afraid she will be this way for a long time yet."

Abby laughed.

"Don't you have any brothers or sisters?" I asked her.

"No." After a long pause she added, "I wasn't supposed to be born."

"What do you mean?"

"I was an accident. My parents didn't want to have any children," she said.

"Why?"

"They didn't want any," she replied, but I sensed there were deeper, darker reasons, reasons she knew but couldn't voice. She had already been more revealing than she'd intended, which was something I attributed to our getting along so well so quickly. It was natural for Abby and I to want to be close. Except for Gisselle, we two were the only girls in the dorm to be attending Greenwood for the first time. I felt that, in time, I could tell her my story; that she was someone I could trust to keep it locked away.

Back in our quad, we tried on our uniforms. Despite the sizes on the labels, they were big enough for us to swim in them. I decided these clothes were designed to keep our femininity a state secret. Dressed in a baggy blouse with a skirt that touched our ankles, we confronted each other in the sitting room and both fell into hysterics. Gisselle looked pleased. Our laughter brought the other girls out of their rooms where they had been organizing their things.

"What's so funny?" Samantha asked.

"What's so funny? Look at us," I said.

"The Iron Lady designed these uniforms herself," Vicki explained. "So don't complain too loudly."

"Or she'll burn you at the stake," Jacqueline added.

"At least we can wear our own clothes on weekends, at the socials, and when we get invited to Mrs. Clairborne's tea," Kate said.

"Mrs. Clairborne's tea?" Gisselle remarked. "I can't wait."

"Oh, she always has the best little cakes," Kate said. "And pralines!"

"A few dozen of which Chubs manages to shove into her purse and then hide somewhere in the room. I don't know why we don't have rats," Jacqueline said.

"What is this tea exactly?" I asked.

"It's not just one tea. It's frequent and by invitation only. Everyone knows who's been invited and who's not, and the teachers think more highly of you if you're invited more than once."

"Three times makes you a Tea Queen," Jacqueline declared.

"Tea Queen?" Abby looked at me, and I shrugged.

"You keep your tea bag each time you're invited and you pin it on a wall in your room like an award or a commendation," Vicki explained. "It's a Greenwood tradition and an honor. Jacki's right. Those who are invited often are treated better."

"She's saying that because she's a Tea Queen," Jacqueline quipped. "She was invited four times last year."

"And what about you?" Gisselle asked.

"Once. Kate was invited twice, as was Saman-tha."

"All new girls are invited to the first tea of the year, but that doesn't count because it's automatic," Vicki continued.

"Where are the teas held?" Abby asked.

"At the Clairborne mansion. Mrs. Penny will take you up there and give you the history of the house. Here it's almost as important to know those facts as it is to know the facts in American or European history," Jacqueline said. Vicki nodded.

"I can't wait," Gisselle said. "Only I'm not sure I can take the excitement." Kate laughed and Samantha smiled, but Vicki looked shocked by what amounted to blasphemy at Greenwood.

"So," Gisselle continued, "when's the first monthly social, the one with boys?"

"Oh, not for nearly a month. Didn't you read the social calendar in your packet?" Jacqueline said.

"A month? I told Daddy this was like being in a nunnery," she wailed at me. "What about getting into the city?" she quickly asked. The girls looked at each other.

"What do you mean?" Vicki said.

"Getting into the city. What's so hard to understand? You're going to be the valedictorian."

Vicki blanched.

"I . . . well . . ."

"None of us ever left the campus on our own," Jacqueline said.

83

"Why not?" Gisselle demanded. "There must be places in the city to go where we can meet boys."

"For one thing, you have to have a permission form on file to be able to leave the campus on your own," Vicki explained.

"What? You mean I'm really a prisoner here?"

"Just call your parents and have them file the form," Vicki said with a shrug.

"What about the rest of you? Are you telling me none of you cared before?" No one spoke. "What are you all? . . . Virgins?" Gisselle cried in frustration. Her face was as red as a steamed lobster claw.

Samantha's mouth dropped open. Kate stared with a half-amused, half-amazed smile on her face. Vicki remained nonplussed, but Jacqueline looked ashamed. Abby and I exchanged quick glances.

"Don't tell me you've been obeying all these dumb rules," Gisselle continued, shaking her head in disbelief.

"Demerits can —" Vicki began.

"Ruin your chances to become a Tea Queen. I get it," Gisselle said. "There are more important things to pin on your walls than old tea bags," Gisselle snapped, then rolled her wheelchair across the room toward Vicki, who stepped back. "Like love letters. Ever get one?"

Vicki looked around and saw that all eyes were on her. She stammered for a moment.

"I . . . I've got . . . to start my assigned reading for European history," she said. "See you later."

She turned and walked quickly to her room. Gisselle spun around and fixed her gaze on Jacqueline.

"Last year a couple of the boys from Rosewood wanted to sneak into our dorm on a weekend night," she revealed.

"And?"

"We didn't have the nerve," Jacqueline confessed.

"Well it's *this* year, and we have the nerve now," Gisselle said. She looked at me. "We'll show them how girls from New Orleans party. Right, Ruby?"

"Don't start, Gisselle. Please."

"Start what? Living? You'd like me to be an obedient little Greenwood girl and roll around quietly in my wheelchair with my mouth shut, my lap full of dried old tea bags, and my knees bound together, wouldn't you?"

"Gisselle, please . . ."

"Who's got a cigarette?" she demanded quickly. Kate's eyes widened. She shook her head. "Samantha?"

"No, I don't smoke."

"Don't smoke. Don't see boys. What do you girls do, read fan magazines and masturbate?"

It was as if thunder had shaken the dorm. I was so embarrassed by my sister's outburst I had to look down at the floor.

"All right," Gisselle continued, "don't worry. I'm here now. Things will be different. I promise. It just so happens," she said with a smile, "I smuggled in some cigarettes of my own."

"Gisselle, you'll get everyone in trouble, and the first day too," I protested.

"You're not chicken, are you?" she asked Jacqueline, Kate, and Samantha. "Good," she said when they didn't respond. "Come into my room. You can help me organize my records and we'll share a cigarette. Maybe I'll get us something better soon," she added, smiling. She spun her chair around and headed for our room. No one moved. "Well?" she snapped.

Jacqueline started after her first, and then Kate and Samantha followed.

"Close the door," Gisselle ordered when they were all in our room.

"I never thought twin sisters could be so different," Abby remarked and then realized what she had said. "Oh, I'm sorry, I didn't mean . . . ."

"That's all right. I never thought so either. Until I met her," I said and bit my tongue. But it was too late.

"Met her?"

"It's a long story," I said. "I wasn't supposed to tell it to anyone here."

"I understand," Abby said. From the way she looked when she said it, I believed she did understand.

"But I don't mind telling it to you," I added. She smiled.

"Why don't we go into my room," she suggested. I looked back at the closed door behind which Gisselle was holding court with her new protegées. It was a scene I wanted no part of at the moment.

"Good idea," I said. "While we talk, I'll organize the things of Gisselle's you had to take. I'd better go through some of it too," I said, throwing a glance back at our room. "No telling what else she smuggled in here."

A little over an hour later, Mrs. Penny came to our quad to see how we were all doing If she had smelled any smoke coming from our room, she didn't reveal it. Frankly, I didn't see how she could miss it. The stench was on the girls' clothing and lingered in the air despite their opening our windows.

"I'm also here to formally pass on Mrs. Clairborne's invitation to Abby, Gisselle, and Ruby to attend tea at her home on Saturday at two," she said. "You can wear what you wish, but you should dress appropriately," she added, winking. "It's a formal tea."

"Oh no! And I left my formal tea dress home," Gisselle said.

"Pardon, dear?"

"Nothing," Gisselle said, smiling. I saw how Samantha and Kate were smiling behind Mrs. Penny's back. Jacki was wearing her usual smirk, but it was clear that all three were still in awe of my sister.

"Good. Well then, dinner's in less than fifteen minutes," Mrs. Penny sang out. "New girls don't have chores until the second week," she added and then sauntered off.

"What was that supposed to mean?" Gisselle inquired, wheeling herself into the center of the sitting room. "What chores?"

"All of us help out in the dining room. The responsibilities are scheduled and posted on the bulletin board in the main lobby," Jacqueline said. "This week Vicki, Samantha, Chubs, and I have bus-girl duties. We have to clean off the tables and bring the dirty dishes and silverware into the kitchen after everyone's finished eating. The girls in B and C quad are waitresses, and the girls in D quad set the table."

"What?" Gisselle spun her chair around to face me. "You didn't tell me this."

"I just found out myself, Gisselle. What's the big deal?"

"What's the big deal? I don't do maid's work."

"I'm sure no one will expect you to do anything since . . ." Vicki started to say but stopped.

Gisselle glared at her. "Since I'm crippled? Is that what you wanted to say?"

"I was going to say 'since you're in a wheelchair.' You can't be expected to carry dishes into the kitchen."

"She can set a table," I said and smiled at my sister, who, if looks were fire, would have burned me to a crisp.

"What I can do and what I will do are two different things. If these other dopes want to pay all this money to go to a private school and work as maids as well, then let them," she said.

"All the girls do it in all the dorms, especially the two big ones," Samantha said. Gisselle threw a glance at her that had the same effect a slap would have had. She bit her lower lip and stepped back. "They do," she muttered to me and Abby.

"Why should any of us be afraid of a little work?" I said.

"You *would* say that. You . . ." Gisselle stopped herself from revealing my Cajun background and glanced quickly at the others. "I'm hungry. Let's go. Samantha," she cried, and Samantha jumped forward to push Gisselle's chair.

In the dining room we met the other girls in our dorm. With the upstairs quads, there were fifty-four in all. Three long tables were set up in the large room that was brightly lit by four big chandeliers. The walls were paneled in a dark wood, with framed prints of plantation scenes and scenes on the bayou evenly hung on each wall. Everyone was chattering excitedly when we arrived, but the sight of Gisselle in the chair quieted them down some. She returned every gaze with her own fierce look of condemnation, causing eyes to shift in every direction but hers. Vicki showed us to our places. Because of her wheelchair, Gisselle was situated at the head of our table, something she enjoyed and quickly used to her advantage. In moments she was determining the subjects of the conversation, ordering this be passed and that be passed and going off on long descriptions of her exciting lifestyle back in New Orleans.

The girls seemed fascinated with her. Some, who

looked even snobbier to me, gazed at her as if she were a ghost from the cemetery of bad manners, but Gisselle let nothing slow her down. She treated the girls who were serving our food as if they were no better than hired servants, demanding, complaining, and never once saying "thank you" for anything.

The food was good, but not nearly as good as the food Nina made for us back home. After the meal had ended and the girls from our quad began clearing the table, Gisselle ordered me to take her back to our room.

"I won't wait for them," she said. "They're absolute idiots."

"No they're not, Gisselle," I said. "They're just participating in what's ours. It's fun. It makes you feel like this is your place, your home away from home."

"Not to me. To me it's a nightmare away from home," she said. "Take me to the room. I want to listen to some records and write some letters to my friends, who will want to know about this poor excuse for a school," she said, loud enough for everyone around us to hear. "Oh, Jacki," she said, calling back. "When you girls are finished with your chores, you can come to my room to listen to my records and learn what's up to date."

I pushed her out as fast as I could. She screamed I was going to crash her into a wall, but that's just what I hoped to do. Abby followed us. We had already decided that she and I would take a walk to the lake after dinner. I was going to ask

90

Gisselle to come along, but since she had already decided on what she wanted to do, I didn't mention it.

"Where are you two going?" she demanded after I had brought her to our room.

"Outside, for a walk. Do you want to come?"

"I don't walk, remember?" she said curtly and shut the door.

"I'm sorry," I said to Abby. "I'm afraid I'll be apologizing for my sister forever."

She smiled and shook her head.

"I thought I had a cross to bear and should feel sorry for myself, but after seeing what you have to put up with . . ." Abby said when we walked out of the dorm.

"What do you mean, you thought you had a cross to bear? What could be your cross? Your parents seemed very nice."

"Oh, they are. I love them very much."

"Then what did you mean? Are you suffering from some disease or something? You seem as healthy as a young alligator."

Abby laughed. "No, thank God, I am very healthy."

"And pretty, too."

"Thank you. So are you."

"So? What's your cross to bear?" I pursued. "I trusted you with my story," I told her after a moment.

She was quiet. We started down the walkway, heading toward the lake. She kept her head down, but I looked up at the half moon peeking over the shoulder of a cloud. The silvery rays coolly illuminated the warm night and made our new world ethereal, like the setting of a dream we were all sharing. Off to our right, the other two dorms were all lit up, and here and there we spotted other girls taking walks or just gathered in small groups talking.

When we made the turn that would take us down to the water, we could hear the bullfrogs, cicadas, and other nocturnal creatures coming alive in their ritualistic night music, a symphony full of croaks and clicks, rattles and thin whistles.

Because we were so far from any highways, the sounds of traffic never reached us, but in the distance I could see the red and green running lights of the oil barges on the Mississippi and imagined the sounds of foghorns and the voices of riverboat passengers. Sometimes, on nights like this, people's voices could carry for more than a mile over the water, and if you closed your eyes and listened, you could feel either your movement or theirs as more and more distance fell between you.

Below us, the lake had taken on a metallic sheen. It was so still that I could barely perceive a bobbing in the rowboats tied at the small dock next to the boathouse as we approached. It was a good-sized lake with a small island in the middle. We were nearly down to the dock before Abby spoke again.

"I don't mean to be so secretive," she said. "I like you and appreciate your trusting me with your story. I don't have any doubts," she added with bitterness, "that most of these girls would look down on you if they knew you came from a poor Cajun background, but that would still be nothing compared to me."

"What? Why?" I said. "What's wrong with your background?"

We stood on the dock now and looked out at the lake.

"Earlier you asked me if I had a boyfriend, and I said yes, and you tried to make me feel better by telling me he would write or call. I told you he wouldn't, and I'm sure you wondered why I was so sure."

"Yes," I said. "I did."

"His name's William, William Huntington Cambridge. He was named after his great-great-grandfather," she said, in that same bitterness she had intoned before. "Who happened to be one of the heroes of the Confederacy, something about which the Cambridges are very proud," she added.

"I suppose if you scratch everyone around here, you'll find most have ancestors who fought for the South," I said softly.

"Yes, I'm sure. That's another reason why I . . ." She spun around, her eyes bright with tears. "I never knew my grandparents on my father's side. They were kept a family secret, which was why they weren't supposed to have me," she explained. She paused as if she expected me to understand everything, but I didn't and I shook my head.

"My grandfather married a black woman, a

Haitian, which made my father a mulatto, but white enough to pass as a white man."

"And that was why your parents never wanted to have children? They were afraid . . ."

"Afraid that I, the offspring of a mulatto and a white woman, would be darker," she said, nodding. "But they had me eventually anyway, which you know makes me a quadroon. We moved around a lot, mostly because whenever we settled somewhere long enough, someone, somehow, suspected."

"And your boyfriend, William . . ."

"His family found out. They consider themselves bluebloods, and his father makes sure that he learns as much as he can about anyone his children get involved with."

"I'm sorry," I said. "It's unfair and stupid."

"Yes, but that doesn't make it any easier to endure. My parents sent me here hoping that by having me surrounded with the crème de la crème, it would rub off and no matter where I went from here on, I would be considered a Greenwood girl first, upper class from a good family, special, and therefore never suspected of being a quadroon. I didn't want to come here, but they want so much for me to escape prejudice and they feel so guilty for having me that I did it for them more than I did it for myself. Understand?"

"Yes," I said. "And thank you."

"For what?" she asked, smiling.

"For trusting me."

"You trusted me," she replied. We started to

hug each other, when suddenly, a man called out from behind us.

"Hey," he cried. A door to the boathouse snapped shut behind him. We spun around to see a tall, dark-haired man no more than twenty-four or -five approaching. He was shirtless, and his muscular upper body gleamed in the moonlight. He wore a pair of tight jeans but was barefoot. His hair was long, down over his ears and most of his neck.

"What are you doing down here?" he demanded. He came close enough for us to see his dark eyes and high Indian cheekbones. The lines in his face were sharp but strong, cutting a firm jaw and a tight mouth. He had a rag in his hands, and he wiped them continuously with it while he looked us over.

"We just went for a walk," I began, "and . . ."

"Don't you know this is off-limits after dark? Want to get me in trouble? There's always one or two of you venturing down here to get me up a tree just to amuse yourselves," he said harshly. "Now you make like two jackrabbits mighty quick or I'll have Mrs. Ironwood on your tails, get it?"

"I'm sorry," I said.

"We didn't come down here to get anyone in trouble," Abby added, stepping forward out of the shadows. When he looked at her, he immediately softened.

"You two are new, huh?"

"Yes," she said.

"Didn't you two read that handbook?"

95

"Not completely, no," she replied.

"Look," he said, "I don't want any problems. Mrs. Ironwood laid out the rules for me. I'm not even supposed to talk to any of you on the grounds without one of the teachers or staff members present after dark, see? And especially not down here!" he added, looking around to be sure no one was listening.

"Who are you?" I asked.

He hesitated a moment before replying.

"Name's Buck Dardar, but it will be Mud if you two don't hightail it outta here pronto," he said.

"Okay, Mr. Mud," Abby said.

"Git," he ordered, pointing at the hill.

We grabbed hands and ran off, our laughter trailing behind us and echoing over the lake. At the top of the hill, we paused to catch our breaths and looked back toward the boathouse. He was gone, but he still titillated our imaginations just like someone and something forbidden would.

Still excited, our hearts pounding, we hurried back to the dorm, new friends drawn closer by our hidden pasts and our hidden hopes for ourselves as well as for each other.

4

My Sister's Keeper

On the first day school life at Greenwood seemed not much different from school anywhere else, except, of course, there were no boys in the corridors and classrooms with us. However, I was impressed with how clean and new everything looked. The marble floors in the corridors gleamed. Our desk tops had barely a scrape on them, and unlike most any other school, none of the chairs or other furniture had any scratches spelling out some cryptic graffiti or revealing some rage and disappointment.

Our teachers made the reason for that perfectly clear the moment we were all seated in their rooms. Each began with a short lecture about how important it was to keep our school looking tidy and new. Their voices boomed as if they wanted to be certain Mrs. Ironwood heard their performances. Almost every teacher wanted it made clear that it was his or her responsibility to keep his or her room looking good, and he or she meant to carry out that responsibility.

"If they don't," Jacki whispered to me, "the Iron Lady will have them whipped."

The lectures bored Gisselle, but even she was impressed with how obedient the student body was when it came to keeping the building immaculate. Whenever a student saw a piece of paper on the corridor floor, she would pause to pick it up. We found the same attention to cleanliness in the cafeteria. Although it was really too early to judge, it seemed like there was a decorum and an orderliness to school life at Greenwood that made our school life in New Orleans look like it had been on the verge of bedlam, despite the fact that we had attended one of the better city schools.

It was just the way my schedule worked out that after the first two periods of classes I had a study period. Gisselle, who had failed algebra last year, had to repeat it at Greenwood. When we first arrived at the main building, I had wheeled her about from homeroom to classes, but at the end of the second period, Samantha arrived on the scene almost by design and offered to take over.

"After this period, we have the next three classes together," Samantha said. Gisselle was obviously pleased with the suggestion.

"All right," I said. "But don't let my sister make you late for your classes."

"If I'm late because it takes me longer to do what I have to do, then they will just have to be understanding," Gisselle insisted. I saw she was already planning to loiter in the bathrooms, perhaps have a cigarette.

"She's going to get you into trouble, Samantha," I warned, but I might as well have been directing my words into the wall. Somehow my sister had quickly turned this naïve girl into her trusted servant. I felt sorry for Samantha; she had little idea what she was in for before Gisselle was tired of her.

I left them and hurried off to my study hall. But just as I sat down to look over my new work, the study-hall teacher informed me that Mrs. Ironwood had asked to see me.

"Her office is right down the corridor to your right and then up a short set of stairs," he told me. "Don't look so worried," he added with a smile. "She often visits with first-time Greenwood students."

Nevertheless, I couldn't help being nervous about it. My heart was thumping as I hurried down the quiet hallway and found the stairs. A short, plump woman with gray-framed bifocals turned from a file cabinet when I entered the outer office. The nameplate on her desk read MRS. RANDLE. She peered at me for a moment and then went to her desk to look at a slip of paper.

"You're Ruby Dumas?" she asked.

"Yes, ma'am."

She nodded, maintaining a stiffly serious expression, and then went to the door of the inner office. After a gentle knock, she opened it and announced my arrival.

"Show her in," I heard Mrs. Ironwood command.

"Right this way, Ruby." She stepped aside and I entered Mrs. Ironwood's office.

It was a good-sized room, but very austere, with dark gray curtains, a light gray rug, a large, dark brown desk, two hard-looking wooden chairs, and a small, stiff-looking charcoal-black settee against the wall on the right. Above it was the only painting in the room, another portrait of Edith Dilliard Clairborne, and as in all the others, she was in a formal gown, either seated in a garden or in a high-backed chair in a study. The other walls had plaques and awards spaced out, awards won by the students of Greenwood for things ranging from debates to oratory contests.

Although there was a large vase of red and pink roses on her desk, the room smelled like a doctor's office, with a heavy scent of disinfectant. The office did look like it had been painstakingly cleaned to the point where the windows were so clear they looked wide open.

Mrs. Ironwood sat erect behind her desk. She lowered her glasses and gazed at me for a long moment, drinking me in as if she wanted to memorize every detail of my face and figure. If there was any approval, she didn't show it. Her eyes remained coldly analytical, her lips firm.

"Sit down, please," she said, nodding at one of the hard wooden chairs. I moved to it quickly and held my books on my lap.

"I called you here," she began, "so that we could

establish an understanding as soon as possible."

"Understanding?"

The right corner of her mouth dipped. She tapped a fat folder on her desk with a pencil.

"This is your file," she continued. "Beneath it is your sister's. I have reviewed them both carefully. Besides your school records, the file contains some important personal information.

"I should tell you," she said, pausing to sit back, "that I had a long, informative talk about you with your stepmother."

"Oh," I said, dropping my voice a couple of octaves. She knitted her dark, thick brows together. Since she had referred to Daphne as my stepmother instead of my mother, it was clear that Daphne had told her about my life as a Cajun.

"She told me of your . . . unfortunate circumstances and expressed her frustration over her failure to bring about the sort of changes required for your adjustment from a rather backward life to a more civilized one."

"My life was never backward, and there is much about my life now that is uncivilized," I said firmly.

Her eyes became small, her lips a bit pale as she tightened them. "Well I can assure you that there is nothing about life at Greenwood that is uncivilized. We have a proud tradition of serving the best families in our society, and I intend to see that continue," she said quickly and sharply. "Most of our girls come from the proper sort of background and are already schooled in how to behave and carry themselves in polite society.

101

"Now then," she proceeded, putting her glasses on and opening my folder, "I see from your schoolwork that you are an excellent student. That bodes well for you. You have the raw material to develop. I also note that you are blessed with some talent. I look forward to your developing it here.

"However," she said, "none of this will be of any good if your social skills, your personal habits, are lacking."

"They're not," I said quickly. "No matter what you might think about the world in which I grew up and no matter what my stepmother might have told you."

She shook her head and then fired her words like bullets.

"What your stepmother told me," Mrs. Ironwood said, "remains locked within these walls. That is what I have brought you here to understand. It is up to you to keep them locked. Despite the circumstances of your birth and childhood, you now come from a distinguished family, and you have an obligation to that family name. Whatever habits, practices, and behavior you engaged in prior to your life in New Orleans must not rear their ugly heads here at Greenwood.

"I have promised your stepmother to watch over you more closely than I watch over my other wards. I wanted you to be aware of that."

"That's not fair. I haven't done anything to deserve being treated differently," I complained.

"And I'm determined to keep it that way. When I promise something to a parent of one of my students, I make sure to keep that promise.

"Which brings me to your sister," she said, moving my folder off Gisselle's so she could open it. "Her schoolwork is disappointing, to say the least, as is some of her past behavior. I realize she has a serious handicap now, and I have made a few accommodations to make her life here comfortable and successful, but I wanted you to know that I hold you responsible for her success and her behavior."

"Why?"

She flicked her stony eyes over me.

"Because you have the full use of your limbs and because your father believes in you so strongly," she replied. "And because you are close to your sister and the most influential person when it comes to advising her."

"Gisselle doesn't take my advice or listen to me most of the time. She's her own person, and as far as her handicap goes, she takes advantage of it more often than not," I said. "She doesn't need accommodations, she needs discipline."

"I think I'll be the one to decide those things," Mrs. Ironwood said. She paused and stared at me a moment, her head bobbing slightly. "I see what it is your stepmother means: You have a strain of independence, that Cajun stubbornness, a wildness that must be kept in tow.

"Well, this is the place where it will be kept in tow," she threatened, sitting forward.

"I want you to maintain your good school achievements; I want your sister to improve her schoolwork; I want you both to behave and to obey our rules to the letter. By the end of this year, I would like your mother to be impressed with the changes in your character." She paused, waiting for my response, but I kept my lips sealed for fear of what might burst out of them if I began.

"Your sister's behavior during the orientation assembly was abominable. I chose to ignore it only because we didn't have this little talk first. Next time she behaves poorly, I'll have both of you on the carpet, understand?"

"You mean I'm going to be punished for the things my sister does too?"

"You are your sister's keeper now, whether you like it or not."

Tears burned beneath my eyelids. A kind of paralyzing numbness gripped me as I thought how pleased Daphne must be to know what she had prepared for me here at Greenwood. It seemed she was determined to put obstacles in my life no matter where, no matter what. Even though I had agreed to come here and to get myself and Gisselle away from her like she wanted, she was still not satisfied. She wanted to be sure she made my life miserable.

"Do you have any questions?" Mrs. Ironwood asked.

"Yes," I said. "If I'm the one who came from a backward world, why am I the one held responsible?"

The question seemed to throw her for a moment. I even saw a flicker of appreciation for my wit flash in her eyes.

"Despite your background," she replied slowly, "you appear to have better raw material, more potential. I am directing myself to that part of you. For now, your sister is still suffering from her accident and impairment. She's not ready for these sorts of talks."

"Gisselle will never be ready for these sorts of talks. She wasn't before her accident," I said.

"Well then, it will be part of your burden to get her ready, now won't it?" Mrs. Ironwood said, smiling coolly. She stood up. "You can go back to your study hall now."

I rose and left the office. Mrs. Randle glanced at me quickly as I passed her desk. Despite my brave facade, I was trembling so hard I could barely walk. I was sure Daddy didn't know the groundwork Daphne had laid here at Greenwood. If he had, he probably wouldn't have brought us. I was tempted to call and tell him, but I imagined Daphne would only find a way to blame me for being ungrateful for this opportunity and for messing up Gisselle's chances to improve.

Frustrated, a black cloud of despair shadowing me, I sank back into my desk in the study hall and pouted. Despite the excitement and the warmth of most of my new teachers, the dark mood the Iron Lady put me in remained with me throughout the rest of the morning and most of the afternoon, only lifting when I walked into Rachel Stevens's art class, which was my last class.

My suspicion that Miss Stevens was uncomfortable dressed in that formal tweed suit and wearing high heels at the assembly proved true when I set eyes on her in our art room. Here she looked more like an artist and far more at ease, her hair loose and brushed down, an artist's smock over her shorter skirt and bright pink blouse. This art class was an elective and consequently had even fewer students in it than our required classes. There were only six of us, which pleased Miss Stevens.

I had no idea that, whereas Daphne had contacted the school and Mrs. Ironwood to reveal my past, Daddy had seen to it that the school and my art teacher knew of my little successes. Miss Stevens was kind enough not to embarrass me in front of the others, but after she had explained our curriculum and set up each girl with workbooks to peruse, she approached me and told me what she already knew.

"I think it's so exciting to have some of your pictures in a gallery already," she said. "What do you like to draw and paint the most? Animals, nature?"

"I don't know. I suppose so," I said.

"Me too. You know what I'd like to do — if you'd like — go down to the river on a Saturday and find things to paint. How would you like that?"

"I'd love it," I said. I felt the curtain of depression lifting. Miss Stevens was so bubbly and so full of excitement. Her enthusiasm inspired my own and revived my need to express myself

106

through my drawings and paintings. So much had occurred in my life recently to draw my attention away from my art. Maybe now I could return with even more energy, more purpose.

While the others continued to look over our workbooks, Miss Stevens lingered to talk to me, quickly becoming the most personal of all my teachers.

"What dorm are you in?" she asked. I told her, and I told her about Gisselle being in a wheelchair. "Does she draw and paint too?"

"No."

"I bet she's proud of you. I bet your whole family's very proud. I know your father is," she said, smiling. She had the warmest blue eyes and the lightest freckles scattered over her cheeks, running up to her temples on both sides. Her lips were almost orange, and there was a tiny cleft in her chin.

Rather than say anything unpleasant about Gisselle or Daphne, I just nodded.

"I started the same way," she told me. "I grew up in Biloxi, so I used to draw and paint a lot of ocean scenes. I sold one through a gallery when I was in college," she told me proudly, "but I haven't sold anything since." She laughed. "It was then I realized I had better go into teaching if I wanted to eat and keep a roof over my head."

I wondered why someone so pretty, sweet, and talented wouldn't consider marriage as another alternative.

"How long have you been an art teacher?" I

asked. A quick perusal of the others told me they were jealous of how much I was dominating our new teacher's time.

"Only two years. In a public school. But this is a wonderful job. I can give my students so much individual attention."

She turned to face the others. "We're all going to have a great time," she declared. "I don't mind if you girls want to bring in some music to listen to while we work, as long as we don't play it too loud and disturb the other classes."

She flashed another welcome smile at me and then went back to describing her goals for our course and how she planned to take us from drawings to watercolors and oils. She described the work we would do in clay, our use of the kilns and the artwork she hoped we would produce. She was so enthusiastic that I was disappointed when the bell signaling the end of the day rang, but I knew I couldn't linger. Gisselle would be waiting at her classroom for me to wheel her back to the dorm. We hadn't made any other arrangements.

But when I arrived, she was already gone. Abby waved from the end of the corridor and hurried to join me.

"Looking for Gisselle?"

"Yes."

"I saw Samantha wheeling her out and Kate and Jacki following. How was your first day?"

"Great, except for a meeting I had with the Iron Lady." I told her about it on our way back to the dorm.

"If I were called to her office I'd be terrified, expecting it would mean only one thing: She had discovered my family background."

"Even if she did, she wouldn't dare —"

"It's happened to me before," Abby said confidently. "It's sure to happen to me again."

I wanted to say optimistic things to her and reassure her, but the Iron Lady had put me into a dark mood too. As we continued down the walkway toward our dorm, we were both silent until we heard the sound of a lawn tractor and looked to the right to see Buck Dardar. He saw us too and slowed down to gaze our way.

"Mr. Mud," Abby said. It brought smiles back to our faces and a spirited energy back to our gait. Risking a reprimand, we both waved at him. He nodded, and even from this distance we could see the whiteness of his teeth when he smiled. Laughing, we clasped hands and broke into a trot all the way back to our dorm.

We arrived only ten or so minutes after Gisselle and the others, but Gisselle acted as if I were an hour behind her.

"Where were you?" she complained as soon as I walked into our room.

"Where was I? Why did you rush out so quickly after the last period? I told you I'd be there."

"You kept me waiting and waiting. How do you think I feel sitting there in this dumb chair while everyone else rushes out to relax? I won't be kept waiting like a piece of furniture."

"I came as soon as the bell ending the period

rang. I only spent a moment talking to my teacher."

"It was a lot longer than a minute, and I had to go to the bathroom! You can get up and go whenever you like. You know what it's like for me to do the simplest things now. You know that and yet you dillydally with your art teacher," she said, wagging her head.

"All right, Gisselle," I said, exhausted from her constant badgering. "I'm sorry."

"Just lucky for me I have other friends now to look after me. Just lucky."

"Okay."

The truth was that I never realized how lucky I was back in New Orleans, having my own room, with walls to separate us. "How were your classes?" I asked, to change the subject.

"Horrible. They're all so small, the teacher hovers over your shoulder and watches every little thing you do. You can't get away with anything here!"

I laughed.

"What's so funny, Ruby?"

"Despite yourself you will likely do a lot better with your schoolwork," I said.

"Oh, forget it. There's no sense in talking to you," she said. "You'll probably sit down and start your homework right now too, won't you?"

"Abby and I are going to do our work now and get it out of the way."

"Peachy. You'll both soon be Greenwood honor students and go to dozens of teas," she quipped and wheeled herself out and into Jacki and Kate's room.

Mrs. Ironwood had said I was to be responsible for Gisselle and her behavior? I might as well try to change the habits of a muskrat or tame an alligator, I thought.

Our first week at Greenwood flew by quickly. Tuesday night I wrote letters to Paul and to Uncle Jean, describing everything. On Wednesday night Beau phoned. We had the use of a telephone in the corridor just outside our quad. Jacki came to our room to tell me I had a call.

"If it's Daddy, I want to talk to him too," Gisselle demanded, eager to continue the flow of her stream of complaints.

"It's not your father," Jacki said. "It's someone named Beau."

"Thank you," I said and rushed out of the room and to the phone before Gisselle could make any of her nasty remarks in front of Jacki.

"Beau!" I cried into the receiver.

"I thought I'd give you a day or so to settle in before I called," he said.

"It's so good to hear your voice."

"And good for me to hear yours. How's it going?"

"Rough. Gisselle has been making life miserable from the moment we arrived."

"I can't say I'm not rooting for her," Beau said, laughing. "If she gets you both kicked out, you'll be back here."

"Don't count on it. If we don't last here, my stepmother will surely find somewhere else to send us, and maybe next time it will be twice as far away. How's school for you?"

"Boring without you, but I keep busy with the football team and all. What's it like there?"

"The school's nice and so are most of our teachers. I'm not fond of the principal. She's a tyrant made of cold stone, and Daphne has already filled her ear with tales about my evil Cajun background. She thinks I might be Annie Christmas."

"Who?"

"The flatboat bully who could chew off a man's ear." I laughed. "She just thinks I might be a bad influence on her preciously perfect young Creole ladies."

"Oh.

"But I am enjoying my classes, especially art."

"And what about . . . boys?"

"There are none here, Beau, remember? When are you coming? I miss you."

"I'm trying to work it out so I can get there weekend after next. With these weekend football practices and all, it's hard."

"Oh, please try, Beau. I'll be half mad with loneliness if you don't come."

"I'll come . . . somehow," he said. "Of course, I've got to do it on the sly, so don't let anyone know . . . especially Gisselle. It would be just like her to get it back to my parents somehow."

"I know. Her mean streak has gotten even thicker since the accident. Oh, I've made friends with one of the girls in my quad, but I'm not sure I want you to meet her."

"What? Why not?"

"She's very pretty."

"I have eyes only for you, Ruby," he said. "Hungry eyes," he added softly.

I leaned against the wall and cradled the receiver against my ear as if I were pressing a precious little baby to my cheek. "I miss you, Beau. I do," I said.

"I miss you, Beau, I do," I heard Gisselle mimic, and I spun around to see her behind me in the corridor with Samantha and Kate at her side, all of them smiling.

"Get away!" I screamed. "This is a private conversation."

"It's against the rules to say sexy things on the telephones in our dorm," Gisselle quipped. "Read page fourteen, paragraph three, line two of our handbook."

Kate and Samantha laughed.

"What's going on?" Beau asked.

"Just Gisselle, up to her usual self," I said. "I can't talk anymore. She's determined to spoil it."

"This is too much of a tease anyway. I'll call you again as soon as possible," he said.

"Try to come, Beau. Please."

"I will," he promised. "I love you and miss you."

"Same here," I said, flashing a look of anger toward Gisselle and the girls. "Bye."

I hung up the phone sharply and spun around.

"Just wait. Just wait until you want some privacy," I told her and marched passed the three of them.

Being angry at Gisselle did little good. If anything, she enjoyed seeing me upset. It was better to simply ignore her. She didn't mind; she had the girls in our quad, who seemed just as comfortable spending most of their time around her during the times before homeroom, between classes, and in the cafeteria. Pushed along by Samantha, with Kate and Jacki at her sides, Gisselle and her entourage quickly became a separate entity, a clique that moved so tightly through the building they all looked attached by invisible wires emanating from Gisselle's wheelchair.

The chair itself metamorphosed into a rolling throne from which Gisselle issued her requests and commands and pronounced her judgments about other students, teachers, and activities. After school the three girls would obediently follow Gisselle back to the dorm, where she continued to hold court, tutoring them in misbehavior, describing her exploits back in New Orleans, getting them to smoke and neglect their homework. Only Vicki, driven by her desire to excel academically, remained aloof which was something for which Gisselle did not forgive her.

Gradually Gisselle turned the other girls against Vicki. Even poor little Samantha, who was quickly evolving into Gisselle's alter ego, spent less and less time with her roommate and began to mimic Gisselle's contempt for her to her face. On Thurs-

114

day night as a practical joke, Gisselle had Samantha steal Vicki's first research report for European history, a report about which she was very proud, since she had gotten right to it and completed it a week ahead of schedule. The poor girl was frantic.

"I know it was with my books in the closet," she insisted, pulling on her hair and biting her lip. Gisselle and the girls sat in the sitting room, listening to her turmoil as she recalled and reviewed her actions, trying to figure out where she could possibly have misplaced it. I took one look at Samantha's face and realized what Gisselle had talked her into doing.

"It was my only copy. I spent hours on it, hours!"

"Knowing you, you probably have it memorized anyway," Gisselle said. "Just start writing it over."

"But . . . my references . . . my quotes . . ."

"Oh, I forgot about quotes," Gisselle said. "Anyone have any quotes?"

I pulled Samantha aside, pinching her upper arm roughly.

"Did you take your roommate's report?" I demanded.

"It's just a little joke. We're going to give it back to her soon."

"It's not funny to put someone through so much pain just to get a laugh for yourself. Give it back to her right away," I commanded.

"You're hurting my arm."

"Do it or I'll go get Mrs. Penny, who will have

to tell Mrs. Ironwood."

"All right." Her eyes were filled with tears of pain, but I didn't care. If she was going to be Gisselle's little slave, she was going to pay for it too.

Vicki went back into her room to tear everything apart again.

"This wasn't funny, Gisselle," I said.

She looked at Samantha and at me. "What wasn't funny?"

"Getting Samantha to take Vicki's report."

"I didn't get her to do anything. She did it herself. Didn't you, Samantha?" Gisselle's fixed gaze was enough. Samantha nodded.

"Give it back to her this minute," I said. Samantha reached under the sofa to pull out the report. There was a look of shock on her face. She knelt down and searched.

"It's not there," she said, surprised. "But that's where I put it."

"Gisselle."

"I don't know anything about it," she said smugly.

Suddenly we heard a scream from Vicki and Samantha's room. All of us rushed in to discover Vicki sitting on the bed, bawling. In her lap was her report, soaked.

"What happened?"

"I found it like this under the dresser," she cried. "Now I'm going to have to copy it all over." She looked at Samantha hatefully.

"I didn't do that," Samantha said. "Honest."

"Someone did."

"Maybe you did it yourself and you're trying to blame it on one of us," Gisselle accused.

"What? Why would I do that?"

"Just to get someone in trouble."

"That's ridiculous. Especially when you consider that I'm going to have to copy it over!"

"Then you'd better start before too much of the ink runs," Gisselle suggested. She turned her chair and the girls followed her out.

"Abby and I will help you, Vicki," I said.

"Thanks, but I'll do it myself." She wiped her cheeks.

"Sometimes, when you rewrite, you make corrections anyway," Abby said.

Vicki nodded. Then she fixed her eyes on me coldly. "We never had things like this happen before," she said.

"I'm sorry," I said. "I'll speak to Gisselle."

Later that night we had an argument about it. Gisselle insisted that she hadn't dipped the report in the toilet and even pretended to be hurt that I would accuse her of such a thing, but I didn't believe her.

The next day Gisselle surprised me with a suggestion.

"Maybe we shouldn't room together," she said. "We don't really get along all that well, and we can't really get to know other people if we see only each other most of the time."

"We don't see each other. I've hardly seen you all week," I said. "But that's not my fault."

"I didn't say it was. I just think it might be better if you roomed with Abby, who you've become close with, and I room with someone else."

"Who?"

"Samantha," she said.

"You mean Vicki doesn't want to room with her since the practical joke, don't you?"

"No. Samantha can't stand rooming with Vicki, who is so involved in her schoolwork, she doesn't even pay attention to personal hygiene."

"Now what are you saying?"

"Samantha said Vicki got her period two days ago but hasn't taken the time to get herself any sanitary napkins. She stuffs her panties with toilet paper," Gisselle replied and grimaced.

"I don't believe it."

"Well, why should I lie? Go ask her yourself. Go in there and ask her what she has in her panties. Go on!" she shrieked.

"Gisselle. All right, relax. I believe you."

"Just don't blame all this on Samantha," she said. "Well?"

"What?"

"Do you want to move in with Abby and let Samantha move in here or not?"

"But what about your special needs?"

"Samantha is willing to do everything I require her to do," Gisselle said.

"I don't know. Daddy might not like this."

"Of course he will like it. If it makes me happy," she added, smiling.

"I don't know how Abby would feel about it,"

I said softly, secretly loving the idea.

"Of course she'll love it. You two have become like . . . sisters," Gisselle said, her eyes fixed on me sharply. Was that jealousy and envy in her eyes or just plain hate?

"I'll talk to Abby," I said. "I suppose I could always move back if it doesn't work out. But what about all your other things, the things you insisted on bringing here? There might not be room enough for my things in Abby's room now."

"I'll have Mrs. Penny put some of it in storage just as she originally suggested," Gisselle replied quickly. Obviously, she would overcome any obstacle to get what she wanted. "Besides, you don't have that much anyway."

"I know why you want to get rid of me," I said sternly. "You don't want me nagging you about your schoolwork. Well, just because I'm in a different room, it doesn't mean I won't try to make sure you do well, Gisselle."

She sighed deeply.

"All right. I promise to work harder. Samantha happens to be a good student too, you know. She's already helped me with math a great deal."

"Did your homework for you is what you really mean. That won't help you learn it," I said. Gisselle rolled her eyes.

I had never told her about my meeting with Mrs. Ironwood on the first day of school. I thought that if she knew what had been said and how I had been given the responsibility of watching over her, she would go into a rage and demand to go home. But I was tempted to tell her about it now.

"If you do poorly, I'll be to blame somehow," I said.

"Why? You'll do well. You always do well," she muttered.

"It's expected of me," I said, coming closer to describing my meeting with Mrs. Ironwood. Of course, Gisselle didn't understand.

"Well, I don't expect it! See, you *do* nag! I need a break. I need to be with different people too."

"All right, Gisselle. Calm down. You'll have all the girls in here."

"Are you going to go ask Abby?"

"Yes," I said. Maybe I shouldn't have given in so easily, but the prospect of escaping from her looked too good. I left and discussed the proposal with Abby, who was very happy about the idea.

That night we made the moves. Vicki, rather than being insulted, was obviously pleased to have a room all to herself. She even helped Samantha carry out her things. Of course, we had to inform Mrs. Penny, who looked very troubled about it at first, but she quickly changed her attitude when she saw how happy Gisselle was.

"As long as you girls all get along, I suppose your private arrangements don't matter," she concluded. "But don't forget, Gisselle: You, your sister, and Abby are going to Mrs. Clairborne's for tea tomorrow. We'll leave the dorm at one-fifty sharp. Mrs. Clairborne likes everyone to be right on time."

"I can't wait," Gisselle said. She flicked her eyelids and turned her shoulder. "I've already picked out my formal afternoon dress and matching shoes. Is light blue an acceptable color?"

"Oh, I'm sure it is," Mrs. Penny said. "Isn't this wonderful? How I wish I were a young girl again, just starting out, just experiencing everything. I suppose that's why I love my work. It gives me an opportunity to be a young woman over and over through you delightful girls."

The moment she was out of earshot, Gisselle slapped her hands together and began to imitate her, performing for her clique.

"How I wish I were a virgin again," she cried, "so I could experience lovemaking over and over."

Gisselle's fan club, as I had soon begun to label them, laughed and encouraged her. Then she drew them all into what had been our room to spin another tale of promiscuity to her faithful audience. I was glad to shut the door and retreat to the quiet of Abby's room, which had now become mine too.

That night we lay awake for hours, telling each other stories about our childhoods. She loved to hear about Grandmere Catherine and her work as a *traiteur*. I explained what a healer was to the Cajuns and the magic Grandmere could work to cure people of their minor ailments and their fears.

"You were very lucky to have a grandmother," Abby said. "I never knew any of my grandparents. Because of all the moving around we've done, I haven't had much contact with any of my family.

Gisselle doesn't know how lucky she is," she added after a moment. "I wish I had a sister."

"You do now," I told her.

She was quiet for a long moment, swallowing her tears back, just like I was swallowing mine.

"Goodnight, Ruby. I'm glad we're roommates now."

"Goodnight. Me too."

I was happy, very happy. I was just worried that Daddy would be upset and that everyone would blame me for being too selfish. But I half-expected Samantha would be overwhelmed by Gisselle soon anyway and would beg to go back to her old room. I might as well enjoy this as long as I could, I thought, and fell asleep contented for the first night since we'd arrived.

5

Sad Songs

Daddy called the next morning, and I immediately told him about Gisselle and I changing roommates. Gisselle was peeved that he had asked to speak with me first, so she sat in her wheelchair and sulked in the hallway, threatening not to speak with him at all while I spoke to him.

"Is that working out?" he asked, his voice full of surprise. "Someone else sharing the room with Gisselle, I mean?"

"Her new roommate's Samantha. You remember which one she was?" He said he did. "She has grown very fond of Gisselle very quickly," I explained.

"I can talk for myself," Gisselle fumed. "Give me the phone." She wheeled up to me, and I handed her the receiver.

"Daddy," she spit into the phone. "I hate it here, but at least I have a roommate that doesn't nag me to death," she said, eyeing me. "Yes," she said, suddenly turning syrupy sweet. "I have gotten off to a good start in my schoolwork. I got an A+ on my math homework and an A on my English just yesterday. And that was without Ruby's help too," she added. "But none of this means I like being here. You can tell that to Daphne," she added and thrust the phone back into my hands.

"Hi, Daddy."

"Should I come up there?" he asked. He sounded so tired, his voice so small and thin.

"No. We'll be all right. Besides, we have the tea at Mrs. Clairborne's house today."

"Oh. Well, that sounds nice. I don't mean to put a great deal of burden on you, Ruby," he said, "but . . ."

"It's all right, Daddy. Gisselle is going to like it here after a while," I said, glaring at her. "I'm sure."

"Is there anything you girls need?"

"No. We're fine, Daddy. Are you all right?"

"I have a little chest cold. Nothing serious. I might be away for a week or so, but I'll try to call you from wherever I am," he promised. "And if you should need me . . . call the office," he added quickly. I knew that meant don't bother calling Daphne.

"Is everything all right at home, Daddy?"

"It's okay," he said.

"How are Nina, Edgar, and Wendy?"

He hesitated a moment. "We've replaced Wendy," he told me.

"Replaced her? But why?"

"Daphne wasn't happy with her work. I saw

to it that she had a good recommendation and a few good leads. We have an older woman now. Daphne picked her out herself at the agency. Her name's Martha Woods."

"I feel so bad for Wendy."

"She'll be all right," he said quickly. "Enjoy your weekend. I love you," he said.

"And we love you, Daddy," I told him.

Gisselle smirked. "What about Wendy?" she asked.

"Daphne had her replaced."

"Good. She was too uppity anyway," Gisselle said.

"That's a lie. She put up with a lot from you, Gisselle. I'm sure the new maid won't."

"Yes she will, or she'll go too," Gisselle promised with a smile. Then she took off, wheeling herself back to her room in a fury. I was sure she would do something to embarrass us at Mrs. Clairborne's tea, maybe by wearing something inappropriate just for spite, but she surprised me by dressing herself in a pretty light blue dress with matching shoes. She had Samantha brush out her hair and pin it back at the sides. Mrs. Penny had told us that Mrs. Clairborne did not like to see her girls wearing makeup, but a slight tinge of lipstick was permissible. I thought Gisselle would be defiant and do her eyelids and her cheeks, but she surprised me again by being conservative with her makeup.

Samantha wheeled her out to the main lobby to join Abby and me at a little before one-fifty.

125

"Chubs asked me to steal a few pralines for her," she told us. "When either of you get a chance, shove some in my purse."

"Kate doesn't need the added calories," I said.

"If she doesn't care, why should you?"

"Good friends try to help each other, not feed each other's weaknesses," I replied.

"Who's saying I'm good friends?" She laughed wickedly. Abby and I looked at each other and shook our heads. A moment later Mrs. Penny appeared dressed in a floral cotton dress with a wide pink sash tied around her waist. She wore a corsage over her right breast and had a sun hat and a matching straw pocketbook with an embroidered rose on each side.

"Well, I declare," Gisselle said. "Scarlet O'Hara." Samantha laughed and ran off to tell the others what Gisselle had said, I was sure.

Mrs. Penny blushed. "You all look so pretty," she said. "Mrs. Clairborne will be very pleased. Right this way, girls. Buck has the station wagon out front," she said.

"Buck?" Abby said, turning to me. We started to laugh.

"Who's Buck?" Gisselle demanded.

"He's the young man in charge of most everything around here," Mrs. Penny said, but Gisselle eyed Abby and me suspiciously as I pushed her out and down the ramp to the wagon.

Close up in the daylight, Buck looked even younger than he had looked at the boathouse or riding on the lawn tractor. He had hair almost as black as Abby's, but his eyes were dark brown. He had a dark complexion, being a Native American. Even in his plaid shirt, we could see how strong he was. He looked taller too, and leaner, with a narrow waist and hips and long legs. The moment he set eyes on us he smiled softly, which was something Gisselle caught.

"Hello, Mr. Mud," Abby quipped. He laughed and then registered a look of surprise and great interest when he saw that Gisselle was my twin.

"Don't tell me there are two like you," he kidded. I just smiled.

"How do you know him?" Gisselle demanded. Neither Abby nor I replied.

"Here, let me help you," he offered Gisselle. He put his left arm around her waist and his right under her legs and lifted her so gently out of the seat, it was as if she weighed no more than ten pounds. She smiled, her face so close to his that her lips could graze his cheek. He placed her comfortably into the wagon and then folded the wheelchair with such expertise, I felt certain he had done this before.

We all got into the car, Mrs. Penny up front.

"Who's wearing all that jasmine?" Gisselle demanded as soon as we were all settled in the station wagon.

"Oh, I am, dear," Mrs. Penny said. "It's Mrs. Clairborne's favorite scent."

"Well it's not mine," Gisselle remarked. "Besides, you should wear what you like, not what some rich old lady likes."

"Gisselle!" I said, widening my eyes. Had she no discretion?

"Well, you should!"

"I like it very much myself," Mrs. Penny said. "Please don't worry. Now, let me tell you about the Clairborne mansion as we drive up. Mrs. Clairborne likes it when the girls know its history. Actually, she expects it," she said in a lower voice.

"Will we be tested later?" Gisselle quipped.

"Tested? Oh no, dear," Mrs. Penny said with a laugh, and then she stopped and thought a moment. "Just be respectful and remember, it's her generosity that keeps Greenwood going."

"And provides a job for her niece," Gisselle muttered. Even I had to smile at that one, but Mrs. Penny, as usual, ignored anything unpleasant and began her lecture.

"The mansion was a very important sugar plantation as recently as ten years ago."

"That's 'recent'?" Gisselle asked.

Mrs. Penny smiled as if Gisselle had said something very silly, something that needed no response.

"The original four-room dwelling was built in the 1790s and is now connected to the main house by an arched carriageway, which serves as a main entrance during inclement weather. At the height of its success as a sugar plantation," she continued, "the estate had four sugar houses, each with a separate planting unit and its own set of slaves."

"My father says the Civil War didn't end slavery, it just raised the cost of labor from nothing to the minimum wage," Gisselle quipped.

I saw a smile break out on Buck's lips.

"Oh dear, dear," Mrs. Penny said. "Please don't say anything like that to Mrs. Clairborne. And whatever you do, don't mention the Civil War."

"I'll see," Gisselle replied, enjoying her hold over our worried housemother.

"Anyway," she continued, catching her breath, "many of the furnishings, such as the armoires, predate the Civil War. The gardens, as you will soon see, are modeled after the French style of the seventeenth century, with marble statues imported from Italy."

A few minutes later we arrived at the entrance to the Clairborne estate, and Mrs. Penny continued in her role as tour guide.

"Look at the magnolias and the old oaks," she pointed out. "Over there, behind that barn, are the family burial grounds. See the iron grillwork fence shaded by the old oaks.

"All of the bookcases inside were hand-made in France. You'll see that most of the windows have brocaded draperies covering rose-point lace curtains and hand-painted linen shades. We will be having tea in one of the pretty sitting rooms. Perhaps you'll have a chance to see the ballroom."

"Is it ever used?" Gisselle asked.

"Not anymore, dear, no."

"What a waste," she said, but even she was impressed with the size of the mansion.

The enormous two-story structure had grand

Doric columns with an upper-level galerie that wrapped around the house. Atop the second story was a glass-windowed belvedere. The west side of the house looked darker, probably because of the huge willow trees whose branches hung as though weighted, casting long, deep shadows over the plastered brick walls and dormer windows.

As soon as we drove up the front door opened, and a tall, lean black man with snow-white hair appeared in the entrance. He was bent forward so that his head projected unbecomingly, making him seem to be climbing hills even while standing in a doorway.

"That's Otis, the Clairborne butler," Mrs. Penny said quickly. "He's been with the Clairbornes for over fifty years."

"Looks like he's been here more like a hundred years," Gisselle quipped.

We got out, and Buck moved around quickly to take out Gisselle's chair. She waited in happy anticipation as he came around to lift her out of the car and place her gently into the chair. Fortunately there were only a few steps up to the portico, something Buck was able to navigate easily. After he had delivered Gisselle in her chair to the front door, he returned to our car.

"Why can't Buck come inside too?" Gisselle asked.

"Oh no, dear," Mrs. Penny said, shaking her head and smiling as if Gisselle had suggested the funniest thing. "This tea is only for new girls today. Mrs. Clairborne sees you in small groups all month."

"Mr. Mud," Gisselle muttered at me. "You'd better tell me how you know him."

I pretended not to hear her as I pushed her chair through the entryway. Otis nodded and greeted Mrs. Penny. Once inside, Mrs. Penny reduced her voice to a whisper as if we had walked into a church or famous museum.

"All of the rooms are furnished with French antiques, and as you will see, all have deep purple divans with scrolled walnut frames."

The marble floors were waxed like glass. In fact, everything from the antique tables and chairs to the statues and walls shone. If there was any dust in here it was hidden under the rugs, I thought, but I noticed that whoever was responsible for the winding of the hickory grandfather clock just inside the entrance hadn't done so, and it was stopped at five after two.

The spacious and airy rooms on the first floor all opened to the central hallway. Mrs. Penny explained that the kitchen was in the rear of the house. About halfway in was the gracefully curved stairway, with its polished mahogany balustrade and marble steps. Above us in the hallway, grand chandeliers were lit and sparkled like drops of ice. In fact, despite its tapestries, its paintings, its great drapes and velvet furniture, there was something cold about the mansion. Even though the Clairbornes had lived here for a long time it lacked the warmth and personality that a family usually

131

imparted to a home. Why, it felt like a cold museum. The pieces looked like things amassed, collected for their value only, and the immaculate condition and appearance of everything around us gave me the impression that these were unused things, things only for show, a home on display, but not a home in which people really loved and lived.

We were brought to a sitting room on the right, where we found a velvet sofa and a matching settee arranged to face a high-backed deep blue velvet chair embroidered with gold, its dark walnut arms and legs scrolled with hand-carved designs. It looked like a throne set atop a large Persian rug. The remainder of the floor was uncovered blond hardwood. Between the chair and the settees and sofas was a long matching walnut table.

After Abby and I took our places on the settee and Gisselle was wheeled in beside us, I had a chance to gaze around at the scenic wallpaper and the framed oil paintings of various scenes on the sugar plantation. On the mantel was another stopped clock with its hands pointing to five after two. Above that was a portrait painting of a distinguished-looking man who had been captured slightly turned and peering down, giving the impression he was someone royal.

Suddenly we heard the definite tap, tap, tapping of a cane on the marble hallway floor. Mrs. Penny, who had been standing near the doorway, remembered something and hurried back to us.

"I forgot to tell you, girls. When Mrs. Clairborne

enters, please stand," she said.

"And how am I supposed to do that?" Gisselle snapped.

"Oh, you're excused, of course, dear," she said. Before Gisselle could say anything else, all eyes turned toward the doorway for Mrs. Clairborne's entrance, and then Abby and I rose.

She paused in the doorway, as if waiting to have her picture taken, and gazed over us, moving slowly from Abby to me and then to Gisselle. Mrs. Clairborne looked taller and stouter than she did in any of the portraits around the school. Also, none of the portraits depicted her with the bluing in her gray hair that now looked thinner and shorter, barely reaching the middle of her ears in length. She wore a dark blue silk dress with a wide collar, buttoned to the base of her throat. Hanging on a silver chain was a pocket watch encased in silver, the small hands frozen at five after two.

I wondered if either Abby or Gisselle had noticed the odd thing about the clocks.

I lifted my gaze to the large teardrop diamond earrings that dripped from her lobes. Her dress had sleeves with frilly lace cuffs that reached the base of her palms. Over her left wrist she wore a diamond and gold bracelet. The long, bony fingers of both her hands were filled with precious-jewel rings, some set in platinum, some in gold and others in silver.

Even in her pictures, Mrs. Clairborne had a narrow face that seemed out of place on her portly body; only in person, it seemed even more so.

Because of the way her long, thin nose protruded, her dark eyes seemed to be set even more deeply than they were. She had a wide, thin mouth, so thin that when her lips were pressed together, it looked like a pencil line drawn from inside one cheek to the inside of the other. Her complexion, unaided by any cosmetic touch whatsoever, was pasty white, spotted with brown aging marks on her forehead and cheeks.

I quickly decided that the artists who had done her portraits had used their imaginations almost as much as they had used her as a model.

She stepped forward and leaned on her cane. "Welcome, girls," she said. "Please, be seated."

Abby and I quickly did so, and Mrs. Clairborne walked directly to her chair, tapping her cane after each step as if to confirm it. She nodded at Mrs. Penny, who sat on the other settee, and then Mrs. Clairborne sat down and hooked her cane over the right arm of the chair before gazing at Gisselle for a moment and then looking at Abby and me.

"I like to have a personal relationship with each of my Greenwood girls," she began. "Our school is special in that we do not, as most public schools are prone to do, treat the students as if they were numbers, statistics. And so, I would like each of you," she said, "to introduce yourself to me and tell me a little about yourself. And then I will tell you why I decided a long time ago to ensure that Greenwood continue, and what I hope will be accomplished there now and in the years to follow." She had a firm, hard voice, as deep as a man's at times. "Afterward," she continued, "tea will be served."

She finally softened her expression, even though it was more of a grimace to me than a true warm smile.

"Who would like to begin?" she asked. No one spoke up. Then she fixed her gaze on me. "Well, since we're all so shy, why don't we start with the twins, just so we won't make any mistakes as to who is who."

"I'm the crippled one," Gisselle declared with a smirk. There was an unheard gasp, as if all the oxygen had been sucked out of the room. Mrs. Clairborne turned to her slowly.

"I hope only physically," she said.

Gisselle's face filled with blood and her mouth fell open. When I looked at Mrs. Penny, I saw she wore an expression of satisfaction. Mrs. Clairborne was heroic in her eyes, and she couldn't be put off balance. I imagined girls a lot smarter than Gisselle had tried and found themselves just as she found herself right now: eating her own words.

"I'm Ruby Dumas and this is my sister, Gisselle." I started quickly so I could fill the embarrassing silence. "We're seventeen years old and we're from New Orleans. We live in what is known as the Garden District. Our father is an investor in real estate."

Mrs. Clairborne's eyes grew small. She nodded slowly, but she studied me so intently I felt I was sitting on a mound of swamp mud and slowly sinking.

"I'm quite familiar with the Garden District, a most beautiful area of the city. There was a time," she said a bit wistfully, "when I used to go to New Orleans quite often." She sighed and then turned to Abby, who described where she and her family now lived and her father's work as an accountant.

"You have no brothers or sisters then?"

"No, madame."

"I see." She sighed again, deeply. "Are you all comfortable in your rooms?"

"They're small," Gisselle complained.

"You don't find them cozy?"

"No, just small," Gisselle insisted.

"Perhaps that's because of your unfortunate condition. I'm sure Mrs. Penny will do everything she can to make you as comfortable as can be while you are attending Greenwood," Mrs. Clairborne said, gazing at Mrs. Penny, who nodded.

"And I'm sure you will find Greenwood a wonderful place in which to be educated. I always say our students come here as little girls and leave as young women, not only highly educated, but morally strengthened.

"I feel," she continued, her face thoughtful, still, "that Greenwood is one of the last bastions of the moral fiber that once made the South the true capital of gentility and grace. Here you girls will get a sense of your tradition, your heritage. In other places, especially in the Northeast and the West, radicals are invading every aspect of our culture, thinning it out, diluting what was once pure cream and turning it into skim milk."

She sighed.

"There is so much immorality and such a lack of respect for what was once sacred in our lives. That comes only when we forget who and what we are, from where we have evolved. Do you all understand?"

None of us spoke. Gisselle looked overwhelmed. I gazed at Abby, who returned my glance quickly with a knowing look.

"Oh well, enough of this deep, philosophical chatter," Mrs. Clairborne said and then nodded toward the doorway, where two maids stood, waiting for the signal to bring in the tea, cakes, and pralines. The conversation became lighter. Gisselle, after a little urging, told the story of her accident, putting the blame entirely on faulty brakes. I described my love of art, and Mrs. Clairborne suggested I look over some of the paintings in the hallways. Abby was the most reticent to talk about herself, of course, something I saw that Mrs. Clairborne noticed but didn't pursue.

About midway through our tea, I asked to be excused to go to the bathroom, and Otis directed me to the closest one, which was on the west side of the house. As I was coming out, I heard piano music coming from a room farther down the corridor. It was so beautiful I was drawn toward it, and I looked through a doorway that opened to a beautiful sitting room, behind which was a patio that opened to the gardens. But to the right of the patio door was a grand piano, the top up so that at first I couldn't see much of the young man who was playing. I took a step in and to the right to see more, and I listened.

Dressed in a white cotton shirt with a buttoned-down collar and dark blue slacks was a slim young man with dark brown hair, the strands thin and loose so that they fell over the sides of his head and over his forehead, settling over his eyes. But he didn't seem to mind — or to notice anything, for that matter. He was so lost in his music, his fingers floating over the keys as if his hands were independent creatures and he was just as much an observer and listener as I was.

Suddenly he stopped playing and spun around on the stool to turn toward me. However, his eyes shifted to my right, as if he were looking not at me but at someone behind me. I had to turn around myself to be sure I hadn't been followed.

"Who's there?" he asked, and I realized he was blind.

"Oh, I'm sorry. I didn't mean to disturb you."

"Who's there?" he demanded.

"My name's Ruby. I'm here for Mrs. Clairborne's tea."

"Oh. One of the greenies," he said disdainfully, the corners of his mouth dipping. Otherwise he had a strong, sensuous mouth, with a perfectly straight nose and a smooth forehead that barely wrinkled even when he smirked.

"I'm not one of the 'greenies,' " I retorted. "I'm Ruby Dumas, a new student."

He laughed, folding his arms across his narrow

torso, and sat back.

"I see. You're an individual."

"That's right."

"Well, my grandmother and my cousin Margaret, whom you know as Mrs. Ironwood, will see to it that you lose that independent spirit soon enough and become a proper daughter of the South, stepping only where you should step, saying only what you should say — and saying it properly — and," he added with a laugh, "thinking only what you should think."

"No one will tell me what to say and think," I replied defiantly. He didn't laugh this time, but he held his smile for a moment and then grew serious.

"There's a different sound in your voice, an accent I detect. Where are you from?"

"New Orleans," I said, but he shook his head.

"No, before that. Come on, I can hear things more clearly, more distinctly. Those consonants . . . Let me think . . . You're from the bayou, aren't you?"

I gasped at his accurate ears. He put up his hand.

"Wait . . . I'm an expert on regional intonations . . ."

"I'm from Houma," I confessed.

He nodded. "A Cajun. Does my grandmother know your true background?"

"She might. Mrs. Ironwood knows."

"And she permitted you to enroll?" he asked with sincere surprise.

"Yes. Why wouldn't she?"

"This is a school for pure bloods. Usually, if you're not a Creole from one of the finest Creole families . . ."

"But I am that too," I said.

"Oh? Interesting. Ruby Dumas, huh?"

"Yes. And who are you?" He was hesitant. "You play beautifully," I said quickly.

"Thank you, but I don't play. I cry, I scream, I laugh through my fingers. The music just happens to be my words, the notes my letters." He shook his head. "Only another musician, a poet or an artist, would understand."

"I understand. I'm an artist," I said.

"Oh?"

"Yes. I have even sold some paintings through a gallery in the French Quarter," I added, finding myself bragging. It was not like me, but something about this young man's condescending, skeptical manner put a steel rod in my spine and hoisted my flag of pride. I might not be blueblood enough for the eyes of Mrs. Clairborne and her grandson, but I was Catherine Landry's granddaughter, I thought.

"Have you?" He smiled, showing a mouthful of teeth almost as white as his piano keys. "What do you paint?"

"Most of my paintings are scenes I did when I lived in the bayou."

He nodded and grew more pensive-looking.

"You ought to paint the lake at twilight," he said softly. "It used to be my favorite place . . .

when the dying sun changes the colors of the hyacinths, shimmering from lavender to dark purple." He spoke about colors as if they were long-lost, dead friends.

"You weren't always blind, then?"

"No," he said sadly. After a moment, he turned back to his piano. "You had better get back to my grandmother's tea before you're missed."

"You never told me your name," I said.

"Louis," he replied and immediately started to play again, only harder, angrier. I watched him for a moment and then I returned to the tea, feeling very melancholy. Abby noticed immediately, but before she could ask me about it, Mrs. Clairborne announced that our tea had come to an end.

"I'm happy you girls could come to see me," she declared and then stood up. Leaning on her cane, she continued. "I'm sorry you have to be going, but I know you young women have things to do. I will ask you all up here again soon, I'm sure. In the meantime, work hard and remember to distinguish yourselves by being proper Greenwood girls." She started out, clicking her cane over the marble, that stopped watch dangling on the chain around her neck like a small but hefty burden she was sentenced to carry the rest of her life.

"Come along, girls," Mrs. Penny said. She looked very pleased. "It was a nice afternoon, wasn't it?"

"I nearly got a heart attack from the excitement," Gisselle said, but she looked at me suspiciously, curious about where I had been and why my mood had changed too. I wheeled her out, and Buck came hurrying up the steps to help get her over the portico. Once again he lifted her gently out of the chair, only this time she deliberately saw to it that her lips grazed his cheeks. He shifted a quick gaze at Abby and me and especially at Mrs. Penny, to see if we'd seen what Gisselle had done. Both of us pretended we hadn't, and Mrs. Penny was too oblivious to have noticed. He looked relieved.

Once we were all inside the car, Abby asked me where I had been so long.

"I met a very interesting but very sad young man," I said.

Mrs Penny gasped. "You went into the west side of the house?"

"Yes, why?"

"I never let the girls go there. Oh dear, if Mrs. Clairborne finds out. I forgot to tell you not to venture off like that."

"Why aren't we permitted to go into the west wing?" Abby asked.

"That's the most private area, where she and her grandson really reside," Mrs. Penny replied.

"Grandson?" Gisselle looked at me. "Is that who you met?"

"Yes."

"How old is he? What does he look like? What's his name?" she followed quickly. "Why wasn't he invited to the tea? At least that would have made

142

it more interesting. Unless he was as ugly as she was."

"He told me his name was Louis. He's blind, but he wasn't always that way. What happened to him, Mrs. Penny?"

"Oh dear," she said instead of replying, "Oh dear, dear."

"Oh stop and just tell us what happened," Gisselle commanded.

"He became blind after his parents died," she said quickly. "He's not only blind but he suffers from melancholia. He usually doesn't speak to anyone. He has been that way ever since the deaths of his parents. He was only fourteen years old at the time. A great tragedy."

"Was Mrs. Clairborne's daughter Louis's mother?" Gisselle asked.

"Yes," Mrs. Penny replied quickly.

"What's melancholia?" she followed. Mrs. Penny didn't respond. "A disease or what?"

"It's a deep mental depression, a sadness that takes over your body. People can actually pine away," Abby said softly.

Gisselle stared at her a moment. "You mean . . . die of heartbreak?"

"Yes."

"That's so stupid. Does this boy ever come out?" Gisselle asked Mrs. Penny.

"He's not a boy, dear. He's about thirty now. But to answer your question, he doesn't come out much, no. Mrs. Clairborne sees to his needs and insists he not be disturbed. But please, please," she begged, "let us not dwell on this anymore. Mrs. Clairborne doesn't like it discussed."

"Maybe she's why he's so sad," Gisselle offered. "Having to live with her." Mrs. Penny gasped.

"Stop it, Gisselle," I said. "Don't tease her."

"I'm not teasing her," she insisted, but I saw the tiny smile sitting comfortably in the corners of her mouth. "Did he tell you how his parents died?" she asked me.

"No. I didn't know they had. We didn't speak very long."

Gisselle directed herself at Mrs. Penny again.

"How did his parents die?" she pursued. When Mrs. Penny didn't reply, she demanded an answer. "Can't you tell us how they died?"

"It's not a fit subject for us to discuss," Mrs. Penny snapped, her face firm. It was the first time we had seen her so adamant. It was clear the answer wasn't coming from her lips.

"Well, why did you start telling us the story then?" Gisselle said. "It's not fair to start something and not finish."

"I didn't start anything. You insisted on knowing why he was blind. Oh dear. This is the first time any of my girls have wandered into the west wing."

"He didn't seem to mind all that much, Mrs. Penny," I said.

"That's remarkable," she said. "He's never spoken to any of the Greenwood girls before."

"He plays the piano beautifully."

"Whatever you do, don't gossip about him with

the other girls, please. Please," she added.

"I don't gossip, Mrs. Penny. I wouldn't do anything to get you in trouble."

"Good. Let's not talk about it anymore. Please. Did you all enjoy the little cakes?"

"Oh, damn," Gisselle said. "I forgot to take some for Chubs." She stared at me a moment, and then she looked at Abby and nodded. "I want to speak to you two as soon as we're alone," she ordered. Then she fixed her gaze on Buck all the way back to the dorm.

Once Mrs. Penny had left us inside, Gisselle spun around in her chair and demanded to know how we knew Buck. I explained about our walk to the boathouse that first night.

"He lives there?"

"Apparently."

"And that's all? That was the only time you saw him?" she asked, obviously disappointed.

"And once mowing the lawn," I said.

She thought a moment. "He's cute, but he's just an employee here. Still," she said thoughtfully, "he's the only game in town right now."

"Gisselle. You stay away from him and don't get him in any trouble."

"Yes, darling sister. Now you tell us about this blind grandson and what really went on between you two or I'll be the one who spreads the gossip and gets Mrs. Penny in trouble," she threatened.

I sighed and shook my head.

"You're impossible, Gisselle. I told you everything. I heard the music, looked into the room, and

145

spoke to him for a few minutes. That was all."

"Did he tell you how his parents died?"

"No."

"Well, what do you think happened?" she asked.

"I don't know, but it must have been something horrible."

Abby agreed.

"Well now," Gisselle said, smiling from ear to ear, "at least we have something to find out and something to hold over Mrs. Penny if she ever so much as threatens us with a demerit."

"Stop it, Gisselle. And don't start anything with your fan club either," I said, but I might as well have been talking to myself. The moment the other girls set eyes on us, Gisselle was ready to tell all, from Buck to Mrs. Clairborne's grandson.

Alone back in our room, after we had taken off our nice clothes and put on jeans and sweatshirts, I did tell Abby more about Louis. We lay on our stomachs, side by side on my bed.

"He doesn't think much of Greenwood girls," I explained. "He thinks Mrs. Ironwood and his grandmother turn us all into puppets."

"He might not be too far off thinking that. You heard Mrs. Clairborne's speech about the traditions we must uphold and how we must behave."

"Did you notice that all the clocks were stopped, even the watch around her neck?"

"No," Abby said. "Were they?"

"All at the same hour and minute: at five after two."

"How strange."

"I was going to ask Mrs. Penny about it, but when she became so agitated over my side trip and my meeting Louis, I decided not to add anymore pepper to the gumbo."

Abby laughed.

"What?"

"Every once in a while your Cajun background sneaks back," she said.

"I know. Louis could detect my accent and knew I was from the bayou. He was surprised I was permitted to enroll, considering I wasn't a true blueblood."

"What do you suppose would happen to me if they found out the truth about my past?" Abby said.

"And what truth is that?" Gisselle demanded.

We both spun around and gasped at the sight of her in our doorway. We were so engrossed in our conversation that we hadn't heard her open the door — or else, knowing her, she had opened it softly just so she could spy on us. She wheeled herself into the room, and I sat up in my bed.

"Having a heart to heart, girls?" she teased.

"You should knock before coming in here, Gisselle. You want *your* privacy, I'm sure."

"I thought you'd be happy to have me come by. I happen to have found out the story of poor Louis," she said, smiling her Cheshire cat smile. Actually, she reminded me more of the sort of muskrat Grandpere Jack trapped.

"And how did you do that?"

"Jacki knew. Seems it isn't all as big a secret

as Mrs. Penny pretended. There are skeletons in Mrs. Clairborne's closets," she sang gleefully.

"What sort of skeletons?" Abby asked.

"What's your secret first?"

"Secret?"

"The thing you don't want Mrs. Ironwood to discover about you. Come on, I heard what you said."

"It's nothing," Abby said, her face turning crimson.

"If it's nothing, tell it. Tell it or I'll . . . I'll make up something."

"Gisselle!"

"Well, it's a fair trade. I'll tell you what I learned, but you've got to tell me something too. I just knew you'd share secrets with her and not with your own twin sister. You probably told her things about us too."

"I did not." I looked at Abby, whose face was drooping with sadness, both for me and for herself. "All right, we'll tell," I said. Abby's eyes widened. "Gisselle can keep a secret. Can't you?"

"Of course. I know more secrets than you'll ever know, especially about the kids back in our old school, even secrets about Beau," she added happily.

I thought a moment and then blurted something I knew Gisselle would accept.

"Abby was suspended once for being caught with a boy in the basement of one of her previous schools," I said. Abby's surprise worked perfectly, because it looked like I had betrayed her. Gisselle

148

gazed from her to me skeptically for a moment and then laughed.

"Big deal," she said. "Unless," she added, "you were naked when you were caught. Were you?"

Abby looked to me for a moment and then shook her head. "No, not completely."

"Not completely? How much then? Did you take off your blouse?" Abby nodded. "Your bra?" Abby nodded again. Gisselle looked impressed. "What else?"

"That's all," Abby said quickly.

"Well, well, little Miss Goody Goody isn't so pure after all."

"Gisselle, remember, you promised."

"Oh, who cares? That's not enough to interest anyone anyway," she said. She thought a moment and then smiled. "Now I suppose you want me to tell you why Louis is blind and what happened to his parents."

"You said you would," I replied.

She hesitated, enjoying her hold over us. "Maybe later, if I feel like it," she said and spun herself around in her chair and wheeled herself out of our room

"Gisselle!" Abby cried.

"Oh, let her go, Abby," I said. "She'll just tease us and tease us."

But I couldn't help wondering myself what it was that had turned that handsome young man into a blind, melancholy soul, revealing his feelings and thoughts only through his fingers on the keys of a piano.

149

6

A Surprising Invitation

Despite my having enough curiosity to fill the eyes of a dozen cats, I didn't give Gisselle the satisfaction of pleading with her to tell us what she had found out, and I certainly didn't go to Jacki. But as it turned out, I didn't have to beg anyone in Gisselle's fan club.

Right after breakfast the next morning, I was called to the telephone to speak to my art teacher, Miss Stevens.

"I was on my way out today to do some work and thought of you," she said. "I know this place just off the highway where we can get a wonderful view of the river. Would you like to come along?"

"Oh yes, I would."

"Fine. It's a bit overcast, but the weatherman guarantees us it will clear up shortly and warm up another ten degrees. I'm just wearing a sweatshirt and jeans," she said.

"So am I."

"Then you're ready. I'll be by in ten minutes to pick you up. Don't worry about supplies: I have everything we'll need in the car."

"Thank you."

I was so excited by the prospect of drawing and painting scenes in nature again that I nearly bowled Vicki over in the corridor. She had her arms filled with books she had just taken out of the library.

"Where are you going so fast?" she asked.

"Painting . . . with my teacher . . . sorry."

I hurried into our room and told Abby, who was curled up on her bed reading her social studies assignment.

"That's great," she said. I started to change from loafers to a pair of sneakers. "You know, I never noticed that string around your ankle," Abby remarked. "What is it?"

"A dime," I replied, and I told her why Nina had given it to me. "I know you think it seems silly, but . . ."

"No," she said, her face dark, "I don't. My father secretly practices voodoo. Remember, my grandmother was Haitian. I know some rituals and . . ." she said, getting up and going to the closet, "I have this." She plucked a garment out of her suitcase and unfolded it before me. It was a dark blue skirt. I thought there was nothing remarkable about it at first, and then she moved the skirt through her fingers until I saw the tiny nest woven with horsehair and pierced with two crossed roots sewn into the hem.

"What's that?" I asked.

"It's for warding off evil. I'm saving this for a special occasion. I'll wear it when I fear I am

151

in some sort of danger," she told me.

"I never saw that before, and I thought Nina had shown me just about everything in voodoo."

"Oh no," Abby said, laughing. "A moma can invent something new any time." She laughed. "I was hiding this from you because I didn't want you to think me strange, and here you are, wearing a dime on your ankle for good gris-gris." We laughed and hugged just as Samantha, Jacki, and Kate came wheeling Gisselle past our doorway.

"Look at them!" my twin cried, pointing. "See what happens when you don't have boys at your school."

Their laughter brought blood to both our faces.

"Your sister," Abby fumed. "One of these days I'm going to push her and that wheelchair over a cliff."

"You'll have to get in line," I told her, and we laughed again. Then I hurried out to wait for Miss Stevens.

She drove up a few minutes later in a brown jeep with the cloth top down, and I hopped in.

"I'm so glad you can come," she said.

"I'm glad you asked me."

She had her hair in a ponytail and the sleeves of her sweatshirt pushed up to her elbows. The sweatshirt looked like a veteran of many hours of painting, because it was streaked and spotted with just about every color of paint. In her beat-up jeans and sneakers, she looked hardly more than a year or two older than me.

"How do you like living at the Louella Clairborne House? Mrs. Penny is sweet, isn't she?"

"Yes. She's always jolly." After a moment I said, "I switched roommates."

"Oh?

"I was rooming with my twin sister, Gisselle."

"You don't get along?" she asked, and then she smiled. "If you think I'm getting too personal . . ."

"Oh no," I said, and I meant it. I remembered Grandmere Catherine used to tell me your first impressions about people usually prove to be the truest because your heart is the first to react. Right from the beginning I felt comfortable with Miss Stevens, and I believed I could trust her, if for no other reason than the fact that we shared a love of art.

"No, I don't get along with her," I admitted. "And not because I don't want to or I don't try. Maybe if we had been brought up together, things would be different."

"If?" Miss Stevens's smile melted with confusion.

"We've only known each other a little more than a year," I began, and I told her my story. I was still talking by the time we arrived at the place that overlooked the river. She hadn't said a word the whole time; she just listened quietly.

"And so I agreed to come to Greenwood with Gisselle," I concluded.

"Remarkable," she said. "And I used to think my life was complicated because I was brought up by nuns at an orphanage, St. Mary's in Biloxi."

"Oh? What happened to your parents?"

"I never really knew. All the nuns would tell me was that my mother gave me over to them shortly after I was born. I tried to find out more about myself but they were very strict about keeping confidences."

I helped her set up our easels and put out paper and drawing utensils. The sky had begun to clear, just as the weatherman had promised, and the thick layers of clouds separated to reveal a light blue sky behind them. Here at the river, the breeze was stronger. Behind us the branches of some red oak and hickory trees shuddered and swayed, sending a flock of chirping sparrows off over the riverbank and then into a quieter section of cottonwoods.

An oil barge and a freighter moved rapidly downriver, while off in the distance, a replicated steamboat carrying frolicking tourists churned its way lazily toward St. Francisville.

"Do you think you'll ever find out about your parents?" I asked.

"I don't know. I've sort of accepted that I won't." She smiled. "It's all right. I have an extended family: all the other orphans I knew, some of the nuns." She gazed around. "It's pretty here, isn't it?"

"Yes."

"What catches your eye?"

I studied the river, the boats, and the shore. Downstream I saw the spiraling smoke from the oil refinery stacks get caught in the wind and disappear against the clouds, but it was a pair of brown pelicans bobbing on the water that held my attention. I told her, and she laughed.

"You're like me. You like to put some animal in your settings. Well, let's begin. Let's work on perspective and see if we can capture the feel of movement in the water."

We started to draw, but our conversation didn't stop as we worked.

"How was your tea with Mrs. Clairborne?" she inquired. I described it and how impressed I was with the house. Then I told her about Louis.

"You actually spoke to him?" she asked, pausing.

"Yes."

"I've heard a great deal about Mrs. Clairborne and her grandson from the other teachers, but there are teachers who have been here for years and never set eyes on him. What's he look like?"

I described him and his beautiful piano playing.

"After I told him I was an artist, he suggested I go down to the lake at twilight and try to paint that scene. He wasn't always blind, and he remembers it vividly," I told her.

"Yes. What a tragic story."

"I don't know it."

"You don't? Yes, I understand why. It is one of the unspoken tales, one of those secrets everyone knows but pretends not to," she said. "It has been made clear to me by the old-timers here on more than one occasion not to be caught gossiping

155

about the Clairbornes."

I nodded.

"But I can tell you the story," she said with a smile. "Even if it does seem like gossip. We're simpatico artists and we're permitted little indiscretions." She grew serious for a moment as she focused on the river. Then she began. "It seems Mrs. Clairborne's daughter, Louis's mother, was having an affair with a younger man." She paused and swung her eyes to me. "A much younger man. Eventually her husband discovered it and was so emotionally wounded and embarrassed, he committed what is known as a murder-suicide. He smothered his wife to death à la Othello, using a pillow in their bedroom, and then he shot himself in the head. Poor Louis somehow witnessed it all, and the traumatic effect put him into a coma, from which he eventually emerged blind.

"From what I've been told, there was a major effort to cover it all up, but the story leaked out over time. To this day, Mrs. Clairborne refuses to accept the actual facts, choosing instead to believe her daughter died of heart failure and her son-in-law, unable to accept her death, took his own life." She paused and then widened her eyes when she looked at me.

"After orientation for the new members of the faculty, we were all invited to a tea at the Clairborne mansion. When you were there, did you notice anything unusual about the clocks in the house?"

"Yes. They're all stopped at two-oh-five."

"That's when Mrs. Clairborne's daughter supposedly died. When I asked one of the older teachers about it, he told me Mrs. Clairborne thinks of time as having stopped for her and makes it appear symbolically that way in her home. It's really a very sad story."

"Then there is nothing physically wrong with Louis, nothing wrong with his eyes?"

"From what I've been told, no. He rarely emerges from that dark section of the mansion. Over the years he's been treated and tutored there, and as far as I know, there have been only a handful of people with whom he has carried on any sort of conversation. You made history," she said, and smiled warmly. "But after knowing you only a short time, it's not hard for me to understand why someone reluctant to talk would talk to you."

"Thank you," I said, blushing.

"All of us have trouble communicating with each other. I know I do. I'd rather communicate through my artwork. I'm especially bashful when it comes to men," she confessed. "Maybe because of how I was brought up." She laughed. "I suppose that's why I feel so comfortable at Greenwood, why I wanted to teach at an all-girls school."

She smiled at me again.

"There. We've traded secrets about ourselves, just like sisters in art should. Actually," she continued, "I've always longed for a sister, someone in whom I could confide and someone who would confide in me. Your twin sister doesn't know what she's missing, treating you the way she does. I envy her."

"Gisselle would never believe anyone envied her. She doesn't want envy anyway; she wants pity."

"Poor dear. A severe handicap after being so active would be devastating, I suppose you'll just have to put up with her. But if there is ever anything I can do to help . . ."

"Thank you, Miss Stevens."

"Oh please, Ruby. Call me Rachel when we're not in class. I really would like to feel we're more friends than simply a teacher and her student. Okay?"

"Okay," I said, surprised but not displeased.

"Oh, look: We've been talking so long we've hardly done anything. Come on. Let's shut our mouths and put our fingers to work," she said. Her soft, happy laughter caught the attention of the pelicans, who looked up at us with what seemed to me to be expressions of annoyance. After all, they were here to fish so they could eat.

"Animals know when you sincerely respect them," Grandmere Catherine once told me. "Too bad people don't."

We worked for about two and a half hours, after which Miss Stevens thought we should go for lunch. She took me to a small restaurant just outside the city. Even before we entered, we could smell the delicious aromas of the crab-boil, sautéed shrimp, and salami, fried oysters, sliced tomatoes, and onions that went into a po'boy sandwich. We had a wonderful time talking, comparing the things we liked and disliked about styles and fashions, food and books. I did feel as if I were with an older sister.

It was midafternoon by the time she brought me back to the dorm. She kept my work, promising to bring it to the art studio for me to complete in school.

"This was fun," she said. "We'll do it again if you want to."

"Oh yes, but I can't let you pay for my lunch all the time."

She laughed. "I have to, otherwise it might be construed a bribe," she teased.

I said goodbye and ran into the dorm, where I found Mrs. Penny wringing her hands and waiting for me. Her hair was unraveled, and she was biting her lip.

"Oh, thank goodness you've returned! Thank goodness."

"What's wrong, Mrs. Penny?" I asked quickly.

She took a deep breath, pressing her right palm to her heart, and sat down on the sofa.

"Mrs. Clairborne called. She called herself. I spoke to her." Mrs. Penny gasped as if she had received a call from the president of the United States. "She asked to speak to you, so I went looking for you, and your roommate, Abby, told me you had gone to someplace on the river to paint with your art teacher. She should know better; she should know better."

"What do you mean, know better?" I asked,

smiling inquisitively. "Better about what?"

"On the weekends especially, if you're going to leave the grounds, you have to have permission. I have to have something on record."

"But we just went down to the river to paint," I explained.

"It doesn't matter. She should know better. I had to tell Mrs. Clairborne you weren't here. She was very disappointed."

"What did she want?"

"Something remarkable has happened," Mrs. Penny said, leaning over and whispering loudly. She looked around to be sure none of the other girls were in earshot.

"Remarkable?"

"Her grandson . . . Louis . . . he asked that you be invited to dinner at the mansion . . . tonight!"

"Oh," I said, surprised.

"None of the girls at Greenwood have ever been asked to dinner at the Clairborne mansion," Mrs. Penny said. I just stared at her. My lack of elation shocked her. "Don't you understand? Mrs. Clairborne called to invite you to dinner. You'll be picked up at six-twenty. Dinner is at six-thirty sharp."

"You told her I would go?"

"Of course. How could you think of not going?" she asked. She studied me a moment, her face trembling. "You will go, won't you?"

"I feel a bit nervous about it," I confessed.

"Oh, that's only natural, dear," she said, relieved. "What an honor. And one of my girls too!" she exclaimed, clapping her hands together. Her smile evaporated quickly. "But I must chastise your art teacher. She should have known better."

"No, you must not, Mrs. Penny. If you do, I won't go to Mrs. Clairborne's," I threatened.

"What?"

"I'll tell her about the rule and I'll see to it that my father provides the necessary permission slip, but I don't want Miss Stevens to get into trouble because of me," I said firmly.

"Well . . . I . . . if Mrs. Ironwood should find out."

"She won't."

"Well . . . you just make sure you tell your teacher and get that permission slip," she said. She paused and returned a happy smile to her face. "Now go find something pretty to wear. I'll see to it that the car is here at six-twenty. Congratulations, dear. One of my girls . . . my girls," she muttered as she hurried off.

I took a deep breath. I couldn't help myself from trembling. How silly, I thought. It was just a dinner. It was not like I was being tested or auditioned for anything.

But now that I knew the dark history of the Clairbornes and why Louis was the way he was, I couldn't help swallowing back lumps. Why had I followed the sound of that sweet, sad music and wandered into that room?

Of course, it would have been impossible to keep

my invitation a secret, even if I had wanted to. Mrs. Penny was determined to brag about it, and in no time all the girls at the dorm had heard about Mrs. Clairborne's call. Gisselle was annoyed because she thought I had known about it since the tea and kept it from her.

"I have to find out about my sister from strangers," she chided after she had wheeled herself through our doorway. As usual, Samantha was at her side, ready to do her beck and call.

"I just returned from painting all day at the river with Miss Stevens, so I just found out myself, Gisselle."

"Painting all day with Miss Stevens. Peachy."

She gazed at the dresses I had laid out on my bed for Abby and I to consider.

"It looks like you've been planning. You must have known about this."

"I haven't. I just this moment took out my clothes, right, Abby?"

"Yes," she said, eyeing Gisselle, who still fumed.

"Well, why did she ask only you?" she demanded.

"I don't know," I said.

"It's because her grandson wants you there, right?" Gisselle followed quickly. Sometimes there was no hiding things from her. Her mind wandered through the labyrinths of deceptions and intrigues so often she knew the routes better than a professional spy.

"I guess," I said.

"He can't even see you and he wants you to come back? What did you two do?"

"Gisselle!" I looked from Abby to Samantha and back to my sister. "We didn't do anything. I spoke to him for a few minutes, listened to him play, and left. I'm very nervous about this as it is, so please don't make it any harder. The truth is, I don't even want to go, but Mrs. Penny's made it seem like the event of the century."

"I like the light blue dress," Abby said. "It's elegant but not too formal."

"Oh, it's just perfect for a little dinner with a blind boy," Gisselle quipped, glaring at me. "You'll be up there having a feast and we'll be down here eating dorm rot."

"We don't eat rot," Abby flared.

"Obviously, you're used to it," Gisselle retorted. "Wheel me out of here, Samantha. The air is too rich for our poor nostrils."

Abby whitened and was about to sting Gisselle with some retort when I looked at her and shook my head. "Don't get yourself upset, Abby," I advised. "That's all she wants anyway."

"You're right," Abby said, and we returned to choosing my wardrobe.

The blue dress was elegant. It had a sweetheart collar that revealed just an inch or so of cleavage, but we decided that with my locket and gold chain it still looked discreet. Abby loaned me a pair of gold-leaf earrings and a gold charm bracelet. We decided I should brush my hair and pin it up. I smeared on a trace of lipstick, sprayed myself with

163

the jasmine cologne Mrs. Penny lent me, and finally went out to wait for the car. Mrs. Penny looked me over one final time and placed her stamp of approval on my appearance.

"This is historic," she continued. "Mark every detail in your mind to remember. I can't wait to hear about it. I'll be right here waiting for you, okay?"

"Yes, Mrs. Penny," I said.

Abby smiled at me. "Have a good time," she said.

"Thanks, but I'm as nervous as a jackrabbit."

"You've got nothing to worry about," Abby said, and winked. "You've still got your good luck gris-gris."

I laughed. I had hidden the dime in my shoe, but it was there.

"The station wagon's here," Mrs. Penny announced. I hurried out. Buck was waiting at the car, holding the door open for me. When he turned, his eyes widened and took on a glint of appreciation, but he said nothing. I got in and he hurried around to the driver's side. Mrs. Penny stood on the steps and waved as we drove off. After we were away, Buck turned around.

"You look very nice," he said.

"Thank you."

"I've been here only three years," he said, "but this is the first time I've taken a Greenwood girl to the mansion for dinner. Are you related to the Clairbornes?"

"No," I said, laughing.

When we arrived at the mansion, he hurried around to open the door for me.

"Thank you," I said.

"Have a good time."

I smiled at him and hurried up the steps. The door opened for me before I reached it and Otis nodded.

"Good evening, mademoiselle," he said, bowing even deeper than usual.

"Good evening."

I entered and he closed the door.

"Right this way, mademoiselle."

He led me down the corridor and off to the right through another hallway that took us deep into the west wing and the dining room. Unlike the other sections of the house, the west wing was somber. The walls had darker paper, the windows darker drapes, and the floors darker carpet. The pictures that were hung depicted the most eerie settings on the river and in the bayou, swamps with ghostly Spanish moss that was caught swaying in the twilight breeze, and the Mississippi at one of its wider points, with the water rust-colored, the boats and ships drifting shadows of themselves. Whatever portraits I saw were portraits of austere ancestors gazing out with looks of disapproval and condemnation.

The long dark oak table was set for three at one end. Two silver candelabra held long, bone-white lit candles, their tiny flames flickering. Above the table the chandelier was only dimly lit. Otis moved to the chair on my right and pulled it out to indicate that was where I was to sit.

"Thank you," I said.

"Madame Clairborne and Monsieur Clairborne will be in shortly," he told me, and then left me sitting there alone in the solemn room. It was deathly quiet for a long moment, and then I heard what was now the familiar tap, tap, tap of Mrs. Clairborne's cane as she came down the corridor outside and finally turned into the dining room.

She wore a black dress with a hem that reached almost to her ankles. The ebony color of her garment made the stopped watch on a chain more prominent as it rested in the valley between her breasts. There were no changes to her hairdo, but she had replaced her diamond earrings with pearl ones and wore a pearl bracelet. Her fingers were still filled with all her rings.

"Good evening," she said, making her way to her chair at the head of the table.

"Good evening." After Otis had pulled her chair out and she sat down, I added, "Thank you for inviting me to dinner."

"I didn't," she said quickly. This close to her, I thought her nose looked sharper. Her pale skin was so thin it was almost transparent. I could see the tiny blue veins in her cheeks and temples, and the hairline above her lip was more conspicuous, darker. She reeked of jasmine, overpowering my own.

"I don't understand," I said.

"My grandson is the one who insisted. As a rule I don't invite the schoolgirls to dinner. There are

166

just too many who deserve it," she said. "I was unaware that you had gone off and met him while you were at tea here."

"I heard him playing the piano when I went to the bathroom and . . ."

"Mrs. Penny should have made it perfectly clear that I —"

"Grandmother, you're not misbehaving now, are you?" we heard, and I spun around to see Louis standing in the doorway. Unlike Mrs. Clairborne, he carried no cane to help him navigate the corridors and rooms, and from what I could see, apparently no one had brought him here.

He looked rather handsome in his dinnerjacket, black tie, and slacks, with his hair brushed neatly back.

"I don't misbehave," Mrs. Clairborne muttered. Louis smiled and walked with perfect precision to his place at the table.

"Don't be impressed, Ruby," he explained as he waited for Otis to pull out his chair. "I've been walking the same paths through this house so long I've worn ditches into the floors, and everyone knows not to change a thing in any of the rooms."

"Which is why I don't permit visitors in this section of the house," Mrs. Clairborne said quickly. "If someone moves a chair or shifts a table . . ."

"Now why would anyone, especially Ruby, do that, Grandmother?" Louis asked. Mrs. Clairborne sighed. She nodded at Otis, who began the dinner service by pouring us some bottled water.

"Aren't we going to have any wine tonight?" Louis inquired.

"I don't serve wine to Greenwood girls," Mrs. Clairborne replied firmly.

Louis held his smile. "At least we have our special dinner tonight, don't we, Grandmother?"

"Unfortunately, yes," she said, and turned to me. "Louis insisted also on having a Cajun menu."

"Let me tell her," Louis said eagerly. "We're beginning with a crawfish bisque and then we're having duck gumbo. But for dessert, I ordered orange crème brûlèe, a New Orleans favorite."

"Sounds wonderful," I said. Mrs. Clairborne groaned. Then she nodded reluctantly and the meal was begun. During it, Mrs. Clairborne said very little. Louis wanted to hear about my paintings and asked me to describe the ones I had sold from the gallery in the French Quarter. He had never been to the bayou and wanted to hear about life in the swamps. A number of times during our conversation, Mrs. Clairborne clicked her tongue and gave me a look of disapproval, especially when I described Grandmere Catherine and her work as a *traiteur*.

"I wonder if a *traiteur* could help me to see again," Louis said aloud. That set Mrs. Clairborne off on a tirade.

"I will not bring these charlatans into this house. The countryside is inundated with fake faith healers and scam artists. Unfortunately, the river has attracted that sort since the colonists arrived. You have the best doctors."

"Who haven't done a thing for me," Louis remarked bitterly.

"They will. We must . . ." She stopped herself.

Louis turned slowly and smiled. "Have faith, Grandmother? Was that what you were about to say?"

"No. Yes. Faith in proven science, in medicine, not in mumbo jumbo. Next thing you know we'll have someone to dinner who believes in voodoo," she said, and I held my breath. There was a moment of silence, and then Louis laughed.

"As you see, my grandmother has definite feelings about everything. It makes things easier," he added sadly. "I don't have to think for myself."

"No one ever said you can't think for yourself, Louis. Didn't I agree to have this young lady to dinner tonight?"

"Yes. Thank you, Grandmother." He turned to me. "Did you enjoy the food?"

"It was delicious."

"It should be. I have the finest cook in Baton Rouge," Mrs. Clairborne said.

"Would you like to hear me play the piano?" Louis asked.

"I'd love to."

"Good. May we be excused now, Grandmother?"

"I have instructed the school driver to be ready to pick her up at nine sharp. The Greenwood girls have their homework and their curfew."

"I've done all my homework," I said quickly.

"Still, you should be returned early to your dorm," Mrs. Clairborne insisted.

"What time is it now, Grandmother?" Louis asked. "What time is it?" he demanded. I held my breath. Would she say, two-oh-five?

"Otis, what is the time?" she asked the butler standing in the doorway.

"It's seven-forty, madame."

"Oh then, we have plenty of time," Louis said. "Shall we go to the music studio." He stood up. I looked at Mrs. Clairborne, who appeared very unhappy, and then stood up too.

"Thank you for a wonderful dinner, Mrs. Clairborne."

Her thin lips moved into a grotesque mockery of a smile. "Yes, you're very welcome," she said quickly.

Louis held up his arm, and I walked around the table and threaded mine through his.

"Wearing Grandmother's favorite scent, I see," he said, smiling. "Someone prompted you, huh?"

"Mrs. Penny, our housemother," I confessed. He laughed and led me out of the dining room and to his study. He did move through the house as confidently as one who could see, and when we arrived at the study, he went directly to his piano without the slightest hesitation.

"Sit beside me," he suggested, making room on the stool. After I did so, he began to play something soft and sweet. The melody seemed to flow out of his fingers and then into the piano. His torso swayed gently, his shoulder grazing mine. I watched his face as he played and saw the tiny movements in his lips and eyelids. When the piece came to an end, he kept his fingers on the keys as if the music still continued to flow from him.

"That was beautiful," I said softly.

"My piano teacher . . . ordinarily a stuffed shirt . . . believes my blindness makes my playing sharper. He sounds almost envious at times. He confessed to me that he has taken to blindfolding himself when he is alone and plays. Can you imagine?"

"Yes," I said.

With his fingers still on the keys, his body postured for him to play another piece, he continued to speak instead. "I've never had a girl . . . a young woman . . . beside me before," he confessed. "I've never been this close."

"Why not?"

He laughed. "Why not?" His smile faded. "I don't know. I've been afraid, I suppose."

"Afraid?"

"Of being at a great disadvantage. For Grandmother's sake, more than my own, I pretend I'm all right. Of course, she doesn't see me groping about. I make sure of that. She doesn't hear my moans. I can't remember the last time she's seen me cry. We do a lot of pretending here. I'm sure you've noticed. We pretend everything's all right. We pretend nothing's happened.

"But I'm tired of pretending," he said, turning

around. "I want . . . some reality too. Is that wrong?"

"Oh no."

"I heard something in your voice when you first came in here, something honest and true, something that put me at ease, that gave me hope. It was almost as if . . . as if I could see you," he said. "I know you're beautiful."

"Oh no, I'm not. I'm . . ."

"Yes you are. I can tell from the way Grandmother speaks to you. My mother was beautiful," he added quickly. I held my breath. My heartbeat started to quicken. Was he going to tell me the tragic tale? "Would you mind if I touched your face, your hair?"

"No," I said, and he brought his fingers up to my temples and slowly, gently, traced the lines of my face, running the tips of his fingers over my lips and down to my chin.

"Beautiful," he whispered. The tip of his tongue swept over his lower lip as he continued down my neck and found my collarbone. "Your skin is so soft. Can I go on?"

My throat felt tight. My heart began to pound. I was confused but afraid to deny him. He seemed so desperate.

"Yes," I said. His fingers moved down to the border of my collar and followed it to my cleavage. I saw his breathing quicken. He ran his hands over my breasts, turning and pressing his fingers as if he were a sculptor shaping them. His hands moved down my ribs to my waist and then back up again

172

so that his palms flowed over my breasts.

Then, suddenly, he pulled them away as if he had touched an uncovered electrical wire. He lowered his head.

"It's all right," I said. Instead of replying, he brought his fingers to the keys again and began to play, only this time his music was loud and hard. A line of sweat broke out along his temple. His breathing quickened. He seemed determined to exhaust himself. Finally he concluded, this time slapping his palms over the keys.

"I'm sorry," he said. "I shouldn't have had Grandmother ask you here."

"Why not?"

He turned his head slowly.

"It's a torment, that's why," he said. "I'm nearly thirty-one years old, and you are the first woman I've touched. My grandmother and my cousin have kept me in mothballs," he added bitterly. "If I hadn't thrown a temper tantrum, Grandmother wouldn't have called you today."

"That's terrible. You shouldn't be kept prisoner in your own house."

"Yes, I am a prisoner of sorts, but my prison isn't the house. It's my own thoughts that lock me up!" he cried, bringing his hands to his face. He groaned deeply. I put my hand on his shoulder. He lifted his hands from his face and asked, "You're not afraid of me? I don't disgust you?"

"Oh no."

"You feel sorry for me, is that it?" he asked bitterly.

"Yes, somewhat, but I also appreciate your talent," I added.

He softened his expression and took a deep breath. "I want to see again," he said. "My doctors tell me I'm afraid to see again. You think that's possible?"

"I guess so."

"Have you ever run away from anything you couldn't face?"

"Oh yes," I said.

"Will you tell me about it sometime? Will you return?"

"If you'd like me to, yes."

He smiled. "I made up a melody for you," he said. "Want to hear it?"

"You did? Yes, please."

He started to play. It was a wonderfully flowing piece that, remarkably, made me think of the bayou, of water and of beautiful birds and flowers.

"It's very beautiful," I said when he had finished. "I love it."

"I call it 'Ruby.' I'll have my teacher write out the notes, and the next time you come I'll give you a copy, if you like."

"Yes, thank you."

"I'd like to know more about you . . . especially how you came to be brought up in the Cajun world but ended up living with a well-to-do Creole family in the Garden District."

"It is a long story."

"Good," he said. "I'd like it to be like Scheherazade and the Arabian Nights. . . . A story that goes on and on, just so you would be here on and on."

I laughed, and he brought his fingers to my face again and again he traced the lines down to my lips, only this time he held his fingers there longer.

"Can I kiss you?" he asked. "I've never kissed a girl before."

"Yes," I said, not quite sure why I was allowing him such intimacies. He leaned toward me and I guided him with my hands to my lips. It was a short kiss, but it quickened his breath. He dropped his hands to my breasts and leaned in to kiss me again, holding his lips to mine longer as his fingers brushed my breasts as lightly as feathers. He tried to push the material away from more of my breasts and was frustrated.

"Louis, we shouldn't . . ."

It was as if I had slapped him. He not only pulled back but this time rose from the stool.

"No, we shouldn't. You should go now," he said angrily.

"I didn't mean to . . ."

"To what?" he cried. "Make me feel like a fool? Well I do. I'm standing here aroused, aren't I?" he asked.

One glance told me it was so.

"Louis."

"Just tell my grandmother I got tired," he said. His arms dropped stiffly to his sides and he started away, moving toward the door.

"Louis, wait," I cried, but he didn't stop. He hurried off. Pity for him flooded through me. I followed to the doorway and gazed down the corridor after him. He seemed to be absorbed by the very darkness in which he dwelt and in moments was gone. I listened for his footsteps, but there was only silence. Curious, I walked farther into the west wing of the house, passing another, smaller sitting room and then going around the corner to stop at the first door. I knocked gently.

"Louis?"

I heard no response but tried the handle anyway. The door opened, and I looked in on a beautiful, spacious bedroom with a grand canopy bed, the mosquito netting around it. The room had a damp, fecund odor, and I saw that the flowers in the vases were all dead. Two small lamps that looked like antique oil lamps were lit. They were on the night stands and threw just enough illumination to outline what looked like someone lying in the bed, but on closer inspection, I saw it was just a woman's nightgown laid out for someone's use.

I was about to close the door when suddenly, an adjoining door on the right was thrust open and Louis appeared. I wanted to call to him but he groaned deeply and slammed his fists into his eyes, falling to his knees at the same time. The act took away my breath. I stood trembling in the doorway. He wrapped his arms around himself and swayed for a moment, then he clawed at the door jamb and pulled himself into a standing position. Head down, he turned and closed the door. I waited a moment, looked over the bedroom once again, and then stepped back and closed the door softly.

Practically tiptoeing, I made my way back to the center of the house and finally to the sitting room in which we had had our tea. Mrs. Clairborne was in her chair, staring up at the portrait of her husband.

"Excuse me," I said. She turned slowly. I thought I saw tears winding down her pale cheeks. "Louis said he was tired and went to his room."

"Oh. Fine," she said, rising. "Your driver is waiting outside to take you back to your dorm."

"Thank you again for dinner," I said.

Otis appeared at the door as if he'd popped out of thin air and opened it for me.

"Good night, mademoiselle," he said, bowing.

"Good night."

I hurried out and down the steps to the car. Buck hopped out quickly and opened the door.

"Have a good time?" he asked.

I didn't respond. I got in and he closed the door. As we drove off, I looked back at the mansion. Louis and his grandmother were about as rich and as powerful as any family I had known or would know, I thought, but that didn't mean that un-happiness stopped outside their door.

How I wished Grandmere Catherine were still alive. I would bring her up here secretly one night, and she would touch Louis and he would see again and put aside all his sadness. Years later, I would

177

attend a concert in some magnificent hall to listen to him play. Before it was over, he would stand up and announce that the next piece was something he had written for someone special.

"It's called 'Ruby,' " he would say, and then he would begin and I would feel like someone who in the spotlight.

Grandmere would say it was all wishful thinking, dreams as thin as soap bubbles. But then she would shake her head sadly and add, "At least you can have dreams. That poor boy . . . he lives in a house without any dreams at all. He truly lives in darkness."

7

So Many Rules

As she had promised, Mrs. Penny was waiting for me in the lobby of the dorm when I arrived. She jumped out of her chair and came rushing to greet me, her eyes full of excitement and expectation.

"How was your dinner?" she cried.

"It was very nice, Mrs. Penny," I said, looking over her shoulder at the girls from the A and B quads who were watching television. Most had turned my way curiously.

"Just nice?" she asked, with disappointment. She looked like a little girl who had been told she couldn't have any ice cream. I knew she wanted a list of superlatives from me, a flood of adjectives, but I wasn't in the mood. She lit up again with a new question. "What did Mrs. Clairborne serve?"

"A shrimp dish," I replied, without mentioning the Cajun recipe. "Oh, and an orange crème brûlèe for dessert," I added. That pleased her.

"I was hoping she would do something special. What did you do afterward? Did you sit and talk in the same sitting room in which we had tea, or did you go on to one of the glass-domed patios?"

"I listened to Louis play the piano. He grew tired and I came back," I summarized.

She nodded "It was an honor," she said, still nodding, "a very high honor. You should be proud of yourself."

For being invited to a dinner? Why wasn't it more of an honor to paint a beautiful picture, or get high marks on a school test? I wanted to ask, but I simply smiled back instead and excused myself.

Gisselle, surrounded by Samantha, Kate, and Jacki, was holding court in the lounge when I arrived. From the pink flush in all the girls' faces I imagined Gisselle had been describing one of her sexual exploits back in New Orleans. They all turned with some disappointment at my interruption, but I had no intention of joining them.

"Well, look who's back," Gisselle quipped, "the princess of Greenwood."

Everyone laughed.

"How was your evening, princess?"

"Why don't you stop making an ass of yourself, Gisselle," I retorted.

"Oh. I'm sorry, princess. I didn't mean to offend your royal bosom," she continued, the laughter of her fan club following quickly. "We poor underlings had a rather uneventful dinner, except for the part where I accidentally spilled my hot soup on Patti Denning." They all laughed again. "How was Louis? At least tell us that much."

"Very nice," I said.

"Did you go groping in the dark with him?" she asked. Despite myself, I couldn't keep my blood from rushing into my cheeks. Gisselle's eyes widened. "Did you?" she pursued.

"Stop it!" I screamed, and crossed quickly to my room. I slammed the door shut to cut off the laughter behind me. Abby looked up from her textbook, surprised at my abrupt entrance.

"What's wrong?"

"Gisselle," I said simply, and she smirked with understanding. She sat up and closed the book on her lap.

"How was your evening?"

"Oh, Abby," I cried. "It was . . . so strange. Mrs. Clairborne didn't really want me there."

She nodded as if she had always known. "And Louis?"

"He's in great emotional pain . . . A very talented, sensitive person, as twisted and knotted inside as swamp grass in a boat motor's propeller," I said. And then I sat down and told her all that had happened. It made us both melancholy, and after we had gotten undressed and into our beds, we lay awake for hours, talking about our pasts. I told her more about Paul and the terrible frustration I had experienced when I learned that the boy I was so fond of was really my half brother. She compared this horrible joke Fate had played on me with her own discoveries about herself and her family lineage.

"It seems both of us have been wounded by events over which we have no control . . . like

181

we're being made to pay for the sins of our parents and grandparents. It's so unfair. We should all have a fresh start."

"Even Louis," I remarked.

"Yes," she said thoughtfully, "even Louis."

I closed my eyes and fell asleep to the memory of his composition entitled "Ruby."

The week that followed began uneventfully, with the promise of being routine. Even Gisselle seemed to calm down and to do some real schoolwork. I noted a remarkable change in her behavior when she was at school. In the two classes we shared, she was quiet and attentive. She even surprised me by stopping her entourage in the hallway after English to have Samantha pick up some gum wrappers someone had discarded near the water fountain. Of course, she still held court in the cafeteria, sitting back like some grand duchess whose words were to be treated with royal respect and commenting on this one and that one, usually in a mocking fashion that stimulated choruses of laughter from the ever-growing audiences she gathered around her.

But the sarcasm that had characterized her replies to questions in class and her ridicule of our teachers and our homework assignments were absent from her speech and behavior. Twice, when Mrs. Ironwood was standing in the corridors observing the students as they passed between periods, Gisselle had Samantha pause so she could greet the Iron Lady, who nodded back with approval.

But watching my sister's unusual good behavior

made me feel like I was watching a pot of milk being boiled. It was bound to bubble up, lift the lid, and simmer over into the flames. I had lived with her long enough to know not to trust her promises, her smiles, and her kind words — whenever any spilled out from her cunningly twisted lips.

What happened next seemed at first totally unrelated. I would have to trace back the zigzag conniving that wrapped itself around my twin sister's evil mind before I could find her true purpose in all this. Ultimately, it stemmed from her initial anger over being brought to Greenwood. Despite her apparent good adjustments, she was still quite upset about it and, as I would learn, quite determined to get back to her old friends and her old ways.

On Wednesday morning, a message was sent into my social studies class, asking me to report to Mrs. Ironwood's office. Whenever anyone was called out of class to see the Iron Lady, the other students looked at the girl with pity and with relief that it wasn't any of them who had been summoned. After having experienced one session with our principal, I understood their fear. Nevertheless, I revealed no nervousness as I stood up and walked out. Of course, my heart was pounding by the time I arrived at the office. One look at the expression on Mrs. Randle's face told me I had trouble.

"Just a minute," she snapped, as if she was an emotional extension of Mrs. Ironwood, mirroring her moods, her thoughts, her angers and pleasures. She knocked on the door and this time whispered my name. Then she closed the door and went back to her desk, leaving me standing in anticipation. She kept her eyes down on her paperwork. I shifted my weight from one foot to the other and sighed deeply. Nearly a minute later, Mrs. Ironwood opened her door.

"Come in," she ordered, and stepped back. I threw a glance at Mrs. Randle, who lifted her eyes and then lowered them instantly, as if looking at me was as deadly as it was for Lot's wife when she looked back at Sodom and was turned into a pillar of salt.

I walked into the office. Mrs. Ironwood shut the door behind me and marched to her chair.

"Sit down," she commanded. I took my seat and waited. She threw me a hard look and began. "By this time it would not be unreasonable of me to expect that one of my new students had read the Greenwood School handbook, especially if that new student was scholastically outstanding," she said. "Am I correct?" she asked.

"Yes, I suppose so," I said.

"You've done so?"

"Yes, although I haven't committed it to memory," I added, perhaps too sharply, for her eyes narrowed into slits and her face whitened, especially at the corners of her mouth. Her frown deepened before she continued.

"I don't ask for it to be committed to memory so it can be recited word for word. I ask that it be read, understood, and obeyed." She sat back and snapped open a handbook, tearing back the pages and then slapping the book open.

"Section seventeen, paragraph two, regarding leaving the Greenwood campus. Before a registered student can leave the school boundaries, she must have specific, written parental permission on file with the administrative office. This must be dated and signed.

"The reasoning behind this is simple," she went on, looking up from the manual. "We incur certain liabilities when we accept a student. If something terrible should happen to you while you are not under our supervision, we would bear the brunt of the blame if we permitted you to gallivant about at your every whim.

"Normally, I don't find it necessary to explain our reasoning, but in this case, with your particular history, I have done so just so that you understand I am not, as some of your type are bound to claim, picking on you.

"Your teacher should have known better than to take you in her automobile. She has already been reprimanded and her indiscretion noted in her file. When her renewal comes up, it will be one of the considerations."

I stared at her. It was difficult to breathe, to not be drowned by everything that was happening so fast. Mrs. Penny had obviously betrayed me, I thought, and after she had promised she wouldn't. Now she had gotten both me and Miss Stevens in trouble.

"That's not fair. She only wanted to provide me an opportunity to paint. We didn't go anyplace terrible. We . . ."

"She took you to lunch too, didn't she?" she demanded, her eyes hardened to rivet on me.

"Yes," I said. Something hard and heavy grew in my chest, making it ache.

"What if you had gotten sick from the food? Who do you think would be blamed? We would be blamed," she replied, answering her own question. "Why, we could even be sued by your parents!"

"It wasn't a dirty little restaurant. It was —"

"That's not the point now, is it?" She sat back again and fixed her gaze on me with those cold steel eyes. "I know your kind," she said disdainfully.

Daring her scorn, I fired back: "Why do you keep saying things like that? I'm not a 'kind.' I'm a person, an individual, just like anyone else who attends this school."

She laughed. "Hardly," she said. "You are the only girl with a rather depraved background. Not one of my other girls has a blemish on her family history. In fact, over eighty percent of the girls in this school come from families that can trace their lineage back to one of the hundred *Filles à la Cassette* or 'Casket Girls' who were originally brought to Louisiana."

"My father can trace his lineage back to them too," I said, even though I didn't place any value on such a thing.

"But your mother was a Cajun. Why, she was probably of questionable mixed blood. No," she continued, shaking her head, "I know your kind, your type. Your bad behavior is more insidious, subtle. You learn quickly who are the most vulnerable, who have certain weaknesses, and you play to those weaknesses, like some sort of swamp parasite," she added. My face flushed so hot I thought the top of my head would blow off. But before I could respond, she added what I realized was her real reason for calling me in.

"Just like you somehow managed to take advantage of my poor cousin Louis and get yourself a dinner invitation to my aunt's home."

The blood started to drain from my face.

"That's not true," I said.

"Not true?" She smiled coyly. "Many young women have dreamed of winning Louis's heart and becoming the one who would inherit this vast fortune, this school, all this property. A young blind man is hardly a catch otherwise, is he? But he is vulnerable. That's why we have been so careful about who he has as company up to this point.

"Unfortunately, you managed to make an impression on him without my aunt's knowledge, but don't think anything will come of it," she warned.

"That was never my intention. I didn't even want to go to dinner at the mansion," I added. She widened her eyes with surprise, her lips curled in a skeptical smile. "I didn't, but I felt sorry for Louis and . . ."

"You felt sorry for Louis? You?" She laughed

coldly. "Don't worry about Louis," she said. "He'll be just fine."

"No he won't. It's wrong to keep him encased in that house like a caterpillar in a cocoon. He needs to meet people . . . especially young women and —"

"How dare you have the impudence and audacity to suggest what is good for my cousin and what is not! I will not tolerate another syllable from your lips about him, is that clear? Is it?" she shrilled.

I looked away, my eyes burning with tears of anger and frustration.

"Now then," she continued, "now that it is well known on this campus, I'm sure, that you have violated section seventeen of our behavior code, it is appropriate that you be punished. Such a violation carries twenty demerits, which automatically invokes a two-week denial of all social privileges. However, since this is your first real offense and since your teacher bears some of the blame, I will limit the punishment to one week. From today until the end of the sentence, you are to report directly back to your dorm after school hours and to remain there throughout the weekend. If you violate this for so much as one minute I will have no alternative but to expel you from Greenwood, which I am sure will impact on your poor crippled sister as well," she said.

Icy tears streamed down my cheeks. My lips quivered and my throat felt as if I had swallowed a lump of coal.

"You can return to your class now," she concluded, slapping the handbook shut.

I stood up, my legs wobbly. I wanted to shout back at her, to defy her, to tell her what I really thought of her, but all I could see was Daddy's disappointed face and hear the deep sadness in his voice. This was just what Daphne would like, I thought. It would reaffirm her accusations about me and make life even more difficult for Daddy. So I swallowed back my indignation and pain and left her office.

For the remainder of the day, I felt numb. It was as if my heart had turned to cold stone. I went through the motions, did my work, took my notes, and walked from class to class with my eyes fixed ahead, not looking from left to right, not interested in any conversations.

At lunch I told Abby what had happened.

"I'm so disappointed in Mrs. Penny," I concluded.

"She must have been frightened into it," Abby said.

"I suppose I can't blame her. The Iron Lady could scare the tail off an alligator."

Abby laughed.

"I won't go anywhere this weekend either," she told me.

"You don't have to do that: to punish yourself unfairly just because I'm being punished unfairly."

"I want to. I bet you'd do it for me," she added wisely. I tried to deny it, but she just laughed as if I were speaking gibberish. "Besides, I don't consider spending time with you a punishment," she put in. I smiled, my heart full at making such a good friend so quickly.

But when I entered the art studio for my last class of the day, I felt as if I had swallowed a cup full of tadpoles. Miss Stevens took one look at me and hurried over to my desk.

"Don't worry," she whispered. "I'll be all right. Actually, I'm sorrier that I got you in trouble than I am about myself."

"That's how I feel about you."

She laughed. "I guess we'll have to take Louis's advice and start painting the lake, since that's on school grounds. Until you get your parents' permission to leave, that is."

"Not for a week," I added.

"In the meantime, you still have the river picture you've started to complete." She squeezed my hand. "Anyway, artists aren't expected to behave and obey the rules. Artists are impulsive and unpredictable. We have to be in order to be creative."

She made me feel better again, and I didn't think about my punishment and my meeting with Mrs. Ironwood until I returned to the dorm and saw Mrs. Penny straightening the furniture in the dorm lobby. I pounced on her.

"I thought we had a deal," I snapped at her. "I thought we agreed."

"Deal?" She smiled in confusion. "What do you mean, Ruby dear?"

"I thought you weren't going to tell about me

and Miss Stevens going to the river to paint," I said.

She shook her head. "I didn't tell. I've been worried about it, but I didn't tell. Why?" She pressed her palms to her bosom. "Did Mrs. Ironwood find out?"

"Yes. I'm confined to the dorm for a week. No social privileges. I'm sure you'll be told about it shortly."

"Oh dear, oh dear," she said, her hands fluttering from her bosom to her plump cheeks as if they were birds looking for a place to alight. "That means she's going to be calling me to find out why I didn't know and why I didn't tell her when I found out. Oh dear."

"Just say I snuck out," I said quickly. "Just say you never knew. I'll confirm that if she asks."

"I don't like lying. See: One falsehood leads to another and another."

"You didn't lie."

"I didn't do what I was supposed to do. Oh dear." She walked away in a daze.

It wasn't until later in the evening, when I had a chance to speak to Gisselle alone in her room, that I realized what had really happened.

"You hate it here now, don't you?" she asked me after I had told her about my meeting with Mrs. Ironwood. "Now maybe you'll tell Daddy we should leave and return to our own school." Her smile turned oily and evil. "I still want to leave, even though the Iron Lady likes me more than she likes you. Why, we're almost pals," she added with a laugh.

And then it came to me: why she had been pretending to be a good student, why she had been behaving. She had ingratiated herself with Mrs. Ironwood and then she had told on me and Miss Stevens.

"You're the one who ratted, aren't you, Gisselle? You got me and Miss Stevens in trouble."

"Why would I do that?" she asked, shifting her eyes away.

"Just so I would be punished and be unhappy and you could pressure me to ask Daddy to get us out of here. And because of your constant jealousy of me," I told her.

"Me? Jealous of you?" She laughed. "Hardly. Even though I'm in this wheelchair, I'm still head and shoulders above you. You've got years and years of swamp life to overcome. You and your Cajun family," she said contemptuously. "Now, are you going to call Daddy or not?"

"No," I said. "I won't break his heart and hand Daphne another victory over us."

"Oh, you and your stupid competition with Daphne. Why don't you want to get back to our school where there's no Iron Lady and none of these stupid rules, where we have boyfriends and fun?" she whined.

Unable to hold back, I flared. "From what I can see," I said, "you're having loads of fun here — and at my expense or someone else's every single day."

Samantha stepped into the room but hesitated

when she saw my face and heard my loud voice.

"Oh, I'm sorry. Did you two want to be alone?"

"Hardly," I said, my face on fire. "And if I were you and your friends, I'd be very careful about what I said and did around here from now on."

"What? Why?" Samantha asked.

I gazed with fury upon my twin sister. "Things have a way of getting back to Mrs. Ironwood," I said, and pivoted to march out of the room.

But Gisselle almost had the victory she wanted when Beau phoned that night. He was very excited about his upcoming trip to Greenwood to see me on Saturday. I had forgotten for the moment because of all the trouble. My heart was breaking; the tears came pouring down my face as I told him.

"Oh Beau, you can't come this weekend. I can't see you. I've been punished and confined to my dorm."

"What? Why?"

Shuddering through my gasps and cries, I told him what had happened.

"Oh no," he said. "We've got an away game the following weekend. I won't be able to come for at least two more weeks then."

"I'm sorry, Beau. You have every right to forget me, to find yourself someone else," I said.

"I won't do that, Ruby," he promised. "I have your picture in the top pocket of my shirt every day, close to my heart. I take it out and gaze at it every now and then in school. Sometimes," he confessed, "I even talk to you through your picture."

"Oh Beau, I miss you."

"Maybe if I come up, you can sneak out and —"

"No, that's just what she wants, Beau. Besides, Gisselle would love to reveal it even if no one else knew, just so she could get me expelled."

"I'm with Gisselle."

"I know, but it would break my father's heart and cause all sorts of new problems at home. Somehow, Daphne would find an even worse situation for me and for Gisselle. And that would be terrible, even though Gisselle deserves it," I added angrily.

Beau laughed. "All right," he said. "I'm going to call you then and I'm going to plead with Father Time to hurry along."

After I had hung up. I stood there sobbing. Mrs. Penny saw me and came hurrying down the corridor.

"What is it now, Ruby dear?" she asked.

"Everything, Mrs. Penny." I ground the tears from my eyes with my small fists and sighed. "Mostly, my boyfriend. He was coming to see me this weekend and I just had to tell him I can't see him."

"Oh. Oh!" she added, wide-eyed. "You spoke to him on the phone?"

"Yes. Why?"

She looked up and down the corridor and shook her head.

"You can't do that, Ruby. You're not permitted to use the phone for social calls for a week. Mrs. Ironwood has made that perfectly clear."

"What? I can't even use the phone?"

"Not for social calls. I'm sorry. All I need is for one more thing to happen that gets Mrs. Ironwood angry at me, and she might give me my discharge," she said sadly. "I'll post that restriction on the bulletin board so all the other girls will know not to call you to the phone. I'm sorry. If you get any social calls, I'll have to talk to the person and explain. I'll give you any messages, however."

I shook my head and then lowered it. Maybe Gisselle was right. Maybe we were better off fleeing from Greenwood and taking our chances with Daphne. My heart felt torn in two: One side was crying for Daddy and what would happen and the other crying for Beau and what had happened.

I returned to my room to bury my sobs in my pillow and do what Beau had said he would do: pray to Father Time and ask him to rush the minutes, the hours, and the days.

I plodded through the remainder of the week, preparing myself for a weekend of what amounted to house arrest, when the second unexpected event occurred. On Friday night after dinner, after most of the other girls in the dorm had gone to the auditorium to see a movie, Mrs. Penny came to my room. Abby and I were amusing ourselves with a game of Scrabble and listening to music. There was a light knocking on the door and I raised my eyes to see our housemother looking rather confused and troubled.

"You had a phone call," she announced. I imagined it had been Beau again. When Mrs. Penny didn't continue but instead wrung her hands and bit on her lower lip nervously, I glanced quizzically at Abby and then turned back to her.

"Yes?"

"It was Mrs. Clairborne's grandson, Louis."

"Louis! What did he want?"

"He wanted to speak to you. I told him why you couldn't come to the phone and he became very . . ."

"Very what, Mrs. Penny?"

"Nasty," she said, with obvious amazement. "I tried to explain how I had no control over the situation, how it wasn't in my power to change things, but he . . ."

"But he what?"

"He just started to scream at me and accuse me of being part of some conspiracy headed by Mrs. Ironwood. Honestly," she declared, shaking her head, "I never heard such talk. Then he slammed the phone down on me. It's given me the shakes," she said, embracing herself.

"I wouldn't worry about it, Mrs Penny. As you said, you don't have any say in the matter."

"Of course, I've never heard him speak before. I . . ."

"Just forget about it, Mrs. Penny. After my period of punishment, I'll try to reach him and see what it was he wanted."

"Yes," she said, nodding. "Yes. Such anger. I feel . . . so shaken," she concluded and walked off.

196

"What do you suppose he wanted from you?" Abby asked.

I shook my head. "I can understand why he feels it's all a conspiracy. His grandmother and the Iron Lady control every moment of his life, especially whom he sees. Mrs. Ironwood made it clear to me she wasn't happy that I went up there for dinner," I said.

But whatever control Mrs. Clairborne and Mrs. Ironwood had enjoyed over Louis seemed to be weakening, for early the next morning, Mrs. Penny returned to my room to announce a new turn of events. She was obviously very impressed and excited about it. Abby and I had barely finished dressing for breakfast when she was at our door.

"Good morning," she said. "I had to come right down to tell you."

"Tell me what, Mrs. Penny?"

"Mrs. Ironwood has called me directly to tell me you will be permitted to go out for two hours this morning."

"Go out? Go where?" I asked.

"To the Clairborne plantation house," she said, her eyes wide.

"She will let me go out and she will let me go to the plantation?" I looked at Abby, who seemed just as amazed as I was. "But why?"

"Louis," Mrs. Penny replied. "I imagine he's insisting on seeing you today."

"But maybe I don't want to see him," I said, and Mrs. Penny's mouth dropped. "I could never get permission to see my boyfriend, who won't be able to come up here now for two weeks and who would have had to drive for hours, but I can be permitted to go up to the plantation house. These Clairbornes play pretty fast and loose with other people's feelings — picking people up and putting them back down again as though we're only pieces on their personal chessboards." I complained and sat back on my bed.

Mrs. Penny wrung her hands and shook her head. "But . . . but this must be very important if Mrs. Ironwood is willing to bend the punishment somewhat. How can you not want to go? It will only make everyone even angrier at you, I'm sure," she threatened. "They might even blame it on me."

"Oh, Mrs. Penny, they can't blame anything on you."

"Yes, they can. I'm the one who didn't tell them that you had left the campus in the first place, remember?" she reminded me. "That's what started all this," she wailed.

The cloud of fear under which everyone at Greenwood lived disgusted me. "All right," I relented. "When am I supposed to go?"

"After breakfast," she said, relieved. "Buck will have the car out front."

Still unhappy and annoyed, I changed into something more appropriate and went to breakfast with Abby. When Gisselle heard where I was going after breakfast, she threw one of her temper tantrums at the table, stopping all other conversation and

198

drawing everyone's attention to us.

"No matter where you go or what you do, you become Little Miss Special. Even the Iron Lady makes special rules for you and not for everyone else," she complained.

"I don't think Mrs. Ironwood is doing anything for me or is very happy about it anyway," I replied, but Gisselle only saw one thing: I was being permitted to break out of my imprisonment.

"Well, if any of us get punished, we're going to remind her about this," she threatened, firing her angry gaze at everyone around the table.

After breakfast I left the dorm and got into the car. Buck said very little, except to mutter about how his repair work kept getting interrupted. Apparently no one was happy about my command appearance at the Clairborne plantation. Mrs. Clairborne didn't even appear to greet me. It was Otis who led me through the long corridor to the music studio, where Louis waited at his piano.

"Mademoiselle Dumas," the butler announced, and left us.

Louis, dressed in a gray silk smoking jacket, white cotton shirt, and dark gray flannel slacks, raised his head. "Please, come in," he said, realizing that I was still standing in the doorway.

"What is it, Louis?" I asked, not disguising the note of annoyance in my voice. "Why did you ask that I be brought back here?"

"I know you're angry with me," he said. "I treated you rather shabbily and you have every right to be mad. I embarrassed you and then ran out on you. I wanted you to come up here so I could apologize to you face to face. Even though I can't see you," he added with a tiny smile.

"It's all right. I wasn't angry at you."

"I know. You felt sorry for me. and I guess I deserve that too. I'm pitiful. No," he said when I started to protest. "It's all right. I understand and accept it. I am to be pitied. I remain here, wallowing in my own self-pity, so why shouldn't someone else look at me pathetically and not want to have anything much to do with me?

"It's just that . . . I felt something about you that drew me a little closer to you, made me less afraid of being laughed at or ridiculed — something I know most girls your age would do, especially Grandmother's precious Greenwood girls."

"They wouldn't laugh at you, Louis. Even the crème de la crème, the direct descendants of the *Filles à la Cassette*," I said with ridicule. He widened his smile.

"That's what I mean," he said. "You think like I do. You are different. I feel I can trust you. I'm sorry I made you feel as if you were summoned to appear in court," he added quickly.

"Well, it's not that, so much as I was punished and . . ."

"Yes. Why were you punished? I hope it was something very naughty," he added.

"I'm afraid it's not." I told him about my painting trip off campus and he smirked.

"That was it?"

200

I wanted to tell him more — how his cousin Mrs. Ironwood had it in for me for meeting him — but I decided not to add fuel to the fire. He looked relieved.

"So I pulled a little rank, so what? My cousin will get over it. I've never asked her for anything before. Grandmother wasn't overjoyed, of course."

"I bet you did more than pull a little rank," I said, stepping closer to the piano. "I bet you pulled a little tantrum of your own."

He laughed. "Just a little." He was silent a moment, and then he handed me a few pages of notes. "Here," he said. "It's your song."

At the top of the page was the title "Ruby."

"Oh. Thank you." I put it into my purse.

"Would you like to take a walk through the gardens?" he asked. "Or rather, I should say, take me for a walk?"

"Yes, I would."

He stood up and offered me his hand.

"Just go through the patio doors and turn right," he directed. He scooped his arm through mine and I led him along. It was a warm, partly cloudy morning, with just a small breeze. With amazing accuracy, he described the fountains, the hanging fern and philodendron plants, the oaks and bamboo trees and the trellises erupting with purple wisteria. He identified everything because of their scents, whether it be camellias or magnolias. He had the surroundings memorized according to aromas and knew just when we had reached a set of patio doors on the west side of the house that, he said, opened to his room.

"No one but the maids, Otis, and my grandmother have ever been in my room since my parents died," he said. "I'd like you to be the first outsider, if you like."

"Yes, I would," I said. He opened the patio door and we entered a rather large bedroom, which contained a dresser, an armoire, and a bed made of mahogany. Everything was very neat and as clean and polished as it would be had the maid just left. A portrait of a pretty blond woman was hung over the dresser.

"Is that a painting of your mother?" I asked.

"Yes."

"She was very beautiful."

"Yes, she was," he said wistfully.

There were no pictures of his father or any pictures of his father and mother together. The only other paintings on the walls were of river scenes. There were no photographs in frames on the dresser either. Had he had all pictures of his father removed?

I gazed at the closed door that connected his room with the room I knew must have been his parents' bedroom, the room in which I had seen him curl up in emotional agony that night.

"What do you think of my self-imposed cell?" he asked.

"It's a nice room. The furniture looks brand-new. You're a very neat person." He laughed.

And then he turned serious, letting go of my arm and moving to his bed. He ran his hand over the footboard and the post. "I've slept in this bed since I was three years old. This door," he said, turning around, "opens to my parents' bedroom. My grandmother keeps it as clean and polished as any of the bedrooms still in use."

"This must have been a nice place to grow up in," I said. My heart had begun to pitter-patter, as if it sensed something my eyes had missed.

"It was and it wasn't," he said. His lips twisted as he struggled with his memories. He moved to the door and pressed his palm against it. "For years and years, this door was never locked," he said. "My mother and I . . . we were always very close."

He continued to face the door and speak as if he could see through it into the past. "Often in the morning, after my father had gotten up to get to work, she would come in and crawl up beside me in my bed and hold me close so I could wake up in her arms. And if anything ever frightened me . . . no matter how late or early, she would come to me or let me come to her." He turned slowly. "She was the only woman I have ever laid beside. Isn't that sad?"

"You're not very old, Louis. You'll find some-one to love," I said.

He laughed a strange, thin laugh.

"Who would love me? I'm not only blind . . . I'm twisted, as twisted and ugly as the Hunchback of Notre Dame."

"Oh, but you're not. You're good-looking and you're very talented."

"And rich, don't forget that."

He walked back to the bed and took hold of the post. Then he ran his hand over the blanket softly.

"I used to lie here, hoping she would come to me, and if she didn't come on her own, I would pretend to have been frightened by a bad dream just to bring her here," he confessed. "Is that so terrible?"

"Of course not."

"My father thought it was," he said angrily. "He was always bawling her out for spoiling me and for lavishing too much attention on me."

Having been someone who never knew her mother, I couldn't imagine being spoiled by one, but it sounded like a nice fault.

"He was jealous of us," Louis continued.

"A mother and her child? Really?"

He turned away and faced the portrait as if he could see it.

"He thought I was too old for such motherly attention. She was still coming to me and I was still going to her when I was eight . . . nine . . . ten. Even after I had turned thirteen," he added. "Was that wrong?" he demanded, spinning on me. My hesitation put pain in his face. "You think so too, don't you?"

"No," I said softly.

"Yes you do." He sat on the bed. "I thought I could tell you about it. I thought you would understand."

"I do understand, Louis. I don't think badly of you. I'm sorry your father did," I added.

He raised his head hopefully. "You don't think badly of me?"

"Of course not. Why shouldn't a mother and a son comfort and love each other?"

"Even if I . . . pretended to need the comfort just so she would come to me?"

"I guess so," I said, not quite understanding.

"I'd open the door a little," he said, "and then I would return to my bed and lay here, curled up like this." He spread himself out and folded into the fetal position. "And I'd start to whimper." He made the small sounds to illustrate. "Just go over to the door," he said. "Go ahead. Please."

I did so, the pitter-patter of my heart growing stronger, faster, as his actions and words became more confusing.

"Open it," he said. "I want to hear the hinges squeak."

"Why?"

"Please," he begged, so I did so. He looked so happy. "Then I would hear her say, 'Louis? Darling? Are you crying, dear?'

" 'Yes, Mommy,' I would tell her.

" 'Don't cry, dear,' she would say." He hesitated and turned his head in my direction. "Would you say that to me? Please?" he asked me.

I was silent.

"Please," he pleaded.

Feeling foolish and a bit frightened now, I did so. "Don't cry, dear."

"I can't help it, Mommy." He held his hand out. "Take my hand," he begged. "Just take it."

"Louis, what . . ."

"I just want to show you. I want you to know and to tell me what you think."

I took his hand and he pulled me toward him.

"Just lay down beside me for a moment. Just a moment. Pretend you're my mother. I'm your little Louis. Pretend."

"But why, Louis?"

"Please," he said, holding my hand even tighter. I sat on the bed and he drew me down toward him.

"She would come just like this and I would stroke her shoulder as she would stroke my hair and kiss my face, and then she would let my hand run down over her breasts," he said, running his hand over mine, "so I could feel her heartbeat and be comforted. It was what she wanted me to do. I did only what she wanted me to do! Was that wrong? Was it?"

"Louis, stop," I pleaded. "You're torturing yourself with these memories."

"Then she would put her hand here," he said, seizing my right wrist and bringing it between his legs, where he had already begun to grow hard. I pulled my hand away as if I had touched fire.

The tears were streaming down his cheeks now.

"And my father. . . he came in on us one day and he grew very angry with both of us and then he had the door locked and if I should cry or complain, he would come in and beat me with a leather strap. Once he did it so much, I had welts over my legs and back and my mother had to put salve over my body afterward, and then she tried to make me feel good again.

"But I couldn't and she became very unhappy too. She thought I had stopped loving her," he said, his face changing into an expression of fury. Then his lips began to tremble as he struggled to bring the words out of them, words that had haunted him. In a gush, he blurted, "So she tried to make another boy her son and my father found out."

He seized my hand with both his hands and brought it to his lips and his face, caressing the back of my hand with his cheeks.

"I've never told anyone that, not even my doctor, but I can't stand keeping it all inside me anymore. It's like having a hive of bees in your stomach and chest. I'm sorry I brought you here and made you listen. I'm sorry."

"It's all right, Louis," I said, stroking his hair with my other hand. "It's all right."

His sobbing grew harder. I put my arms around him and held him close as he cried. Finally he grew quiet and still. I lowered his head to the pillow, but when I let go of his hand, he seized mine again.

"I'm afraid I've made a mess of this visit too, but just stay a little while longer," he said. "Please."

"All right. I will."

He relaxed. His breathing grew softer, more regular. As soon as he was asleep, I slipped off the bed and tiptoed out the patio door. I walked quickly through the garden and back through the studio. Hurrying down the corridor toward the front door, I glanced to my right when I saw a shadow move. It was Mrs. Clairborne, peering out of a doorway. I stopped and started to turn to her but she closed the door. I hesitated only a moment longer before fleeing the plantation full of shadows and pain.

8

Suspicions

By the time I returned to the dorm, something hard and heavy had grown in my chest, making it ache, so I was grateful that for once Gisselle and her clique were not in the lounge waiting to pounce on me when I entered our quad. Listening to Louis's revelations about himself and his mother and father, I felt as if I had trespassed and wandered into a confessional, overhearing someone else's sins. Abby took one look at my face and knew I had gone through something terrible.

"Are you all right?" she asked softly.

"Yes," I said.

"What happened?"

I shook my head. I couldn't get myself to talk about it, and she understood. Instead, I dove into my homework and began studying for upcoming exams in math and science. I dreaded facing Gisselle's biting questions and remarks later. I don't know whether she was just trying to show she wasn't interested in the things I did or whether she really didn't care, but neither at lunch nor at dinner did she inquire about my visit at the plantation. She looked like she was still smarting over the fact that my punishment had been mitigated.

Actually, we had a very quiet Sunday night. Jackie, Katie, and Vicki left the dorm to go to the school library, which was open until nine, and Gisselle and Samantha spent most of their time in their room or out in the lobby, watching television and talking to girls from the other quads.

I soaked in a hot bath and then went to bed early. Before I fell asleep, Abby asked me again what it was Louis had wanted. I took a deep breath before I replied.

"Mostly to apologize for his behavior the last time," I told her. I didn't even know how to begin telling her about the things he told me concerning his relationship with his mother and father.

"Are you going back there to visit him?"

"I don't want to," I admitted. "I feel sorry for him — I really do — but there are more dark turns and swamp holes in that plantation house than there are in the bayou. Being rich and coming from a distinguished family background doesn't guarantee happiness, Abby. In fact, it might make happiness harder to find because you have to live up to all that expectation."

Abby agreed and then she wished for something.

"I wish my parents would stop trying to hide the truth and keep people from knowing I'm descended from a Haitian woman. I'm a quadroon, and there's no sense pretending otherwise. I think we'd all be happier being who we are."

"We all would," I said.

Louis didn't call or contact me the next day, but on Tuesday, Mrs. Penny brought me a letter that Louis had had delivered to the dorm. She stood in the doorway of my room for a few moments, hoping I would open it in her presence, I suppose, but I simply thanked her and put it aside. My fingers trembled when I opened it later.

Dear Ruby,

I just wanted to scribble out this note to thank you for coming to see me again after I had been so unpleasant to you the first time. I was surprised when I woke up in my room hours after you had apparently left and found myself alone. I don't even remember what I did or said prior to your leaving, but I hope it wasn't anything that upset you. Naturally, I hope you will visit with me again.

And now for a piece of exciting news. Yesterday I woke up and for the first time saw a hazy light. I can't see anything really, but I can suddenly distinguish between light and shadows. It might not sound like much to someone with sight, but to me it's almost a miracle. Grandmother is excited about it too, and so is my doctor, who wants me to spend time in an institute for the legally blind. I'm not ready to leave home and do that and I have continued instead with my periodic doctor's visits at the house. So if you so decide, I will be here and can see you almost any time you wish. I would like that very much. I hope you enjoy the song I wrote for you.

With deepest regards,
Louis

I put the note in with my box of letters I had received from Paul and from Beau. Then I sat down and wrote a short note expressing my happiness for Louis and hope that his sight was really returning. I made no specific mention about another visit but instead made a vague promise to see him again soon. Mrs. Penny said she would see to it that my letter was delivered promptly.

About midweek, the excitement over our first social, the Halloween dance, began building. It was practically the only subject the girls wanted to discuss at dinner. I was surprised to learn that costumes weren't permitted. Abby and I were discussing it when we saw Vicki sitting in the lounge, reading a biography of Andrew Jackson. We asked her about the prohibition. Annoyed with the interruption, she looked up from her reading and shifted her glasses back on the bridge of her nose.

"Because some of the costumes girls chose to wear at past Halloween dances were deemed inappropriate dress, it was decided there wouldn't be any costume ball as such," she explained.

"Oh, too bad," I said, just imagining some of

the costumes Miss Stevens and I could have created. I had remained after school all week to help Miss Stevens, who had been given the assignment to decorate the gymnasium. We drew and cut out pumpkins and witches, goblins and ghosts. On Saturday, she and I and some members of the school's social committee would put everything up in the gymnasium, along with cray paper streamers, Japanese lanterns, and tons of tinsel.

"So then what should we wear?" Abby asked Vicki.

"You can wear what you want, but I'll warn you that anyone whose clothes are too sexy or too revealing will be stopped at the gym door."

"Really?"

"Yes. Mrs. Ironwood stands off to the side and either nods or shakes her head when we enter, and then the teacher on duty, usually Mrs. Brennan or Miss Weller, our librarian, admits or refuses to admit you. If you're refused admittance, you have to go back to your dorm and change into something considered more appropriate.

"Inappropriate dress includes anything that reveals even a smidgen of cleavage, a skirt that shows your knees, or a blouse or sweater that is too tight around your bosom. One time last year a girl was sent back because she wore a blouse too thin. It revealed the outline of her bra."

"Why don't we just dress in our uniforms and forget it," Abby suggested with disgust. "Or is that considered a costume?"

"Some girls do wear their uniforms."

"You're kidding?" I said. "To a dance?"

Vicki shrugged, and I wondered if she hadn't been one to have worn her uniform.

"What is the dance like?" Abby asked.

"The boys gather on one side of the gym and we on the other. Just before or just after the music starts, they cross and ask us to dance. They must ask properly, of course."

"Of course," I said. She smirked.

"Didn't you read the section in the handbook concerning the proper behavior at school socials?" she asked us. "Naturally, smoking or drinking anything alcoholic is strictly forbidden, but there is also an acceptable and unacceptable way to dance. It specifically says that there should be a clear inch or so between you and the boy when you're on the dance floor."

"I didn't read that," Abby said.

"It's in there. Check the footnotes."

"Footnotes!" I moaned and then laughed. "What are they afraid will happen on a dance floor?"

"I don't know," Vicki said, "but that's the rule. You're not supposed to leave the gym with a boy alone either, but a lot of girls get around that by leaving separately and then meeting someplace outside," Vicki said. "Anyway, the dance lasts two and a half hours exactly, after which Mrs. Ironwood announces it has come to an end and stops the music. The boys are told to board their bus and the girls are told to return to their dorms. Some girls escort the boys they've met to the bus, but Mrs. Ironwood is out there watching to see how they say goodbye. Passionate kissing is strictly forbidden, and if she should catch a girl permitting a boy's hands to wander, that girl will get a note about it and some demerits, which might prohibit her from attending the next social."

"Mrs. Ironwood should come to one of the fais dodos in the bayou," I whispered to Abby, who laughed.

Vicki frowned.

"Anyway," she concluded, "the refreshments are usually very good."

"Sounds like . . . loads of fun," Abby said, and we giggled so much that Vicki went back to her reading.

But despite the rules and restrictions and the promise of being followed by Mrs. Ironwood's eagle eyes and the eyes of other teachers on duty, excitement over the social continued to build all week long.

Gisselle, who was normally bitter about the fact that she couldn't get up and dance, was quite enthusiastic about all this party preparation. Her devoted followers gathered around her more often and more closely to listen to her experienced advice about boy-girl relations. She obviously enjoyed tutoring them in the ways of a coquette, describing the things she did to tease and torment and draw a boy's attention. On Thursday and Friday night, she actually sat in the lounge and instructed Jacki, Samantha, and Katie on how to walk, turn their shoulders, flutter their eyelashes, and how to find ways to brush their bosoms against the arms and chests of the boys they fancied. Vicki stood in her doorway scowling, but listening and observing like someone who wished she could enter a forbidden world; while Abby and I kept off to the side, smiling but saying nothing to bring on one of Gisselle's nasty tirades.

Then on Saturday morning, just before I went off to help set up the decorations, Gisselle surprised me by wheeling into our room to talk to Abby. Samantha was at her side.

"It's none of my business, I know, but you really ought to wear your hair down and pin the sides up so that more of your forehead and face are visible. We all voted and agree you are the prettiest, Abby," she said. "You have the best chance to be chosen queen of the dance tonight, and that would make us all very proud."

For a moment Abby was speechless. She looked at me and I looked back, smiling and shaking my head. What was my sister up to now? I wondered.

"Here," she said, offering Abby a white silk ribbon. "This would look perfect in your ebony hair."

Hesitantly, Abby took the ribbon. She studied it for a moment, as if she expected it would explode in her hands, but it was nothing more than a pretty silk ribbon.

"Are you going to wear something blue or pink?" Gisselle followed.

"I was thinking of my dark blue dress. It's one that definitely meets the skirt-length requirement," she added, laughing.

"Nice choice," Gisselle said. "What about you, Ruby?"

"I thought I'd wear the Kelly green."

"Then so will I. We'll be real twins on Saturday night," she added. "Why don't we all go over to the gymnasium together and enter as a unified quad?"

Abby and I looked at each other again, suspicion and surprise still in both our faces.

"Okay," I said.

"Oh," Gisselle said after she had started to turn her wheelchair. "I almost forgot. Susan Peck has been telling her brother about Abby. He's very anxious to see and meet her," she added. "You remember everyone talking about Jonathan Peck, how they all drool over him every time Rosedown is brought to Greenwood for a social."

"Susan?" Abby said. "I don't think she's said a word to me since I've been here."

"She's shy," Gisselle explained. "But Jonathan's not," she added with a wink. We watched her turn her chair and then waited as Samantha took over and wheeled her out.

"What was all that about?" Abby asked.

"Don't ask me. My sister is more mysterious than an owl peering out from behind Spanish moss in the swamp. You never know what you'll find until you drift by, and by then it's usually too late."

Abby laughed.

"Nice ribbon, though," she said, then tied it in her hair and gazed at herself in the mirror. "I think I will wear it."

As the day wore on, the air of excitement became contagious. Girls from all the quads were coming around to see each other, show off a new dress, pair of shoes, bracelet, and necklace, or just talk about hairstyles and makeup. At the socials the Greenwood girls were permitted to indulge in makeup, as long as they didn't go overboard and, as the handbooks said, "appear clownish."

Gisselle and Samantha's room took on more importance as the girls from the other quads paid visits, as if to pay homage to someone whom everyone now accepted as the most experienced girl in the dorm. Despite her handicap, Gisselle sat back confidently and arrogantly in her chair and approved and disapproved garments, hairstyles, even make up, as if she had been in charge of costumes and makeup at some Hollywood studio all her life.

"This is a school full of social retards," she whispered to me later when we met in the hallway. "One girl thought an orgasm had something to do with mining zinc. Get it? *Ore-gasm.*"

I had to laugh. In a way I was happy Gisselle was really enjoying herself. I had feared that as the social between Greenwood and Rosedown drew closer and closer, she would become more and more depressed and bitter; but the exact opposite had happened, and I felt relief. I myself wasn't looking to find a new boyfriend or anything, but I was eagerly anticipating the distraction the dance would provide. What I was really looking forward to, of course, was Beau's arrival the following weekend. I was determined not to do anything to endanger that visit, a visit I had been anticipating for so long.

Late in the afternoon after I had returned from helping put up the decorations, Daddy called. Gisselle spoke to him first and talked so long and so much about the dance, he had to laugh about her when I took the phone and began speaking.

"I'll be up to see you girls on Wednesday," he promised. Despite his happiness over Gisselle's apparently settling down at Greenwood, there was something in his voice that put a heaviness in my chest and made my heart thump.

"How are you, Daddy?" I asked.

"I'm fine. A little tired, maybe. I've been running around too much. We've had some business problems I've had to fix."

"Maybe you shouldn't make the trip up to see us then. Maybe you should just rest, Daddy."

"Oh no. I haven't seen my girls for some time now. I can't neglect them," he said, laughing, but the laughter was followed with a stream of coughing. "Just a stubborn chest cold," he said quickly. "Well, enjoy yourselves. I'll see you soon," he concluded before I could pursue him and his health any further.

I was troubled by our conversation, but I didn't have time to dwell on it. The hours were ticking by. We were all getting ready to shower, and dress, and fix our hair. Fun was so rare at Greenwood that everyone wanted to hoard it and cherish it and make it into something greater than it was. I couldn't blame them. I felt that way myself.

As Gisselle had unexpectedly requested, the girls from our quad all left the dorm together to go to the gymnasium. Gisselle was ready at seven-thirty. With Samantha pushing her at the forefront, we walked to the main building, our voices full of excitement. Everyone — even Vicki, who ordinarily neglected her coiffeur and clothes — looked very pretty. Seeing ourselves day in and day out dressed in the Greenwood uniform, we welcomed the dramatic changes in style, material, and color. It was as if we had all gone into our respective dormitories as dull-colored caterpillars so identical we looked like clones and emerged as monarch butterflies, each unique and beautiful.

Thanks to Miss Stevens and our committee, the same could be said about our gymnasium. The decorations and the lights, the streamers and the tinsel transformed it into a dazzling ballroom. The six-piece orchestra was set up in the far left corner, all the musicians in black tie and tuxedos. At the head of the room was a small desk and podium with a microphone for Mrs. Ironwood to make her announcements and declarations, and from which the queen of the dance would be declared and crowned. The trophy, a golden Greenwood girl twirling on a pedestal, glittered from its place at the center of the small table.

Off to the right were the long tables for the buffet that had been prepared by all the chefs in all the dorms. One table was dedicated to desserts and was covered with a variety of sweets and party breads ranging from almond tarts and brownies with caramel icing to old-fashioned pumpkin bread and orange muffins. There were crepes and French market doughnuts, sheets of pralines, and pecan crisps.

"That's where Chubs will camp out, won't you, Chubs?" Gisselle quipped as soon as we set eyes on the dessert table.

Katie blushed. "I'm going to be a good girl tonight and not overdo it."

"How boring," Gissell replied.

We all passed through the entryway, the eyes of the chaperones sweeping up from our feet to our hair, while off to the left Mrs. Ironwood stood glaring analytically at each and every one of her wards to be sure she was properly attired. The faculty surrounded her and mingled around their own refreshment table.

Chairs for the Greenwood girls had been set up on the left side of the gymnasium and chairs for the Rosewood boys on the right. Just like the other girls, we headed directly for the punch bowl first, got our cups to hold and sip, and found places on our side of the gymnasium as we waited for the arrival of the Rosewood boys. A little before eight o'clock, Suzzette Huppe, a girl from Quad A in our dorm, came rushing in to announce that the Rosewood buses had driven up. All of us lowered our voices in anticipation as the Rosewood boys began entering in an orderly fashion.

They were all dressed in their dark blue blazers and matching slacks. On the breast pocket of each blazer was the Rosewood insignia, a gold-embroidered shield with Latin words that Vicki said meant "Excellence is our tradition." The design was supposedly the original Rosewood family emblem that originated in England.

The boys were all well groomed, their haircuts nearly identical. Just like the girls of Greenwood, the boys of Rosewood gathered in small cliques. They gazed across the gymnasium floor nervously. Some who recognized girls they had met before at previous socials waved. Then they all huddled around the punch bowls as we had and filled their cups. The sound of laughter and conversation rose as the last group of Rosewood boys streamed into the ballroom.

"There's Jonathan." Jacki indicated with a nod. We all gazed at a tall, dark-haired, handsome boy who seemed to be the center of his group. He was tan with broad shoulders, and he looked like a heartthrob movie star. It was easy to understand why he was so popular with the Greenwood girls. But he stood, spoke, and moved as if he knew it. Even from across the gymnasium, I could sense that Southern arrogance that some aristocratic young men inherited. As his eyes swept the Greenwood girls, he smiled disdainfully, muttered something to his pals that caused them all to laugh, and then stood back expectantly, as if this whole social were being given in his honor.

Then everyone grew silent as Mrs. Ironwood

went to the podium to welcome the Rosewood boys.

"I don't see any reasons to remind you all that you are the young women and young men of distinguished families who are attending two of the most highly respected schools in the state, if not the country. I'm sure you will all behave properly and leave as you have arrived: proud and deserving of the honor and respect your families enjoy. In exactly one hour we shall interrupt the dancing so we can all partake in the wonderful and delicious foods our Greenwood chefs have prepared for this occasion."

She nodded at the orchestra leader, who turned to his musicians and started the first musical number. Those Rosewood boys who were familiar with a girl or two at Greenwood started across the floor to ask them for a dance. Gradually other boys built up their courage and began to approach the girls. When Jonathan Peck started toward us, we all assumed he was going to approach Abby, just as Gisselle had suggested; but he surprised us all by stopping in front of me and asking for a dance. I glanced at Abby, who smiled, gazed at Gisselle, who wore a gleeful expression, and then accepted Jonathan's hand. He took me out to the center of the floor before placing his right hand on my hip and holding my left up at the classic ballroom level, even with my chin. With the perfect precision of a schooled dancer, he began to move and turn me to the rhythm and beat, holding that confident look in his face, his eyes fixed on mine.

"I'm Jonathan Peck," he said.

"Ruby Dumas."

"I know. My sister has told me all about you and your twin sister, Gisselle."

"Really? What did she tell you?"

"Only nice things," he said with a wink. "As you probably know by now, Rosewood and Greenwood are practically sister and brother schools anyway. We Rosewood boys usually get to hear all the nitty-gritty about the girls of Greenwood. You girls can't hide anything from us," he added smugly and glanced back at Gisselle, whom I noticed had already attracted the interest of half a dozen Rosewood boys. But what surprised me more was Abby. She was standing off, to the side. None of the Rosewood boys had asked her to dance; nor did any who were around Gisselle, laughing and joking, show any interest in her. Even Katie had been asked to dance.

"For instance," he continued, "I know you fancy yourself an artist, right?"

"I don't 'fancy' myself anything. I *am* an artist," I fired back.

His smile widened and he threw his head back with a short and what I thought artificial laugh. "Of course. You are an artist. How rude of me to imply otherwise."

"And what are you, besides a walking encyclopedia about the nitty-gritty details on the girls of Greenwood?" I snapped. "Or is that your only ambition?"

"Wow! Susan was right. You and your sister

are two balls of fire."

"Be careful then," I warned. "You might get burned."

This brought another peal of laughter from him. He winked and smiled at his companions and twirled me a little more firmly, but I didn't lose my poise. Having danced at a Cajun fais dodo more than a dozen times in my life, I had no trouble keeping my balance and looking graceful in Jonathan Peck's hands.

"This is going to be a very interesting night," he predicted as the first number came to an end. "I'll call on you again," he promised, "but first I have a few fans to please."

"Oh, don't strain yourself," I said. My stern retort stunned him for a moment. I turned and left him standing there and hurried back to Abby's side.

"What's wrong?" she asked, seeing the flush in my cheeks.

"He's obnoxious, more arrogant than a cottonmouth snake, and probably just as poisonous. I bet he has mirrors on every wall in his room."

Abby laughed. Another number began and I was approached by a different boy, one somewhat on the shy side, which I thought was a welcome change. The boys who were around Gisselle remained, one rushing off to get her another glass of punch. Once again, when I looked back from the dance floor, I noted that all of the girls in our quad had been asked to dance but Abby. Left alone for the second time, she looked uncomfortable but tried to keep her happy demeanor, smiling and nodding at me.

"I'm sorry," I told the boy with whom I was dancing, "but my ankle's started to ache. I sprained it a few days ago. Why don't you ask my girlfriend to continue?" I nodded in Abby's direction. The boy, a redhead with a splatter of freckles on both his cheeks, gazed at her and then shook his head quickly.

"That's all right," he said. "Thanks." He let go of me and hurried back to his companions.

"What happened?" Abby asked when I returned to her side.

"I must have twisted my ankle out there before. It started to ache, so I asked to stop dancing." I didn't tell her about the boy's refusal to ask her to dance.

"The music's very good," she said, swinging to the rhythm.

Why weren't any of these boys coming over to her? So many of them stood on the other side of the gymnasium looking anxious to ask a girl to dance. I glanced at Gisselle, who threw her head back to laugh at something one of the boys had told her. She took his hand and pulled him down so she could whisper something in his ear that lit his eyes like Christmas lights. His face turned crimson, and then he grinned nervously at his friends. Gisselle looked over at us and flashed a smile full of self-satisfaction.

At the start of the third number, I felt confident someone would ask Abby to dance, especially when two boys headed directly for us. But one veered off to ask Jacki to dance and the other approached me instead.

"No, thank you," I said. "I have to rest a sprained ankle. But my friend's free," I added, tilting my head toward Abby. He gazed at her and, without a word, turned and hurried down the line to ask someone else.

"Did I put on the wrong perfume or something?" Abby wondered.

My heart began to flutter as a small panic began in the base of my stomach and climbed its way into my breast. Something was going on here, something very strange, I thought, and I looked toward my sister again. She looked smug and content. Dance after dance, boys would approach me, and if I refused and suggested they ask Abby, they flew off muttering excuses and approached someone else. It not only amazed me but annoyed me how the girl who was beyond a doubt one of the prettiest, if not *the* prettiest, in the school could go this long without being asked to dance. Just before the break for refreshments was announced, I pulled Gisselle's wheelchair aside.

"Something's going on here, Gisselle," I told her. "Not one boy has asked Abby to dance and none will if I suggest he ask."

"Really? How remarkable," she said.

"You have a way of keeping your ear to the wall, Gisselle. What's going on? Is this some sort of practical joke, because if it is . . ."

"I don't know anything about any practical

227

jokes. No one's asked me to dance either, you'll notice, but I don't see you being so concerned about my feelings," she snapped back.

"But you look like you're having a good time. All those boys . . ."

"I'm just teasing them for my own amusement. You think I enjoy being trapped in this chair while everyone else gets to dance and move about the ballroom? Poor Abby . . . poor, poor Abby," she said, turning down the corners of her mouth. "You've made her into your sister because she's a whole person with no handicap."

"That's unfair. You know that's not true. You're the one who wanted to change roommates and —"

The music stopped and Mrs. Ironwood announced the serving of refreshments. A great cheer went up and everyone began moving toward the tables.

"I'm hungry and I've promised those boys I'd sit with them and let them feed me," she said slyly. "You can go and sit with poor Abby." She whirled away and into the awaiting clump of Rosewood boys she had somehow turned into flypaper. They argued over which one of them would assume Samantha's assignment and wheel Gisselle across the floor. She turned back to flash a look of deep pleasure at me and then laughed shrilly and reached up to take another boy's hand while his companions hovered around her.

"My sister is being her infuriating self," I told Abby. Many of the boys were being perfect gentlemen and getting food for a Greenwood girl before they got any for themselves, but no one offered to get anything for Abby and me. Boys cleared a space for me at the food tables but they didn't for Abby. After we had gotten what we wanted, we found a table off to the side. No one joined us, not even the other girls from our dorm. We were left alone.

Mrs. Ironwood walked around the tables with Miss Weller, greeting some of the Rosewood boys, talking to some of the girls. When they came around toward our table, Mrs. Ironwood paused, glared our way, and then turned down another aisle.

"I don't have the measles broken out over my face or anything, do I?" Abby asked.

"No. You look . . . beautiful."

She smiled weakly. Neither of us had a great appetite, but we ate just to fill the empty time. Way off to our right, Gisselle sat at a table with only boys. Whatever she was telling them had them in stitches. They couldn't do enough for her. She merely had to glance at something, and two or three of them would nearly fall over each other to get it.

"Was your sister always this popular with boys?" Abby asked enviously.

"As long as I've known her, yes. She has a way of appealing to a side of them that titillates. Who knows what sort of promises she's been making," I added angrily.

The social committee fanned out and handed the girls their ballots for queen of the dance. Two girls followed afterward with boxes into which we were to throw our choices.

"I bet Gisselle has everyone voting for her," I muttered.

"I'm voting for you," Abby said.

"And me, you."

We laughed, then filled out our ballots and deposited them.

After we had had some dessert, Abby and I went to the girls' room to freshen up. It was jammed with everyone gossiping and laughing, but the moment we walked in a great deal of the talk ended. It was as if we were pariahs, lepers who had the others terrified we might touch or infect them. We gazed thoughtfully at each other, wondering.

The second half of the evening proved no different from the first, only the longer I stood beside Abby, the less and less I was approached too. By the time the next-to-last musical number was played, Abby and I were the only ones not dancing. Just before the last dance of the night, Mrs. Ironwood went to the microphone once again.

"It is a tradition here at Greenwood, as most of you know, that at the end of a social event, especially at the end of a formal dance, the girls choose their queen of the dance. The social committee has tallied the votes and asked that I call up Gisselle Dumas to announce the results."

Abby and I looked at each other with surprise. When did Gisselle arrange this? I wondered. She backed herself away from her male admirers and wheeled herself across the floor to the sound of applause. Then she turned and faced the party-goers, a happy smile across her face. One of the members of the social committee then brought the results to Gisselle. The microphone was lowered so she could speak into it.

"Thank you for this honor," she said. "It's just peachy." She turned to the girl who had the results. "The envelope, please," she said, as if it were the Academy Awards. Everyone laughed. Even Mrs. Ironwood relaxed her lips into something of a smile. Gisselle tore open the folded paper and read it to herself. Then she cleared her throat.

"We have a somewhat surprising choice," she declared. "A first for Greenwood, according to what the committee has written here." She gazed at Mrs. Ironwood, who now looked more intense, more interested. "I shall read the winner's name and exactly what the committee has written after it." She looked our way. "The girls of Greenwood have chosen Abby Tyler," she declared.

Abby's eyes widened with surprise. I shook my head in wonder, but it was as if the first shoe had dropped. The room became silent. Abby started to stand up. My heart began to pound when I looked around at the faces of the other girls. They all seemed to be holding their breaths.

Gisselle gazed at the card and then brought her mouth to the microphone to add, "Who is the first quadroon ever to have been chosen."

It was as if we had fallen into the eye of a storm. There wasn't a giggle or even a cough. Abby froze.

She looked down at me, her eyes filled with shock. So this was why none of the boys would ask her to dance. They had been told she was a quadroon. And this was why Gisselle had been so sweet and offered the white silk ribbon for Abby's hair: so all the boys would know who she was the moment they set eyes on her.

"Who told her?" Abby whispered.

I shook my head in denial. "I would never . . ."

"Come get your trophy," Gisselle screamed into the microphone.

Abby stood in front of me, even straighter and taller than she usually did, looking for all the world like a beautiful princess. "Don't worry, Ruby," she said, "it's okay. I had already decided to tell my parents that they must stop living a lie. I relish each and every part of my ancestry and never again will I hide any of it." She walked across the room and out the door.

"I guess she didn't like our trophy," Gisselle quipped. There was a roar of laughter that continued even after I had run from the ballroom after her. I flew into the hallway and hurried to the side door that just closed behind my friend. By the time I was outside, she was halfway across the campus, her pretty head held high, walking into the darkness.

"Abby! Wait!" I called, but she didn't stop. By now she was crossing down to the driveway that led to the road away from the school. I started in that direction too, when I heard my named called.

"Ruby Dumas."

I turned to see Mrs. Ironwood standing behind me in the pool of illumination from the lights above the doorway of the school.

"Don't you dare set foot off the grounds of this school," she warned.

"But Mrs. Ironwood, my friend . . . Abby . . ."

"Don't you dare."

I turned and looked in Abby's direction, but all I could see was darkness now, darkness and deep shadows that reached back and extended deep enough to drape over my own broken heart.

9

A Friend in Need

"I'd advise you to get yourself back to your social," Mrs. Ironwood warned. She had stepped up and now hovered behind me like a hawk about to pounce. The sky had turned stormy and foreboding in the distance, heralding rain and wind. For a moment I continued to stare into the darkness of the road, hoping to see Abby reappear, but I saw nothing. I stood like an island with the sea eddying around me, so miserable and unhappy. "Did you hear what I said?" she snarled.

With my head down, I turned back toward the building and walked past Mrs. Ironwood without so much as glancing at her.

"Never have I seen such behavior," she continued, following me and chanting. "Never. Never. Never have one of my girls so openly embarrassed the school."

"How could having a bright, beautiful, and kind student like Abby ever be an embarrassment? I hope she will be proud of her heritage, just like I am of my Cajun past," I shot back. She hoisted her shoulders and glared down at me with her stone-cold eyes. Silhouetted against the increasingly foreboding sky, she had become as ominous and as dark as one of Nina's voodoo spirits.

"When people go where they don't belong, they only make problems for themselves," she declared with her imposing, authoritative tone.

"Abby belongs here more than anyone else," I cried. "She's the smartest, nicest . . ."

"This is not the time nor the place to discuss such matters, and anyway, it is no concern of yours," she spit out, using her words like tiny knives to cut away my complaints. "Your concern should be about yourself and your own behavior. I thought I made that quite clear the last time we had a talk."

I stared at her a moment as a terrible anger washed over me. Grandmere Catherine had taught me to respect my elders, but surely she had never anticipated me having to show a woman like Mrs. Ironwood respect. Her age and her position shouldn't shield her from justifiable criticism, I thought, even if it came from someone as young as I was, but I bit down on my lower lip to keep my fiery words locked inside my mouth.

The Iron Lady seemed to enjoy my struggle to keep control. She glared back at me, waiting, hoping to see me become insubordinate so she could justify a harsher punishment, perhaps even have me expelled and keep me from ever seeing Louis again, which, I suspected, had become her real motive.

I swallowed back my tears and fury, spun away from her, and returned to the ballroom, where I found the last dance in progress. Most of the girls glanced my way with interest, most with smiles on their faces. Whatever they uttered to their male companions brought laughter. It sickened me to see such joviality after what had been done to Abby.

Over by the tables, Gisselle held court, surrounded now by more followers and admirers, including Jonathan Peck. Her laughter was so shrill it could be heard over the music.

"I bet that's the first time a girl's turned down the Greenwood dance trophy," she said as I approached, more for my benefit than anyone else's. There was more laughter. "Oh, here's my sister. Give us a report, Ruby. Where's the quadroon gone?"

"Her name is Abby," I fired back. "And thanks to you she left."

"What do you mean, thanks to me? All I did was read the results of the vote, and why would anyone run off after winning?" Gisselle asked with an expression of utter innocence. The others nodded and smiled, gleefully anticipating my response.

"You know very well why, Gisselle. You did a very mean thing tonight."

"Don't tell me you condone the presence of mixed bloods at Greenwood," Jonathan remarked. He pulled his shoulders back and pressed down the sides of his hair with his palms as if he were standing in front of a mirror instead of a dozen admiring females. I turned on him.

"What I don't condone is the presence of cruel and vicious people at Greenwood, nor do I condone the presence of snobs and arrogant young men who think they're somehow God's gift when in truth they're more in love with themselves than they could ever be with anyone else," I retorted.

Jonathan's face flushed red. "Well, I see where you stand when it comes to associating with people of a lower class. Perhaps you're in the wrong place too," he said, looking to the young men and women who had gathered around us for support. Almost all nodded in agreement.

"Maybe I am," I said, hot tears burning under my eyelids. "I'd rather be in a swamp surrounded by alligators than here with people who look down on other people because of their background."

"Oh, stop being such a goody-goody," Gisselle complained. "She'll get over it."

I drew closer to her, my eyes so filled with fury that the girls around her parted to make way. Hovering over her chair, I folded my arms under my breasts and spit my question down at her.

"What did you do, Gisselle? Listen with your ear to our door?"

"You think I'm so interested in your private talks? You think there's anything you've done that I haven't read about or seen?" she replied, reddening under my accusation. "I don't have to put my ear to the door to know what goes on between you and your quadroon friend. But," she said,

237

smiling and sitting back, "if you would care to confess, to describe what it was like sleeping beside her . . ."

"Shut up!" I screamed, unable to hold back my flood of emotion. "Shut your filthy mouth before I —"

"Look how she's threatening her crippled sister," Gisselle cried, cringing theatrically. "You see how helpless I am, how helpless I've been. Now you all know what it's like to be a crippled twin and have to live day in and day out watching your sister have fun, go wherever she wants, do whatever she wants."

Gisselle covered her face in her hands and began to sob. Everyone glared at me angrily.

"Oh, what's the use?" I moaned, and turned away just as the music came to an end.

Mrs. Ironwood was immediately at the microphone. "It looks like a storm's brewing," she advised. "The boys should move right to the waiting buses and the girls should head back to their dorms immediately."

Everyone started toward the exits, but Miss Stevens hurried to my side.

"Poor Abby. What they did to her was horrible. Where did she go?" she asked.

"I don't know, Miss Stevens. She ran down the driveway and down the road. I'm worried about her, but Mrs. Ironwood wouldn't let me go after her."

"I'll get into my jeep and see if I can find her," Miss Stevens promised. "You go back to the dorm and wait for me."

"Thank you. There really is a bad storm coming, and she might get caught in it. Please, if you find her, tell her I had nothing to do with what Gisselle did tonight. Please, tell her."

"I'm sure she doesn't think that anyway," Miss Stevens said, with a smile of kindness. We saw Mrs. Ironwood watching us from the side as we followed the crowd out of the ballroom.

A streak of lightning cut a white gash in the dark and foreboding sky. Some of the girls squealed with excitement. Some of the Rosewood boys stole quick goodbye kisses before mounting their buses. Jonathan Peck had a crowd of at least half a dozen doting Greenwood girls around him, waiting and hoping for him to press his precious lips to theirs, or at least to their cheeks.

Another crack of thunder caused more shouting and scurrying about. I saw Miss Stevens hurry away to get to her jeep and I looked hopefully down the driveway for a sign of Abby before I turned to walk quickly back to our dorm. Perhaps she had circled around and gone back herself, I anticipated; but when I arrived, I found our room empty. I went back to the main lobby to wait for Miss Stevens. All the other girls arrived, bubbling over with excitement about the dance and the boys they had met. I ignored them, and for the most part, they ignored me.

The storm came over the campus rapidly, blowing in from the river. Soon the wind was turning and twisting the branches of the great oak trees.

The world outside grew darker and darker and the rain began to fall in sheets, thumping on the windows and bouncing off the walkways. The railings around the galerie were dripping in a continuous stream, and the lightning continued to flash in the dark, illuminating the school and the grounds for a split second of white light and then leaving it in darkness again. What if Miss Stevens hadn't found Abby? I imagined her terrified under a tree somewhere on the road that led up to Greenwood. Perhaps she had made it to one of those nice houses that were on that road, and the people had been kind enough to take her in until the storm ended.

Nearly an hour had gone by before I looked through the lobby windows and saw the headlights of a car. Miss Stevens's jeep pulled up in front of our dorm and Miss Stevens emerged, her raincoat pulled up and over her head as she ran toward the dorm. I greeted her at the front door.

"Has she returned?" she asked me, and my heart sank.

"No."

"No?" She shook the water from her hair. "I drove up and down the road. I went miles more than she could have gone even if she had run the whole way, but I didn't see any sign of her. I was hoping she had turned back on her own."

"What could have happened to her?"

"Maybe someone stopped for her."

"But where would she go, Miss Stevens? She doesn't know anyone in Baton Rouge."

She shook her head, her face revealing worry as both of us thought of the same sort of terrible possibilities that might befall a beautiful young girl, wandering alone at night in a storm on a quiet highway.

"Maybe she just found shelter somewhere and is waiting for the storm to end," she offered.

Mrs. Penny came up beside us, her hands twisting, her face full of concern.

"I just had a call from Mrs. Ironwood, who wanted to know if Abby had returned. Where did she go, Ruby?"

"I don't know, Mrs. Penny."

"She left the grounds, and at night! . . . In a storm!"

"It wasn't something she wanted to do, Mrs. Penny."

"Oh dear," she moaned. "Oh dear. We've never had these sorts of problems at Greenwood before. It has always been such a delightful job for me, such a delightful experience."

"I'm sure everything will be all right," Miss Stevens told her. "Just leave the front door unlocked for her."

"But I always lock the door after curfew. I have all these others girls to think about too. What am I to do?"

"Don't worry about the door, Mrs. Penny. I'm going to sit right here and wait for Abby to return," I said, planting myself on the sofa in the lobby.

"Oh dear," she said. "And social evenings were always such a wonderful time."

"If you need me, call me," Miss Stevens said in a low voice. "Call me if she returns anyway. I'd like to know she's all right."

"Thank you, Miss Stevens," I said after she gave me her phone number. I followed her to the door to see her off. She squeezed my hands between hers.

"Everything will work out. You'll see," she promised, to boost my morale. I struggled to form a smile and watched her put her coat over her head again as she prepared to run the gamut between the dorm and her jeep. The rain was still coming down that strong. I waited at the door until she drove away. A few moments later, Mrs. Penny came up behind me and locked the doors.

"I've got to call Mrs. Ironwood," she told me. "She's going to be very angry. Let me know if she returns soon, will you, dear?"

I nodded, then returned to the sofa and sat staring at the door and listening to pounding raindrops that seem to fall just as hard on my heart as they did on the walls and roof of the dorm. I fell asleep on and off, waking abruptly a few times when I thought I heard someone at the door, but it proved to be only the wind. Exhausted from worry and fatigue, I finally got up and went to our room. I didn't even get out of my clothing. I collapsed on my bed, sobbing for Abby for a while, and then fell into a deep sleep, not waking up again until I heard the girls moving through the lounge preparing to go to breakfast. I turned quickly to look at Abby's bed, and my heart sank at the sight of it, untouched.

Rubbing the sleep from my eyes, I sat up and thought a moment. Then I went to the bathroom and dabbed ice-cold water on my face. I heard Gisselle's ripple of laughter and pulled open the door to confront her as she was being wheeled by.

"Good morning, Sister, dear," she said, looking up at me and smiling. She appeared fresh and happy and full of gloating satisfaction. "You look like you stayed up too late. Is your . . . friend back?"

"No, Gisselle. She never came back."

"Oh no! What will we do with the trophy?" she wondered aloud, and looked at Jacki, Katie, and Samantha, who flashed smiles back at her, but then those smiles evaporated quickly when they gazed at me. At least they showed some remorse, Samantha looking the saddest.

"It's not funny anymore, Gisselle. Something terrible might have happened to her last night. Where would she go? What would she do?"

"Maybe she found refuge in a sharecropper's shack. Who knows?" she said, shrugging. "It might even be one of her long-lost relatives." She laughed hysterically. "Let's go," she commanded Samantha. "I'm ravishingly hungry this morning."

Embarrassed and disgusted over the fact that this was my sister, I lowered my head and returned to my room. I had little appetite and wasn't looking forward to sitting down at breakfast with the girls, who would only be waiting to hear and see what I would do and say. Nevertheless, I changed my clothes. Just as I was about to go to the dining room, Mrs. Penny arrived. One look at her face told me she knew about Abby. The fingers of her hands were locked around each other as if she were holding onto herself for dear life.

"Good morning, dear," she said.

"What's happened, Mrs. Penny? Where's Abby?"

"Mrs. Ironwood just called to tell me that her parents will be stopping by later today to pick up her things," she said in one gasp and sighed.

"Then she's all right? They've found her?"

"Apparently she went into the city last night and called them. Now she'll be leaving the school. She would have been expelled for running off the school grounds in the middle of the night anyway," she added.

"Oh, she would have been expelled, Mrs. Penny, but not for running off," I said, shaking my head and fixing my angry gaze on our housemother. "That wouldn't have been Mrs. Ironwood's true reason."

Mrs. Penny lowered her eyes and shook her head sadly. "We never had such problems," she muttered. "It's so troubling." She looked up and quickly gazed around the room. "Anyway, I know how you girls are always bunching your things together. I wanted you to separate whatever is yours from whatever is hers so that they can come and go as quickly as possible. This won't be pleasant for anyone, especially for them," she added.

"I imagine not. All right. I'll take care of it," I promised, and began sorting things out, packing Abby's things in her suitcases and boxes so it would be that much easier for her parents, the tears dripping off my cheeks as I worked.

By the time the girls had returned from breakfast, I had most everything organized and was sitting dumbly on the edge of my bed, staring at the floor. Gisselle paused in the doorway, Samantha right behind her.

"What's going on?" she demanded, looking at the packed suitcases and boxes. "Mrs. Penny wouldn't say a word."

I raised my head slowly, my eyes bloodshot.

"Abby's parents are coming for her things. She's leaving Greenwood. Are you satisfied now?" I demanded sharply. Samantha bit down on her lower lip and shifted her eyes away quickly.

"It's better for all concerned," Gisselle said. "It would have happened eventually anyway."

"If she had to leave, she should have left because she wanted to, not because she was embarrassed by you and your followers in front of the whole student body and all those boys," I complained.

"It's the risk someone like that takes when she tries to be one of us," Gisselle replied, without a note of contrition in her voice. She was so self-satisfied, so confident, it made me sick to my stomach.

"I don't want to talk about it anymore," I said

and turned away from her.

"Fine with me," she said and had Samantha wheel her away.

But early in the afternoon, just before Abby's parents arrived, Samantha came to my door alone. She had left Gisselle in the lobby with the others and come back to fetch something for her.

"What do you want?" I demanded sharply.

"Gisselle wanted me to get a record out of the box stored in Abby's closet," she said meekly. "She's loaning it to one of the girls from B quad."

I turned my back as she came into the room and knelt down to search through the boxes on the closet floor. She quickly located what she wanted and started out. Then she stopped in the doorway and turned back to me.

"I'm sorry about Abby," she said. "I didn't expect something like this would happen."

"Well what did you expect would happen when someone is exposed like that in front of all those people? And why? What did she ever do to you or to any of the other girls to deserve that?"

Samantha looked down.

"How did my sister find out about her?" I asked after a moment. "Did she listen at the door to our conversations?" Samantha shook her head. "Well, how then?"

Samantha gazed to her right first before turning back to answer.

"When she came in here to get something else of hers that Abby was keeping in her closet, she looked at her letters from her parents," Samantha

246

revealed. "But please don't tell her I told you. Please," she begged, real fear in her eyes.

"Why, what will she reveal about you?" I asked sharply. Samantha's anxiety made her eyes wide and her otherwise cherry cheeks white.

"You shouldn't have told her anything about yourself you didn't want anyone to know," I chastised.

Samantha nodded, that piece of advice coming too late. "Anyway," she said. "I'm sorry about Abby."

I wasn't in a forgiving mood, but I saw she was sincere, so I nodded. She stood there a few more moments and then hurried away.

Shortly afterward, Abby's parents arrived.

"Mrs. Tyler," I cried, jumping to my feet when she and her husband appeared in the doorway. "How's Abby?"

"She's just fine," Mrs. Tyler said, her face firm, her lips tight. "My daughter's got more grit in her than any other girl at this precious school," she added bitterly. Abby's father shifted his eyes from me quickly.

"I must talk to her, Mrs. Tyler. She must know I had nothing to do with this terrible incident."

Mrs. Tyler raised her eyebrows. "It was your twin sister who did the dirty work, as I understand," she said.

"Yes, but we're two different people, even though we are twins, Mrs. Tyler. Abby knows that."

I saw from the way she gazed at her husband

that Abby had said that too.

"Where are her things?" Mrs. Tyler demanded.

"Everything's set aside. All of her things are there." I pointed to where I had organized everything. Her father looked grateful. "How can I talk to her? When can I see her?"

"She's in the car outside," Mr. Tyler revealed.

"Abby's here?"

"She didn't want to come in here with us," her mother said.

"I don't blame her," I said as I hurried past them and out. In the lobby the girls were keeping their comments under their breaths while Abby's parents were in the building. Even Gisselle's voice was subdued. I didn't pause to look at them. Instead, I rushed out the front door. I saw Abby sitting in her parents' automobile and hurried down the steps and over to it. She rolled down the window as I approached.

"Hi," I said.

"Hi. I'm sorry I kept running away from you last night, but I just couldn't stop once I had started. All I wanted to do was get out of there."

"I know, but I was so worried about you. Miss Stevens went driving around looking for you, because Mrs. Ironwood wouldn't let me leave the grounds."

She smirked and muttered, "The Iron Lady."

"Where were you?"

"I hid for awhile until the rain slowed some and then I got a ride into the city and called my parents."

"Oh, Abby, I'm so sorry. It's so unfair. My sister is more horrible than I ever imagined. I found out she snooped into your things and read some letters from your parents."

"That doesn't surprise me. Anyway, it wasn't all just her doing, I'm sure," Abby said. "Although she did seem to relish her part, didn't she?" she added. I nodded. She smiled at me and got out of the car. "Let's take a little walk," she suggested.

"What are you going to do now?" I asked.

"Enroll in the public school. In a way this was a good thing. My parents have decided to stop trying to ignore who I am and who they are. No more moving all around the country, no more pretending to be someone I'm not." She gazed around at the campus. "No more fancy schools."

"I've had my fill of fancy schools too."

"Oh no, you're doing well here, Ruby. All of our teachers like you and you have a great relationship with Miss Stevens. You'll do great things with your artwork. Take advantage of the opportunities and ignore the rest."

"I don't like being in a place where there is so much hypocrisy. Grandmere Catherine wouldn't want me here."

Abby laughed. "From the way you described her to me, I think she'd tell you to dig in like a clam, shut yourself off from the phonies like an oyster, and clamp down on what you want like an alligator. Besides," Abby said in a whisper, "you know how to get the bad gris-gris off you. My mistake was last night, when I didn't wear the blue skirt with the good gris-gris sewn in." She winked and we laughed. It felt good, only I realized I wouldn't be hearing her laughter anymore; I wouldn't be having our girl-to-girl talks anymore, and we wouldn't be sharing our dreams and fears anymore. Gisselle was right to have been jealous: Abby had been the sister I never had, the sister Gisselle, despite our identical faces, would never be.

"I wish there was something more I could do for you," I moaned.

"You've done a lot. You've been a good friend, and we can still be good friends. We'll write to each other. Unless Mrs. Ironwood has your mail screened," she added.

"It wouldn't surprise me."

"I'll tell you what you can do for me," Abby said, suddenly animated. "Next time you're called into Mrs. Ironwood's office, for any reason, see if you can find one of her hairs lying about on the desk or floor. Put it in an envelope and send it to me and I'll give it to a momma to use to make a doll into which I can stick pins."

We laughed, but Abby wasn't just kidding. Behind us, her parents were completing loading the car. We paused and watched them a moment.

"I'd better get going," she said.

"I'm glad I got a chance to see you."

"It's really why I came along," she revealed. "Goodbye, Ruby."

"Oh Abby."

"No tears or you'll start me crying and give

Gisselle and her friends just what they want," she said with defiance. "They probably all have their noses to the windows right now, watching us."

I looked back at the dorm. I swallowed my sobs down quickly and nodded. "Probably," I said.

"Don't get too involved with Louis," she warned, her eyes small and thoughtful. "I know you feel sorry for him, but there are a great many ghosts wandering through the Clairborne family's dreams."

"I know. I won't."

"Well . . ."

We hugged quickly and she started toward the car.

"Hey," she called back, smiling. "Don't forget to say goodbye to Mr. Mud for me."

I laughed. "I will."

"I'll write as soon as I can," she promised.

Her father slammed the trunk closed and her mother got into the car. She got in also and her father sat behind the wheel. Then he started the engine and pulled away. As they went by, Abby turned to wave. I waved back until the car was gone. Then, with a chest that felt full of cement, I returned to the dorm and my half-emptied room.

The remainder of the day felt like a period of mourning. Last night's storm had passed, but it had left thick, long clouds behind it, clouds that hovered threateningly above Baton Rouge and the surrounding area well into the night. I went to dinner mainly because I hadn't eaten anything all day. The girls were quite exuberant and loud, some still discussing Abby, but most were on to other things as if Abby hadn't even existed. Gisselle certainly was. She was waxing on and on about boys she had known who were so handsome they made Jonathan Peck look like Frankenstein's monster. According to what she was telling everyone, she had dated practically every heartthrob in America.

Disgusted and emotionally exhausted, I retreated from dinner as soon as I was able and sat alone in my room. I decided to write a letter to Paul. It went on for pages and pages as I described all that had happened, all that Gisselle had done.

"I don't mean to unload all my misery on you, Paul," I wrote toward the end.

But even to this day when I think of someone in whom I can confide my innermost feelings, I think of you. I suppose I should think of Beau, but there are things a girl would rather tell a brother than she would her boyfriend, I suppose. I don't know. I'm so confused right now. Gisselle is getting her way after all. I now hate it here and I am on the verge of calling Daddy and asking him to do the very thing she wanted me to do from the start — get us out of Greenwood. The only person I will miss will be Miss Stevens.

On the other hand, I'm tempted to stay here and put up with it, just so Gisselle won't get her way. I don't know what to do. I don't know what's right anymore. The good suffer and the bad don't so often, I wonder if the world is filled with more bad gris-gris than good. I miss Grandmere Catherine so; I miss her wisdom and her strength. Anyway, I'm looking forward to your visiting us in New Orleans during the Christmas holidays as you promised. I've already told Daddy, and he's looking forward to seeing you too. I think anyone or anything that reminds him of our mother fills him with an inner happiness and peace he will reveal only to us through his smile.

Write soon.

Love,
Ruby

It wasn't until I started to fold the letter to put it in an envelope that I saw the stains from my teardrops.

The next morning I got up, dressed, and had my breakfast silently, barely looking or speaking to anyone except Vicki, who asked me if I was ready for our social studies test. We talked about it on the way to the main building. Throughout the day, I couldn't help but feel that everyone's eyes were on me. News about Abby had spread quickly, and it was only natural that the other girls would wonder and watch to see how I reacted and behaved. I decided not to give any of them the satisfaction of seeing me unhappy, something I was more easily able to do when I entered Miss

Stevens's art class.

She taught her lesson and we all began our work. It wasn't until the bell rang to end the period that she came over to me to talk about Abby. I told her how Abby seemed relieved and even happier now that it was over.

She nodded. "Whatever doesn't destroy you, makes you stronger. Hardships have a way of toughening us, if they don't kill us," she said, smiling. "Look at you and the hard things you've had to endure."

"I'm not a tough person, Miss Stevens."

"You're tougher than you think you are."

I looked down at my desk. "I was thinking about asking my father to take Gisselle and me out of Greenwood," I said.

"Oh no. I'd hate to lose you. You're the most talented student I have, and probably ever will have. Things will get better for you. They have to," she promised. "Try not to think of the bad things. Lose yourself in your art. Make art everything," she advised.

I nodded. "I'll try."

"Good. And don't forget, I'll be here for you whenever you need me."

"Thank you, Miss Stevens."

Buoyed by our little talk, I did turn from the dark and unhappy events to look forward to Daddy's arrival on Wednesday and Beau's arrival on Saturday. At least two of the people I loved most in the world would soon be with me and would bring rays of sunshine back into the world that had become dismal and gray.

And then when I returned to the dorm, I found that a letter had arrived from Paul, even before mine to him had been posted. His was full of optimism and happy news: how well he had been doing in school, how much his family's business had improved, and how his father was giving him more and more responsibility.

Although I still have time to take my pirogue and pole up the bayou to do some fishing at my secret spots. Yesterday I just lay back in the canoe and watched the sun turn red as it began to fall between the branches of the sycamores. The scattered light made the Spanish moss look like sheets of silk. Then the nutrias started to come out more boldly. The dragonflies did their ritualistic dances over the water, and the cream and white crappie rose and fell in the canals as if I, fishing pole and all, weren't even there. A snowy egret swooped down so low I thought it was going to land on my shoulder before it veered and went farther downstream.

I turned to see a white-tailed deer poke its head through the branches of a cottonwood on shore and watched me drift for a while before disappearing in the willow.

All of this made me think of you and our wonderful late afternoons together, and I wondered how it must be for you to live someplace else now, away from the bayou.

It made me sad, until I remembered how completely you absorbed everything and then, with that wonderful artistic talent, brought it out again to last forever on some canvas. How lucky will be the ones who buy your paintings.

> Looking forward to seeing you,
> Paul

His letter filled me with a delicious sort of happiness, the kind that mixed melancholy with joy, memories with hope. I felt aloof, above the fray. I must have had a smile of such deep satisfaction on my face that evening at dinner. I saw how Gisselle kept gazing at me with frustration.

"What's wrong with you?" she finally demanded. All the girls around us who had been talking spiritedly stopped to look and listen.

"Nothing. Why?"

"You look stupid sitting there with that grin on your face, like you know something we don't," she said.

I shrugged. "I don't," I said. Then I thought a moment and put down my fork. I folded my hands in front of me and fixed my gaze on all of them. "Except I know that many of the things you all think are so important, things like family lineage and great wealth, don't guarantee happiness."

"Oh no?" Gisselle whined. "Then what does?"

"Liking yourself," I said, "for who you really are and not what others want you to be." Then

I got up and went back to my room.

I reread Paul's letter, made a list of things I wanted to do before Daddy and Beau's visits, completed my homework, and went to sleep. I lay there with my eyes open, staring up into the dark ceiling and imagining I was in the pirogue with Paul, drifting. I thought I could even see the first star.

In the morning I awoke filled with all sorts of plans for pictures I wanted to do under Miss Stevens's guidance. Her love of nature was as strong as mine, and I knew she would appreciate my visions. I washed and dressed eagerly and was one of the first at the breakfast table, something else that seemed to annoy Gisselle. I saw she was becoming more and more intolerant and impatient with Samantha too, snapping at her for not doing things fast enough for her.

Our quad had cleanup duty again. Gisselle, of course, was excused from the chores, but she made it more difficult for me and the others by lingering at the table. It nearly made us all late for school, and I had an English test to take.

I was ready for the test and eager to take it, but right in the middle of the exam, a messenger came into the room. She went right to Mr. Risel and whispered in his ear. He nodded, then looked out at the class and announced that I was wanted at Mrs. Ironwood's office.

"But my exam . . ." I muttered.

"Just bring up what you've completed," he said.

"But . . ."

"You'd better go quickly," he added, his eyes dark.

What could she want now? I wondered. What could she possibly accuse me of doing this time?

Filled with rage, I pounded through the corridor and walked into the principal's office. Mrs. Randle looked up from her desk, but this time she didn't look annoyed or upset with me. She looked sympathetic.

"Go right in," she told me. My fingers trembled a bit on the doorknob. I turned it and entered, surprised to discover Gisselle sitting there in her wheelchair, her handkerchief clutched in her hand, her eyes bloodshot.

"What is it?" I cried, looking from her to Mrs. Ironwood, who was standing by her window.

"It's your father," she replied. "Your stepmother has just called me."

"What?"

"Daddy's dead!" Gisselle screamed. "He had a heart attack!"

Somewhere deep inside myself, a scream became a cry, the sort of cry that lingered over the water, that wove itself around the trees and bushes, that made day turn into night, that made sunny skies turn gray, and that turned raindrops into tears.

Behind my eyelids, slammed shut to lock out the faces and the moment, I recalled an old nightmare I had often had as a child. In it I was running over the marshland, chasing after a piroque that was picking up speed to round a turn in the bayou and carrying away the mysterious man I wanted to call Daddy.

The word got stuck in my throat, and a moment later he was gone.

And once again I was all alone.

10

Orphaned Again

As far as I was concerned, Daddy's funeral began with our ride back to New Orleans. Even Gisselle became dark and quiet just before we were to leave, her usual banter of complaints reduced to a few grievances about the speed with which she had to get her things together and the manner in which she was transferred from her wheelchair to the limousine Daphne had sent. The driver hadn't been told that one of his passengers was handicapped and was quite unprepared for the experience. He didn't know how to fold the chair and get it as well as our luggage into the trunk. Fortunately, Buck Dardar came by to help, which immediately cheered up my sister and, for the moment, returned a look of flirtatious delight to her eyes.

"Thank goodness your Mr. Mud happened by," she declared loud enough for Buck to hear as he assisted with the folding of the wheelchair. "Otherwise poor Daddy would be buried a week before we left here."

I flashed a furious gaze at her, but she rolled it away with one of her flighty little laughs and then poked her head out of the window to flutter her eyelashes at Buck as she thanked him profusely for coming by.

"I can't thank you properly just now," she told him. "We have to leave right away, but when we come back . . ."

Buck glanced toward me and then hurried back to his tractor to continue his work on the grounds. The chauffeur got in and we were off. All of the other students were in class. Gisselle had managed to tell her clique about Daddy and then sponge up their condolences and sympathy. Miss Stevens was the only person I had told. She was very upset, her eyes actually filling with tears when she gazed into my devastated face.

"Now I'm really an orphan, just like you," I told her.

"But you have your stepmother and your sister."

"It's the same as being an orphan," I replied.

She bit down on her lower lip and nodded without challenging my declaration. "You'll always have family here," she said, hugging me. "Be strong."

I thanked her and returned to the dorm to pack my things.

Now the limousine was carrying us off on a journey that seemed more like a nightmare, a trip through what, to me at least, was an endlessly dark tunnel whose walls were woven from the fabric of my most dreaded fears, the foremost of which was the fear of being alone. From the moment I was old enough to understand that my mother had died and my father had, I was told, deserted me, I felt this cavernous pit in my heart, this great sense of being tethered to the shore by only a slim line of woven hemp. More than one night I was awakened by the nightmarish vision of myself being tossed about while I slept at the bottom of my pirogue. The storm that whipped through the bayou lashed at the slim line of hemp until it ripped it in two and sent me rushing downstream into the night and the unknown.

Of course, Grandmere Catherine's reassuring embrace and soothing words put me at ease. She was my slim line of hemp, she was my only sense of security; and when she died, I would have felt lost and at the mercy of these terrible winds of Fate had she not given me new hope just before her passing by telling me my father's name and encouraging me to go to him. Like a hobo looking for a handout of love, I went knocking on his door, but my heart was cheered by the overwhelming manner in which he had accepted and welcomed me into his home and his own heart. Once again I felt secure, and my dreams of being lost in a raging storm all but disappeared.

Now Daddy was gone too. Those prophetic paintings I had done as a young girl, paintings in which I envisioned my mysterious father drifting away, had all unfortunately come true. The dark shadows were rushing back, the wind began its howling. Numb to the very core of my soul, I sat in the limousine and stared out at the scenery that flowed by with a gray fluidity that made it seem as if the dreary world were draining down behind us and we would soon be left dangling in empty space.

Finally, unable to keep silent a moment longer, Gisselle poured forth a new stream of complaints.

"Daphne's going to really lord it over us now," she moaned. "Anything we've inherited will be in trust. We'll have to do whatever she says, whatever she wants." She waited for me to join her with my own rendition of grievances, but I remained silent, gazing out, listening to her ramble on, but barely acknowledging her presence. "Didn't you hear what I said?"

"I don't care, Gisselle. It's not important right now," I muttered.

"Not important?" She laughed. "Just wait until we get home and you find out how right I am. Then we'll see how important it is," she declared. "How could he die?" she screamed shrilly, not because she was saddened by our daddy's death but because she was angry at him for succumbing to it. "Why didn't he see he wasn't well and go to a doctor? Why wasn't he well anyway? He wasn't old."

"He had more heartache to contend with than a man twice his age," I said sharply.

"Oh, and what's that supposed to mean, Ruby? Huh? What exactly is Miss Goody Two-Shoes saying now?"

263

"Nothing," I said with a sigh. "Let's not argue today. Please, Gisselle."

"I'm not arguing. I'd just like to know what you meant, that's all. Did you mean it's all my fault, because if you did . . ."

"No, I didn't mean that. Daddy had a lot on his mind besides you and me. He had poor Uncle Jean and Daphne and his business problems . . ."

"That's right," she said, liking my explanation. "He did. But still, he should have taken better care of himself. Look at how he's left us now. I'm crippled and I have no father. You think Daphne's going to give me the things I want when I want them? Never. You heard her when we left. She believes Daddy spoiled us, spoiled me!"

"Let's not jump to any conclusions," I said in a tired, small voice. "Daphne must be devastated too. Maybe . . . maybe she'll be different. Maybe she'll need us and love us more."

Gisselle made her eyes small as she thought about what I had said. I knew she was simply trying to figure out how to take advantage of the situation if what I said were true, how she could impose upon Daphne's great grief and maneuver to get what she wanted. She sat back to think about it some more, and the remainder of our ride went quietly, even though it seemed to take twice as long. I fell asleep for a while and woke up to see Lake Pontchartrain looming ahead. Soon the skyline of New Orleans came into view, and we were traveling through the city streets.

Everything looked different to me. It was as if

Daddy's death had changed the world. The quaint narrow streets, the buildings with their scrolled iron balconies, the little gardens in the alleyways, the cafés, the traffic, and the people all seemed foreign. It was as if the soul of the city had left along with Daddy's soul.

Gisselle did not have the same reaction. The moment we entered the Garden District, she wondered aloud if she would soon see her old friends.

"I'm sure they've all heard about Daddy. They're bound to come visiting us. I can't wait," she said. "I'll find out all the gossip." She smiled gleefully.

How could she be so selfish? I wondered. How could her mind and her heart not be filled with gloom? How could she not be thinking about Daddy's smile, Daddy's voice, Daddy's embrace? And how could she not be weighed down with a sorrow that turned her very bones to stone and made her blood run cold? Would I have turned out this way had I been the first baby born and the one given to the Dumas family? Did the evil of that act settle in her tiny heart like a lump of coal and infect her every thought and feeling? Would that have happened to me?

As if he had been standing at the door for hours and hours, Edgar was there when we drove up. He looked years older, his shoulders slumped, his face pale. He hurried down to help with our things.

"Hello, Edgar," I said.

His lips trembled as he tried to greet me, but just the pronunciation of my name, a name Daddy had loved to call, made his eyes tear and his tongue stumble.

"Get me out of here already!" Gisselle screamed. The chauffeur hurried around to the trunk and Edgar went to help him with Gisselle's wheelchair. "Edgar!"

"Oui, mademoiselle, I'm coming," he replied, hobbling around the rear of the car.

"So's Christmas."

They got the wheelchair unfolded and Gisselle into it. The moment we entered the house, I felt the cold gloom that permeated the very walls. All the lights were subdued, the shades still drawn. A tall, thin man in a black suit and tie emerged from the parlor. He had a narrow face that brought his nose and even his chin to a point, reminding me of a pelican. His bald head was spotted but shiny, with two tufts of light brown hair just above his ears. He seemed to slink along, gliding over the floor, moving with barely a sound.

"Madame wanted the wake to be held here," Edgar warned us. "This is Monsieur Boche, the undertaker."

Monsieur Boche's smile was sickly smooth. His lips lifted off his gray teeth as though his mouth was a curtain hinged at the corners. He pressed his long hands together and then slid his right palm over his left hand, giving me the impression he had to wipe it dry before extending it to greet us.

"Mademoiselles," he said. "My deepest condolences. I am Monsieur Boche, and I am here to see that all your bereavement needs are satisfied. If there's anything you want, simply —"

"Where's my daddy?" I demanded with more authority than I had intended. Even Gisselle's eyes widened.

"Right this way, mademoiselle," he said, bowing and turning with one smooth motion.

"Ugh," Gisselle said. "I don't want to look at him now."

I spun on her. "He was your father. You won't look on him ever again."

"He's dead," Gisselle complained. "How can you want to look into a coffin?"

"Don't you want to say goodbye?" I asked.

"I said goodbye. Edgar, take me to my room," she demanded.

"Very good, mademoiselle." He lifted his eyes to me and then turned Gisselle toward the stairway. I followed Monsieur Boche to the parlor where Daddy lay in his open coffin. Over it and around it were dozens and dozens of multicolored roses. The room reeked of the scent. Beside the coffin, large candles flickered. The sight of it all put a lump in my throat. It was true; none of this was a dream.

I turned because I felt Daphne's eyes on me. She was sitting in a high-backed chair. Bedecked in black with a black veil pulled off her face, she sat like a dowager queen, expecting me to kneel at her feet and kiss her hand. She didn't look as pale and sick with grief as I had anticipated. Though she had kept rouge off her cheeks, she still wore her favorite shade of lipstick and had some eyeliner on. Her hair was pinned back with pearl combs, and she did have an elegance about her that was intimidating.

"Where's Gisselle?" she demanded.

"She wanted to go to her room," I replied.

"Nonsense," she said and rose from the chair. "She's to come directly in here." She walked out and I approached the coffin. I heard Daphne shout her orders to Edgar, demanding that he bring Gisselle back down the stairs.

My heart was pounding; my legs felt wobbly. I gazed down at Daddy. He was dressed in his black tuxedo, and except for his pasty-white complexion, he looked like he was just taking a catnap. Monsieur Boche stepped up beside me so silently that I nearly jumped when he whispered into my ear.

"He looks good, doesn't he? One of my best jobs," he bragged. I glared at him with such fury, he simply bowed and retreated quickly, floating away on those oily feet. Then I reached into the coffin and took hold of Daddy's right hand. It didn't feel like a hand anymore, but I willed the cold, hard sensations out of my mind and forced myself to think of him smiling, warm and loving.

"Goodbye, Daddy," I said. "I'm sorry I wasn't here when you needed me the most. I'm sorry I didn't have you with me when I grew up. I'm sorry we had so short a time together. I know my mother loved you very much and I know you loved her. I think I've inherited the best of that love. I will miss you forever and ever. I hope you're with Mommy and you've made your peace and the two of you are floating happily along in a pirogue somewhere in the bayou of heaven."

I leaned over and kissed his cheek, desperately ignoring the sensation that I was kissing a cold face. Then I knelt down and said a little prayer for him. I stepped away from the coffin just as Gisselle was being wheeled in, her complaints loud and clear.

"I'm tired. It was a long, boring trip. Why do I have to come in here?"

"Be quiet," Daphne ordered. She nodded at Edgar, which meant he should leave, and then she returned to her high-backed chair. Gisselle glared at me and then at her and pouted. "Bring her closer," Daphne commanded me in an icy tone. I went to Gisselle's chair and rolled it toward Daphne. "Sit down," she said, nodding at the chair across from her. I did so quickly.

"Why can't we just rest first?" Gisselle moaned.

"Shut up," Daphne snapped. Even Gisselle was frightened and impressed with her sharpness. With her mouth open, she sat back. Daphne glared at her with eyes that seemed able to penetrate into her thoughts. "For a long time, I've had to put up with your whining and crying and moaning. Well, that's over with, you hear? Look over there," she said, nodding toward Daddy. "You see what comes of worrying about everyone

269

else's problems, everyone else's needs, everyone else's likes and dislikes? You die young, that's your reward.

"Well, it's not going to be mine. There are going to be some serious changes around here now, and it's best you two understand that immediately. I'm still a very young woman. I don't intend to let these events age and sicken me, and that's just what they would do if we continued the way things were."

"Events?" I said.

"Yes, events. Everything's an event." She turned her lips into a twisted smile. "Oh, don't start with your histrionics, Ruby. I know you better than you think." Her smile faded and was replaced by a look of firm anger. "You came here from the swamps and you won your place in your father's heart, conniving, reminding him of his great romance in the bayou, just so you would get your piece of inheritance. I'm sure that grandmother of yours put you up to it."

I felt the blood rush into my cheeks, but before I could respond, she continued.

"Don't worry, I don't blame you for it," she said. "I would probably have done the same thing if I had been in your moccasins. Well, what's done is done. You're in your father's will and you will get your piece. Both of you will," she added, turning to Gisselle. "And it will start when you're both twenty-one. Until then, everything you've inherited is in trust, with me as the executor. I will be the one to decide what you get now and what you don't. I will be the one who tells you where you will go and what you will do."

Gisselle smirked. "You always wanted to be the boss, Mother," she said, nodding.

"I always was, you little fool. Did you really believe it was your father who was running the business? He had no real business sense. He didn't have the heart for it. He could never make the tough decisions if it involved taking from someone or cutting someone out. He was too soft to be in business. If it weren't for me, we wouldn't have half what we have; and now you two are going to inherit a big piece of that. Too much of it, if you ask me, but that's the way it is.

"I don't expect you two to be grateful, but I do expect you to be obedient and cooperative," she continued. "The funeral will be over in two days," she said, pulling herself up even firmer in the seat. "After that, you are to return to Greenwood."

"Oh, but Mother," Gisselle moaned.

"Yes, you are," Daphne hammered. "I don't have the strength or the patience to deal with you two and your problems on a day-to-day basis right now. I want you to return, to do well, to obey all the rules and not get into a bit of trouble, you hear? I warn you: If you cause even an iota of aggravation, I'll have the two of you sent to an even stricter place. If you really annoy me, I will see about nullifying your inheritances, understand? Then they'll stick you into a home for crippled people and you'll really be sorry. And you,"

271

she said, focusing her anger at me, "you will be sent back to the bayou to live with whatever Cajun relatives are left."

Gisselle lowered her head and grimaced. I simply glared at Daphne. She had become the ice queen. Freezing water ran through her veins. I was sure that if I touched her, she'd feel colder than Daddy now felt. I should have realized she would be like this. Gisselle had been right: Daphne despised the sight of us more than she had loved Daddy.

"Take your sister upstairs now and prepare yourselves to greet the many mourners who will come here shortly to pay their respects. Make sure you both dress properly and act properly."

"Has Uncle Jean been told about Daddy?" I asked.

"Of course not," she replied. "What would be the point?"

"He has a right to know. It's his brother."

"Please, the man doesn't know what day it is, where he's at, or even his own name anymore."

"But . . ."

She rose, towering over us, her beauty hardened so that she looked statuesque, poured into a mold.

"Just do what I tell you to do and worry about yourselves. It seems to me," she added, looking at Gisselle and then back at me, "that there's enough there to worry about." She gave us her wintry smile before turning to leave.

Gisselle wagged her head and groaned.

"I told you so, didn't I? Didn't I?" she complained. "Now she's sending us back to Greenwood. I didn't even have a chance to tell her why she shouldn't. Maybe later, you can say something. She'll listen more to you. I just know it."

"I don't want to stay here," I said, furious. "As bad as Greenwood is, I'd rather be there than here with her."

"Oh, damn you for being so stupid. She won't bother us after a while. She'll do her own things and leave us alone. We'll be better off here, and you can be with Beau."

"I don't want to think about that right now. I just want to think about Daddy," I said, and began to push her out.

"Daddy's dead. He can't help us. He can't help himself!"

Edgar was waiting at the foot of the stairs to assist with Gisselle.

"Where's Nina?" I asked him.

"She's in her room. She spends most of her time there now," he said, and he shifted his eyes so I would understand that Nina had turned to her voodoo for solace and protection. We heard someone on the stairs and looked up to see the new maid, Martha Woods, a stout, elderly woman with gray hair chopped at her ears, dark brown eyes, and a rather large mouth with a thick lower lip. She had neglected to pluck some face hairs that were curled back on her chin.

"Oh, this is Mademoiselle Gisselle and Mademoiselle Ruby," she said, clapping her hands together. "I'm sorry I wasn't here to greet you before, but I've been preparing your rooms.

Everything's spick-and-span clean and organized," she declared. "And madame insists we all keep it that way."

"Oh no," Gisselle groaned. "Just take me to my room, Edgar."

"I'll help," Martha said.

"Edgar can do it himself," Gisselle snapped. "Just go wash a toilet someplace."

Martha gasped and looked at me.

"I'm going to see Nina," I muttered, and hurried away. I found her seated in her soft-cushioned chair, surrounded by lit blue candles. She wore her red tignon in her hair with the seven knots all pointing straight up. When she saw me, her eyes took on some of the light and she smiled. She rose to hug me.

"Nina be thinking about you all day," she said. She gazed around fearfully. "This house be filled with evil spirits crawling through every crack since Monsieur Dumas's death. Nina have this ready for you." She reached down to get a leg bone that was on the small table. "This be mojo, the leg bone of a black cat killed exactly at midnight. Strong gris-gris. Put this in your room."

"Thank you, Nina," I said, taking it.

"Someone must've burned a candle against poor Monsieur Dumas. The evil spirits snuck into the house when Nina be sleeping one night and they go and sink their teeth into him." She looked guilty.

"Oh Nina, it wasn't your fault. My father had too much on his mind and didn't watch his health.

He would be the last to blame you, Nina."

"Nina tried. I pray to Virgin Mary. I go to cemetery and make the four corners, stopping at each corner to make wish for Monsieur Dumas to be healthy again. I say prayer before the statue of St. Expedite, but the bad gris-gris find a welcome mat," she said, making her eyes small. She nodded. "The door be left open."

"Daphne," I said.

"Nina speak no ill about the madame."

I smiled. "I missed you, Nina. I could have used some of your candles and powders at Greenwood."

She smiled back at me. "I cook all day to make food for the wake. You be sure you eat. You gonna need your strength," she said.

"Thank you, Nina." We hugged again, and then I went up to my room to call Beau and let him know I was home and needed him at my side, desperately.

"I'm sorry that this is the reason that brought you home," Beau said, "but I can't wait to see you."

"I can't wait to see you either," I echoed.

"My parents and I are coming to pay our respects. I'll be there soon," he told me.

After we spoke, I changed into something appropriate for the wake and went next door to see if Gisselle had done the same. She hadn't even started; she was still on the telephone, catching up on news with her old friends.

"Daphne wants us downstairs to greet the mourners," I told her. She grimaced and continued gossiping as if I weren't in the room. "Gisselle!"

"Oh, wait a minute, Collette." She put her hand over the mouthpiece and turned roughly toward me. "What do you want?"

"You've got to dress and come downstairs. People will be arriving."

"So? I don't know why I've got to rush about now. This is worse than . . . than being at Greenwood," she said and turned back to her phone conversation. Whatever patience I had left evaporated. I pivoted and marched out of her room. Gisselle was Daphne's problem, I told myself. She was the one who'd brought her up, who'd given her these values and taught her how to be self-centered. They deserved each other.

People had begun to stream in: neighbors, business associates, employees, and, of course, Daphne's social acquaintances. Most went up to Daddy's coffin, knelt, and said a prayer, after which they joined Daphne, who was greeting people with a quiet elegance that indeed made her seem like someone with royal blood. I noticed that Bruce Bristow, Daddy's business manager, was constantly at Daphne's side, ready to do her every bidding. Occasionally I saw her lean over and whisper something to him. Sometimes he would smile, and sometimes he would nod and go off or approach one of the distinguished mourners, shake his hand, and bring him to Daphne.

Bruce wasn't much older than my daddy, if he

was older at all. He was taller and a bit stouter, with dark brown hair and sideburns. I had met him only two or three times before, and I was always a little bothered by the way he drank me in with those hazel eyes, smiling coyly as he lowered his gaze down to my breasts, fixed his eyes there for a moment, and then lowered and lowered his gaze again until he was practically looking at my feet before lifting his eyes to travel upward ever so slowly. I always felt uncomfortable in his presence, felt as if I had been undressed in his imagination and stood totally naked before him.

Also, he had a nickname for me from the very first time he set eyes on me. He called me La Ruby, as though I were the jewel I had been named after. And then, when he took my hand to kiss it, his lips would linger for a moment longer than they should, sending a nervous tingle up my arm.

During a moment when she had no one speaking to her, Daphne marched across the parlor to me.

"Where's your sister? Why isn't she down here already?" she demanded, her hands on her hips.

"I don't know, Mother," I said. "I told her to get dressed, but she won't get off the telephone."

"March yourself up there and get her down here this instant," she commanded.

"But . . ."

"I know," she said with a crooked smile, "that you are just sitting here waiting for your precious boyfriend Beau to arrive with his parents." Her smile faded. "If you don't get Gisselle down here, I'll see to it you don't spend a moment alone with him. Not now, not ever."

"Why do I have to be responsible for Gisselle? She —"

"Because you're her dear twin sister, whole, with no handicap," she replied, smiling again. "And it's only an opportunity for you to do a good deed, perform a blessing. I'd like all these people to see how well you look after your more unfortunate sister. Now do it!" she ordered. Just as she did so, Beau and his parents entered the parlor. The sight of him lifted the crust of ice from my heart. "First things first," Daphne said, throwing a gaze Beau's way. "Go get Gisselle."

"Very well, Mother," I said, getting up.

Beau looked at his parents and then hurried to me. "Ruby," he said, taking my hand and speaking loud enough in his formal tone to please his parents and those around them. "I'm so sorry about Pierre. Please accept my deepest regrets."

"Thank you, Beau. I have to go help Gisselle for a moment. Please excuse me."

"Of course," he said, backing up.

"I'll be right back," I mouthed, and hurried upstairs to find my stubborn sister plucking chocolates from a box on the night stand beside the bed as she talked to one of her old boyfriends.

"Gisselle!" I cried, anger and frustration flooding my face. She turned with surprise. "Your absence has become an embarrassment for Mother and for me, as well as for Daddy's memory." I stormed across the room and seized the receiver. She screamed in protest when I slammed it down in its cradle. "You're going to put on your black dress right now and come right down with me."

"How dare you!"

"Now!" I screamed, and turned her around roughly in her chair, pushing her toward the bathroom. "Wash off that makeup while I get your dress, or I swear," I said, "I'll push you down the stairs."

She took one look at my infuriated face and gave in. Of course, she was as uncooperative as could be, forcing me to do all the work in removing what she was wearing and putting on the proper dress and shoes, but finally I was able to wheel her to the top of the stairway.

"I hate things like this," she whined. "What am I supposed to do, sit there sobbing?"

"Just let people offer their condolences and sit quietly. If you're hungry, you can eat something."

"I am hungry," she said. "Yes. That's a good reason to go down."

Edgar came up and helped me get her down the stairway in the lift. We got her into the downstairs wheelchair and I rolled her into the parlor. Many more mourners had arrived. Everyone turned our way, some of the women smiling softly and sadly. Those who had brought their children sent them to us to offer their sympathies. Finally Beau joined us, leaning down to kiss Gisselle.

"Well, it's about time," she told him. "And you

279

don't have to kiss me as if I'm someone's old grandmother."

"I gave you the proper kiss," he replied, his eyes full of laughter when they were turned to me.

"I bet you'll give Ruby the proper kiss later," she said.

I saw that Daphne was watching us, nodding with satisfaction.

After a while Gisselle became involved with some of the other young people, and Beau and I were able to slip away. We went out to the gazebo.

"It's been so long since I was alone with you," he said. "I feel a little nervous."

"Me too," I confessed.

"It's so hard to believe that Pierre is dead. I haven't been by for some time, so I didn't see how he had changed, but my father said he just knew something bad was going to happen to him. He always had this tired, troubled look and had lost his mirth. He wasn't joining his gentlemen friends for their usual card games, or attending the theater. They rarely saw him and Daphne out at any of the fine restaurants."

"If only we hadn't been sent away to school," I moaned. "I might have seen what was happening and done something. The last time he called me, he sounded so tired, but he insisted it was nothing."

Beau nodded. "Are you going back to Greenwood?"

"Daphne insists we do."

"I thought she might. Don't worry. I'll get up there to visit you often now. The football season is winding down."

"At least that will make it more bearable," I told him. "And the holidays are coming in a few weeks and we'll be back home."

He nodded and took my hand. We sat on the bench and looked out at the partly cloudy night that permitted only a few stars to show their brilliance. "Before I leave, I've got to go see my uncle Jean, Beau. He's got to know what's happened to Daddy. He probably wonders why Daddy doesn't come to visit him. It's not fair. Daphne doesn't care to tell him; she says he won't understand, but I've seen him; I know he will."

"I'll take you," Beau promised.

"You will?"

"Yes. Just say when," he said firmly.

"What about your parents? Won't they be angry?"

"They don't have to know. When?"

"Tomorrow. We'll go as soon as you can."

"I'll cut practice. The coach will understand. I'll come by about three o'clock," he said.

"Daphne won't let me go. I'm sure. I'll just meet you outside the gate. I hate doing sneaky things, but she makes me."

"It's all right," Beau said, slipping his arm around my shoulders. It felt so good to be in his arms. "It's all right to do something sneaky if it's going to result in something good."

"Oh Beau, I'm all alone now. I really am," I

cried with a little more desperation than I had intended.

His eyes filled with sadness. "No you're not. You have me, Ruby. You'll always have me," he swore.

"Don't make promises, Beau," I said, putting my forefinger on his lips. "It's better not to make a promise than to make one you can't keep."

"I can keep this one, Ruby," he pledged. "And I'll seal it with a kiss."

He brought his lips to mine. They felt so good, but I felt guilty for enjoying his kiss while Daddy lay dead in the parlor. My mind and heart should be directed only to him, I thought and pulled back.

"We'd better return before we're missed, Beau."

"Okay. Tomorrow, at three," he repeated.

Although the mourners left relatively early, it seemed very late to me. I hadn't realized how tiring emotional sadness could be. Beau and his parents were some of the last people to leave. He winked conspiratorially at me and continued to act formal and proper as we said our goodbyes.

After everyone had gone, Bruce Bristow and Daphne went into Daddy's office to discuss some necessary business affairs, and Gisselle and I went up to our rooms. I could hear her talking to her old friends on the telephone late into the evening. In fact, the drone of her voice and silly laughter sent me into a welcomed sleep.

Daphne didn't come down to breakfast, but the

priest arrived at lunch to discuss the final arrangements for the funeral. Some of Gisselle's friends came to visit her, more out of curiosity than loyalty, I thought. I let them go off on their own and retreated to what had been my art studio. I recalled how happy and excited Daddy was when he had first brought me to see it. And then my heart fluttered with the tingle of excitement that warmed my breasts when I thought about the day I began painting Beau in the nude. One thing led to another so quickly and so intently that even now I could experience the deliciously ecstatic descent I had taken into the depths of my own sexuality when I embraced him and kissed him and surrendered to his own driving desires. I was so lost in these memories, I almost missed our rendezvous in front of the house.

I hurried out the side entrance and down the drive to the sidewalk to wait for him at three. He was right on time. I got into his car quickly and in moments we were speeding off to the institution in which my father's poor younger brother languished in a world of confusion and mental anguish. I couldn't help but be nervous and afraid. Beau knew that Daphne had once tried to have me confined in the same place as a way of getting me out of her life.

"I know how frightening that place must be to you. You sure you can do this?" he asked.

"No," I said. "But I feel I have to for Daddy. It's something he would want me to do."

A little more than half an hour later, we pulled

up to the four-story, gray stucco structure with bars on its windows. I got out of the car slowly and with Beau at my side entered the institution. The nurse behind the glass enclosure directly before us didn't look up until we were practically at her desk.

"I'm Ruby Dumas," I said. "I want to see my uncle Jean."

"Jean Dumas?" she said. "Oh yes. We just moved him to his new facilities this morning."

"New facilities? He's still here, isn't he?"

"He's here, but he is no longer housed in a private room. He's in a ward now."

"But . . . why?" I asked.

She smirked. "Because whoever is paying for him has stopped paying the extra stipend, and he is covered only by basic insurance now," she replied.

I looked at Beau. "She didn't waste a minute, did she?" I said. "Can we see my uncle, please?" I asked the nurse.

"Yes. Just a moment." She pushed a button, and a few moments later a male attendant appeared. "Take these people to Ward C to visit Jean Dumas."

"Lord Dumas," he said, smiling. "Sure. Right this way," he said, and we followed him through a door and down a corridor.

"Why do you call him Lord Dumas?" Beau asked.

"Oh, it's just a little joke among the staff. Despite his problems, Jean loves his clothes and looks after his appearance. At least he used to."

"What do you mean, 'used to'?" I asked.

"Since he's been moved and even a little before, he stopped caring. The doctors are concerned. Usually we take him to the game room after lunch, but he's been a bit more depressed lately, so he goes back to the ward."

I glanced at Beau. "What is this ward like?" I wondered aloud.

The attendant paused. "It ain't the Ritz," he said.

That was an understatement. The men's ward simply consisted of a dozen beds in a row, each with its own metal locker. There were three windows spaced out on one side and two on the other, all the windows lined with bars. The floor was cement and the walls were a dull brown color. The lighting was dull, but we could see Uncle Jean at the far end, sitting at the edge of his bed. A nurse had just given him something and was coming toward us.

"I have a couple of visitors for Jean," the attendant told her.

"He's a bit more down today. He wouldn't even eat much lunch. I had to give him some medicine. Are you relatives?" she asked us.

"I am his niece, Ruby."

"Oh," she said, smiling. "The Ruby who sends him letters from time to time?"

"Yes," I replied, happy he was getting them.

"He cherishes those letters, although I sometimes wonder if he actually reads the words. Sometimes he sits with one for hours and hours, just staring at it. When he was in his own room, I would read him one occasionally. They've been very nice letters."

"Thank you. Is he getting worse?"

"I'm afraid so. The move and all hasn't helped, either. He used to be so proud of the way he kept his room."

"I know," I said. "I remember."

"Oh, you've seen him there?"

"Not exactly," I said. This nurse hadn't been working here when I had been forced to stay, so she didn't remember me. But I saw no point in bringing all that back.

With Beau still right beside me, I walked down to Uncle Jean, who sat staring at his hands. His golden hair was disheveled, and he wore a pair of creased pants and a creased white shirt with some food stains on the front of it.

"Hello, Uncle Jean," I said, sitting down beside him. I took his hands into mine and he turned, first to look up at Beau and then to look at me. I saw a note of recognition in his blue-green eyes and a small smile start at the corners of his mouth.

"Do you remember me? . . . Ruby? I'm Pierre's other daughter. I'm the one who's been sending you all the letters." His smile widened. "I've come home from school because . . . because there's been a tragedy, Uncle Jean, and now I've come to tell you because I think you have a right to know. I think you should know." I looked up at Beau, to see if he thought I should continue or not. He nodded. Uncle Jean was still gazing at me, his eyes moving slightly from side to side as he studied my face.

"It's Daddy, Uncle Jean . . . he's . . . his heart gave out on him and he's . . . he's dead," I said. "That's why he hasn't been here to see you; that's why you've been moved to this ward. But I'm going to complain about it to Daphne and I'm going to see to it that they get you back in your room. At least I'll try," I said.

Gradually, the small smile that had been on his lips wilted, and his lips began ever so slightly to tremble. I put my hand on his shoulder and rubbed it gently.

"Daddy would have wanted me to come here, Uncle Jean. I'm sure. He was very unhappy about what had happened between the two of you and he was very sad about your sickness. He wanted so much to see you get better. He loved you very much. He really did," I said.

Uncle Jean's lips quivered more. His eyes began to blink, and then I felt a trembling in his hands. Suddenly, he shook his head, softly at first, and then more vigorously.

"Uncle Jean . . ."

He opened his mouth and then closed it, shaking his head harder. The nurse and the attendant drew closer. I looked up at them when Uncle Jean began to make an unintelligible sound.

"Aaaaaaa . . ."

"Jean," the nurse said, rushing over to him. "What did you tell him?" she demanded.

"I had to tell him his brother — my father — has died," I said.

"Oh dear. Easy, Jean," she said.

His shoulders began to shake and he opened and closed his mouth to make the ugly sound.

"You two had better go now," the nurse said.

"I'm sorry. I didn't mean to cause trouble, but I thought he should know."

"It's all right. He'll be all right," she assured us, but she was anxious for us to leave.

I stood up, and Uncle Jean gazed up at me with desperation. He was silent for a moment, and I decided to hug him quickly and did so.

"I'll be back another time, Uncle Jean," I promised through my tears and then turned away. Beau followed me toward the door. We were nearly there when Uncle Jean screamed.

"P-P-Pierre!"

I turned to see him bury his head in his hands. The nurse eased him back on the bed and lifted his legs up so he was lying quietly.

"Oh, Beau," I said. "I shouldn't have come. Daphne was right. I shouldn't have told him."

"Of course you should have come. Otherwise he would have felt deserted when Pierre never showed up. At least now he understands why and he knows he still has you," Beau said, putting his arm around me.

I let my head fall against his shoulder and then I let him take me out and home to where Daddy lay waiting for his final goodbyes.

288

11

The Gloves Are Off

I told Beau to pull up to the walk a block before my house.

"I feel like Gisselle, sneaking around like this," I said, "but I'd rather Daphne didn't see you dropping me off."

He laughed. "That's all right. Sometimes Gisselle's scheming comes in handy. Too bad she can't learn from you as well." He leaned over to give me a quick kiss on the lips before I stepped out of the car.

"I'll be here tonight," he called after me. I waved and ran up the walk to sneak back in through the side entrance.

The house was very still when I entered. I went around quietly and started up the stairs, which seemed to creak extra loudly just because I was trying to be discreet. I was nearly to the top when Daphne called up to me. I turned and glared down at her. Bruce Bristow was at her side.

"Where were you?" she demanded, her hands on her hips. She wore one of her business suits,

289

rouge, lipstick, and eyeliner, but she had her hair unpinned.

"I went to see Uncle Jean," I confessed. I had made up my mind that I wouldn't lie if she caught me, and anyway, I wanted to question why she had cut back on the funds for Jean at the institution and had him transferred.

"You did what? Get down here this instant," she demanded, stabbing her right forefinger toward the floor. She spun around and marched into the sitting room behind her. Bruce gazed up at me, that somewhat impish smile couched comfortably in the corners of his mouth. Then he turned to follow Daphne. I was nearly halfway down when Gisselle called from the top of the stairway, where she had wheeled herself to watch my confrontation with our stepmother.

"I would have covered for you," she said, "but you didn't even tell me where you were going." She wagged her head. "I couldn't even make anything up when she came around looking for you."

"That's all right. I'm not happy about lying and sneaking around anyway."

"Too bad," she said. "Now you're getting into trouble." She gave me an oily smile of glee before spinning around in her chair to return to her room. I continued downstairs quickly and entered the sitting room. Daphne was seated on the sofa, but Bruce was standing beside her, his hands clasped before him. He was scowling, which was a face he wore more for her sake than for mine.

"Get in here," Daphne said when I paused just

inside the doorway. I approached her, my heart pounding. "I thought I told you not to go to Jean. I thought I told you not to tell him anything," she said quickly.

"Daddy would have wanted him to know," I replied. "And besides, if I hadn't told him, he would have been waiting for Daddy and wondering why he never came."

She smirked. "I'm sure he doesn't wonder about anything." Her eyes became thin slits and her lips tightened for a moment. "Who took you? Beau?" I didn't respond, and she nodded with that cold smile. "His parents are not going to be happy to hear that he was party to this disobedience. Since you've been at Greenwood, he hasn't been in any trouble, but as soon as you return . . . ."

"Please don't get him into trouble. He wasn't party to anything. He was just nice enough to drive me up there."

She shook her head and gazed at Bruce, who mirrored her disdain.

"Anyway," I continued, gathering my courage, "now I know the real reason why you didn't want me to go to see him." I spoke so sharply that Bruce's eyebrows lifted. "Secretly you had Uncle Jean moved from his private room into a ward."

She sat back and crossed her arms under her bosom.

"Secretly?" She laughed a hollow, thin laugh before looking at Bruce and then turning to me with a frown. "I don't have to do anything secretly. I don't need your or your sister's or anyone else's

291

permission to do anything that regards this family."

"Why did you do it?" I cried. "We can afford to have him in his own room."

"A private room was a waste of money. I always thought it so," she said. "Not that I have to explain myself to you or your sister."

"But he's regressing now. The staff says so. He no longer cares about himself the way he used to and —"

"He wasn't making any real progress either way. All Pierre was doing was soothing his own troubled conscience by lavishing the extra money on Jean. It was a ridiculous expenditure."

"It wasn't," I insisted. "I saw the difference; you haven't."

"Since when did you get a degree in mental illness?" she shot back. Then she smiled coldly again, a smile that put chills into my spine. "Or have you inherited some magical powers from your faith-healing grandmere?"

A heat came into my face. Daphne never missed an opportunity to mock my grandmere's memory. She loved ridiculing the Cajun world. I took a deep breath and stood my ground firmly.

"No, I simply inherited compassion and human kindness," I said. My words cut so deeply, she winced. Bruce no longer had a smile on his face, impish or otherwise. He shifted his weight from one leg to the other and gazed apprehensively at Daphne.

"That will be enough of that," she said slowly,

her eyes as dark as shadows in the swamp. "You disobeyed me. I want you to understand right from the start what it means to be insubordinate. Your father is no longer here to make excuses for you." She pulled herself back and her shoulders up to pass sentence on me. "You are to go upstairs and remain in your room until it is time to attend your father's funeral. I will have Martha bring up your meals, and you are not to see anyone."

"But the wake . . . greeting mourners . . ."

"We'll make excuses for you, tell people you aren't feeling well, and that way prevent everyone from knowing about your misbehavior," she said curtly.

"But it wasn't misbehavior," I insisted. "I have a right to see Uncle Jean, and he should have been told about Daddy, and you shouldn't have had them move him into the ward."

For a moment, my continued defiance disarmed her. Then she gathered all her bitterness and leaned forward.

"When you are twenty-one," she replied, her eyes somewhat wider, "you will be able to make financial decisions without my interference or opinions. You can take your entire inheritance and waste it on Jean, for all I care. Until then, I'm the only one who makes the decisions about how to spend the Dumas fortune. I have an expert in these matters," she said, nodding toward Bruce, "so I don't need to hear from you. Do you understand? Do you?" she hammered when I didn't reply.

"No," I said, nailing my feet to the floor in defiance. "I don't understand how you could do this to poor Uncle Jean, who has no life, who has nothing but his own troubled mind."

"Good. So you don't understand." She sat back again. "Whatever," she said, waving her hand. "But for now, march yourself upstairs and close the door behind you or I'll call Beau's parents and have them bring him over here right now to hear what you and he did," she threatened, "and then punish you twice as severely."

My eyes burned with the hot tears of anger and frustration.

"But I have to be at the wake. . . . I should be —"

"You should listen to what you are told to do," she said firmly, punching out the words. She extended her arm, her forefinger pointing toward the stairway. "Now march!"

I lowered my head.

"Can't you find some other way to punish me?" I begged, the tears running down my cheeks.

"No. I don't have the time, nor do I have the energy to sit here and dream up ways to reward you for insubordination, especially when you are disobedient under these circumstances. I have a husband to bury. I don't have time to be a nursemaid to spoiled, defiant young girls. Just do what I say. Do you hear!" she shrilled.

I sucked in my breath, turned, and walked out slowly, my stomach feeling as if I had swallowed a gallon of swamp mud. When I got to my room,

I threw myself on my bed and sobbed. I realized I wouldn't be able to help Uncle Jean; I couldn't even help myself.

"So where did you go?" Gisselle asked from the doorway. I turned slowly and wiped the tears from my cheeks. "Over to Lake Pontchartrain?" she asked, a smile of lewd suggestion washing over her lips. "To neck?"

"No. Beau took me to see Uncle Jean," I said, and described what I had found. "And so she's had him moved into a ward where he has only his bed and a beat-up metal locker," I concluded.

She shrugged, barely showing any interest. "It doesn't surprise me. I told you what Daphne was capable of doing, but you just don't listen. You think the world's all birds and roses. She's going to cut back plenty on what we get too. You'll see," she said. She wheeled herself closer and lowered her voice to a whisper. "It's better that we stay here rather than return to Greenwood. Put your brilliant mind and your time to figuring out a way to get her to let us stay," she said.

"Let us stay?" I laughed so madly I even frightened myself. "She can't stand the sight of us. You're the one who's dwelling in a world of illusion if you think Daphne would even consider having us around now."

"Well, that's just great," Gisselle moaned. "You just want to give up?"

"It's the way it is," I said with a tone of fatalism that shocked her. She remained there staring in at me as if she expected me to snap out of my mood and tell her the things she wanted to hear.

"Aren't you going to get washed and dressed for the wake?" she finally asked.

"Because I disobeyed Daphne and went to the institution to see Uncle Jean, I am not permitted to go to the wake. I'm being punished."

"Can't go to the wake? That's your punishment? Why can't I be punished too?" she cried.

I spun around on her so abruptly she wheeled herself back.

"What's wrong with you, Gisselle? Daddy loved you."

"He did until you arrived. Then he practically forgot about me," she moaned.

"That's not true."

"It is, but it doesn't matter anymore. Oh well," she said, sighing deeply and fluffing her hair. "Someone's got to entertain Beau when he arrives. I guess I'll fill in." She smiled and rolled herself back to her room.

I got up and gazed out the window, wondering if I wouldn't be better off just running away. I might have seriously considered it if I didn't recall some of the promises I had made to Daddy. I had to remain here to look after Gisselle, as best I could, to succeed at my art and become a credit to his memory. Somehow, I would overcome the obstacles Daphne was sure to place in my path, I vowed, and some day I would do just what she had said I would do: I would help Uncle Jean.

I returned to my bed and lay there thinking and dozing off until I heard Gisselle go to the stairway and have Edgar help her down to attend the wake. Then I got down on my knees and recited the prayers I would have recited at Daddy's coffin.

Martha brought up a tray of food for me, and even though she had explicit orders from Nina commanding me to eat, I just picked and nibbled, my appetite gone, my stomach too tight and nervous to accept much more.

Hours later, I heard a gentle knock on my door. I was lying there in the dark, with just the moonlight spilling through my window illuminating the room. I leaned over, flicked on a lamp, and told whoever it was to enter. It was Beau, with Gisselle right behind him.

"Daphne doesn't know he's up here," she said quickly, a capricious smile on her face. How she so enjoyed doing forbidden things, even if it meant doing something for me. "Everyone thinks he's wheeling me around the house. There are so many people here, we won't be missed. Don't worry."

"Oh Beau, you'd better not stay here. Daphne threatened to bring your parents to the house and get you in trouble because you drove me to the institution," I warned.

"I'll risk it," he said. "Why was she so angry anyway?"

"Because I found out what she had done to my uncle," I said. "That's the main reason."

"It's so unfair for you to suffer anything at this time," he said, and our eyes locked for a moment.

"I could leave you two alone for a while," Gisselle suggested when she saw the way we were gazing at each other. "I'll even go to the top of the stairway and be a love sentry."

I was about to protest, when Beau thanked her. He closed the door softly and came to sit beside me on the bed and put his arm around my shoulders.

"My poor Ruby. You don't deserve this." He kissed my cheek. Then he looked around my room and smiled. "I remember being in here once before . . . when you tried some of Gisselle's pot, remember?"

"Don't remind me," I said, smiling for the first time in a long time. "Except I do remember you were a gentleman and you did worry about me."

"I'll always worry about you," he said. He kissed my neck and then the tip of my chin before bringing his lips to mine.

"Oh Beau, don't. I feel so confused and troubled right now. I want you to kiss me, to touch me, but I keep thinking about why I am here, the tragedy that has brought me back."

He nodded. "I understand. It's just that I can't keep my lips off you when I'm this close," he said.

"We'll be together again and soon. If you don't get up to Greenwood during the next two weeks, I'll see you when we return for the holidays."

"Yes, that's true," he said, still holding me close to him. "Wait until you see what I'm getting you for Christmas. We'll have great fun, and we'll celebrate New Year's together and —"

Suddenly the door was thrust open and Daphne stood there, glaring in at us.

"I thought so," she said. "Get out," she told Beau, holding up her arm and pointing.

"Daphne, I . . ."

"Don't give me any stories or any excuses. You don't belong up here and you know it.

"And as for you," she said, spinning her gaze at me, "this is how you mourn the death of your father? By entertaining your boyfriend in your room? Have you no sense of decency, no self-control? Or does that wild Cajun blood run so hot and heavy in your veins, you can't resist temptation, even with your father lying in his coffin right below you?"

"We weren't doing anything!" I cried. "We —"

"Please, spare me," she said, holding up her hand and closing her eyes. "Beau, get out. I used to think a great deal more of you, but obviously you're just like any other young man. . . . You can't pass up the promise of a good time, no matter what the circumstances."

"That's not so. We were just talking, making plans."

She smiled icily. "I wouldn't make any plans that included my daughter," she said. "You know how your parents feel about your being with her anyway, and when they hear about this . . ."

"But we didn't do anything," he insisted.

"You're lucky I didn't wait a few more moments. She might have had you with your clothes off, pretending to he drawing you again," she said. Beau flushed so crimson I thought he would have a nosebleed.

"Just go, Beau. Please," I begged him. He looked at me and then started for the door. Daphne stepped aside to let him pass. He turned to look back once more and then shook his head and hurried away and down the stairs. Then Daphne turned back to me.

"And you almost broke my heart down there before, pleading to have me let you attend the wake . . . like you really cared," she added, and closed the door between us, the click sounding like a gunshot and making my heart stop. Then it started to pound and was still pounding when Gisselle opened the door a few moments later.

"Sorry," she said. "I just turned my back for a moment to get something, and the next thing I knew, she was charging up the stairs and past me."

I stared at her. It was on the tip of my tongue to ask if the truth wasn't that she really had made herself quite visible so Daphne would know she and Beau had come up, but it didn't matter. The damage was done, and if Gisselle was responsible or not, the result was the same. The distance between Beau and me had been stretched a little farther by my stepmother, who seemed to exist for one thing: to make my life miserable.

Daddy's funeral was as big as any I had ever seen, and the day seemed divinely designed for it: low gray clouds hovering above, the breeze warm but strong enough to make the limbs of the sycamores and oaks, willows and magnolias wave and bow along the route. It was as if the whole world wanted to pay its last respects to a fallen prince. Expensive cars lined the streets in front of the church for blocks, and there were droves of people, many forced to stand in the doorway and on the church portico. Despite my anger at Daphne, I couldn't help but be a little in awe of her, of the elegant way she looked, of the manner in which she carried herself and guided Gisselle and me through the ceremony, from the house to the church to the cemetery.

I wanted so much to feel something intimate at the funeral, to sense Daddy's presence, but with Daphne's eyes on me constantly and with the mourners staring at us as if we were some royal family obligated to maintain the proper dignity and perform according to their expectations, I found it hard to think of Daddy in that shiny, expensive coffin. At times, even I felt as if I were attending some sort of elaborate state show, a public ceremony devoid of any feeling.

When I did cry, I think I cried as much for myself and for what my world and life would now be without the father Grandmere Catherine had brought back to me with her final revelations. This precious gift of happiness and promise had been snatched away by jealous Death, who always lingered about us, watching and waiting for an opportunity to wrench us away from all that made him realize how miserable his own destiny was eternally to be. That was what Grandmere Catherine had taught me about Death, and that was what I now so firmly believed.

Daphne shed no tears in public. She seemed to falter only twice: once in the church, when Father McDermott mentioned that he had been the one to marry her and Daddy; and then at the cemetery, just before Daddy's body was interred in what people from New Orleans called an oven. Because of the high water table, graves weren't dug into the ground, as they were in other places. People were buried above ground in cement vaults, many with their family crests embossed on the door.

Instead of sobbing, Daphne brought her silk handkerchief to her face and held it against her mouth. Her eyes remained focused on her own thoughts, her gaze downward. She took Gisselle's and my hand when it was time to leave the church, and once again when it was time to leave the cemetery. She held our hands for only a moment or two, a gesture I felt was committed more for the benefit of the mourners than for us.

Throughout the ceremony, Beau remained back with his parents. We barely exchanged glances. Relatives from Daphne's side of the family stayed closely clumped together, barely raising their voices above a whisper, their eyes glued to our every move. Whenever anyone approached Daphne to offer his or her final condolences, she took his hands and softly said *"Merci beaucoup."* These people would then turn to us. Gisselle imitated Daphne perfectly, even to the point of intoning the same French accent and holding their hands not a split second longer or shorter than

Daphne had. I simply said "Thank you," in English.

As if she expected either Gisselle or me to say or do something that would embarrass her, Daphne observed us through the corner of her eye and listened with half an ear, especially when Beau and his parents approached us. I did hold onto Beau's hand longer than I held onto anyone else's, despite feeling as if Daphne's eyes were burning holes in my neck and head. I was sure Gisselle's behavior pleased her more than mine did, but I wasn't there to please Daphne; I was there to say my last goodbye to Daddy and thank the people who really cared, just as Daddy would have wanted me to thank them: warmly, without pretension.

Bruce Bristow remained very close by, occasionally whispering to Daphne and getting some order from her. When we had arrived at the church, he offered to take my place and wheel Gisselle down the church aisle. He was there to wheel her out and help get her into the limousine and out of it at the cemetery. Of course, Gisselle enjoyed the extra attention and the tender loving care, glancing up at me occasionally with that self-satisfied grin on her lips.

The highlight of the funeral came at the very end, just as we were approaching the limousine for our ride home. I turned to my right and saw my half brother, Paul, hurrying across the cemetery. He broke into a trot to reach us before we got into the car.

"Paul!" I cried. I couldn't contain my surprise

and delight at the sight of him. Daphne pulled herself back from the doorway of the limousine and glared angrily at me. Others nearby turned as well. Bruce Bristow, who was preparing to transfer Gisselle from her chair into the car, paused to look up when Gisselle spoke.

"Well, look who's come at the last moment," she said.

Even though it had only been months, it seemed ages since Paul and I had seen each other. He looked so much more mature, his face firmer. In his dark blue suit and tie, he appeared taller and wider in the shoulders. The resemblances in Paul's, Gisselle's, and my face could be seen in his nose and cerulean eyes, but his hair, a mixture of blond and brown — what the Cajuns called *chatin* — was thinner and very long. He brushed back the strands that had fallen over his forehead when he broke into a trot to reach me before I got into the limousine.

Without saying a word, he seized me and embraced me.

"Who is this?" Daphne demanded. The final mourners who were leaving the cemetery turned to watch and listen, too.

"It's Paul," I said quickly. "Paul Tate."

Daphne knew about our half brother, but she refused to acknowledge him or ever make any reference to him. She had no interest in hearing about him the one time he had come to see us in New Orleans. Now she twisted her mouth into an ugly grimace.

"I am sorry for your sorrow, madame," he said. "I came as quickly as I could," he added, turning back to me when she didn't respond. "I didn't find out until I called the school to speak with you and one of the girls in your dorm told me. I got into my car right away and drove straight to the house. The butler gave me directions to the cemetery."

"I'm glad you've come, Paul," I said.

"Can we all get into the car and go home," Daphne complained, "or do you intend to stand in a cemetery and talk all day?"

"Follow us to the house," I told him, joining Gisselle.

"He looks very handsome," she whispered after we were seated. Daphne just glared at the two of us.

"I don't want any more visitors in the house today," Daphne declared when we turned into the Garden District. "Visit with your half brother outside and make it short. I want the two of you to start packing your things to return to school tomorrow."

"Tomorrow?" Gisselle cried.

"Of course, tomorrow."

"But that's too soon. We should stay home at least another week out of respect for Daddy."

Daphne smiled wryly. "And what would you do with this week? Would you sit and meditate, pray and read? Or would you be on the telephone with your friends, having them come over daily?"

"Well, we don't have to turn into nuns because

305

Daddy died," Gisselle retorted.

"Precisely. You'll go back to Greenwood tomorrow and resume your studies. I've already made the arrangements," Daphne said.

Gisselle folded her arms under her breasts and sat back in a sulk. "We should run away," she muttered. "That's what we should do."

Daphne overheard and smiled. "And where would you run to, Princess Gisselle? To your half-witted uncle Jean in the institution?" she asked, glancing at me. "Or would you join your sister and return to the paradise in the swamps, to live with people who have crawfish shells stuck in their teeth?"

Gisselle turned away and gazed out the window. For the first time all day, tears flowed from her eyes. I wished I could think it was because she really missed Daddy now, but I knew she was crying simply because she was frustrated with the prospect of returning to Greenwood and having her visit with her old friends cut short.

When we arrived at the house, she was too depressed even to visit with Paul. She let Bruce put her into the chair and take her in without saying another word to me or to Daphne. Daphne gazed back at me from the doorway when Paul drove in behind us.

"Make this short," she ordered. "I'm not fond of all sorts of Cajuns coming to the house." She turned her back on me and went inside before I could respond.

I went to Paul as soon as he emerged from his

vehicle and threw myself into his comforting arms. Suddenly, all the sorrow and misery I had been containing within the confines of my battered heart broke free. I sobbed freely, my shoulders shaking, my face buried in his shoulder. He stroked my hair and kissed my forehead and whispered words of consolation. Finally I caught my breath and pulled back. He had a handkerchief ready and waiting to wipe my cheeks, and he let me blow my nose.

"I'm sorry," I said. "I couldn't help it, but I haven't really been able to cry for Daddy since I came home from school. Daphne's made things so hard for all of us. Poor Paul," I said, smiling through my tear-soaked eyes. "You have to be the one to endure my flood of tears."

"No. I'm glad I was here to bring you any comfort. It must have been horrible. I remember your father well. He was so young and vibrant when I last saw him, and he was very kind to me, a real Creole gentleman. He was a man with class. I understood why our mother would have fallen in love with him so deeply."

"Yes. So did I." I took his hand and smiled. "Oh Paul, it's so good to see you." I looked at the front door and then turned back to him. "My stepmother won't let me have visitors in the house," I said, leading him to a bench over which was an arch of roses. "She's sending us back to Greenwood tomorrow," I told him after we had sat down.

"So soon?"

"Not soon enough for her," I said bitterly. I took a deep breath. "But don't let me focus only on myself. Tell me about home, about your sisters, everyone."

I sat back and listened as he spoke, permitting myself to fall back through time. When I lived in the bayou, life was harder and far poorer, but because of Grandmere Catherine, it was much happier. Also, I couldn't help but miss the swamp, the flowers and the birds, even the snakes and alligators. There were scents and sounds, places and events I recalled with pleasure, not the least of which was the memory of drifting in a pirogue toward twilight, with nothing in my heart but mellow contentment. How I wished I was back there now.

"Mrs. Livaudais and Mrs. Thirbodeaux are still going strong," he said. "I know they miss your grandmere." He laughed. It sounded so good to my ears. "They know I've kept in contact with you, although they don't come right out and say so. Usually they wonder aloud in my presence about Catherine Landry's Ruby."

"I miss them. I miss everyone."

"Your grandpere Jack is still living in the house and still, whenever he gets drunk, which is often, digging holes and looking for the treasure he thinks your grandmere buried to keep from him. I swear, I don't know how he stays alive. My father says he's part snake. His skin does look like he's been through a tannery, and he comes slithering out of shadows and bushes when you least expect him."

"I almost ran away and returned to the bayou," I confessed.

"If you ever do . . . I'll be there to help you," Paul said. "I'm working as a manager in our canning factory now," he added proudly. "I make a good salary, and I'm thinking of building my own house."

"Oh Paul, really?" He nodded. "Have you met someone then?"

His smile faded. "No."

"Have you tried?" I pursued. He turned away. "Paul?"

"It's not easy finding someone to compare to you, Ruby. I don't expect it to happen overnight."

"But it has to happen, Paul. It should. You deserve someone who can love you fully. You deserve a family of your own someday too."

He remained silent. Then he turned and smiled. "I really enjoyed your letters from school, especially all the things you've told me about Gisselle."

"She's been more than a handful, and I just know things are going to get worse now that Daddy's gone, but he left me promising to look after her. I'd rather look after a barrel of green snakes," I said. Paul laughed again, and I felt the weight of sorrow lift from my breast. It was as if I could suddenly breathe again.

But before we could continue, we saw Edgar approaching. He looked glum.

"I'm sorry, mademoiselle, but Madame Dumas

wants you to come into the house and go directly to the parlor now," he said, raising his eyebrows to indicate how sternly she had given the command.

"Thank you, Edgar. I'll be right along," I said. He nodded and left us.

"Oh Paul, I'm so sorry you've come so far to spend so short a time with me."

"It's all right," he said. "It was worth it. A minute with you is like an hour back home without you anyway," he added.

"Paul, please," I said, taking his hands into mine. "Promise me you'll look for someone to love. Promise me you'll let someone love you. Promise."

"All right," he said. "I promise. There isn't anything I wouldn't do for you, Ruby, even fall in love with someone else, if I could."

"You can; you must," I told him.

"I know," he said in a whisper. He looked like I had forced him to swallow castor oil. I wanted to stay with him, to talk and remember the good times, but Edgar was standing in the doorway as a way of showing me Daphne was being very insistent.

"I've got to go inside before she makes a scene that embarrasses us both, Paul. Have a safe trip back and call and write to me at school."

"I will," he said. He kissed me quickly on my cheek and hurried to his car, forcing himself not to look back. I knew it was because he had tears in his eyes and he didn't want me to see them.

I felt an ache in my heart when he drove off, and for a moment I could see that look in his face again on the day he learned the truth about us, the truth we both wished had been buried in the swamp with the sins of our fathers.

I sucked in my breath and hurried to the front entrance to see what new rules and orders Daphne wanted to lay on my sister's and my head now, now that we had no one to stand between her and us and protect us anymore.

She was waiting in the parlor, sitting back in her chair. Gisselle had been wheeled in and she waited too, fidgeting and looking very unhappy. I was surprised to see Bruce seated at the dark pine secretary. Would he be present at all our family discussions now?

"Sit down," Daphne ordered, nodding at the chair beside Gisselle. I took it quickly.

"Is Paul gone?" Gisselle asked.

"Yes."

"Quiet, the two of you. I didn't gather you here to discuss some Cajun boy."

"He's not a boy; he's a young man," I said. "And the manager of his father's factory."

"Fine. I hope he becomes king of the swamp. Now," she said, putting her hands on the arms of the chair, "the two of you will be leaving early in the morning, so I wanted to get some matters straightened out and some business conducted before I retire to my suite. I'm exhausted from all this."

"Then why do we have to leave tomorrow?"

Gisselle whined. "We're exhausted too."

"It's settled: You're leaving," Daphne said, her eyes big. She calmed herself again and continued. "First, I'm cutting in half the amount of money your father was sending you. You have little or no use for spending money while you attend Greenwood anyway."

"That's not true!" Gisselle countered. "In fact, if you give us permission to leave the grounds —"

"I'm not about to do that. Do you think I'm a fool?" She glared at Gisselle as if she expected an answer. "Do you?" she taunted.

"No," Gisselle said, "but it's boring having to stay on the grounds, especially on the weekends. Why can't we take taxis to the city, go to a movie, go shopping?"

"You're there to study and work, not vacation. If you need more money for some emergency, you can phone Bruce at the office and explain what it is and he'll see to it the money is delivered — taken from your trust, of course.

"Neither of you need anything new in your wardrobe. Your father overindulged you both when it came to clothing. He insisted I take you shopping when you first arrived, Ruby. Remember?"

"I thought you wanted to do that," I said softly.

"I did what I had to do to maintain some social dignity. I couldn't have you living here and looking like a runaway Cajun, could I? But your father didn't think I had bought enough. There was never enough for his precious twins. Between both your closets, I could open a department store. Bruce knows our bills. Isn't that so, Bruce?"

"Quite true," he said, nodding and smiling.

"Explain the trust to them simply and quickly, Bruce, if you please," Daphne told him.

He pulled himself up and gazed at some documents on the desk. "Quite simply, all your basic needs are provided for: your schooling, your travel expenses, necessities, and some money for luxuries, gifts, et cetera. As it is required, it is drawn out when Daphne signs for it. If you need an extra stipend, put it in writing and send it to the office, and I'll look into it."

"Put it in writing? What are we, employees now?" Gisselle demanded.

"Hardly employees," Daphne said, her voice hard, her smile faint and sardonic. "Employees have to work for what they get."

She and Bruce exchanged a look of satisfaction before she turned back to us.

"I want to reiterate what I told you about your behavior at Greenwood. Should I be called by the principal because of some misbehavior, the consequences will be dire for you, I assure you."

"What could be more dire than having to stay at Greenwood?" Gisselle muttered.

"There are other schools, farther away, with rules far stricter than the rules at Greenwood."

"You mean reform schools," Gisselle said.

"Gisselle," I said, "stop arguing. It's no use."

She gazed at me with her teary eyes.

313

I shook my head. "She almost had me committed once. She's capable of anything."

"That's enough," Daphne snapped. "Go up and pack your clothes and remember my warnings about your behavior at school. I don't want to hear a bad word. It's enough that Pierre went and died and left me to be guardian over the offspring resulting from his wild indulgences. I don't have the time nor the emotional strength for it."

"Oh, you have the strength, Daphne," I said. "You have the strength."

She stared at me a moment and then put her hand on her chest. "My heart is beating a mile a minute, Bruce. I have to go up. Will you see to it that they do what they're told and the limousine is here to take them to school in the morning?"

"Of course," he said.

I rose quickly and pushed my sister out of the parlor. Maybe she realized it now; maybe she understood that when Daddy died, we had become orphans, albeit orphans from a rich family, but poorer than the poorest when it came to having someone to love and someone to love us.

12

Dark Clouds

Despite what Gisselle had heard and seen in the parlor the day before, she somehow blamed me, insisting I hadn't done enough to persuade Daphne to let us remain at home and return to school in New Orleans.

"At least you have something there you like," she moaned before we went to sleep the night before. "You have your precious Miss Stevens and your artwork to occupy yourself and you can run up to the Clairborne mansion to tease Mrs. Clairborne's blind grandson, but all I have is this group of stupid, immature girls with which to amuse myself."

"I don't tease, Louis," I said. "I feel sorry for him. He's someone who's suffered great emotional pain."

"And what about me? Haven't I suffered great emotional pain? I nearly died; I'm crippled. We're sisters. Why don't you feel sorry for me?" she cried.

"I do," I said, but it was half a lie. Despite

Gisselle's being confined to a wheelchair, I found it more and more difficult to sympathize with her plight. Most of the time, Gisselle managed to get what she wanted no matter what, and usually at someone else's expense.

"No you don't! And now I've got to go back to that . . . that hellhole," she groaned.

She threw a tantrum and wheeled herself about her room, knocking things off the dresser and scattering clothing everywhere. Poor Martha had to come in and straighten it all out before Daphne discovered what Gisselle had done.

In the morning she sat rigidly in her wheelchair, as stiff as she would be had she been calcified, not moving a limb and making the transference from chair to chair to car that much more difficult. She refused to eat a morsel of breakfast and kept her lips so tightly pressed together, they looked stitched closed. Although Gisselle was doing all this for our stern mother's benefit, Daphne witnessed none of her tantrum. She merely sent down orders for Edgar, Nina, and the chauffeur and reminders with warnings attached for us. Bruce Bristow arrived just before we were to leave to make sure our departure went smoothly and on schedule. It was the only time Gisselle uttered a word.

"Who are you now," she taunted, "Daphne's little gofer? Bruce, go for this; Bruce, go for that." She laughed at her own derisive comment. Bruce's face turned pink, but he simply smiled and then went to see to the luggage. Frustrated and furious,

Gisselle gave up and sat back with her eyes closed, resembling one of the patients strapped in a strait-jacket in Uncle Jean's institution.

The trip back to Greenwood was almost as depressing as our journey home to Daddy's funeral. It was far more bleak, the dark gray skies following us all the way, with some light sprinkles dotting the windshield and creating a need for the monotonous sweep of the wipers. Gisselle closed up as tightly as a clam in her corner of the rear seat, not so much as gazing out the window once we left New Orleans. Occasionally, she would throw me a hard look.

For my part I found myself looking forward to doing just what Gisselle had said: returning to work with Miss Stevens and throwing all my energies and attention into the development of my artistic talents. After spending days under Daphne's glaring eyes and oppressive thumb, I actually welcomed the sight of Greenwood when we pulled up the drive and saw the girls scurrying about the grounds after class, all of them laughing, giggling, talking with an animation I now envied. Even Gisselle permitted herself to brighten a bit. I knew she wouldn't show her defeat and disappointment to her disciples.

In fact, once she was back in our dorm, she immediately reverted to her previous demeanor and behavior, refusing to acknowledge anyone's expression of sympathy, acting as if Daddy's death and funeral had been just a terrible inconvenience. She wasn't in her room two minutes before she

317

opened fire on her new whipping boy, her roommate Samantha, screaming at her for having the nerve to move some of her things while she was away. All of us heard the commotion and came out to see what was happening. Samantha was in tears in the doorway where Gisselle had driven her during her tirade.

"How dare you touch my cosmetics? You stole some of my perfume, didn't you? Didn't you?" she hammered. "I know there was more in the bottle."

"I didn't."

"Yes you did. And you tried on some of my clothes too." She spun around in her chair and glared at me. "Look at what I have to put up with since you forced me to move out of your room and share a room with her!" Gisselle screamed.

I nearly burst out laughing at the lie. "Me? *I* told you to move? *You* were the one who wanted to move, Gisselle. You were the one who insisted," I said. Vicki, Kate, and Jacki all looked at me sympathetically because they knew what I said was the truth. But none was willing to come to my defense and risk Gisselle's wrath.

"I did not!" Gisselle yelled, her face so red with anger and frustration, she looked like the top of her head would blow off. She pounded the arms of her wheelchair with her fists and shook her body from side to side so vigorously, I thought she would topple over. "You wanted to be with that quadroon so bad you drove me out." She pulled her eyes back under her trembling lids and foamed at the lips, gagging and choking. Everyone thought she was going into a convulsion, but I had seen her behave this way many times before.

"All right, Gisselle," I said with a tone of defeat, "calm down. What do you want?"

"I want her out of here!" she demanded, pointing her right forefinger at Samantha, who looked as confused and frightened as a baby bird driven out of its nest.

"Do you want to move back in with me, then? Is that what you want?" I asked, slowly closing and opening my eyes.

"No. I'll live by myself and take care of myself," she insisted, wrapping her arms around her body and sitting back firmly in her chair. "Just as long as she's out of here."

"You can't toss people in and out of your room like you would one of your stuffed animals, Gisselle," I chastised. She turned her head slowly and fixed her eyes on little Samantha, burning her gaze into the diminutive strawberry blonde, who stepped farther back.

"I'm not tossing her out. She wants to leave, don't you, Samantha?"

Samantha turned helplessly and gazed at me.

"You can move in with me, Samantha," I said, "if my sister is so positive she can be on her own."

Now that Daphne had forced us to return to Greenwood, I knew that all Gisselle was out to do was make everyone else's life as miserable as her own.

"Sure," she whined, "take someone else's side, just like you always do. We're twins, but do you ever act like we are? Do you?"

I closed my eyes and counted to ten.

"All right, what is it you want, Gisselle? Do you want Samantha to move out or don't you?"

"Of course I do! She's a pathetic little . . . virgin!" she thundered. Then she twisted her lips into a wry smile before adding, "Who dreams of sleeping with Jonathan Peck." She wheeled toward her. "Isn't that what you told me, Samantha? Don't you wonder what it would be like to have Jonathan touch your precious little breasts and kiss you below your belly button? And bring the tip of his tongue —"

"Stop it, Gisselle," I screamed. She smiled at Samantha, who now had large tears streaming down her cheeks. She didn't know how to react, how to deal with this violent betrayal.

"Get your things together, Samantha," I told her, "and bring them into my room."

"And I want any of my things that were left in there brought into MY room," Gisselle commanded. "Kate will help, won't you, Kate?" she asked, smiling at her.

"What? Oh, sure."

Gisselle widened her smile for me, glared at Samantha, and then twirled her wheelchair about to return to her room, mumbling loudly about having to check all her things now to see what else Samantha had stolen or used.

"I didn't take any of her things. Honest,"

Samantha exclaimed again.

"Just move out, Samantha, and don't try to explain or defend yourself," I advised.

I didn't mind having a new roommate and I thought it would serve Gisselle right to have to struggle on her own for a while. Maybe then she would appreciate the help everyone else gave her. But whether it was out of spite or out of defiance, she surprised me by unpacking her own things, changing her dress and shoes for dinner, and fixing her own hair. Kate was given the privilege of wheeling her about now that Samantha was persona non grata. At least for a while, it looked like things would calm down.

After dinner that night, while Vicki was helping me catch up with the work I had missed in the classes she and I shared, Jacki came to my doorway to tell me I had a phone call. I hurried out, assuming it was either Beau or Paul, but it turned out to be Louis.

"I found out from Mrs. Penny about your father," he began. "I wanted to call you in New Orleans, but my cousin wouldn't give me the telephone number. She said it was inappropriate. Anyway, I'm sorry."

"Thank you, Louis."

"I know what it means to lose a parent," he continued. He was silent for a moment and then he changed his tone of voice. "I've been making slow but definite progress with my eyesight," he said. "I can distinguish shapes even better and more clearly. There's still a gray haze over everything, but my doctors are very optimistic."

"I'm happy for you, Louis."

"Can I see you soon? That sounds so great to say, 'see you.' Can I?"

"Yes, of course."

"Come tomorrow. For dinner," he said excitedly. "I'll have the cook prepare a shrimp gumbo."

"No, I can't for dinner. I have serving duty, and it wouldn't be right to ask anyone to take my place."

"Then come after dinner."

"I'll probably have loads of schoolwork to catch up on," I said.

"Oh." Disappointment dripped through the phone.

"Just give me a little while to catch up on everything," I pleaded.

"Sure. I'm just so anxious to show you my progress. Progress," he added softly, "that came after I met you."

"That's nice of you to say, Louis. But I don't know what I could have had to do with it."

"I do," he said cryptically. "I'm warning you. I'll drive you crazy until you visit me," he teased.

"All right," I said, laughing. "I'll come up on Sunday after dinner."

"Maybe by then I'll make even more progress and surprise you by telling you the color of your hair and the color of your eyes."

"I hope so," I said, but after I hung up the phone, I felt a dark anxiety spiral its way up from the bottom of my stomach to my heart, where it settled like a dull ache. It was nice to have Louis feel that I was helping him, and it was flattering to think I could have such a dramatic impact on so serious a problem as blindness, but I knew he was putting too much importance on me and developing too much reliance on my company. I was afraid he would think he was falling in love with me and that he might even imagine that I was falling in love with him. Soon, I promised myself, soon I would tell him about Beau. Only now I was afraid it might shatter his delicate improvement; and his grandmother and his cousin, Mrs. Ironwood, would only have something else to blame on me.

I returned to my room and to my work and buried myself in the reading, the notes, and the studies because it kept me from thinking about all the sad things that had occurred and the heavy burdens I had been left to bear. The next day all of my teachers were understanding and cooperative, the warmest being Miss Stevens, of course. Returning to her class was like coming out of a dark, summer storm into the brightness of sunlight again. I returned to my unfinished paintings and we made a tentative date to meet at the lake on the school grounds Saturday morning to start some new work.

Over the next few days, Gisselle continued to surprise me and the others with her new independence. Except for Kate's wheeling her about at times, she took care of her own needs. She kept the door to her room shut tight whenever she was in there. Samantha, on the other hand, looked sad and lost. Whenever Gisselle was with Kate and Jacki, the three ignored her. She trailed after them like a puppy dog who had been kicked and driven from its home but had nowhere else to go. Obviously under Gisselle's orders, Jacki and Kate joined her and refused to acknowledge or speak to Samantha. They acted as if she were invisible.

"Why don't you try to make new friends, Samantha," I told her. "Perhaps you should even go to Mrs. Penny and request to be moved to a new quad."

She shook her head vigorously. The thought of making such a dramatic break, even under these conditions, terrified the shy, insecure girl.

"No, it's all right. Everything will be all right," she said.

On Thursday night, however, I returned from the library with Vicki and found Samantha curled up in her bed, sobbing softly. I closed the door and hurried to her bedside.

"What is it, Samantha? What's my sister done now?" I asked in a tired voice.

"Nothing," she moaned. "Everything's fine. We're . . . friends again. She's forgiven me."

"What? What are you talking about? Forgiven you?"

She nodded, but kept her back to me, the covers tightly wrapped around her body. Something about her behavior triggered my darker suspicions. My heart began to beat quickly in anticipation when I put my hand on her shoulder and she jumped as if I had touched her with fingers of fire. "Samantha, what happened here while I was away?" I demanded. She simply cried harder. "Samantha?"

"I had to do it," she moaned. "They all made me. They all said I had to."

"Do what, Samantha? Samantha?" I shook her shoulder. "Do what?"

Suddenly she turned around and buried her face against my stomach while throwing her arms around my waist. Her body shook with sobs.

"I'm so ashamed," she cried.

"Ashamed of what? Samantha, you must tell me what Gisselle made you do. Tell me," I insisted, seizing her shoulders firmly. She sat back slowly, her eyes closed, and let her head fall back to the pillow. I realized she was naked under the blanket.

"She sent Kate in to tell me to come into her room. When I did, she asked me if I wanted to be part of the group again. I said yes, but she said . . . she said I had to do penance."

"Penance? What sort of penance?"

"She said that while she was away, I dreamt of being like her. I wanted to be her, and that was why I used her lipstick and her makeup and her perfume. She said I was so sexually frustrated, I even put on her panties, but I didn't," Samantha insisted. "Honest, I didn't."

"I believe you, Samantha. Then what happened?"

325

Samantha closed her eyes and swallowed.

"Samantha?"

"I had to take off my clothes and get into the bed," she blurted.

I held my breath, knowing what sort of sordid things Gisselle was capable of making her do.

"Go on," I said in a breathy whisper.

"I'm so ashamed."

"What did she make you do, Samantha?"

"They all did," she cried. "They taunted and cheered until I gave in."

"Gave in to what?"

"I had to take a pillow and pretend it was . . . Jonathan Peck They made me stroke it and kiss it and . . ."

"Oh no, Samantha." She shuddered with sobs.

I stroked her hair. "My sister is a sick person. I'm sorry. You shouldn't have listened to her."

"They all hated me," she cried in defense, "even the other girls in the dorm and the girls in our classes. No one would talk to me in the girls' room or in the lockers, and someone poured a bottle of ink over my social studies notebook today, blotting out all the pages." She cried harder.

"All right, Samantha. It's all right," I said. I rocked her until her sobbing subsided. Then I stood up. "My sister and I are going to have a little chat right now."

"NO!" Samantha said, seizing my hand. "Don't." Her eyes were wide with terror. "If you get her angry, she'll turn the girls against me again. Please," she begged. "Promise you won't say anything. She made me promise not to tell you what they made me do and she'll just accuse me of betraying her again."

"She would make you promise that because she knows I'll go right in there and heave her out the window," I said. Samantha bit down on her lip, the alarm filling her face. "All right, don't worry. I won't do anything, but Samantha, are you all right?"

"I'm okay," she said, wiping her face quickly. She forced a smile. "It wasn't so bad, and it's over. We're all friends again."

"With friends like that, you don't need enemies," I said. "My grandmere Catherine used to say that even if we lived in a world without sickness and disease, without storms and hurricanes, droughts and pestilence, we would find a way to make the devil comfortable in our own hearts."

"What?" Samantha asked.

"Nothing. Are you moving back in with her?"

"No. She still wants to live alone," Samantha said. "Is it all right if I continue to room with you?"

"Of course. I'm just surprised. The second shoe hasn't dropped yet," I muttered, wondering what scheme Gisselle was designing to make life more unbearable for everyone, especially me, at Greenwood.

The remainder of the week passed quickly and without incident. I didn't know whether being alone in the dorm and being responsible for taking care of her own basic needs was what exhausted her, but every morning when Kate finally wheeled her to the breakfast table, Gisselle looked half drugged. She sat there with her eyelids drooping and nibbled on something, barely paying any attention to the chatter around the table. She was usually the first to interrupt or to ridicule something someone else said.

Then on Friday Vicki stopped me in the corridor after science class to tell me she had heard that Gisselle had fallen asleep in remedial reading. I imagined Gisselle was too stubborn to admit that caring for herself was draining her of whatever energy she possessed. Toward the end of the day, I stopped her in the corridor.

"What is it?" she snapped. Fatigue made her even more irritable than usual.

"You can't go on like this, Gisselle. You're dozing in class, dozing at lunch, moping in your chair. You need help. Either take Samantha back in with you or move back with me," I said.

The suggestion brought color to her face and perked her up.

"You'd like that, wouldn't you?" she replied in a voice loud enough to attract everyone nearby. "You want me to be dependent, to have to scream for help whenever I want to brush my hair or my teeth. Well, I don't need you or darling Samantha in order to get myself around this school. I don't need anyone," she added and whipped the wheels of her chair hard to push herself off. Even Kate was left standing with her mouth open.

"Well," I said, shrugging, "I'm glad she's trying

to be independent. Let me know if she seems to be getting sick, though," I told Kate, who nodded and then ran after Gisselle. I went on to my art class.

That night Beau phoned. I had been waiting anxiously for his call all week.

"I thought I would sneak away tomorrow and come up to Baton Rouge to see you, but my father has restricted my use of the car since Daphne had a talk with him and my mother. She told them about my taking you up to the institution."

"And that made them that angry?"

"She said we disturbed Jean so much he has had to be given shock treatments."

"Oh no. I hope it's a lie," I cried.

"My father was furious, and then when she told them I was up in your room during the wake . . . I think she exaggerated what we were doing too."

"How could she be so horrible?"

"Maybe she takes lessons," Beau jested. "Anyway, I expect my restriction will be lifted at holiday time. It's only another ten days, right?"

"Yes, but will your parents permit you to have anything whatsoever to do with me now?" I wondered aloud.

"We'll manage. There's no way anyone can keep me from seeing you when you're here," he promised.

He asked me about school, and I told him about Gisselle and how she was making everyone's life as miserable as she could.

"You really have your hands full. It's not fair."

"I made promises to my father," I said. "I have to try."

"I overheard my father talking to my mother last night about Daphne," Beau said. "She and Bruce Bristow have made some drastic moves, foreclosing on some businesses and tenants to seize their property. My father said Pierre would never have been so cruel, even though it made good business sense."

"I'm sure she's enjoying it. She has ice water running through her veins," I told him. Beau laughed and described again how much he missed me, how much he loved me, and how much he looked forward to our being together. I could almost feel his lips on mine when he threw me a kiss through the phone.

When I returned to the quad, I half expected that Gisselle would be waiting for me in the lounge to interrogate me about the call, but she had the door to her room shut tight. Kate informed me that Gisselle had decided to go to sleep early. I thought about checking on her and reached for the doorknob, only to find she had locked the door. Surprised, I knocked gently.

"Gisselle?"

She didn't reply. Either she was already asleep or she was pretending to be.

"Are you all right?"

I waited, but there was no response. If that was the way she wanted it, I thought, that was the way it would be. I went to my own room to read and to write a letter to Paul before going to sleep. Miss Stevens and I had made a date to paint at the lake after breakfast the next day, and I was finally closing my eyes and looking forward to something again.

Saturday morning was beautiful. The December sky was more of a crystalline blue, even the clouds looking like glazed alabaster. Miss Stevens was already at the lakeside, setting up our easels. I saw she had spread out a blanket as well and had brought a picnic basket along. The lake itself had a silvery blue sheen. Although the sun was bright, the air felt cool and invigorating. Miss Stevens saw me approaching and waved.

"What a challenge it's going to be to mix paints to duplicate this color," she said, looking out over the water. "How are you?"

"Fine and eager," I said, and we began. Once we got started, we both lost ourselves for a while in our work, the process itself absorbing us, seizing our minds. Often, I would imagine myself to be one of the animals I painted in my settings, seeing the world from the eyes of a tern or a pelican, or even an alligator.

We both had our concentration broken by the sound of hammering and looked at the boathouse to see Buck Dardar pounding on a lawn-mower blade. He paused as if he could feel our gazes and looked our way for a moment before starting again.

Miss Stevens laughed. "For a while there I forgot where I was."

"Me too."

"Want something cold to drink? I've got iced tea or apple juice."

"Iced tea will be fine," I replied. "Thanks."

She asked me how Gisselle was coping since Daddy's death and our return, and I described her behavior. She listened keenly and nodded thoughtfully.

"Let her alone for a while," she advised. "She needs to succeed at being independent. That will make her stronger, happier. I'm sure she knows you're there if and when she needs you," she added.

I felt better about it, and then we painted some more before stopping to enjoy the picnic lunch she had prepared. As we sat on the blanket and ate and talked, other students walked by, some waving, some gazing curiously. I saw many of my teachers and even spotted Mrs. Ironwood watching us for a few moments before crossing the campus.

"Louis was right about this lake," I said when we resumed our work. "It does have a magic to it. It seems to change its nature, its color, and even its shape as the day moves on."

"I love painting scenes with water in them. One of these days, I'm going to take a trip to the bayou. Maybe you'll come along as my swamp guide," she suggested.

"Oh, there's nothing I'd love better," I said. She smiled warmly at me, and I felt as if I did have a big sister. It turned out to be one of the best days I had had at Greenwood.

That night there was a pajama party at our dorm. Girls from the other dorms came over to listen to music, eat popcorn, and dance in the lounge. Afterward, they slept over, some sharing beds, some sleeping on blankets on the floors. During the night tricks were played. Some of the girls from the B quad downstairs went upstairs and knocked on a door. When the girls opened it, they threw pails of cold water over them and ran. Naturally, the girls upstairs had to respond. Somehow they had captured a couple of bullfrogs and cast them into the B quad lounge, sending the girls screaming through the corridors. Mrs. Penny was beside herself running from one section of the dorm to the other.

To my surprise, Gisselle found all this immature and stupid, and rather than participating and devising things for her little group to do, she retreated again to the confines of her room, locking the door behind her. I began to wonder if she wasn't falling into a deep depression and if that wasn't partly responsible for her fatigue every morning.

On Sunday I caught up on all my homework, studied for my English and math tests with Vicki, did my chores at dinner, and then dressed to go up to visit Louis. I told him not to bother Buck. I'd rather walk to the mansion. It was that nice a night, with a sky just blazing with stars, the Big and Small Dippers rarely as clearly delineated. I felt a pair of eyes on me as I walked and looked up and to my right to see an owl. I imagined that a human being walking alone at night through his domain was more of a curiosity to him than he was to me. It made me recall my life in the bayou and the feeling I used to have that animals there had grown accustomed to me.

The deer had no fear about drawing closer. Bullfrogs practically hopped over my feet; ducks and geese flew so low over my head, I felt the breeze from their wings stir the strands of my hair. I was part of the world in which I lived. Maybe the owl here sensed I was a kindred spirit. He didn't hoot; he didn't fly away. He just lifted his wings gently, as if in greeting, and remained like a statue on a branch, watching.

The large plantation house loomed ahead of me, lights burning brightly on the galeries, even though many of the windows were dark. As I drew closer, I could hear the melodious tones of Louis's piano. I rapped on the door with the large brass ball knocker and waited. A few moments later Otis appeared. He wore a troubled look when he set eyes on me, but he bowed and stepped back.

"Hello, Otis," I said cheerfully. His eyes shifted to the right to be sure Mrs. Clairborne wasn't watching from a doorway before he returned my greeting.

"Good evening, mademoiselle. Monsieur Louis is waiting for you in the music studio. Right this way," he said, and began to lead me through the long corridor quickly, but I looked to my left just in time to see a door closing and thought I caught a glimpse of Mrs. Clairborne. Otis brought me to the studio doorway before nodding and retreating. I entered and watched Louis play for a few moments before he realized I had arrived. He wore a dark blue velvet sports coat with a white silk shirt and a pair of blue slacks. With his hair neatly brushed, he looked handsome. When he turned toward the door, he stopped instantly and sprung from his stool. I immediately noticed something different about the way he looked in my direction and the confidence with which he now walked.

"Ruby!" He stepped quickly across the room to take my hand. "I can see you silhouetted clearly," he declared. "It's so exciting, even to view the world in grays and whites. It's so wonderful not to worry about bumping into anything. What's more, occasionally I get a flash of color." He reached up to touch my hair. "Maybe I'll see your beautiful hair before the evening comes to an end. I'll try. I'll think about it and I'll try. If I concentrate hard enough . . .

"Oh," he said, stepping back a bit, "here I am going on and on about myself and not even asking you how you are."

"I'm fine, Louis."

"You can't be fine," he insisted. "You've been through a terrible time, a terrible time. Come, sit on the settee and tell me everything, anything," he said, still holding my hand and leading me toward the sofa. I sat down and he sat beside me.

There was a new and brighter radiance in his face. It was as if with every particle of light that pierced the dark curtain that had fallen over his eyes, he came back to life, drew closer and closer to a world of hope and joy, returning to a place where he could smile and laugh, sing and talk and find it possible to love again.

"I don't mind your being selfish, Louis, and talking about your progress. I'd rather not talk about the tragedy and what I've just been through. It's still too fresh and painful."

"Of course," he said. "I only meant to be a sympathetic listener." He smiled. "Someone on whose shoulder you could cry. After all, I cried on yours, didn't I?"

"Thank you. It's nice of you to offer, especially in light of your own problems."

"We're better off not worrying about ourselves, and to do that, we have to worry about others," he said. "Oh, don't I sound like some wise old man. I'm sorry, but I've had a lot of time to sit and meditate these past few years. Anyway," he said, pausing to sit up straight, "I've decided to give in and go to the clinic in Switzerland next month. The doctors have promised me that I would stay there only a short time, but in the interim, I could attend the music conservatory and continue with my music."

"Oh Louis, how wonderful!"

"Now," he said, taking my hand into his and softening his voice, "I have asked my doctor why my eyes have suddenly come alive again and he assures me it's because I have found someone I could trust." He smiled. "My doctor is really more what you would call a psychiatrist," he said quickly. "The way he describes my condition is that my mind dropped a black curtain over my eyes and kept it there all this time. He said I wouldn't let myself get better because I was afraid of seeing again. I felt safer locked in my own world of darkness, permitting my feelings to escape only through my fingers and into the piano keys.

"When I described you and the way I felt about you, he agreed with me that you have been a major part of the reason why I am regaining my sight. As long as I have you nearby . . . as long as I can depend on you to spend time with me . . ."

"Oh Louis, I can't bear to have so much responsibility."

He laughed.

"I just knew you would say something like that. You're too sweet and unselfish. Don't you worry. The responsibility is all mine. Of course," he added, sotto voce, "my grandmother is not at all pleased with all this. She was so angry she wanted to employ another doctor. She had my cousin over here to speak to me to try to convince me I felt the way I felt because I am so vulnerable. But I told them . . . I told them how it was impossible for you to be the sort of girl they were describing: someone who connives and takes advantage.

"And then I told them . . ." He paused, his face becoming firm. "No, I didn't tell them — I demanded — that you be permitted to visit me whenever you can before I go off to the clinic. In fact, I made it very clear that I would not go if I didn't see you as often as I wanted, and . . .

of course, as often as you wanted to see me.

"But you do want to see me, don't you?" he asked. His tone sounded more like a pleading.

"Louis, I don't mind coming up here whenever I can, but . . ."

"Oh, wonderful. Then it's settled," he declared. "I'll tell you what I will do: I will continue to write an entire symphony. I'll work all this month, and it will be dedicated to you."

"Louis," I said, my eyes tearing, "I must tell you . . ."

"No," he said, "I've already decided. In fact, I have some of it already written. That's what I was playing when you arrived. Will you listen to it?"

"Of course, Louis, but . . ."

He got up and went to the piano before I could say another word and began playing.

My heart was troubled. Somehow I had gotten myself into Louis's world so deeply, it seemed impossible to climb out without hurting him terribly. Perhaps after he went off to the clinic and when his eyesight returned fully, I could get him to understand that I was involved with someone else romantically. At that time he could endure the disappointment and go on, I thought. Until then, I could do nothing but listen to his beautiful music and encourage him to continue with his efforts to regain his sight.

His symphony was beautiful. His melodies rose and fell with such grace that I felt swept away. I relaxed with my eyes closed and let his composition take me back through time until I saw myself as a little girl again, running over the grass, Grandmere Catherine's laughter trailing behind me as I squealed with delight at the birds that swooped over the water and the bream that jumped in the ponds.

"Well," Louis said when he finished playing, "that's all I have written so far. How's it coming?"

"It's beautiful, Louis. And it's very special. You will become a famous composer, I'm sure."

He laughed again.

"Come," he said. "I asked Otis to have some Cajun coffee and some beignets shipped up from the Cafe du Monde in New Orleans waiting for us in the glass-enclosed patio. You can tell me all about your twin sister and the terrible things she's been doing," he added. He held out his arm for me to pass my arm under and then we left the music studio. I looked back once as we walked through the corridor. In the shadows behind us, I was sure I saw Mrs. Clairborne standing and staring. Even at this distance, I felt her displeasure.

But it wasn't until the next morning at school that I was to discover how determined she and her niece, Mrs. Ironwood, were to get me out of Louis's life.

13

False Accusations

My homeroom teacher had just begun to read the day's announcements when a messenger arrived from Mrs. Ironwood's office with the order for me to appear immediately. I glanced at Gisselle and saw that she looked just as confused and as curious about it as everyone else. Without a word I left and walked quickly down the corridor. When I reached Mrs. Ironwood's office, I found Mrs. Randle standing in the inner-office doorway, a tablet in her hand.

"Come right in," she said, stepping back to let me enter.

With my heart pounding so hard I thought it would crack open my chest, I walked into Mrs. Ironwood's office. She was seated behind her desk, her back rigid, her lips pursed, her eyes more filled with fury than I had ever seen them. She had her hands on the desk, palms down over some documents.

"Sit down," she commanded. She nodded at Mrs. Randle, who stepped in after me and then closed the door. Mrs. Randle then moved quickly to a seat beside the desk and put her notepad down. Her hand was poised with her pen clutched in her fingers.

"What's wrong?" I asked, not able to stand the long, ominous silence that had fallen over me.

"I can't recall summoning another student to my office as frequently in so short a time as I have had to summon you," Mrs. Ironwood began, her dark eyebrows knitted together. She glanced at Mrs. Randle for confirmation and Mrs. Randle nodded slightly, closing and opening her eyes at the same time.

"That's not my fault," I said.

"Humm," Mrs. Ironwood muttered. She looked at Mrs. Randle as though the two of them heard voices I didn't hear. "It's never their faults," she said with a smirk, and Mrs. Randle nodded again, closing and opening her eyes as before. She resembled a puppet, the strings of which were in Mrs. Ironwood's hands.

"Well, why have you sent for me?" I asked.

Before replying, Mrs. Ironwood pulled her shoulders back and up even straighter and firmer. "I have asked Mrs. Randle in here to take notes, since I am about to commence a formal expulsion hearing."

"What? What have I done now?" I cried. I looked at Mrs. Randle, who this time kept her eyes down. I returned my gaze to Mrs. Ironwood, who was staring at me with such intensity, I thought I felt her gaze pass through me like a beam of heat.

"What haven't you done? is more like it." She shook her head and looked down at me from the height of her contempt. "Right from the start, from the background on you that your stepmother so frankly confessed, from the arrogance and disdain you exhibited during our initial conference, from your attitude about our rules, violating the off-grounds restrictions almost immediately, from the manner in which you defied my wishes, I knew your attendance at Greenwood was a mistake of gargantuan proportions and destined for horrible failure.

"Punishments, warnings, even friendly advice did little or no good. Your kind rarely changes for the better. It's in your blood to fail."

"Exactly what am I being accused of doing?" I fired back defiantly.

Instead of replying immediately, she cleared her throat and put on her pearl-framed reading glasses. Then she lifted the papers under her hands to read from them.

" 'This is to formally commence step one of the expulsion procedure as outlined in the governing bylaws of Greenwood School as set down by the board of directors. The student under question,' " she read, and looked over her glasses at me, " 'one Ruby Dumas, has, on the date described herein, been summoned to be informed of her hearing and to hear the charges levied against her by the administration of Greenwood Schools.

" 'Number one,' " she began in an even more authoritative voice, " 'she has willfully and knowingly trespassed on a well-designated off-limits location on the Greenwood campus and remained at this location after curfew.' "

"What?" I cried, looking again at Mrs. Randle, who had her head lowered and was scribbling rapidly on her notepad. "What location?"

" 'Number two, she has willfully and knowingly participated in immoral behavior on school property while under school supervision.' "

"Immoral behavior?"

" 'The above charges will be levied and adjudicated at a formal expulsion hearing this afternoon at four P.M. in this office.' "

She lowered the papers and then her glasses.

"I am to instruct you as to our procedure. A panel consisting of two faculty members and your student body president, Deborah Peck, will hear the charges and the proofs and render judgment. I will oversee the proceedings, of course."

"What charges? What proofs?"

"I've read you the charges," she said.

"I haven't heard anything specific. Where am I supposed to have gone that's off-limits on the campus? The mansion? Is that what this is about?" I demanded. Her cheeks reddened as she shot a quick glance at Mrs. Randle and then looked at me.

"Hardly," she replied. "You were seen at the boathouse after hours."

"Boathouse?"

"Where you went to have an illicit rendezvous with an employee, Buck Dardar."

"What? Who saw me?"

"A member of this faculty, a well-respected, long-time member of this faculty, I might add."

"Who? Can't I know the name of my accuser?" I demanded when she hesitated.

"Mrs. Gray, your Latin teacher. So there is no question she would be able to recognize you," she concluded.

I shook my head. "When?"

She looked at the papers as if it was a great effort to do so and said, "You were seen entering the boathouse at seven-thirty last night."

"Last night?"

"And you remained after curfew," she added. "The remaining details of Mrs. Gray's testimony will be given at the formal hearing."

"It's a mistaken identity. I couldn't have been in the boathouse at seven-thirty last night. Just call Buck in here and ask him," I advised.

She smirked. "Don't you think I had enough sense to do just that? He was called in here first thing this morning, and he did write out a confession," she said, holding up another document, "corroborating what our eyewitness saw."

"No," I said, shaking my head. "He's mistaken or he's lying. You'll see when he comes to the hearing and sees me and realizes . . ."

"Buck Dardar is no longer on these grounds. He has been relieved of his duties and he has already left the school," she said.

"What? He's been fired because of these false charges against me? But that's not fair."

"I assure you," she said, smiling coldly, "he thought my offer to him was quite fair. You girls are all under age. If not for the potential scandal, I would have turned him over to the police."

"But this isn't true. Just ask your aunt where I was last night."

"My aunt?" She pulled herself in like an accordion. "You want me to involve Mrs. Clairborne in this loathsome and vulgar affair? How dare you suggest such a thing. Is there no bottom to the depth of your immorality?"

"But I was at the mansion last night, and I was back in the dorm well before the curfew."

"I assure you," Mrs. Ironwood said slowly, "Mrs. Clairborne would never consent to give such testimony." She looked so confident and smug about it.

"But then just call Louis . . ."

"A blind man? You want to bring him into this too? Are you out to disgrace this distinguished family? Is that your motive? Some sort of sick Cajun jealousy?"

"Of course not, but this is all a mistake," I cried.

"That's for our panel to decide at four o'clock. Be here on time." She closed her eyes and then opened them. "You can bring someone to speak in your defense." She paused and leaned forward, a curt smile on her lips. "Of course, if you want to avoid all this unpleasantness, you can confess and admit to these charges and accept your expulsion."

"No," I said, infuriated. "I want to face my accusers. I want everyone who is party to these lies to have to look into my eyes and understand what they're doing."

"Suit yourself." She sat back again. "I knew you would be defiant to the end, and I had little hope of making things easier for your family, even after the tragedy your stepmother has just recently endured. I feel sorry for you, but you are probably better off returning to your own kind."

"Oh, there's no question I'm better off doing that, Mrs. Ironwood," I said. "My kind doesn't look down on people just because they don't happen to be rich or descendants of some noble family. My kind don't plot and connive," I snapped. My tears were hot under my lids, but I kept them locked in my eyes so as not to give her the satisfaction of seeing me brought down. "But I won't be paddled out of here in a canoe built out of fabrications and hateful deceit."

She gazed at Mrs. Randle, who quickly looked down at her notepad again.

"For the record," Mrs. Ironwood dictated, "let it be noted that the student, Ruby Dumas, denies all charges and wishes to go forward with the formal hearing. She has been informed of her rights —"

"Rights? What rights do I have here?" I said with a sarcastic laugh.

"She has been informed of her rights," Mrs. Ironwood repeated pointedly. "Do you have all this, Mrs. Randle?"

"Yes," she replied quickly.

"Let her sign the notes as prescribed by the by-laws," Mrs. Ironwood said. Mrs. Randle turned her pad toward me and pushed it closer, handing me a pen at the same time.

"You sign right here," she instructed, pointing to a line drawn at the bottom of the page. I plucked the pen out of her fingers and started to sign.

"Don't you want to read it first?" Mrs. Ironwood asked.

"What for?" I said. "This is all a well-rehearsed play, with the outcome predetermined."

"Then why continue it?" she demanded quickly.

Yes, I wondered, why continue it? Then I thought about Grandmere Catherine and about all the times she was called to face the hardest of challenges, the unknown, the dark; and how she always went willingly to do battle for what was right and what was good, no matter how terrible the odds against her success were.

"I will continue it so that all those who are part of this conspiracy can face me and have me lay heavy on their consciences," I replied.

Mrs. Randle's eyes widened with surprise and a little appreciation, appreciation she was sure Mrs. Ironwood did not see.

"You can return to your classes now," Mrs. Ironwood said. "You have been told to appear at four. If you should fail to appear, you will be judged in absentia."

"I have no doubt of that," I said and got up. My legs wanted to wobble, but I closed my eyes and willed a stream of hard, cold strength from my proud heart down through my veins and to the bottoms of my feet. With my shoulders straight and my head high, I turned and walked out of Mrs. Ironwood's office, not faltering until I set myself down in my desk in my first class and realized just what it was that was about to happen now. A kind of paralyzing numbness gripped me.

I moved like a zombie throughout the day. I told no one about my meeting with Mrs. Ironwood and what I had been accused of and what that meant, but I didn't have to whisper a word to a living soul. As soon as Deborah Peck was informed she would be sitting in on an expulsion hearing, the news wove its way through every corridor and every classroom faster than an eel in the swamp going after its supper. By midafternoon, everyone knew and everyone was talking about me. Just before my last class period, Gisselle cornered me in the hallway, first to chastise me for not coming directly to her with my problem, and then to express her pleasure because if I were forced out of Greenwood, so was she.

"I didn't tell you just because of the way you're acting right now, Gisselle," I said. "I knew how you would gloat and be pleased."

"Why are you bothering with the hearing? Let's just call Daphne and tell her to send the limousine."

"Because it's a pack of lies, that's why, and I don't intend to let the Iron Lady get away with it, if I can help it," I replied. "I won't be driven

348

out of here on a rail, tarred and feathered."

"Well you can't stop it, and you're just being Cajun stubborn and Cajun stupid. You don't go to that hearing, Ruby," she ordered. "Did you hear what I said? You don't go."

"Let me go to my class, Gisselle. I don't want to add a lateness to everything else and give her any more reason to pick on me," I said, starting around the wheelchair.

She seized the sleeve of my blouse. "Just don't go, Ruby."

I pulled my arm free.

"I'm going," I said, my eyes so full of fire my cheeks felt singed.

"You're wasting your time," she called after me. "And it's not worth it! This place isn't worth it!" she screamed. I walked faster and entered the art room just at the bell. One look at Miss Stevens's face told all: She knew and she was very upset for me. She was so upset she put the others to busy work and pulled me aside at the rear of the room, where she asked me to tell her everything.

"I'm not guilty, Miss Stevens. These are trumped-up charges. I couldn't have been at the boathouse last night. Mrs. Gray is mistaken."

"Why couldn't you be?" she asked.

I told her about my visit with Louis.

"Only they say Mrs. Clairborne won't testify for me and they won't let Louis do it either," I explained.

She shook her head, her eyes dark with troubled thoughts. "I can't see Mrs. Gray as part of any underhanded conspiracy to have you thrown out of Greenwood. She's a fine woman, a very kind person. Don't you get along with her in class?" she asked.

"Oh yes. I think I have an A-plus in her class."

"She's been like a mother to me," Miss Stevens said, "advising me, helping me right from the start. She's a churchgoing lady too."

"But I wasn't there, Miss Stevens! Honest. She has to be mistaken."

Miss Stevens nodded, thoughtful.

"Maybe she'll realize that and recant her testimony."

"I doubt it. Mrs. Ironwood looked too pleased and too assured of herself, and with Buck already fired and gone, it's going to be my word against Mrs. Gray's and that fiction they made Buck sign," I moaned.

"Why is Mrs. Ironwood so adamantly against you?" Miss Stevens wondered.

"Because of Louis, mainly, but she never liked me from the start and made that perfectly clear the first time we met in her office. My stepmother put a dark cloud over me here immediately. I don't know why she would do that, except to make sure my stay here would be horrible. She wants me to fail, to look bad, just so she will have reason to get rid of me . . . and Gisselle," I said.

"You poor dear. Do you want me to come to the hearing with you and testify about your talents and success?"

"No. That won't matter, and it would only bring

you into this dirty mess. I just want to go there and spit back in all their faces."

Miss Stevens's eyes filled with tears. She hugged me and wished me well and then returned to the front of the class to give instruction, but I heard nothing and saw nothing. After school I returned to the dorm, floating in a daze and not even re-membering the walk. As soon as I was back in my room, I began to pack some of my things. When Gisselle arrived, she was ecstatic.

"You've decided to take my advice and give up? Good. When is the limousine coming?"

"I'm just preparing for what I know is inevi-table, Gisselle. I'm still attending the hearing, which will begin in an hour. Do you want to come along?"

"Of course not. Why would I do such a thing?"

"To be with me."

"You mean to be embarrassed with you. Thanks, but no thanks. I'll wait here and start packing my things too. Thank goodness we'll be able to tell this place and everyone in it good riddance," she said, not caring that some of the girls would over-hear.

"I won't be so happy about it, Gisselle. Daphne will have some other torment awaiting us. You'll see. We'll be shipped off to another school, a worse place, just as she threatened."

"I won't go. I'll tie myself to my bed!"

"She'll have the movers pack the bed too. She's determined."

"I don't care. Anything is better than this," she

insisted, and spun away to begin her packing. I returned to my own packing and then took the time to fix my hair so I would look as presentable and as self-assured as I could.

I started back to the school at a quarter to four. Many of the girls in the dorm were downstairs in the lounge talking about me. They grew silent when I appeared and watched me leave, some going to the windows to stare out as I paraded up the path, my head high. I had taken nothing with me, but I made sure Nina's good gris-gris, the dime on a string, was around my ankle.

The sky had turned ominously gray, the thick overcast moving quickly to block out any sight of blue until the world looked dark and dreary, reflecting the way I felt in my heart. There was even a surprising chill in the air, so I hurried into the building.

At this time of the day, there were few students wandering about the halls. Those who were there stopped whatever they were doing to stare and then whisper as I made my way down the corridor toward Mrs. Ironwood's office. The door to her inner office was closed and Mrs. Randle was not at her desk. I took a seat and waited, watching the clock tick closer and closer toward four. At exactly four the door to the inner office was opened. Mrs. Ironwood herself stood there, a look of both disappointment and disgust on her face when she saw me waiting.

"Come in and take your seat," she ordered, and

pivoted to return to her desk.

The room furniture had been rearranged so that it appeared more like a courtroom. A chair for witnesses had been placed to the left of Mrs. Ironwood's desk. Mrs. Randle, who was there to record the hearing, sat at a small table to the right of the desk. To the left of what would be the witness chair sat the panel of judges: Mr. Norman, my science teacher; Miss Weller, the librarian; and Deborah Peck, who wore a smirk of satisfaction that made my stomach churn with anger. I was sure she would be on the phone to her brother the moment this had ended. Mrs. Gray sat to the left on the settee, looking very unhappy and very troubled.

There was a seat for me, the accused, facing the desk, which Mrs. Ironwood indicated with a nod for me to take. I did so quickly, my eyes fixed on the panel. I was determined not to look frightened or guilty, but my chest felt as if I had swallowed a clump of swamp mosquitoes, all of which buzzed and bit around my pounding heart.

"This formal hearing to determine whether or not to expel student Ruby Dumas will commence," Mrs. Ironwood began. She put on her glasses to read the charges once again. While she read, I felt everyone's eyes on me, but I didn't change expression. I kept my eyes fixed on her, my back straight, my hands comfortably in my lap. "Do you plead guilty or not guilty to these charges?" she asked in conclusion.

"Not guilty," I said. My voice threatened to

crack, but I held it together. Mrs. Ironwood straightened up.

"Very well. We shall continue then. Mrs. Gray," she said, turning to the small-framed, dark-brown-haired lady with soft blue eyes. I knew that up until now she had been very fond of me, often complimenting me on my class work. She looked like she had a broken heart and was doing something terribly painful to her, but she stood up, took a deep breath, and went to the witness chair.

"Please describe to the panel what you know and what you have seen, Mrs. Gray," Mrs. Ironwood instructed.

Mrs. Gray glanced at me quickly and then directed herself to the three who were to pass judgment. "Last night at approximately seven-twenty, seven twenty-five, I was returning from having dinner with Mrs. Johnson, the dorm mother at Waverly. I had left my car in the faculty parking lot and walked. When I rounded the turn, I saw someone hurrying toward the lake and the boathouse, moving surreptitiously through the shadows. Curious because I knew it had to be one of our students, I turned down the path to the lake."

She paused to take a deep breath and swallow.

"I heard the door of the boathouse open. I heard what was definitely female laughter, and then I heard the door close. I went down to the dock and continued. When I reached the boathouse, I paused because the window was open and I had a clear view of what was going on inside."

"And what was going on inside?" Mrs. Ironwood

asked when Mrs. Gray hesitated. She closed her eyes, bit down on her lower lip, and then took another breath and resumed.

"I saw Buck Dardar wearing only his briefs, embracing a girl. When he pulled back a bit, I had a full view of the girl."

"And who was this girl?" Mrs. Ironwood demanded quickly.

"I saw Ruby Dumas. Naturally, I was shocked and disappointed. Before I could utter a sound, she unbuttoned her white blouse and began to take it off. Buck Dardar embraced her again."

"What was she wearing at this point?" Mrs. Ironwood asked.

"She was . . . half nude," Mrs. Gray said. "She wore only her skirt."

I saw Deborah Peck's mouth drop open. Miss Weller shook her head in disgust. Mr. Norman only closed his eyelids a bit but kept his face frozen, his lips unmoving, his eyes directed at Mrs. Gray.

"Go on," Mrs. Ironwood instructed.

"I was so astonished and disappointed, I felt weak and nauseated," Mrs. Gray said. "I turned away and hurried up the path."

"After which you called me to make your report. Isn't that true?"

Mrs. Gray looked at me and nodded.

"Yes."

"Thank you."

"It wasn't me, Mrs. Gray," I said softly.

"Quiet. You will have your time to speak," Mrs.

Ironwood snapped. "You can leave now, Mrs. Gray," she said, nodding.

"I'm sorry. I had to tell what I saw," she said to me as she stood up. "I'm very disappointed."

I shook my head, my tears building behind my lids.

"After this report was made to me," Mrs. Ironwood began as soon as Mrs. Gray had left, "I called Buck Dardar to this office early in the morning. I confronted him with Mrs. Gray's testimony and I took out Ruby Dumas's file and showed him her picture so he could confirm that the girl Mrs. Gray reported with him in the boathouse was indeed Ruby Dumas. I will now read his sworn and signed statement."

She picked up a document.

" 'I, Buck Dardar, do hereby admit that on the occasion noted and on a number of previous occasions,' " she read, raising her eyebrows and looking at the panel, " 'I did have intimate relations with Ruby Dumas. Miss Dumas came to my quarters on at least a half dozen previous occasions to flirt and offer herself to me. I confess to accepting her advances. On the occasion cited, Ruby Dumas arrived at the boathouse at seven-thirty and she didn't leave until after nine-thirty. I do regret my involvement with this student and accept the punishment rendered by Mrs. Ironwood on this date.'

"As you can see," she concluded, handing the document to Miss Weller, "he has signed it."

Miss Weller gazed at the paper, nodded, and

then passed it to Mr. Norman. He glanced at it and handed it to Deborah, who held it the longest before returning it to Mrs. Ironwood. Looking as satisfied as a raccoon with its belly full, she sat back in her chair.

"You may offer your defense now," Mrs. Ironwood said.

I turned toward the panel. "I don't doubt that Mrs. Gray saw someone go to the boathouse last night at seven-thirty, and I know she believes she's telling the truth, but she is mistaken. I was not in there. I was —"

"I'll tell them where you were," we heard. I spun around in my chair to see Miss Stevens leading Louis through the door.

"What is the meaning of this?" Mrs. Ironwood demanded.

I think I was just as shocked as she was. Louis, in a jacket and tie, his hair brushed neatly, nodded.

"I'm here to testify for the defendant." He smiled in my direction. "Ruby Dumas," he said. "May I?"

"Of course not. This is a school matter and I —"

"But I have information pertaining to the case," he insisted. "Is that the witness chair?" He nodded in the right direction.

Mrs. Ironwood threw a furious, hot glance at Miss Stevens and then looked at the panel, all of whom were looking at her and waiting.

"This is highly irregular," she said.

"What's irregular about it? This is a hearing, and a hearing is the place to bring evidence, is it not?" Louis asked. "I'm sure you want to get at the truth," he added with a smile.

Everyone looked from Louis to Mrs. Ironwood. Louis moved toward the chair when she was silent. He sat down and pulled himself up comfortably.

"My name is Louis Turnbull. I am Mrs. Clairborne's grandson, and I reside in the Clairborne mansion, as it is known." He turned in Mrs. Ironwood's direction. "Do I have to give my age, occupation?"

"Don't be ridiculous, Louis. You have no business being here."

"I have business being here," he replied firmly. "Now then, as I understand it, the issue is whether or not Ruby Dumas was at the boathouse last night at seven-thirty and after, correct? Well, I can assure the panel she wasn't. She was with me. She arrived at seven-fifteen and remained until nine o'clock."

A leaden silence fell over the room, making the tick-tock of the grandfather clock seem much louder than it was.

"Isn't that the issue?" Louis pursued.

"Very well. If you wish to carry on like this: How can you be sure of the exact time?" Mrs. Ironwood challenged. "You are blind." She gave the panel a look of superiority.

Louis turned to the panel as well. "I have, it is true, been suffering with an eyesight problem.

But of late, I have made significant progress," he said, then glanced toward me and smiled. He turned toward the grandfather clock in the corner of the office. "Let's see. According to my cousin's office clock, it is now four-twenty . . . two," he said. He was exactly right. I looked at the panel. All of them were impressed.

"Of course, I can have you verify all of this by calling in our butler, Otis, who greeted Mademoiselle Dumas and saw her out at the end of the evening. He also served us tea while she visited. So you see, there is no physical way for her to have been at the boathouse last night at seven-thirty, eight, eight-thirty, nine," he chanted.

"A well-respected member of my faculty says otherwise, and I have a signed confession —"

"Please go out to the car and ask Otis to come in," Louis said to Miss Stevens.

"That won't be necessary," Mrs. Ironwood countered quickly.

"But if my testimony is under some doubt . . ." He turned toward Mrs. Ironwood. "If need be, I'm sure I can convince my grandmother to corroborate my testimony too."

She stared at him. The fury that built in her face had turned her cheeks red and spread down her neck, making it crimson as well.

"You're not doing anyone any good, Louis," Mrs. Ironwood muttered.

"Except Mademoiselle Dumas," he said.

She bit down on her lower lip and then sat back,

swallowing her rage.

"Very well. Under the circumstances, with this contradiction of facts, I don't see how we can ask our panel to render a clear judgment. I'm sure you all agree," she said. Mr. Norman, Miss Weller, and Deborah, her eyes wide, all nodded.

"Accordingly, I am declaring this hearing ended without concluding the question. I want to emphasize that this is not to say that the student in question has been exonerated. It's merely a declaration that a clear conclusion is not possible at this time."

She looked at me.

"You are dismissed," she said. Then she turned away, her frustration causing her to fume so intently, I thought I saw smoke come out of her ears. My heart was pounding so hard, the thumping echoing in my ears, I was sure everyone in the room heard it as clearly. "I said, the hearing is ended," Mrs. Ironwood snapped when I didn't get up quickly. I stood up.

Louis rose and walked out with me and Miss Stevens.

"Why did you bring him, Miss Stevens?" I asked as soon as we were out of the inner office. "Mrs. Ironwood is so angry she's liable to take it out on you."

"I thought about it and decided I couldn't lose my best artist," she said, smiling. "Besides, once Louis heard what was happening to you, I couldn't have kept him away, could I, Louis?"

"Absolutely not," he said, smiling.

"And your eyesight is so improved, Louis!" I exclaimed. "You read the time to the minute."

He smiled again, and Miss Stevens laughed.

"What's so funny?"

"Louis anticipated being challenged with his eyesight and asked me the exact time just before we entered the office," Miss Stevens explained.

"I knew if I was off a minute or so it would still be impressive," he said.

"But you weren't. You were right on the minute," I cried. I hugged him. "Thank you, Louis."

"It was fun. I've finally done something for someone else," he said.

"And you'll probably get in trouble with your grandmother for it," I said.

"It doesn't matter. I'm tired of being treated like a child. I can make my own decisions and answer for my own actions," he declared proudly.

We continued down the hallway toward the exit, the three of us holding hands. Suddenly I burst out laughing.

"Why are you laughing?" Louis asked, a smile of anticipation on his face.

"My sister, Gisselle. I can't wait to tell her and see the expression on her face."

"What!" Gisselle shrilled. "You're not expelled from Greenwood?"

"The hearing ended without conclusion, thanks to Louis and Miss Stevens. You should have been there, Gisselle," I said, so full of self-satisfaction my cheeks glowed shamelessly. "You would have so enjoyed the look on Mrs. Ironwood's face when she had to swallow her hard words and threats."

"I wouldn't have enjoyed it. I thought we were going home! I even packed most of my things!"

"We are going home soon . . . for the holidays," I sang, and left her burning with almost as much frustration as Mrs. Ironwood.

Just as word of the accusations and my hearing had swept through the school with the speed of a hurricane, so did the news of my not being expelled. The entire episode had an effect opposite to the one Mrs. Ironwood had anticipated, I was sure. Instead of making me a pariah in the eyes of the other students, I was suddenly cast as a heroine. I had withstood the fire and brimstone, the fury and power of our feared principal. I was the David who had battled our Goliath and survived. Wherever I went, the girls gathered around me to hear the details, but I didn't gloat, and I know they were disappointed in my answers.

"It wasn't very pleasant," I said. "I don't like to keep talking about it. A number of people were hurt by all this."

I thought about poor Buck Dardar, who had lost his job, and I bore no anger toward him for signing that false confession. I was sure he had been intimidated and had done it only under the dire threat of being arrested and disgraced. But Mrs. Gray remained a mystery, a mystery that wasn't to be solved until after I had attended her class the next day.

"Ruby," she called as soon as the bell to end the period rang.

I waited for the others to leave before approaching her.

"Yes, Mrs. Gray?"

"I want you to know that I didn't make up my story," she said firmly and with such sincerity, I couldn't take my eyes off hers. "I am aware of the testimony Mrs. Clairborne's grandson gave at the hearing, but it doesn't change what I saw and what I said. I don't lie, nor do I conspire against anyone."

"I know, Mrs. Gray," I said. "But I wasn't there. Honest, I wasn't."

"I'm sorry," she said. "But I don't believe you." She turned away and I left with a heavy heart.

Mrs. Gray's face of firmness haunted me for the remainder of the day. It was almost as if Mrs. Ironwood had cast a spell over her and caused her to see what she wanted her to see and say what she wanted her to say. How I wished I had Nina with me for only a few minutes so she could concoct some voodoo ritual or charm to change things.

I recalled Grandmere Catherine once telling me about a man who had lost his five-year-old daughter in a boating accident in the swamp. Even though her body was recovered, he continued to believe she was lost out in the bayou, swearing he heard her calling to him at night and even swearing that he saw her from time to time.

"He wanted so much for it to be true," she told

me, "that to him it *was* true, and no one could tell him otherwise."

Maybe Mrs. Gray didn't have that clear a view and wasn't as positive when she first told Mrs. Ironwood, and maybe Mrs. Ironwood convinced her it was I she had seen.

It continued to trouble me. On the way back to the dorm at the end of the day, I stopped to gaze down at the boathouse. If only I could find Buck, I thought, and get him to tell me the truth. Maybe I could get him to tell Mrs. Gray. I hated the fact that she continued to think so poorly of me.

I was surprised to find that Gisselle wasn't back in the dorm yet when I arrived, but Samantha appeared soon after to tell me Gisselle had been made to remain with Mrs. Weisenberg and review her terrible math scores. I knew she would be in a fury when she finally returned.

I had unpacked all the things I had packed just before the hearing and then peeked into Gisselle's room to see if she had done the same. Her room was a mess. In her frustration and rage, she had tossed everything out of her suitcase. Dresses, skirts, and blouses lay over chairs and the bed, and some garments were even on the floor. I started to pick things up, folding and hanging her clothing neatly. As I placed a silk white blouse with pearl buttons on a hanger, I paused, recalling some of Mrs. Gray's testimony.

Didn't she say the girl had unbuttoned her white blouse? I wore no white blouse; I wore only my Greenwood uniform. My eyes drifted down to

Gisselle's shoes lined up on the floor of the closet. Something caught my eye. My heart began to pitter-patter as I knelt slowly and picked up the loafers, the bottoms and the sides of which were caked with mud. But how . . .

The sound of my sister's loud voice declaring her complaints about being kept after school preceded her arrival in the quad. I heard her ranting as Kate wheeled her down the corridor. I stood up, holding my breath. My mind was reeling with possibilities, thoughts that seemed too fantastic. Just before she was wheeled to the door of her room, I backed into the closet and closed the sliding door almost all the way.

"Where's my sister?" Gisselle demanded.

"She was in your room," Samantha told her. "Straightening up your clothes."

Gisselle gazed in and smirked.

"Who asked her to? Anyway, she's not in here now."

Samantha came up beside her and looked into the room.

"Oh. She must have left when I was in the bathroom."

"Great. I want her to know just what that horrible Mrs. Weisenberg made me do until I got the answers right."

"Should I look for her?" Samantha asked.

"No. I'll tell her later. I have to get some rest," she said, and wheeled herself into the room, slamming the door behind her. She sat for a moment, staring at her bed. Then she reached back and snapped the lock on the door. I held my breath. As soon as she had locked the door, she stood up without wobbling, without much effort.

And I realized my sister could walk!

I slid open the closet door slowly, without much sound, but she sensed my presence and turned. Her eyes widened in astonishment, but I was sure they weren't as wide as mine.

"What are you doing?" she gasped. "Spying on me?"

"You can stand and you can walk. *Mon Dieu,* Gisselle!"

She sat herself back down in the wheelchair.

"So what?" she said after a moment. "I don't want anyone to know it just yet."

"But why? How long have you been able to stand and walk?"

"Awhile," she admitted.

"But why have you kept it a secret?"

"I get treated better," she confessed.

"Gisselle . . . how could you do this? All these people, everyone slaving over you . . . Could you walk before Daddy died? Could you?" I demanded when she didn't respond, but she didn't have to respond. I knew she could. "How horrible! You could have made him feel so much better."

"I was going to tell him as soon as we were permitted to go home and leave this terrible place, but as long as I had to stay here, I wasn't going to tell anyone," she said.

"How did it happen? I mean, when did you realize you could stand?"

"I was always trying to do it, and one day I just did."

I sat down on her bed, my mind in turmoil.

"Oh, stop making such a big thing over it," she ordered. She stood up and walked to the closet. The sight of her walking so easily seemed so incongruous. It was as if I had fallen into a dream. At full height again and able to use her limbs, Gisselle appeared changed to me. It was as if she had grown taller and stronger while confined to her wheelchair. I watched her brush her hair for a few moments, everything I had suspected now rushing over me.

"It was you, wasn't it?" I cried, pointing at her.

"Me? Whatever are you talking about now, Ruby?" she asked, pretending ignorance.

"It was you who was with Buck Dardar that night, wasn't it? That's why your shoes are caked with mud. You snuck down there and —"

"So what? He was the only game in town, although I must admit, he was quite a good lover. I hated to see him go, but when you were accused of being there, I thought it was perfect. Finally we'd get out of here too. Then your own loverboy had to appear and get you off the hook. Crummy luck."

"Did Buck think you were me? Did you tell him your name was Ruby?"

"I did, but I don't know whether he believed it or not. Let's just say he was happy to pretend I was anyone I wanted to be as long as I appeared."

"How often . . . All those times you kept this door locked," I said, turning to her door. I looked at the window.

"That's right. I would crawl out the window and have my rendezvous. Pretty exciting, huh? I bet you wish you had thought of it now."

"I do not." I pulled myself up. "You're going to march out of here right now and tell the truth," I said. "Especially to Mrs. Gray."

"Oh, am I? Well I'm not ready to let people know I can stand and walk," she said, returning to her chair.

"I don't care if you're ready or not. You will tell," I assured her, but she didn't seem intimidated. She wheeled herself toward me and looked up at me with hard, cold eyes.

"I will not," she said, "and if you so much as breathe a word of this to anyone, I'll tell Mrs. Ironwood about you and your precious Miss Stevens. That oughta do her in for sure."

"What? What are you saying?"

She smiled.

"Everyone knows about pretty little Miss Stevens who's afraid of boys but who likes to be around girls," she said, smiling. "Especially you, huh?"

It was as if a match had been lit in my stomach. The flame of anger singed my heart and sent smoke into my brain. I gasped.

"That's a disgusting, terrible lie, and if you tell anyone such a thing . . ."

"Don't worry. I'll keep your secret as long as

you keep mine," she said. "Is it a deal?"

I stared down at her, my mouth open, but words not coming, my tongue numb.

"I take your silence to mean it's a deal. Fine." She turned and wheeled herself to the door to unlock it. "Now, I do need some rest before dinner. Oh, and thanks for straightening up my room. I have been too hard on myself, trying to be independent. I might call on you to do little things for me from time to time. As long as we stay here," she added.

"Of course, once we're gone from this place . . ."

"You're blackmailing me," I finally accused. "That's what you're doing."

"I'm just trying to get along as easily and as comfortably as I can. If you were a good sister and if you really cared about me, you would do what I want for a change."

"So you're going to stay in that wheelchair and let everyone think you're still crippled?"

"As long as it suits me," she said.

"I hope it suits you forever," I snapped, and marched to the door. "I feel sorry for you, Gisselle. You hate yourself so much, you don't even realize it."

"Just remember what I said," she retorted, her eyes small and spiteful. "I meant it."

I opened the door to get a breath of fresh air as much as to get away from my twin sister, whose vicious, selfish face, despite the resemblances, made it clear we were truly strangers.

14

Unexpected Gifts

From my expulsion hearing until the start of our holiday break, I did the best I could to avoid and ignore Gisselle. It was obvious that she took delight in holding the dark cloud of her threat over me, and if I should so much as stare distastefully at her while she pretended to struggle along in her wheelchair or cried out for one of her entourage to do something for her, she would give me that icy smile and ask, "How is Miss Stevens?" I would simply shake my head in disgust and either walk away or return to what I was reading or doing.

Because of this constant tension between us at Greenwood, I looked forward eagerly to the holiday break. I knew that back in New Orleans Gisselle would amuse herself with her friends, and I could avoid her even more. Of course, I was anxious to see Beau, who was phoning me almost every night, but before I left, I knew that I had to visit Louis. He called to tell me he had decided that he would rather begin his stay at the clinic in Switzerland and attend the music conservatory during the holidays than remain at the Clairborne mansion for what he called another dreary Christmas. He anticipated an even more cheerless time because of my absence and his grandmother's and his cousin's lingering displeasure over what he had done for me at the hearing.

So I went up to the mansion to have dinner with him the night before the school vacation commenced. His grandmother did not appear anywhere in the house, not even to peer at me through a partially open doorway, much less come to the table. Louis and I sat alone in the large dining room, with the candles burning, and had a delicious duck dinner, followed by a French chocolate silk pie.

"I have two presents for you," Louis declared at the end of the meal.

"Two!"

"Yes. I've been to the city for the first time in . . . I don't even remember how long . . . and bought you this," he said, and then he produced a small box from his dinner-jacket pocket.

"Oh Louis, I feel terrible. I haven't brought you anything."

"Of course you have. You brought me your company, your concern, and you've given me the desire to want to see and be productive again. There's no way to measure the value of such a gift, but I assure you," he said, taking my hand for a moment, "it's worth far more than anything I could possibly give you in return."

He felt for my hand and then brought it to his

lips and kissed my fingers.

"Thank you," he said in a deep whisper. Then he sat back and smiled. "And now open your first gift and don't swallow any reactions. I don't see clearly yet, but I can hear very well."

I laughed and untied the tiny ribbon so I could peel off the pretty paper without tearing it. Then I opened the small box and looked at what had to be a full carat ruby set in a gold ring. I gasped.

"Is it as beautiful as I have been told?" he asked.

"Oh Louis, it's the most beautiful ring I've ever seen! It must have cost a fortune."

"If it doesn't fit, I'll have it sized for you. Put it on," he said, and I did.

"It fits perfectly, Louis. How did you do it?"

"I've memorized every part of you that I have touched," he said. "It was easy. I felt the finger of the saleswoman in the store and told her you were two sizes smaller." He smiled proudly.

"Thank you, Louis." I leaned forward and kissed him quickly on the cheek. His expression changed into a serious one instantly. Then he brought his fingers to his cheek as if he could feel the warmth of my lips still lingering.

"And now," he said firmly, bracing himself for my words, "you must tell me if what I see with my heart is true."

I held my breath. If he was going to ask me if I loved him . . .

"You love someone else," he said instead. "Don't you?"

I turned from him and looked down, but he

reached out to lift my chin.

"Don't look away, please. Tell me the truth."

"Yes, Louis, I do. But how did you know this?"

"I heard it in your voice, in the way you held back whenever you spoke softly to me. I felt it just now in your kiss, which was the kiss of a good friend and not the kiss of a lover."

"I'm sorry, Louis, but I never meant to . . ."

"I know," he said, finding my lips with his fingers. "Don't think you need make excuses. I don't blame you for anything and I don't expect anything more from you. I am still forever in your debt. I hope only that whoever you love is deserving of your love and will love you as strongly as I would."

"So do I," I said.

He smiled.

"Now let's not get melancholy. As we French Creoles say, *Je ne regrette rien,* eh? I regret nothing. Besides, we can always be good friends, can't we?"

"Oh yes, Louis. Always."

"Good." He beamed a bright smile. "I can't ask for any better Christmas present. And now," he said, rising, "your second gift. Mademoiselle Dumas," he requested, holding up his arm for me to take, "permit me to escort you, *si'l vous plaît.*"

I took his arm and we walked out of the dining room and into the music study. He brought me to the settee first and then he went to the piano and took his seat. "Your symphony is complete," he announced.

I sat there and listened to him play the most wondrous and beautiful melodies. I felt swept away by the music; it was truly a magic carpet taking me to the most marvelous places in my imagination and in my memory. Sometimes the music reminded me of the sound of the water flowing through the canals in the bayou, especially after a heavy downpour; sometimes I heard the morning songs of birds. I saw sunsets and twilights and dreamt of blazing night skies when the stars were so bright they lingered for hours on the surface of my eyes even as I slept. When the music ended, I was disappointed it was over. Louis had outdone anything I had heard him do before.

I rushed to him and threw my arms around his neck.

"That was wonderful! Too wonderful for words!"

"Hey," he said, overwhelmed by my reaction.

"It's incredibly beautiful, Louis. Really. I have never heard anything like it."

"I'm so glad you like it. I have something special for you," he said, and he reached under the stool to bring up another gift-wrapped box, this one much larger. I unraveled the ribbon quickly and peeled off the paper to open the lid of the box and look in at a record.

"What is this, Louis?"

"It's my symphony," he said. "I recorded it."

"You recorded it? But how . . ."

I gazed at the label on the record. It read, "Ruby's Symphony, composed and played by Louis Turnbull."

"Louis, I can't believe it."

"It's true," he said, laughing. "They brought the machinery to the house one day and I recorded it right in this studio."

"It must have cost a lot of money."

He shrugged. "I don't care what it cost," he said.

"It's such an honor. I'll play it for anyone who'll listen. How I wish Daddy was still alive to hear this," I said. I didn't mean to inject the note of sadness, but I couldn't help it. My heart was so full, and I didn't have anyone I loved with me to share it, not Grandmere Catherine, not Daddy, not Paul or Beau.

"Yes," Louis said, his face darkening. "It's painful not to have people you really love with you when something nice happens. But," he added cheerfully, "all that will end for both of us now. I'm hopeful, aren't you?"

"Yes, Louis."

"Good. Merry Christmas, Ruby, and may you have the healthiest and happiest new year of your life."

"You too, Louis." I kissed him on the cheek again.

That night, when I walked back to the dorm, I felt lightheaded. It was as though I had drunk two bottles of Grandmere Catherine's blackberry wine. All the way back, I was followed by a black-crowned night heron who called to me with its staccato quack.

"Merry Christmas yourself," I called up to it when it swung by to alight on the limb of an oak tree. Then I laughed and hurried into the dorm. From the open doorway of her room, Gisselle saw me enter the quad and wheeled herself out to block my path.

"Have another lovely dinner up at the mansion?" she teased.

"Yes, it was lovely."

"Humph," she said, and then she noticed the box I was carrying. Her eyes brightened with curiosity. "What do you have under your arm?" she demanded.

"A gift from Louis. A record," I said. "It's a symphony he composed and had recorded."

"Oh. Big deal," she said, smirking and starting to back away.

"It is a big deal. He composed it for me and it's called Ruby's Symphony."

She stared at me a moment, her face filling with envy.

"Do you want to hear it?" I asked her. "We'll play it on your phonograph."

"Of course not," she said quickly. "I hate that kind of music. It puts me to sleep." She started to turn when she spotted my ring. This time her eyes nearly popped out of her head.

"Did he give you that too?"

"Yes," I said.

"Beau's not going to like this," she declared after

376

narrowing her eyes. She shook her head. "Another man giving you expensive gifts."

"Louis and I are just good friends. He understands that and accepts it," I said.

"Sure. He goes and spends all this money and time on you, and all you've been giving him is conversation," she replied with a twisted smile on her lips. "Who do you think you're talking to, some dumb Cajun girl who believes in tooth fairies?"

"It's true, and don't you tell anyone anything different," I warned her.

"Or?" she challenged.

"Or I'll . . . break your neck," I threatened. I stepped toward her and she gazed at me with surprise. Then she backed away.

"Some sister," she moaned, loud enough for everyone in the quad to hear. "Threatening her crippled twin with violence. Merry Christmas," she screamed, spinning around in her chair to wheel herself back to her room.

I couldn't help laughing at her this time, which only infuriated her more. She slammed her door shut and I went into my room to pack for our trip home for the holidays.

The next day we had an abbreviated schedule, at the end of which we were all marched into the auditorium to hear Mrs. Ironwood's speech, which was supposed to be a short holiday talk, wishing us all a good vacation and a happy new year, but instead it turned into a heavy series of threats, warning us about failing to do our term papers and reminding us that shortly after our return we would be facing midyear exams.

But nothing she could do could diminish the excitement in the air. Parents were arriving to pick up their daughters, limousines were everywhere, and wherever I looked, girls were hugging each other and wishing each other happy holidays. Our teachers stood around to greet parents and wish students a good holiday too.

Our limousine was one of the last to arrive, which put Gisselle into a small rage. Mrs. Penny felt obligated to stay with her and comfort her, but that just gave Gisselle an ear to fill with her ranting. Shortly before our limousine did arrive, Miss Stevens appeared to say goodbye and to wish me a happy new year.

"I'm going to spend the holidays with one of the sisters from my old orphanage," she told me. "It's something of a tradition. We've spent dozens of Christmases together. She's the closest to being my mother."

Gisselle watched from the portico of the dorm as Miss Stevens and I hugged and kissed.

"I never thanked you enough for what you did for me at the hearing, Miss Stevens. It took courage."

"Sometimes doing the right thing does take more courage, but the feeling it gives you deep inside makes it worth it. That may be something only we artists understand," she said with a wink. "Do something with your spare time at home. Bring me back a picture of a setting in the Garden District," she said, getting into her jeep.

"I will."

"Happy new year, Ruby."

I watched her drive off and felt a sudden wave of sadness rush over me. I wished I could bring Miss Stevens back home with me. I wished I had a real home with parents who would welcome her happily and we could all enjoy the music, the food, the brightness and warmth of Christmas together.

Her jeep disappeared around the turn just as the limousine appeared. Gisselle cried out her joy, but when the driver pulled up to put our things in the trunk, she berated him unmercifully for being so late.

"I left when Madame Dumas told me to leave," he protested. "I'm not late."

Gisselle's mumbling wore down like the gradually lowering thunder of a departing storm in the bayou as we drove away from the school and headed toward New Orleans. When familiar scenery appeared, she brightened with excitement and expectation. I knew she had made phone calls to some of her old girlfriends and they had begun making preliminary plans for parties over the holidays. I just wondered what sort of greeting Daphne would give us.

To my utter surprise, we didn't find the house dark and deserted. Daphne had had the Christmas decorations hung and there was a tree bigger than last year's in the main sitting room, under which was a pile of gifts. Moments after we had arrived and gazed in at the holiday splendor, the front door was thrust open and Daphne came bursting in with a peal of laughter. She wore a white fox jacket, riding pants, and a smart pair of leather boots. She had her hair pinned up under a matching fur hat. Her full carat diamond earrings glittered in her lobes, adding even more brightness to her undeniably vibrant and beautiful face. Her cheeks were flushed, and I had the feeling that she had been drinking. There was no question that whatever period of mourning she had undergone for Daddy's death was over. Bruce, laughing almost as hard, was at her side. The two stopped in the entryway and looked at Gisselle and me.

"Why here are the little dears," Daphne said. "Home for the holidays." She pulled off her silk gloves and Bruce helped her off with her coat and then handed it to Martha, who waited obediently in the wings. "And how are the precious Dumas twins?"

"We're fine," I said sternly. Her buoyancy and happy demeanor annoyed me. This would be a Christmas without Daddy. His passing was still as painful as a raw wound, and yet Daphne behaved as if nothing had changed; if anything had, it was for the better.

"Good. I've decided to have a few holiday dinners, so there will be guests coming and going during your stay here. I myself have been invited to a friend's beach house for New Year's Eve, so I will be depending on you girls to be at your best behavior.

"You can invite friends over and go to proper parties," she declared. Her leniency and generosity took us both by surprise. "We're going to be together for years and years, and it's best to co-exist on the best of terms," she added, gazing at Bruce, who was beaming like someone about to explode with one happy declaration after another. "This is the jolliest time of the year. I've always enjoyed it, and I don't intend to spend a sad moment. Behave yourselves, and we'll all get along just fine.

"All of those gifts under the tree are for the two of you and the servants," she concluded. Neither Gisselle nor I knew how to respond. We gazed at each other with surprise and then looked at Daphne.

"Go freshen yourselves up and put on something nice. We're having the Cardins for dinner. You might remember that Charles Cardin is one of our biggest investors. Bruce," she said, turning to him. He snapped to attention and followed her into the study.

"Are my ears on right?" Gisselle asked. "I can't believe what I heard. But this is wonderful. All those gifts for us!" I shook my head. "What's the matter, Ruby?"

"Somehow all this seems wrong," I said. "With Daddy's death so recent."

"Why? We weren't buried in the vault with him. We're still alive and Daphne's right: This is the jolliest time of the year. Let's have fun. Martha!" she shouted. She looked up at me and winked.

"Yes, mademoiselle?"

"Help me up the stairs," Gisselle ordered. How long would she keep up this charade? I wondered, but I wasn't about to expose her and have her spread disgusting, untrue stories about Miss Stevens. I let her moan and groan and struggle like the cripple she wasn't.

However, afraid that Daphne would return to her domineering and restrictive ways, Gisselle was a perfect little lady at dinner that night. I never saw her so polite and charming. She spoke about Greenwood as if she loved the school and bragged about my artwork as though she were a proud sister. Daphne was very pleased and rewarded us by permitting us to be excused as soon as the dinner ended, so that we could call our friends and make plans to invite them over. Daphne, Bruce, and the Cardins were adjourning to the parlor for after-dinner cordials, but as we all started to leave the dining room, Daphne called to me.

"I just want to speak with Ruby for a moment," she told her guests and Bruce. "I'll be there momentarily." She nodded toward Bruce and he led the Cardins out. Gisselle wheeled herself into the corridor, peeved at not being part of the conversation.

"I'm very pleased with the two of you," Daphne began. "You're accepting the new order of things sensibly."

Apparently Mrs. Ironwood had not informed her of the hearing or the circumstances surrounding it; or if she had, Daphne was ignoring it since the outcome was favorable, I thought.

"If you mean accepting that Daddy is gone, that's something we have to accept."

"Of course it is," she said, smiling. "You're smarter than Gisselle is. I know that, Ruby, and I know that your intelligence permits you to make the wiser decisions. That's why I always agreed with Pierre that you should be the one to look after Gisselle. I will be giving the two of you more freedom than I usually do because of the holidays, but I will be depending on you to make sure everyone behaves."

"I thought I was the hot-blooded Cajun," I replied.

Her smile faded and her eyes narrowed for a moment, but then she smiled again. "We all say things we don't mean when we're angry. I'm sure you understand. Let this be a real new year, a real new beginning for all of us," she said. "We'll wipe the slate clean and forget all the bad episodes in the past. Let's see if we can all get along and, who knows, be a family again. Okay?"

Her changed attitude bothered me. I sensed she was conniving, preparing us for something, and I couldn't help being anxious.

"Yes," I said cautiously.

"Good, because anything else would just make life unpleasant for us all," she concluded, the veiled threat clear.

I watched her leave and then followed. Gisselle was waiting in the corridor.

"What did she want?" she demanded.

"She wanted to tell me she hoped we would

all have a new beginning, forget all of our past mistakes, and love each other like a family again."

"So why do you look so unhappy about that?"

"I don't trust her," I said, looking toward the parlor.

"You would say something like that. You're always imagining the worst. You're always looking at the dark side, almost hoping things will be terrible, just so you can be miserable. You like suffering. You think it's noble," she accused.

"That's ridiculous. No one likes to suffer and be unhappy."

"You do. I heard someone say your paintings show your melancholy. Even the birds look like they're about to burst into tears. Well, I'm not about to let you put a cloud over my sunny sky." Then she wheeled herself off to call her girlfriends and start to make her holiday plans.

Was she right? I wondered. Was I prone to sadness and melancholy? How could anyone like that? It wasn't that I wanted it; it was that I was so used to hard rains, I couldn't help expecting a cloudburst every time something nice happened and sunshine beamed down over me. But perhaps I should try to be a little like Gisselle, I thought, a little more carefree. I went up to my room and waited for Beau's phone call. When it came, it was so good to hear his voice and know he was so close.

"My parents are resigned to the fact that I will be seeing you," he said. "Apparently they spoke to Daphne, and she was more reasonable about

384

it. What's going on?"

"I don't know. She's acting different, but . . ."

"But you don't trust her?"

"Yes. Gisselle thinks I'm being unnecessarily skeptical, but I can't help it."

"I don't care what Daphne's motives are as long as I can see you," he said. "Let's not even think about her."

"You're right, Beau. I'm tired of being unhappy anyway. Let's just enjoy ourselves."

"I'll come by after breakfast," he said. "I'll spend every possible waking moment with you, if you like."

"I'd like nothing better," I told him.

The days before Christmas were full of fun and excitement. As soon as I could, I told Beau all about Louis and played the symphony for him. I didn't want Gisselle planting any bad thoughts in his mind. He was understandably jealous, but I assured him Louis was someone whom I had just befriended and who had befriended me. I told him about Mrs. Ironwood's expulsion hearing and how Louis had testified on my behalf, even though it meant he would be in the doghouse with his grandmother and cousin.

"I wouldn't blame him if he did fall in love with you," Beau said.

"He asked me if I loved someone else, and I told him yes."

Beau brightened.

"And he understands," I added.

Confident now that Gisselle couldn't plant any

nasty seeds of doubt in Beau's mind, I relaxed and enjoyed our time together. Beau and I went for rides, took walks, and spent hours cuddling on the sofa talking. We had been separated by time and distance and events so long, it was as if we had to get to know each other again, but if it was possible to fall in love with the same person twice, I did.

At first I thought Gisselle would be envious, since she didn't have a steady boyfriend. But most of her old friends were drawn back to her, parading in and out of the house day and night. She had private parties in her room whenever Daphne left. I knew they were smoking pot and drinking, but as long as they kept the door closed and didn't bother any of the servants, I didn't care.

Daphne went out every night to parties and dinners with Bruce, but on Christmas Eve we had a special early dinner for just the three of us because Daphne was going to a Christmas party in the French Quarter.

"I thought we would have a quiet family dinner together to celebrate the holiday," she declared at the table. She was radiantly beautiful in her black velvet dress with her diamond brooch and matching earrings. Her hair had never looked softer or richer. She had planned our menu for our Christmas Eve dinner herself, asking Nina to prepare trout amandine. The dessert tray was filled with delectable choices, including tarte aux pêche, banana nut bread, lemon mousse, and chocolate rum soufflé. Gisselle sampled everything, but Daphne barely nibbled on some lace cookies. She had often told both Gisselle and myself that a lady leaves the table a bit hungry. That was the way to keep your figure.

"Well, what have you two decided to do for New Year's Eve?" she asked.

Gisselle looked at me and then blurted: "We'd like to have a party here for just a few friends." She held her breath, expecting Daphne to reject the idea.

"Good. I'll feel better knowing you two are safe at home and not riding around the streets of the city."

Gisselle beamed. Daphne had permitted us to have friends over this night too.

Why was she indulging us so? I continued to wonder, but, like Gisselle, I wasn't about to look a gift horse in the mouth.

After our Christmas dinner, Bruce arrived to escort her to the party. He brought gifts for both of us and placed them under the tree.

"It'll take you two hours tomorrow morning to unwrap everything you've been given," he declared, gazing at the pile. I had to admit it was overwhelming.

"Enjoy your evening, Mother," Gisselle said as they started to leave.

"Thank you, dear. You two enjoy yours. And remember, everyone leaves by twelve," she said.

"We'll remember," Gisselle replied, then looked conspiratorially at me. The truth was that there were only two people coming to our house for Christmas Eve: Beau and Gisselle's newest boyfriend, John Darby, a good-looking dark-haired boy whose family had moved to New Orleans just this year. He had been on the football team with Beau.

Before they arrived, Edgar informed me that I had a phone call. I went into the study to take it. It was Paul.

"I was hoping you were home so I could wish you a merry Christmas," he said.

"Merry Christmas to you too, Paul."

"How are things there?"

"Something of a truce has been declared, but I keep expecting my stepmother to pop out of a closet with a whip in her hand."

He laughed. "We have a houseful of people for dinner."

"I bet you have beautiful decorations and a nice tree."

"We do," he said wistfully, "as always, but . . . I wish you were here. Remember our first Christmas together?"

"Of course," I said sadly. "Do you have any friends over, any special friends?"

"Yes," he said, but I could hear the lie. "Anyway," he added quickly, "I just wanted to wish you a quick holiday greeting. I've got to get back. Wish Gisselle a merry Christmas and happy new year for me."

"I will," I said.

"I'll speak to you soon," he promised, and hung

up. I wondered if the telephone wires could withstand all of the laughter and tears, the happiness and sadness that would pass through them this night.

"Who was that?" Gisselle demanded from the doorway.

"Paul. He wants me to tell you merry Christmas and happy new year."

"That's nice, but why do you have that gloomy look on your face? Wipe it off," Gisselle ordered. She had a bottle of rum in her hands and she smiled, holding it up. "We're going to have a good time tonight."

I stared at her, my twin sister, indulgent, spoiled, capricious, and self-centered, sitting in her own wheelchair, milking everyone around her of their sympathy and using her false condition to get people to do and give her anything she wanted. At this moment on Christmas Eve, I saw her as the embodiment of all the evil inclinations in my own heart and imagined I was looking at the darker part of myself, almost like Dr. Jekyll peering into a mirror and seeing Mr. Hyde. And like Dr. Jekyll, I couldn't hate this side of myself as much as I wanted because it was still part of me, part of who I was. I felt trapped, tormented by my longings and dreams. Maybe I was just tired of being who Gisselle said I was: Miss Goody Two-Shoes.

"You're right, Gisselle. We're going to have a good time."

She laughed gleefully and we went into the parlor to wait for Beau and John.

Less than half an hour after Beau and John arrived, Gisselle had John take her upstairs to her room and Beau and I were left alone. The house had grown very quiet. Nina had gone to her room, and Edgar and Martha were in their quarters. Only the occasional bong of the grandfather clock in the hallway interrupted the silence.

"I thought and thought for months about your Christmas present," Beau said after we had kissed passionately for a few moments. "What could I give a girl who has everything?"

"I'm hardly the girl who has everything, Beau. True, I live in this luxurious house and I have more clothes than I know what to do with, but . . ."

"What do you mean? You have me, don't you?" he asked, laughing. "You promised you were not going to be serious, that we'd relax and have fun, and here you are taking everything I say literally."

"You're right. I'm sorry. What did you buy the girl who has everything?"

"Nothing," he said.

"What?"

"Oh, I did buy this solid gold chain to hold it around your neck," he said, plucking the chain and his school ring out of his pocket. My breath caught in my throat. For a young Creole man in New Orleans, the giving of his school ring or his fraternity pin was a step below the giving of an engagement ring, It meant that all the words and vows we had whispered to each other and pledged over the telephone would be consummated. I would be his girl and only his girl, and he would be my young man, not only in our own eyes but in the eyes of our families and friends.

"Oh, Beau!"

"Will you wear it?" he asked.

I looked into his soft blue eyes, eyes filled with promises and love. "Yes, Beau. I will," I said, and he put it around my neck, and then with his fingers he followed the chain down to the valley between my breasts where his ring sat snugly. I thought I could feel its warmth through my blouse, a warmth that traveled with electric speed to my heart and started it racing. He brought his lips to mine and I moaned, feeling my body soften and mold to his embrace. The parlor was only dimly lit by the illumination of one small table lamp and the flickering flames in the fireplace. Beau reached over and turned off the lamplight. Then he turned my shoulders and I permitted my body to slide under him on the sofa. His lips were on my neck, his fingers unbuttoning my blouse so he could follow my breasts to their fullness.

Filled with abandon, tired of the anguish and agony that had pursued me relentlessly these past months, I turned myself to Beau with kisses that were even more demanding. Everywhere his fingers traveled I welcomed them, and when he lifted the cups of my bra away and nudged my nipples with his tongue and then his lips, I sank deeper and deeper into the warm pool of ecstasy that had flowed down from my shoulders, over my waist and legs, and brought tingling to the tips of my toes.

I kept my eyes closed and just listened to the rustling of his clothing and felt his fingers move under my skirt and slip my panties down. I raised my legs and let him take them off completely. The realization of my nudity drove my excitement to an even higher pitch. I tasted his tongue, his lips, and kissed his closed eyes. Both of us were whispering "Yes" into each other's ears. I opened my eyes for just a moment and saw the shadows and light from the fire dancing on the walls and even over us. For a moment, perhaps because of the heat between us, I felt as if we were in the fire, consuming ourselves with our own flames. But I wanted it, I wanted it very much.

I opened myself to him and he pressed himself forward and inward, calling my name as if he feared he would lose me even at this moment. I clutched his shoulders, pulling down on his back and joining him in the undulation that would make us feel as if we had become one entity. Wave after wave of passion washed over us. I couldn't distinguish one kiss from another. It became one long kiss, one long embrace, one graceful turn after another.

"I love you, Ruby. I love you," he cried at his climax. I muffled my own cries in his shoulder and hung onto him with all my might as if that would prolong the ecstatic moments. Then we stopped moving and simply held each other and breathed hard, waiting for our pounding hearts to slow down.

It had all happened so quickly. There hadn't been much of a chance to reconsider, not that I thought I would have. I had welcomed him, welcomed the relief and the passion, the love and the tenderness, the beautiful feeling; and in moments, I had smothered the darkness and the sadness that had haunted me for so long. As long as I had Beau, I thought, I would have sunshine.

"Are you all right?" he asked. I nodded. "I didn't mean to be so . . ."

"It's all right, Beau. Let's not make each other feel guilty or dirty. I love you and you love me. Nothing else matters, and that makes whatever we do good and pure, because it's good and pure to us."

"Oh Ruby, I do love you. I can't imagine loving anyone else as much."

"I hope that's true, Beau."

"It is," he promised.

The sound of Gisselle's laughter coming from the stairway sent us both into a frenzy. We replaced our discarded clothing quickly and he turned on the lamp. Then I straightened my hair. He rose from the sofa and went to the fireplace to stir the logs just before John, carrying Gisselle in his arms, entered the parlor.

"We decided to see what you two have been up to," she said. "And John's so strong, it's faster and easier for him to carry me up and down the stairs than for me to use that stupid electric chair." She clung to him like a baby chimp holding onto its mother, her arm wrapped around his neck, her cheek against his chest.

Kneeling at the fire, Beau looked at me and then up at her.

"I know that expression on your face, Beau Andreas." She smiled at me. "Don't try to hide anything from your twin sister, Ruby." She looked up at John, who was holding her as if she hardly weighed a thing. "Twins sense things about each other, did you know that, John?"

"Oh?"

"Yes. Whenever I'm unhappy, Ruby senses it quickly, and when she's been excited . . ."

"Stop it, Gisselle," I said, feeling the heat return to my cheeks.

"Wait a minute," she said. "John, bring me to the sofa." He did so, and she gazed down at me. "What's that around your neck? Is that your ring, Beau?"

"Yes," he said, standing up.

"You gave her your ring! What are your parents going to say?"

"I don't care what they say," Beau replied, coming to my side. He took my hand. I saw Gisselle's look of surprise change quickly into a look of green envy.

"Well, there's someone back at Greenwood who's going to be heartbroken," she quipped.

"I've already told Beau about Louis, Gisselle."

"You did?" she asked, dripping with disappointment.

"Yes, she did," Beau said. "I must see if I can thank him for helping her at the hearing," he added. Gisselle smirked and then beamed with excitement, her facial expressions clicking on and off and changing as if her face were a television screen changing channels.

"Well let's celebrate your giving Ruby your ring. Let's all go someplace. How about the Green Door? They don't check for IDs, or at least they never used to."

"We told Daphne we were staying at home tonight and it's late already, Gisselle. She'll be home soon."

"No she won't, and what's the difference what we said? She's being different, isn't she?"

"Which is why I don't want to upset her," I replied. "How about popcorn? We'll make it in the fireplace and play backgammon."

"Oh, that's just bundles of fun. Come on, John. Let's go back up to my room and leave these two old people knitting in the parlor." She ran her hand along John's upper arm. "Isn't he strong? I feel like a baby in his arms." She kissed him on the neck, and John blushed and smiled at Beau. "I'm so helpless," she wailed. "But John is gentle, aren't you, John?"

"What? Sure."

"Then let's go up. I need my diaper changed," she said, and laughed. I thought John was going to drop her, but he turned away, his face crimson, and hurried out of the parlor with her bouncing in his arms and giggling.

"I can't help wondering," Beau said, "why I ever started with her."

"It was Fate, Destiny. If you hadn't," I told him, "you and I might never have met."

"I love you, Ruby. I love the way you can find the good in things, even in someone like Gisselle."

"That's a challenge," I admitted, and we laughed. Then he asked me to play Louis's symphony. We sat listening with his arm around me.

"It's wonderful how you inspired someone to do something so beautiful," he confessed.

At twelve we went upstairs to call John out of Gisselle's room. She complained, of course, and did her best to try to get him to stay, if simply to violate Daphne's curfew. But Beau wasn't taking any chances about riling Daphne again. He told John sternly to come out and he did so.

I kissed Beau goodbye at the door and then went upstairs. Gisselle was waiting in her doorway. The sight of her standing, even though I knew she was capable of doing it any time she wanted, still looked incongruous and surprising.

"Well aren't you the happy one now," she said. "You've got Beau Andreas forever and ever."

"Do you want someone forever and ever too?" I asked.

"Of course not. I'm too young. I want to explore, have fun, have dozens of different boyfriends, before I marry someone just dripping with money," she said.

"So why are you jealous?"

"I'm not jealous." She laughed. "I'm hardly jealous."

"Yes you are, Gisselle. You won't admit it, not even to yourself, but you want someone to love you, only . . . no one's going to love someone so selfish."

"Oh, don't start one of your lectures," she whined. "I'm tired. John's a very good lover, you know," she added, smiling. "A bit stupid, but a good lover. My pretending to be so helpless turns him on. It turns them all on, you know. Men like feeling in charge, even though they're not. I could play him like a . . . a flute," she said, laughing.

"So then you're going to keep pretending to be crippled?"

"Until I don't feel like it anymore. And if you have any ideas about exposing me . . ."

"I really don't care what you do, Gisselle, as long as you don't hurt anyone I care about," I said. "Because if you do . . ."

"I know. You'll break my neck. The only neck that's going to be broken around here is yours when Beau's parents find out what he's given you. You'll have to give it back, you know. You had better prepare yourself for it. Good night, dear sister, and oh . . . merry Christmas."

She closed her door and left me trembling in the hallway. She was wrong; she had to be wrong, I thought. Besides, tomorrow morning I would show Nina Beau's ring and ask her to prepare a chant or find a ritual that would throw a blanket of protection around our love.

I went to sleep, curling up in my wonderful memories of lovemaking with Beau, memories and feelings that were still so vivid, it was as if he were still beside me. I even stretched out my arm and pretended he was there.

"Good night, Beau," I whispered. "Good night, my darling Beau."

With his kiss still on my lips, I drifted back into the warm darkness of my own love-filled heart.

15

Bought and Paid For

Even I slept late the next morning. When I was a little girl, I hated the hours of sleep between Christmas Eve and Christmas morning. It was torture waiting for the sun to come up so I could go downstairs and unwrap my presents. No matter how poor our year had been, Grandmere Catherine always managed to have wonderful gifts for me, and all of her friends brought things over for me as well. There was always one secret gift, a present without a name on a card to tell from whom it had come. I liked to pretend it was from my mysterious father, and maybe Grandmere Catherine let me imagine such a thing so I would continue to believe I had a father waiting for me out there. Prophet that she was, she anticipated the day I would leave to find him.

But with Grandmere Catherine gone and now Daddy gone too, the excitement and the joy of Christmas morning had diminished until it was practically reduced to just another day. I thought this was true for Gisselle as well, but for different reasons, even though she bragged to everyone about the pile of gifts for us under the tree. With all that she had — the tons of clothes in her closets and dresser drawers, the mountains of cosmetics and the rivers of perfume, a queen's stash of jewels and more beautiful watches than there were hours in the day — I wondered what she could possibly be given and what would possibly excite her. I'm sure she felt the same way, for neither the morning sunlight nor the bong of the clock stirred her from her stupor. I knew she had to be suffering a hangover after all she had drunk the night before.

I myself lay with my eyes open, thinking only about Beau and the promises he and I had made to each other. I wished I could jump ahead years until the day of our wedding, a wedding that would take me from this fractured family and place me on the threshold of a new life, one filled with hope and love. I imagined Gisselle off to the side with the wedding party, where she glared at us with green eyes, her envy curling her lips into a crooked, hard smile as I pledged my love and faithfulness to Beau and he did the same to me. Daphne, I thought, would simply be happy I was out of her hair.

My stream of imaginings was broken when I suddenly heard a loud "Ho, ho, ho," and the ringing of sleighbells.

"Get up, you sleepyheads," Bruce called from the top of the stairway. I rose and peered out my door to see him dressed in a Santa Claus costume and wearing a fake Santa beard. "Daphne and I are anxious to see you open your gifts. Come on. Wake up." He walked up to Gisselle's door and shook the strap of bells hard. I heard her scream and curse and laughed to myself envisioning what that sound must be like to someone with her size hangover.

"I'm coming," I shouted, after he did the same to me.

I washed, then dressed in a white silk blouse with a lace collar and cuffs and a peasant skirt. I tied my hair with a matching silk ribbon, even though I had little excitement and felt I was just going through the motions. Martha Woods had been sent up to speed Gisselle along, but she was still standing outside Gisselle's door, wringing her hands and mumbling "Oh dear, oh dear," when I stepped out to go downstairs.

I gazed through Gisselle's door and saw her rolled up into a ball under her blankets with just some strands of her hair leaking out.

"Just tell them she doesn't care about her gifts," I said, loud enough for Gisselle to hear. Instantly, she threw back the blanket.

"You tell them no such thing," she screamed, and then moaned. "Oh, why did I yell like that? Ruby, help me. My head feels like there are bowling balls rolling back and forth inside it."

I knew that Nina had a recipe for an elixir that would cure a bad hangover.

"Start getting dressed," I said, "and I'll bring something up that will help."

She sat up hopefully. "Will you? Promise?"

"I said I would. Just get dressed."

"Martha, get in here," she commanded. "Why aren't you getting out my things?"

"Oh, what am I to do? First she tells me to get out and then she screams for me to come in," she said, and she hurried in behind me.

I went downstairs and directly to the kitchen, where I found Nina preparing our Christmas Day breakfast.

"Merry Christmas, Nina," I said.

"You be merry Christmas too," she replied with a smile.

"I need two things from you, Nina, if you'll be kind enough to do them," I said.

"What you want, child?"

"First," I said, grimacing, "Gisselle has a head this big," I said, holding my hands near my ears, "from drinking too much rum."

"This not be the first time," Nina said, smirking. "It don't help her none to make it easier for her."

"I know, but she'll just make things miserable for everyone else if she's miserable, and then somehow Daphne will find a way to blame me."

Nina nodded. "Okay," she said. She went to a cabinet and began taking out the ingredients. "Best if we have a raw egg with a blood spot in it," she mumbled as she began to mix things together. "I been savin' one I found yesterday." I smiled, knowing that if Gisselle discovered what it was she was about to drink, she wouldn't do it. "Here," Nina said after she was done. "Have her drink this in one gulp, no air. That be most important."

"All right."

"What else? You said two things you want from Nina."

"Beau gave me his school ring last night, Nina," I said, showing it to her. "He's pledged his love for me and I've pledged mine to him. Can you burn a candle for us?"

"You need brimstone, not a candle, especially if the love was pledged in this house," she added with wide eyes. "You bring Monsieur Beau to Nina's room later and Nina do it for the two of you while you hold hands."

"I'll tell him, Nina," I said, smiling to myself and wondering what Beau would say when I proposed we do it. "Thank you."

I hurried back upstairs in time to find Gisselle tearing into Martha Woods unmercifully for choosing the wrong clothing and the wrong shoes.

"The woman has no sense of taste. Look! She wanted me to wear this blouse with this skirt and shoes."

"I just thought she'd want to wear Christmas colors today and . . ."

"It's all right, Martha. I'll help her."

"Oh. Okay," she said with relief. "I do have other duties this morning." She hurried out.

"What's that?"

"Nina's cure. You have to drink it in one gulp. If you don't, it won't work," I said.

She eyed it suspiciously. "Did you ever drink it?"

403

"I drank something like it for an upset stomach," I replied.

She grimaced. "I'll do anything. I might even cut off my head," she cried and took the glass from me. She sucked in her breath and then brought it to her lips. Her eyes bulged as the elixir rolled over her tongue and taste buds.

"Don't stop," I ordered when it looked like she would stop drinking. I had to admit I enjoyed her discomfort. She drank it all down and then gasped, pressing her hand to her heart.

"Ugh. That was awful. It was probably poison. What was in it?"

"A raw egg, I know. Some herbs. Some powder that might be rattlesnake bone —"

"Oh no. Don't tell me anymore," she cried with her hands up. She swallowed hard. "I think I'm going to vomit." She lunged out of her chair to the bathroom, but she didn't throw up. A few minutes later she emerged, the color restored to her face.

"I think it's actually working," she declared happily.

"Pick out your clothes. They're waiting for us in the living room. Bruce is wearing a Santa Claus costume and beard."

"Oh, how peachy," she said.

When we went down, we found Daphne, dressed in her red Chinese robe and slippers with her hair neatly brushed and pinned and her face made up as if she had gotten up and prepared herself hours ago. She was sitting in a high-backed French Provencal chair, sipping coffee from a silver cup. Bruce was standing by the tree in his Santa outfit, beaming.

"Well, it's about time you prima donnas came down. When I was a little girl I couldn't wait to open my gifts."

"We're not little girls, Mother," Gisselle said.

"When it comes to getting presents, a woman is always a little girl," Daphne replied, and she winked at Bruce, who laughed, holding in his false stomach. "It's time, Santa," she said.

"Ho, ho, ho," he cried, scooping up some gifts to bring to us. I sat on the settee to open mine and Gisselle opened hers in her wheelchair as Bruce made frequent trips back to the tree. We got more clothes, expensive designer sweaters and blouses, as well as skirts. We both received new leather half coats with matching boots and fur hats we would probably never wear. Bruce gave us charm bracelets, and there were gift packages of bath oils, talcum powders, and perfumes. As soon as Gisselle ripped one thing open and gazed at it, she was ripping at another.

"This is so much," I said. I was still baffled by Daphne's new generosity.

"There is a gift here I thought you'd like to bring to your uncle Jean," she said, holding up a package. "It's half a dozen of the silk shirts he always loved."

"You'll let me go to the hospital?" I asked, amazed.

"I'll have our driver take you tomorrow, if

you like," she replied.

I turned to Gisselle. "Would you like to come along?"

"To the nut house? Are you crazy?"

"You used to go," I reminded her.

"Once in a blue moon and only because of Daddy," she said. "I hated it."

"But . . . just for Christmas."

"Pleeeze," she moaned.

"Take Beau, if you like," Daphne said. I stared at her in disbelief. I was speechless. "There are gifts here from your Cajun half brother, I believe," she said. "Bruce."

He fetched them quickly and brought them to us. They were beautiful diaries with hand-carved cyprus wood covers depicting a scene in the swamp with Spanish moss, an alligator poking up its head, and terns swooping toward the water.

"A diary!" Gisselle blurted. "Like I would ever write down my secrets." She laughed.

"Well," Daphne said, looking first at Bruce, "we have a secret that we're about to announce. It's another Christmas present," she said. Gisselle widened her eyes and sat back in her chair as Bruce moved closer to Daphne. She reached up to take his hand and then turned to us and said, "Bruce and I are going to be married."

"Married! When?" Gisselle demanded.

"After the proper length of time since your father's death passes." She stared at us, her eyes raking our faces for clues to our true reactions. "I hope the two of you will be happy for us and welcome Bruce to the family as your new father. I know it's a bit overwhelming for you at first, but it would be best if we would be seen as a united family. Can I depend on the two of you?" she asked, and suddenly I realized why she had been so sweet.

This wedding was going to be a major social affair among the upper classes in New Orleans, and it was important to Daphne that it go as perfectly as a royal event. It would be in all the social columns and our family would be the center of attention from the day of announcement to the actual wedding. Important people would be invited to dinners between now and then, and Daphne certainly wanted us all to be seen together at the theater or the opera.

"I know I can't replace your father in your eyes," Bruce began, "but I'd like the chance to try. I will do all that I can to be a real father to you."

"Can you talk our mother into letting us come back home to live and go to school?" Gisselle demanded quickly.

Daphne's smile faded. "Just finish out the year at Greenwood, Gisselle. Bruce and I have a lot to do without worrying about you and your sister's daily needs. I'll give you permission to leave the grounds and I'll see to it that your allowances are increased," she added.

Gisselle weighed the compromises.

"We haven't heard a word from you yet, Ruby," Daphne said, focusing on me.

"I hope you'll both be happy," I said. We fixed

our eyes on each other for a moment, gazing across the room like two gladiators considering whether to begin a new battle or settle for a truce. She decided to accept my cold blessing.

"Thank you. Well, now that all this has ended, we can go and have our Christmas Day breakfast." She put down her coffee cup and started to stand.

"Wait," Gisselle cried. She threw a look at me and then smiled at Daphne and Bruce. "I do have a surprise, something I've been saving for my Christmas present to you, Mother. And now," she added, "it can be your first wedding present too."

Daphne sat back cautiously. "And what would that be, Gisselle?"

"This!" Gisselle said, and she started to rise out of the chair, pretending it was a mammoth struggle. Daphne's face went from bewilderment to glee. Bruce laughed and put his hand on Daphne's shoulder. I watched as Gisselle tottered, steadied herself took deep breaths, grimaced as if in pain, and then let go of the arms of her chair to stand free. She wobbled with her eyes closed and then, pretending it took all her concentration and strength, made one small step forward and then another. She looked like she was going to fall, so Bruce raced to embrace her and she collapsed in his arms.

"Oh Gisselle, how wonderful!" Daphne cried. Gisselle gulped in some air, her hand pressed to her chest, milking the event for all it was worth.

"I've been working on it," she gasped. "I knew I could get up and I have taken a step or two before, but I wanted to walk all the way to you. I'm so disappointed," she moaned. "I'll try again."

"That's all right. Your just doing this much is a wonderful Christmas present, isn't it, Bruce?"

"It sure is," he said, still holding her firmly. "You'd better take it easy." He guided her back to her wheelchair. As he helped her into it, she glanced triumphantly at me.

"Did you know about this, Ruby?" Daphne asked.

I looked at Gisselle and then at Daphne. "No," I said. This was a house and a family built on lies. My addition wouldn't even be noticed, and I was convinced Daphne and Gisselle deserved one another's deceit and conniving.

"What a surprise. And to keep it from everyone, even your twin sister, just so you could do it first for us. This is very nice of you, Gisselle."

"I promise, Mother," Gisselle pledged, "that I will work hard at regaining my ability to walk and be right behind you when you go down the aisle to marry Bruce."

"That would be . . . just fantastic." She looked at Bruce. "Think of how the wedding guests will react. Why, it's as if . . . as if my new marriage restored the health of this family."

"So you see, Mother," Gisselle said, "I can't go back to Greenwood now. I need daily rehabilitation work and Nina's good cooking instead of that dormitory slop. Just get me a tutor and let me stay here."

Daphne pondered for a moment. "Let me think

about it," she said.

Gisselle beamed. "Thank you, Mother."

"Now then, I'm really hungry this morning. This has been a far better Christmas than I had anticipated," Daphne said, rising. "Santa?" She held out her arm and Bruce rushed to take it. I watched them leave and then turned to Gisselle. She was beaming from ear to ear.

"She'll let us stay home now. You'll see."

"Maybe she'll let you stay home, but not me," I said. "I don't have a handicap to miraculously overcome."

Gisselle shrugged. "Anyway, thanks for keeping your mouth shut and going along."

"I didn't go along. I just stood to the side and watched you two fill each other with lies," I said.

"Whatever. Here," she said, thrusting Paul's gift at me. "You probably have so many secret thoughts, you can fill two of these in a day."

I took the diary and started to follow as she wheeled herself out, but at the doorway, I paused to look back at the tree and the obese pile of open gifts. How I longed for a real Christmas morning again, when the truly important gift was the gift of love.

Beau arrived shortly after his own family had exchanged gifts, and I gave him my present, which was a gold identification bracelet I had bought him the day after Gisselle and I arrived home. Underneath I had the jeweler inscribe, "With all my love, always, Ruby."

"I have three of these that lay in my drawer at home," he said, putting it on, "but none of them had any meaning until now." He kissed me quickly on my lips before anyone came into the parlor.

"Now I have a favor to ask of you," I said. "And you can't laugh."

"What could that be?" He smiled widely in anticipation.

"Nina's going to burn some brimstone for us, to bless our love and keep the evil spirits from destroying it."

"What?"

"Come on," I said, taking his hand. "It doesn't hurt to be safe."

He laughed as we hurried down the corridor to Nina's room. I knocked on the door and entered when she said for us to come in. Beau nearly gasped at the sight of the small room cluttered with voodoo paraphernalia: dolls and bones, chunks of what looked like black cat fur, strands of hair tied with leather string, twisted roots, and strips of snakeskin. The shelves were crowded with small bottles of multicolored powders, stacks of yellow, blue, green, and brown candles, jars of snake heads, and a picture of the woman I knew to be Marie Laveau sitting on what looked like a throne. Nina often burned white candles around it at night when she chanted her prayers.

"Who's that?" Beau asked.

"You be New Orleans boy and you don't know that be Marie Laveau, Voodoo Queen?"

411

"Oh yes. I've heard of her." He glanced at me and bit down on his lower lip.

Nina went to her shelves to fetch a small ceramic jar. She and I had performed a similar ceremony when I had first arrived from the bayou.

"You both hold it," she commanded. She lit a white candle and mumbled a prayer. Then she brought the candle to the ceramic jar and dipped the flame toward the contents so the brimstone would burn, but it didn't catch on. She glanced at me and looked worried and then tried again, holding the candle longer until a small stream of smoke twisted its way up. Beau grimaced because the stench was unpleasant, but I had been expecting it and held my breath.

"Both close your eyes and lean over so the smoke touches your faces," she prescribed. We did so. We heard her mumble something.

"Hey, this is getting hot," Beau complained. His fingers slipped and I fumbled with the jar to keep from dropping it. Nina plucked it from my hand and held it firmly.

"The heat be nothing," she chastised, "compared to the heat of evil spirits." Then she shook her head. "Nina hope it be enough brimstone smoke."

"It's enough," Beau assured her.

"Thank you, Nina," I said, seeing how uncomfortable he was. She nodded, and Beau urged me toward the door.

"Yes, thank you, Nina," he added. He pulled me out.

"Don't laugh, Beau Andreas."

"I'm not laughing," he said, but I saw he was very happy we had left and were returning to the parlor.

"My grandmere taught me never to laugh at anyone's beliefs, Beau. No one has a monopoly on the truth when it comes to spiritual things."

"You're right," he said. "And anyway, whatever makes you comfortable and happy makes me comfortable and happy. I mean that," he promised, and kissed me.

A moment later Gisselle wheeled herself in, looking very full of herself. All the talk at breakfast had been about her wonderful recuperation. Edgar and Nina were told, but both looked so unimpressed Gisselle suspected I had told them.

"Am I interrupting anything?" she asked Beau coyly.

"As a matter of fact, you are," he replied, smiling.

"Too bad. Did you tell him yet?" she asked me.

"Tell me what?"

"I guess you haven't, because it's not as important to you as it is to everyone else." She turned to Beau, took a dramatic breath, and announced, "I'm regaining the use of my legs."

"What?" Beau looked at me, but I said nothing.

"That's right. My paralysis is going away. Soon I will be competition for Ruby again, and she's not too happy about that, are you, Sister dear?"

"I've never been in competition with you,

413

Gisselle," I retorted.

"Oh no? What do you call your hot romance with my old boyfriend here?" she snapped.

"Hey, I think I might have something to say about all this," Beau told her. "And besides, Ruby and I were seeing each other way before the accident."

She smirked and then laughed her thin, sardonic laugh. "Men think they've made a decision, but the truth is, we have them wound around our little finger. You were always a bit too conservative for me, Beau. It was my decision to leave you behind. I was the one who made it possible for you two to meet and . . ." — she twisted her lips into her condescending smile — "get to know each other."

"Yeah, right," Beau said, peeved.

"Anyway, New Year's Eve, I'll be dancing again and I expect to dance with you. You won't mind, will you, Sister dear?"

"Not in the least," I said. "That is, if Beau doesn't."

She didn't like my tone, and her smile evaporated quickly.

"I've got to call John and give him the good news. It might break his heart. He so enjoyed my helplessness last night."

"Just don't recuperate that fast then," I suggested, but instead of getting angry, she laughed.

"Maybe I won't. Don't knock it unless you try it," she added with narrowed eyelids. Then she laughed again and wheeled herself out.

"Is she telling the truth about her recovery?"

"No."

"She can't move her legs?"

"Yes, but she could do it weeks, maybe even months ago." I quickly related the incident at school and why I was blamed.

"Well, I'll be damned. You've had your share of surprises," Beau said.

"There's more."

"Oh?"

"Daphne is permitting me to take Uncle Jean his Christmas gift. She said you could go with me, if you like."

"Really?" He shook his head in amazement and sat back. Then I told him why she was being so nice to Gisselle and me. "Married? So soon?" he said.

"She said after a proper period of mourning, but who knows what she considers proper."

"My parents had suspicions," he told me in a whisper.

"The two of them have been seen everywhere together." He looked down and then up again to add, "There were suspicions even before your father's death."

"I don't doubt it. I don't care what she does with herself now, and I don't want to talk anymore about it," I said angrily.

"Well then, why don't we just go visit Jean today and have lunch at one of the roadside restaurants on the way back," he suggested.

I went to get Uncle Jean's gift and told Daphne we were leaving.

"Make sure he knows that's from me," she said.

But when we arrived at the institution and were brought to him in the lounge, I knew immediately that not only wouldn't he understand who the gift was from, he wouldn't even realize he had visitors. Uncle Jean had become little more than a shadow of his former self. Like one of Nina's zombies, he sat staring blankly ahead, his eyes turned inward, where he could revisit all the places and times he had formerly experienced. When I spoke to him and held his hand, there was only a slight blinking and a tiny light in his eyes.

"He's like a clam closing its shell!" I moaned to Beau. "He barely hears me."

We sat in the lounge. It had started raining on our trip out, and the rain built a frantic tattoo on the window we now gazed through. It matched the rhythm of my heart. Uncle Jean looked so much thinner, the bones in his nose and cheeks more prominent. He looked like someone who was dying slowly from within.

I tried again, talking about Christmas, some of the things I had done at school, the decorations at the house. But his expression didn't change, and he wouldn't turn his eyes to me. After a while, I gave up. I leaned over and kissed him goodbye on the cheek. His eyelids fluttered and his lips trembled, but he said nothing, nor did he really look at me.

On the way out, I stopped to talk to his nurse.

"Does he ever speak?"

"He hasn't for a while now," she admitted. "But sometimes," she added, smiling, "they do return. There are new medications coming out every day."

"Would you see that he puts on his new shirts? He used to be so proud of his clothes," I said sadly. She promised she would, and Beau and I retreated. Visiting Uncle Jean had made this Christmas Day even more gloomy than the dark clouds and rain. I barely spoke, and I had little appetite when we stopped for lunch. Beau carried most of the conversation, describing plans for us for the near future.

"I've already decided: We'll both apply to Tulane. That way we'll be in New Orleans and together. My teachers think I should look toward a career in medicine because I do so well in the biological sciences. Doctor Andreas . . . how does that sound?"

"It sounds wonderful, Beau."

"Well, your grandmere was a healer. We've got to keep up the tradition. I'll practice medicine and you'll paint and become one of New Orleans's leading artists. People will come from everywhere to buy your pictures. On Sundays after church, we'll walk along the streets in the Garden District and I'll brag to our baby that his mother has a picture in that house and that, and two more in that. . . ."

I smiled. Grandmere Catherine would have liked Beau, I was sure.

"Good. You're smiling again. You're ravishingly beautiful when you're happy, Ruby. I want to keep you continuously happy for as long as I live," he said. His words brought the blood to my face again and the warmth to my heart.

When he brought me home, I found Daphne in Daddy's office, talking on the phone. Apparently, even on Christmas Day, she was all business. She was dressed in a smart, light blue tweed skirt and vest with a white lace silk blouse and had her hair tied in a French knot.

"And how is Jean?" she asked with half interest as she moved some papers around.

"He's become a vegetable," I said. "Won't you reconsider and put him back in his own room?"

She sat back and stared at me a moment. "I'll make you a trade," she said.

"Trade?" What could I possibly have that she wanted? I wondered.

"I'll move Jean back into private quarters if you convince Gisselle to return to Greenwood. I don't want her in my hair during this particularly difficult period."

"She won't listen to me," I moaned. "She hates the restrictions and the rules."

Daphne gazed down at her paperwork again.

"That's my offer," she said coldly. "Find a way."

I stood there for a moment. Why should Uncle Jean's welfare be tied to Gisselle's selfish wishes? How could anything be more unfair? More pessimistic than a nutria locked in the jaws of an alligator, I lowered my head and left her, never missing Daddy more.

I spent the remainder of Christmas Day in my art studio, working on the drawing and painting for Miss Stevens. The studio and my artistic work was the only refuge in this house of deceit. I had chosen to draw the view from my studio, to capture the sprawling oak tree and the gardens. I decided to have a red-winged blackbird strutting proudly on the wall in the background. It was good to lose myself in my work. While I painted I played Louis's symphony, and I didn't hear Bruce come in behind me.

"Ah, so here is where La Ruby hides herself," he said. I spun around. He stood there with his hands on his hips, looking over the studio and nodding. He had changed into a pair of dark gray wool slacks and a shirt made of the softest white Egyptian cotton. "Very nice. And that looks like it's going to be a pretty picture," he said, gazing at my easel.

"It's too soon to tell," I replied modestly.

"Well, I'm no art critic, but I know the value of good art on the market, of course." He focused his gaze intently on me for a moment and then smiled and stepped closer. "I was hoping to have a short tête-à-tête with both you and Gisselle today. I've already spoken to your sister, who has begged me to use my influence with Daphne to permit her to remain and return to public school here in New Orleans. Apparently, if I win her that favor, she will accept me into the family with open arms.

"And now," he said, inching toward me, "what can I do to win the same acceptance from you?"

"I have no requests for anything for myself, but if you want to do something to please me, get Daphne to move Uncle Jean back into his private room."

"Ah ha, a selfless demand. You are what you seem to be after all, aren't you, La Ruby? . . . A spotless jewel, genuine, virtuous. Are you as innocent as you appear, as innocent as the flowers and animals in your pictures?"

"I'm no angel, Bruce, but I don't like to see anyone in unnecessary pain, and that's what Uncle Jean is in right now. If you want to do something good, help him."

He smiled and reached out to touch my hair. I cringed and started to step back, but he put his hand on my arm just above the elbow.

"You and Gisselle are twins," he said in a voice barely above a whisper, "but a man would have to be blind not to see the differences. I'd like to be someone you can love and trust. You know, I've always admired you, La Ruby. But you've been tossed from one world to another, and just when you needed a true guardian, you lost him. Will you let me . . . be your guardian, your protector and champion? I'm a man of great taste. I can make you into the princess you deserve to be. Trust me," he said, raising his hand to my shoulder. He was so close I could see the tiny beads of sweat over his upper lip and smell the aroma of the last cigar he smoked. He held me firmly in his grasp and then brought his lips to my forehead. I heard him inhale as he took in the scent of my hair. I let him embrace me, but I didn't return his affection.

"That's all right," he said, feeling my stiffness and stepping back. "I don't blame you for being cautious. I'm the new man in your life and you don't really know all that much about me. But I intend to spend as much time with you as you will permit so we can get to know each other as intimately as possible. Will that be all right?"

"You're my stepmother's new husband-to-be," I said, as if that were enough of an answer.

He nodded. "I'll speak to Daphne. Maybe I can find a sensible financial arrangement and get her to do what you want. I can't make promises, but I'll try for you."

"Thank you."

"La Ruby," he said with that deep, licentious smile on his lips. He looked around again. "You have a nice hideaway. After I've married Daphne, perhaps you will let me share it with you from time to time, *n'est-ce pas?*"

I nodded, even though I detested the thought.

"Good," he said. "We're going to be a wonderful family, even more highly respected than we are now, and you and your sister will be the crème de la crème of New Orleans. That's a promise," he said. "I'll let you go back to your wonderful work. We'll speak later."

I watched him leave and then sat down because my heart was still thumping so hard,

I thought I might faint.

Despite Bruce's promise, nothing more was said about Uncle Jean during the days between Christmas and New Year's Eve. Feeling trapped by Daphne's offer, I tried on a number of occasions to get Gisselle to reconsider her demand to remain in New Orleans.

"You've made new friends, and they all look up to you and depend on you now," I told her just before we were about to go to sleep. It was the night before New Year's Eve. "You're their leader."

"You can have that honor," she replied.

"But think of what you can do now that you'll be walking. And there's the Valentine's dance coming up too."

"Peachy. The Valentine's dance. Don't get too close and don't hold hands too long. And just when you get to meet someone, you have to say good-bye. And that stupid curfew, even on the weekends."

"Daphne's going to permit us to go off the campus. We'll meet boys in the city."

"You wouldn't do that," she said. "You're too head over heels in love with Beau. Wait a minute." She scrutinized me with her suspicious eyes. "Why are you trying to get me to go back to Greenwood? What's going on?"

"Whenever you want, I'll take trips into Baton Rouge with you," I promised, ignoring her question.

"There's more to this, Ruby. What is it? You better tell me. One thing's for sure, I'll never go back if you don't tell me the truth."

I sighed and leaned back against her door jamb.

"I asked Daphne to move Uncle Jean back to his private room. He's nothing more than a vegetable now. He's lost all desire to live, to communicate. He's retreated into his own world."

"So what? He was nuts anyway."

"He wasn't. He was making progress. If he had a loving family around him again . . ."

"Oh, stop being Miss Goody Two-Shoes. What does that have to do with my returning to Greenwood?"

"Daphne said if I got you to go back, she would return Uncle Jean to his room."

"I thought there was something behind your sweettalk. Well, you can forget it," she said, turning away to look at herself in her vanity mirror. "I'm not going back to Greenwood. Right now I'm enjoying John, and I don't intend to give him up just so my crazy uncle can have his own room in a nut house." She smiled. "Daphne's going to let me stay for sure then. She doesn't want me to upset the apple cart. Good. Thanks for telling me."

"Gisselle . . ."

"I said I'm not going back. That's final," she hammered. "Now stop thinking about sad things and help me plan out our New Year's Eve party. I've invited nearly twenty friends. Claudine and Antoinette are coming over to help decorate the living room tomorrow. For refreshment, I thought we'd have those twelve-foot po'boy sandwiches. We'll work up a fruit punch and wait until Daphne and Bruce leave. Then we'll spike it with rum. What do you think?"

"I don't care," I said glumly.

"You better not be a lump of swamp mud around here tomorrow night. I'm warning you not to spoil the fun."

"That's the last thing in the world I would want to do, Gisselle, spoil your fun. Heaven forbid," I spit out, then left her room before I pulled out each and every strand of hair on her head.

16

A Brave Front

Despite my gloomy feelings, I tried not to walk about with downcast eyes and let everyone know just how unhappy I was. Gisselle's friends were very excited about the New Year's Eve party, and I had never seen Daphne so friendly and outgoing toward them. She came into the living room in the afternoon and made suggestions for the decorating. Of course, all the girls were in awe of her. I could see from the way they gazed at her that they thought she was akin to a movie star: beautiful, rich, elegant, and full of style.

But Gisselle kept herself the center of attention, revealing the miraculous recovery of her limbs and promising to dance for the first time since the accident. She got Edgar to bring in a ladder and then had the girls string streamers from one side of the ceiling to the other. They blew up balloons and placed them in a net to be released at midnight. While they worked, they gossiped about the boys who would be attending the party, and Gisselle described the girls of Greenwood, bragging about the things she had taught them concerning sex and boys. From time to time, she shifted her eyes toward me to see if I would contradict her, but I was barely listening after a while.

I was looking forward to spending the evening with Beau. I took my time choosing my dress and settled on a strapless black velvet gown with a deep, sweetheart neckline. The dress fit snugly at the waist and then had a full skirt that ended about six inches above my ankles. I had planned to wear a string of pearls around my neck but decided at the last minute simply to wear Beau's chain and ring, excited by the way the gleaming jewelry heightened that part of my bosom and cleavage. When I closed my eyes, I could almost feel his fingers softly gliding down, over my collarbone toward my breasts.

I put on a pair of delicate gold and pearl hoop earrings and decided to wear the ring that Louis had given me. Gisselle and I had each been given half a dozen different perfumes. I chose one that suggested the fresh aroma of blossoming roses. I had decided to wear my hair down but pinned back at the sides. My bangs needed a bit of trimming and I smiled to myself, recalling how Grandmere Catherine used to do it for me and even sit talking to me for what seemed like hours and hours while she brushed my long ruby hair, telling me again and again how she used to do the same thing for my mother.

Gisselle surprised me by choosing a dress similar to mine in dark blue. She bedecked herself with far more jewelry, wearing two strings of pearls, long dangling pearl earrings, a gold bracelet on one wrist and Bruce's charm bracelet Christmas gift on the other, as well as half a dozen rings spaced over her two hands. She wore a gold anklet as well. She left her hair down as well, not even pinning the sides, and she had caked on makeup, eyeliner, and lipstick so thick, she could kiss for hours before reaching her skin.

"How do I look?" she asked after coming to my doorway.

"Very nice," I replied. I knew that if I criticized her she would only resent it and rant and rave about how jealous I was.

" 'Nice'? What's that like, 'neat'?" she said, grimacing. She studied me a moment, making comparisons. "Why don't you put on more makeup? I can still see those freckles on your cheeks."

"They don't bother me," I said. "Or Beau," I added pointedly.

"They used to," she remarked, her eyes twinkling with mischief. When I didn't bite, she stopped smiling. "I'm going down."

"Be right there," I said. A short while later, I found her seated in her wheelchair in the center of the living room, gazing about with satisfaction.

"This is going to be the greatest party ever," she declared. "You'll never forget this New Year's Eve." She stared at me a moment. "Did you ever have a good New Year's Eve in the swamps?"

"Yes."

"Doing what, fishing?" she asked disdainfully.

"No. We would have a party in the town. All of Main Street would be closed down, and the merchants as well as other people would set out food. There were fireworks and continuous music making for a grand fais dodo."

"Fais dodo, I forgot. You danced in the streets?" she asked.

I nodded, remembering. "It was as if we had all become one family, celebrating," I said wistfully.

"Sounds . . . stupid," she said, but I could see she was trying to convince herself.

"You don't need to spend a lot of money and have expensive clothing to have a good time, Gisselle. A real good time starts here," I said, pointing to my heart.

"I would have pointed someplace else," she retorted, and laughed.

"What's so funny?" Daphne asked as she and Bruce entered the living room. They were dressed and ready to leave. Bruce did look handsome in his tuxedo, and I had to admit that Daphne was never more striking. She wore a long narrow gown in the deepest, richest burgundy color that had a beaded rhinestone bodice and a bolero jacket with a beaded collar. The bodice of the gown dipped in one graceful swoop over the tops of her breasts, revealing just enough cleavage to be enticing. She wore no necklace to take away from the jeweled clothing, but she had rhinestone earrings. Her hair was up in a French knot with bangs.

428

"Cajun New Year's Eve," Gisselle quipped.

"Oh," she said, nodding as if to say she understood why that would be a topic for humor. "Well, we just stopped by to wish you two a happy new year. Remember, I don't want to see a lot of drinking and wildness. Respect the house. Enjoy yourselves, but be ladies," she added.

"Of course we will, Mother. You have a good time too," Gisselle said.

Daphne looked at me. "You both look very nice," she said.

"Thank you," I replied.

"Can I give my soon-to-be stepdaughters a New Year's Eve kiss now?" Bruce asked.

"Sure," Gisselle said. He leaned over and kissed her quickly on the cheek. She had closed her eyes, expecting a kiss on the lips. He approached me, smiling, and put his hands on my shoulders.

"You are as beautiful as always," he said softly, and then leaned in to kiss me. I turned just in time to direct him from my lips to my cheek. He stared at me for a moment and then laughed.

"Happy new year, girls," he cried, then joined Daphne to leave for their gala affair.

"Good riddance," Gisselle muttered. "Let's have a drink alone before the others arrive," she said and wheeled herself to our bar. "What do you want, rum and coke?" She started to get up to make them.

"I'll pour my own drinks, thank you," I said, recalling how Gisselle tried to get me drunk before.

"Good. Make mine too then," she said, sitting down again. I did so and handed it to her. "Well, dear Sister, here's to a happier year than the one we just had. May it be filled with fun, fun, fun."

"For everyone we love," I added. She shrugged.

"Sure, for everyone we love." We drank and, a moment later, heard the doorbell.

"Here we go," Gisselle cried, wheeling herself toward the doorway. She was keeping herself in the wheelchair just so she could make her standing and walking look that much more dramatic later.

All of Gisselle's guests arrived a little early. Word about the party's prospects had spread quickly. By the time Beau appeared, everyone was there, and most of them had had more than one drink. The music was blaring, and some of the food had already been eaten.

"You're even more beautiful than I imagined you would be," Beau told me when I greeted him at the door. We kissed and then entered the party. Everyone was talking loudly; some had already had more to drink than they could tolerate and were acting silly.

"Looks like one of Gisselle's typical parties," Beau cried over the noise. We danced, ate something, and had our drinks along with everyone else.

At ten o'clock, as she had planned, Gisselle had the music turned down and announced her intention to dance for the first time since the accident.

John stood by her as she pretended to struggle out of the chair. She fell into his arms, regained her composure, and took what she wanted everyone to think were her first dance steps. The party guests clapped and whistled as Gisselle and John moved over the dance floor. Not long afterward, Gisselle told one of the girls to turn the lights low and the real partying began. Everyone paired off.

"I don't care where you go in the house," Gisselle announced, "as long as it doesn't look like you've been there. The upstairs is off-limits, of course."

"Let's get away from all this," Beau said. When no one was looking, we slipped out. He paused, wondering where we should go. I pulled him forward and we scampered up the stairs and into my room.

"I don't want to spend my New Year's Eve with them anyway," I told Beau. "They're like strangers to me now."

"Me too," he said. We kissed and then both of us gazed at my bed. I sat down and Beau sat beside me.

"I can put on my radio," I said. I got up quickly and turned the dial, searching for a good station. I don't know why I was suddenly so nervous, but I was. My fingers trembled around the knob and I felt a tingling in my stomach. It was almost as if Beau and I were on our first date. I finally settled on a station that was broadcasting from the grand ballroom of one of the downtown hotels. We could hear the excitement of the people dancing as well as the music. The announcer came on to tell everyone how close we were to midnight.

"Why is New Year's Eve so special?" I asked.

Beau thought a moment.

"I suppose it gives people a chance to hope for better things." He laughed. "I used to have this toy, a magic slate. You wrote or drew on it and then, just by pulling up the plastic cover, everything you did disappeared and you could start new. Maybe everyone feels that on New Year's Eve: They can pull up the magic sheet and rewrite their lives."

"I wish I could. But I wish I could go back, much further back than just one year."

He nodded, his eyes soft and sympathetic.

"Well-to-do young people like Gisselle and myself, like all those downstairs drinking too much, couldn't even begin to understand how hard your life has been, Ruby." He reached up and took my hand, his eyes still fixed on me. "You're like a wildflower. The rest of us have been cared for, nourished, given the best of everything, while you've had to struggle. But you know what, Ruby? The struggle has given you more strength and more beauty. Just like that wildflower, you've blossomed high and above the ordinary, the weeds. You're special. I always knew you were, right from the first moment I set eyes on you."

"Oh Beau, that's so sweet."

He pulled me toward him and I let myself fall against him, our lips meeting, his hands around my shoulders. Then, gently, gracefully, he turned himself and me so that we were side by side on my bed. He kissed my hair, my forehead, my eyes, the tip of my nose, before pressing his lips to mine again. When our tongues touched, I felt myself soften everywhere.

"You smell so good," he whispered. "I feel like I'm standing in the middle of a garden."

He dropped his hands below my shoulders and found the zipper on my dress. As he lowered it and the garment became loose around my bosom, I moaned and let my head fall back to the pillow. He brought his lips to my chin and then moved over my throat and down into the valley between my breasts.

"Beau, we're not being careful," I whispered, but I held him to me as if I wanted to disagree with myself and contradict everything I knew was right.

"I know," he said. "We will," he promised, but he started to slip my dress over my shoulders and down my arms. I let the bodice fall to my waist. Beau sat back and peeled off his sports jacket, loosened his tie, and unbuttoned his shirt while I stared up at him, his face now illuminated by the moonlight that came pouring through my window. He looked ghostlike, part of a dream, my wildest fantasy personified. I closed my eyes and didn't open them again until I felt him over me, his shirt stripped off. He toyed with my bra until he had it unfastened and then his lips were against my naked breasts, kissing each of them softly, until I pulled him away and put my lips to his.

His hands were under my dress, groping for my panties. I should have stopped him then, but instead I let him slip my panties off, and then I heard him moan and whisper my name as he brought his hard manliness to me.

"Beau," I cried weakly.

"It's good, Ruby. It's beautiful. It's meant to be. Otherwise we wouldn't love each other as much as we do."

I didn't resist. I let him enter me and touch me even more deeply than he had touched me before. I rose and fell, imagining myself in a pirogue near the ocean where the water would ripple with waves. Each time I was lifted, I felt myself become lighter. I thought I would eventually float off like a balloon.

I don't know how many times Beau cried my name. I can't remember what I was saying, but this time our lovemaking was so intense, it brought tears to my eyes. For a few moments it was as though we had melted into each other. We were that hot. I embraced him so tightly, one would have thought I was afraid of being thrown out of my bed.

We reached our climaxes simultaneously, ravishing each other with kisses, moving our lips over one another's faces like two people starving for affection, for the touch of another human being, hungry for love. We smothered our cries against one another's neck and shoulders and wound ourselves down with deep gasps, our hearts pounding against one another's, both of us so surprised at our passion we could only laugh.

"Feel this," Beau said, placing my palm over his heart.

"And you feel mine."

We lay beside each other, our heartbeats tapping against our hands, the rhythms traveling down our arms and back into our own hearts.

We lay side by side, silent for a long while. Then Beau sat up and leaned over me, gazing down at me.

"You're wonderful," he said. "I love you. I can't say it enough."

"Do you, Beau? And will you love me forever and ever?"

"I can't see why not or how I could stop," he said, and kissed me softly.

On the radio, the announcer, in a very excited voice, began a countdown. "Ten, nine, eight . . ."

Beau took my hand and we recited the rest of the numbers together.

"Five, four, three, two, one — HAPPY NEW YEAR!"

"Auld Lang Syne" began to play on the radio.

"Happy New Year, Ruby."

"Happy New Year, Beau."

We kissed again and held each other, and for a moment it did seem like nothing in this world was strong enough to tear us apart. I hadn't felt this happy and this contented for a long time. It was a good feeling. I had hungered for it more than I had realized.

We got dressed, fixed our hair, and straightened

ourselves up so that we looked almost as prim and neat as we had at the beginning of the evening. Then we left to go downstairs to see what Gisselle and her friends were up to.

I wish we hadn't. It looked like two boys had rushed down the corridor to get to a bathroom and hadn't made it. They were vomiting and spitting over the same area, alternating their moaning with stupid laughter. The house reeked from the sickeningly sweet stench of wine and whiskey.

All of the party decorations had been pulled down in a mad frenzy at the midnight hour. Balloons had been popped and lay everywhere. The living room was a mess. What's more, it looked like — and we later found out this was so — there had been a food fight. Drinks had been spilled on the floor; there was cake and pieces of po'boy sandwiches on the furniture, mustard and mayonnaise smeared on the walls and over the tables; there was even some of it smeared on the windows.

Some of the party guests were sprawled on the floor, wrapped in each other's arms, laughing and giggling stupidly. Others, feeling their overindulgence, sat with their eyes closed, their hands on their stomachs. Two boys were still at the bar, challenging each other with drinks. Naturally, the music had been turned up until it was nearly deafening.

"Where's Gisselle?" I screamed. Some gazed at me indifferently. Antoinette broke out of the arms of the boy who was sleeping on her shoulder and

436

walked over to us.

"Your sister left the party about an hour ago with John."

"Left the party? Where did they go?"

Antoinette shrugged.

"Did she leave the house?"

"I don't think so," Antoinette said, and laughed. "She wasn't feeling any pain. Oh. Happy New Year, Beau," she said, leaning over to kiss him.

"Happy New Year," he replied, kissing her quickly on the cheek. She backed up, disappointed, and returned to her drunken partner.

"She didn't go up to her room," I told Beau. "We would have heard her for sure. Daphne is going to be furious when she comes in and sees this. We'd better find Gisselle and have her order these people to clean up and leave."

"Doesn't look too promising," Beau said, gazing around. "But let's see if we can find her."

We went through most of the downstairs area, found a couple entwined in Daphne's office and shooed them out, but we didn't locate Gisselle. I ran upstairs to check the other bedrooms and came down to report no one there. We went through the kitchen and even looked down by Edgar's and Nina's rooms.

"Maybe she went out to the cabana," Beau suggested.

We checked but found no one there or around the pool.

"Where could she be? She must have left the house," Beau reasoned.

"There's only one place we haven't checked, Beau."

"Where?"

I took his hand and led him back into the house. We stepped over a boy sprawled across the hallway floor asleep and went down to my studio. As we approached the door, I heard Gisselle's giggling. I looked at Beau and thrust the door open. For a moment, neither of us believed what we were seeing.

John was naked on the sofa and Gisselle, dressed only in her bra and panties, was painting him. She had smeared red and green paint over his shoulders and chest and made long streaks of yellow down his legs, but at this moment she was dabbing black over his private parts. John was obviously too drunk to care. He laughed with her.

"Gisselle!" I screamed. "What are you doing?"

She turned and swayed for a moment as she tried to focus on us.

"Oh . . . look who's here . . . the lovers," she muttered, and then laughed again.

"What do you think you're doing?"

"Doing?" She looked down at John, who had his eyes closed and wore a dumb smile on his face. "Oh. I'm painting John. I told him I had just as much art talent as you did, and if you could paint Beau, I could paint him. John agreed." She laughed and poked him. "Didn't you, John?"

"Yeah," he said.

"Get your ass off that sofa," Beau commanded, "and get dressed, you idiot."

John lifted his head. "Oh, hi, Beau. Is it New Year's Day yet?"

"For you it's the end of the year if you don't get up and get dressed and fast."

"Huh?"

"Gisselle, did you see what your friends did to the house? How long have you been away from the party?"

"How long have you been away, dear Sister?" she countered, smiling licentiously and swaying.

"They've wrecked the house! There are kids vomiting in the halls. The walls are smeared with food —"

"Oops. Sounds like an emergency."

"Beau," I cried. He rushed forward and grabbed John by the arms, pulling him up. Then he shoved him toward the rear of the studio and forced him to start putting on his clothes.

"Get dressed, Gisselle, and march down to the party. You've got to get them to start cleaning up before Daphne returns."

"Oh, stop worrying about Daphne. Daphne — she's going to be very nice to us now because she wants to marry Bruce and make us look like a happy, respectable New Orleans family. You were always too frightened of Daphne. You're frightened of your own Cajun shadow," she quipped.

I stepped up to her and thrust her dress into her face.

"I'm not too frightened to break your neck. Put on this dress. Now!"

"Stop yelling, It's New Year's Eve. We're sup-

439

posed to be having a good time. You had a good time, didn't you?"

"I didn't wreck anything. Look at my studio!" I cried. Gisselle had spilled paints, torn canvases, and smeared clay over the tables and tools.

"The servants will clean up after us. They always do," she said. She started to put on her dress.

"Not this mess and the mess in the living room. Even a slave would rebel," I said. But it didn't matter what I said.

Gisselle was too drunk to listen or care. She wobbled, laughed, and got herself together. Beau managed to get John dressed, and then we pulled the two of them out of the studio and marched them back to the party. Even Gisselle was surprised at the extent of the damage. Some of the kids, realizing what had been done, had already left. The ones who remained were not in the best condition to help clean up and restore the living room.

"Happy New Year!" Gisselle cried. "I guess we better try to clean up." She giggled and started to gather up glasses, but she took too many too fast and dropped them, breaking three.

"She's worthless," I told Beau.

"I'll get her to sit down and stay in one place," he said. While he did that, I tried to get some of the kids to help me pick up plates and glasses that were left on the floor. We found some under the sofas, some behind the chairs, glasses on the bookshelves and under tables.

I went into the kitchen and got a pail of soapy

water with some sponges. When I returned, I found that more of the party guests had deserted. Those who were left tried to help. Antoinette and I went around the room and scrubbed as much as we could off the walls, but some of the food had made deep stains. It was overwhelming.

"It's going to take an army to fix this, Beau," I cried.

He agreed.

"Let's just get them all out of here," he said. We announced the party had ended. Beau helped some of the boys out of the house, making sure the ones who were driving were the most sober. After everyone was gone, we surveyed what was left to be done. Gisselle was sprawled out on the living-room floor by the settee, snoring.

"You'd better go too, Beau," I told him. "You don't want to be here when Daphne arrives."

"Are you sure? I could testify about it and . . ."

"And say what, Beau? That we were upstairs in my room making love while Gisselle and her friends wrecked the house?"

He nodded. "Oh boy," he said. "What are you going to say?"

"Nothing. It's better than lying," I replied.

He shook his head.

"You want me to help you get her upstairs?" he asked, nodding toward Gisselle.

"No, leave her there."

I walked him to the door, where we kissed good night.

"I'll call tomorrow . . . sometime," he said, raising his eyebrows. I watched him leave and then I closed the door and walked back to the living room to wait for the inevitable storm that would soon break and rage over my head.

I sat in the easy chair across from Gisselle, who was still sprawled out and dead to the world on the floor. She had vomited but was too out of it to notice or care. The clock ticked and bonged at two. I closed my eyes and didn't open them again until I felt someone shaking me roughly. I looked up into Daphne's enraged face and for a moment forgot where I was and what had happened. She wouldn't let that moment last long.

"What did you do! What did you do!" she screamed down at me, her mouth twisted and her eyes wide. Bruce stood in the doorway shaking his head, his hands on his hips.

"I didn't do anything, Daphne," I said, sitting up. "This is what Gisselle and her friends call a good time. I'm only a backward Cajun. I wouldn't know what a good time is."

"What are you saying? This is how you repay me for being understanding and kind to you?" she shrilled.

Gisselle's loud moan spun Daphne around.

"Get up!" she screamed over her. "Do you hear me, Gisselle? Get up this minute!"

Gisselle's eyes fluttered, but they didn't open. She groaned and went quiet again.

"Bruce!" Daphne cried, turning to him.

He sighed and stepped forward. Then he knelt down, put his arms under Gisselle, and, not without great effort, lilted her off the floor.

"Take her upstairs this minute," Daphne commanded.

"Upstairs?"

"This minute, do you hear? I can't stand the sight of her."

"I'll use the wheelchair," he said, and dropped her in it, disregarding the piece of cake smeared over the back of the seat. She sat limply, her head on her shoulder, and moaned again. Then Bruce wheeled her out the way Grandpere Jack would wheel a wagonful of cow manure, his head back and his arms extended so the stench would be as far away from him as possible. The moment Bruce and Gisselle were out of the room, Daphne was on me again.

"What went on here?"

"They had a food fight," I said. "They drank too much. Some of them couldn't hold their liquor and threw up. The others were too drunk to be careful. They broke glasses, dropped food, fell asleep on the floor. Gisselle told them they could go anywhere in the house but upstairs. I found a couple in your office."

"My office! Did they touch anything?"

"Just themselves, I imagine," I said dryly. I yawned.

"You're happy this happened, aren't you? You think this proves something."

I shrugged. "I've seen people get drunk and

sloppy in the bayou," I said, thinking about Grandpere Jack. "Believe me, I have, and drunken rich young Creoles are no different."

"I was depending on you to keep things in order," she said, shaking her head.

"Me? Why always me? Why not Gisselle? She was brought up better, wasn't she? She was taught about all the finer things in life, given all this!" I cried, holding out my arms.

"She's crippled."

"No she's not. You saw she's not."

"I don't mean her legs, I mean . . . her . . . her . . ."

"She's just the spoiled, selfish young lady you created," I said.

Daphne stood there fuming.

"I don't care about making appearances anymore," she said. "When she wakes up, you can tell her that, come hell or high water, you and she are going back to Greenwood. That's final." She looked about. "I'll have to contract with a cleaning agency to come in here and clean and repair this house, and the expense will come out of y'all's spending money. Tell her that too."

"Maybe you should tell her yourself."

"Don't you be insolent." She nodded. "I know why you let this go on. You were probably not even here when it all happened, were you? You and your loverboy were probably somewhere else, weren't you?" she accused. I felt my face turning crimson. It convinced her she was right. "Well, I'm not surprised," she said. "So much for giving people second chances."

"I'm sorry this happened, Daphne," I said. I didn't want her to find a way to blame Beau. "I really am. I couldn't stop it from happening. Gisselle was in charge. These were all her friends. I'm not trying to pass the blame. That's just the way it was. They wouldn't have listened to me no matter what. Whenever I complain about something they do, Gisselle laughs at me and calls me names. She turns them against me, and I have no power or authority over them."

"This is your house too, you know," Daphne said pointedly.

"You've never let me feel that way. But I'm still sorry this happened," I said.

"Just go to sleep. We'll deal with it tomorrow. Up until now, this was one of the best New Year's Eves I've had in a long time."

She started out.

"Happy New Year to you too," I mumbled, then went up to bed.

Gisselle didn't stir until after twelve the next day, but neither did Daphne. I had breakfast with Bruce.

"She's pretty angry," he said. "But I'll calm her down. I don't think I can keep her from sending you both back to Greenwood, however."

"I don't care," I said. At this point I just wanted to get away. After breakfast, I went out on the patio by the pool and slept in the sun. A little after one o'clock, I felt a shadow move over me and opened my eyes to see Gisselle. She looked devastated. Her hair was disheveled, her face was as pale as a dead fish. She wore a pair of sunglasses and a robe, under which she was still dressed in last night's lingerie.

"Daphne said you blamed it all on me," she said.

"I just told her the truth."

"Did you tell her you were upstairs with Beau all night?"

"We weren't upstairs all night, but I didn't have to tell her. She figured it out."

"Couldn't you make something up, blame it on one of our guests or something?"

"Who would believe such a story, Gisselle? What's the difference? You didn't care very much last night when I tried to get you and your friends to clean up. Maybe if we had, it wouldn't have been as bad."

"Thanks," she said. "You know what she said now, don't you? We have to go back to Greenwood. She won't listen to anything I say. I've never seen her so angry."

"Maybe it's for the best."

"You would say that. You don't care: You're having a good time at Greenwood, doing well in your work, enjoying your Miss Stevens and Louis."

"Louis is gone, and I would hardly say I was having a good time at a school where the principal tried to expel me because of something you did," I reminded her.

"So why do you want to go back?"

"I'm just tired of fighting with Daphne. I don't know. I'm just tired."

"Just stupid is more like it. Stupid and selfish."

"Me? You're calling me selfish?"

"You are." She pressed her hands to her temples. "Oh, my head. It feels like someone's playing tennis in it. Don't you have a hangover?" she asked.

"I didn't drink all that much."

"You didn't drink all that much," she mimicked. "Miss Goody Two-Shoes strikes again. I hope you're happy," she moaned. She spun around, but she didn't rush away. She had to walk slowly to keep her head from pounding.

I smiled. Just desserts, I thought; she'd been taught a lesson. Only I knew that whatever promises she had made and however she swore to repent, she would forget it all as soon as her pain subsided.

Two days later we had our things packed for the trip back to Greenwood, only this time the wheelchair was left at home. Gisselle wanted to bring it along, claiming she wasn't confident enough to walk all the time, but to Daphne's credit, she didn't buy the story. She wasn't going to let Gisselle revert to her former ways, drawing on everyone's sympathy, using her condition as an excuse for her bad behavior.

"If you can walk around here, dance and make a mess, you can walk to and from your classes," Daphne told her. "I've already called your house-mother and given her the good news," she added, "so by now everyone knows about your miraculous recovery. Now I hope your schoolwork undergoes a similarly miraculous recovery."

"But Mother," Gisselle pleaded, "the teachers hate me at Greenwood."

"I'm sure they hate you here as well," Daphne said. "Remember what I told you: If you misbehave there, it's off to a stricter school, one with barbed wire around it," she quipped, leaving Gisselle standing with her mouth open. That was Daphne's version of a motherly goodbye.

We rode back in funereal silence, Gisselle sniveling from time to time and sighing deeply. I tried to sleep most of the way. When we arrived at the dorm, it was as if we were homecoming heroines — or at least Gisselle was. For the moment it brought a blush of pleasure to her cheeks. Mrs. Penny was out front with the girls of our quad to greet Gisselle and witness the wonder of her miraculous recovery. The moment she saw them, her mood changed.

"Ta-da!" she announced, stepping out of the car. Mrs. Penny clapped her hands together and rushed down to hug her. All the girls gathered around, each firing question after question: How did it happen? When did you first realize? Did it hurt? What did the doctors say? What did your mother say? How far have you walked?

"I'm still a bit weak," Gisselle declared, and she leaned on Samantha. "Can someone get my jacket?" she asked weakly. "I left it on the seat."

"I will," Vicki said, hurrying to do so.

I raised my eyes to the sky. Why was it that

no one but me could see through Gisselle's facade? Why were they all so eager to be taken in by her, fooled and made fools of by her? They deserved her mistreatment; they deserved to be taken advantage of and used and manipulated, I thought, and I made a promise to myself right then and there that I would close my eyes to everything but my art.

So it was with genuine excitement that I hurried to class our first day back. I was looking forward to my first session with Miss Stevens. I was sure she would ask me to stay after class and we would talk and talk about our holidays. In my mind and deep in my putaway heart, Miss Stevens had become my older sister. One day soon, I thought, I would even tell her so.

But the moment I entered the building and started down the corridor toward homeroom, I sensed something was wrong. I felt it when I observed the small clumps of girls whispering here and there, all of them appearing to gaze my way as I passed them. Without knowing why, my heart began to pitter-patter, and an uneasiness couched itself in my stomach, making it feel as if a hive of bees were buzzing around inside. I had come to school ahead of the others, so I had some time. It had been my intention to stop by and say hello to Miss Stevens before homeroom anyway. I hurried down to the art suite and rushed through the doorway, expecting to see her standing there in her smock, her hair up, her face full of smiles.

But instead I confronted an elderly man in an

artist's smock. He was seated at the desk, sifting through some student drawings. He looked up, surprised, and I gazed around the room.

"Well, good morning," he said.

"Good morning. Isn't Miss Stevens here yet?" I asked.

His smile faded. "Oh. I'm afraid Miss Stevens won't be here anymore. My name is Mr. Longo. I'm her replacement."

"What?" For a moment the words seemed utterly ridiculous. I just stood there with this wide, incredulous smile on my face, my heart still racing.

"She won't be coming back," he said more firmly. "You're an art student, I take it?"

I shook my head.

"It can't be true. Why won't she be coming back? Why?" I demanded.

He sat up. "I don't know the details, Mademoiselle . . ."

"Dumas. What details?"

"As I said, I do not know, but . . ."

I didn't wait for him to finish. I spun around and ran out of the room. I ran down the corridor, confused, the tears streaming down my cheeks. No Miss Stevens? She was gone? How could she do this without telling me? Why wouldn't she tell me? My hysteria grew. I didn't even know where I was running; I was just running from one end of the building to the other. I turned a corner and headed back toward the front. When I was nearly there, I heard Gisselle's shrill ripple of laughter. More girls had gathered around her to hear the story of her miraculous recovery. I stopped running and walked slowly toward them. The group parted so that Gisselle and I faced each other.

"I just heard," she said.

I shook my head. "What did you hear?"

"Everyone's talking about it this morning. Your Miss Stevens was fired."

"That can't be. She's a wonderful teacher. It can't be."

"I guess it wasn't her teaching that got her fired," Gisselle said, and she looked knowingly at the others, who also wore smug smiles.

"What was it? What? Was she fired for helping me at the hearing?" I demanded. I turned on them. "Someone tell me. Who knows?"

There was a moment of silence. Then Deborah Peck stepped forward. "I don't know the exact details," she said, gazing back at the others, "but the charge against her had to do with her immorality."

"What? What immorality?" They only smiled widely in response. I spun on Gisselle.

"Don't blame me," she cried. "The Iron Lady found out about her on her own."

"Found out what? There was nothing to find out."

"Found out why she never goes out with men," Deborah said. "And why she wanted to teach in an all girls' school," she replied. There was a titter of laughter. My heart stopped and then started again, this time pounding angrily.

"Those are lies, all lies."

"She left, didn't she?" Deborah said. The warning bell rang. "We'd better get to homeroom. No one wants to get a demerit the first day back."

The group started to break up.

"Lies!" I screamed at them.

"Stop making a fool of yourself," Gisselle said. "Just go to class. Aren't you happy? You're back at your precious Greenwood!"

"You did this!" I accused. "Somehow, some way, you did this, didn't you?"

"How could I do this?" She raised her arms and turned to Vicki, Samantha, Jacki, and Kate. "I wasn't even here when it all happened. See? See how she's always blaming me for everything?"

They all turned and gazed at me. I shook my head and stepped back, and then I turned and ran down the corridor to Mrs. Ironwood's office. Mrs. Randle looked up with surprise as I burst through the doorway.

"I want to see Mrs. Ironwood," I said.

"You have to make an appointment, dear," Mrs. Randle replied.

"I want to see her now!" I ordered.

She sat back, shocked at my insistence. "Mrs. Ironwood is very busy with her work reopening the school at this moment, and —"

"NOW!" I screamed.

Mrs. Ironwood's door opened and she stood there glaring at me.

"What is the meaning of this?"

452

"Why was Miss Stevens fired?" I demanded. "Was it because she came to my assistance at the hearing? Was it?"

Mrs. Ironwood looked at Mrs. Randle, then straightened her shoulders.

"First," she began, "this is not the time nor the place to discuss such matters, even if it were proper to do so with a student, which it is not. Second, who do you think you are storming in here and making demands on me?"

"It's not fair," I said. "Why take it out on her? It's not fair. She was a wonderful teacher. Don't you want good teachers? Don't you care?"

"Of course I care, and I care about your insolence too," she said. I wiped the tears from my cheeks and stood there. She seemed to soften. "The conduct of faculty affairs is none of your business but I will tell you that Miss Stevens was not fired. She resigned."

"Resigned?" I shook my head. "She would never . . ."

"I assure you, she resigned." The homeroom bell rang. "That was the final bell. You're late for homeroom, two demerits," she snapped, then spun around and went back into her office, closing the door behind her and leaving me confused and lost in her wake.

"You'd better get to your homeroom, mademoiselle, before you make things even worse for yourself," Mrs. Randle warned.

"She wouldn't resign," I insisted, but I turned and walked back to my homeroom.

Later in the day, however, I tapped into the line of gossip and learned that Miss Stevens had indeed resigned.

She had been accused of immoral behavior and given the opportunity to resign and not be charged and dragged through a nasty hearing. The word was that one of the students had come forward and confessed to having been seduced by Miss Stevens. No one knew who the student was, of course, but I had my suspicions.

Gisselle couldn't have looked more satisfied, and Ironwood had gotten her pound of flesh.

17

A Waking Nightmare

During the days that followed, I resembled a somnambulist. I walked the corridors and grounds of Greenwood, my eyes focused on nothing, my gait slow. I barely heard anyone speaking to me or around me. I didn't know whether the sun was shining or not. One afternoon I was surprised to arrive at the dorm and discover I was wet, that it had rained and I hadn't even been aware of it.

Every day that I returned to the dorm after classes I hoped I had a message from Miss Stevens, but there were never any. I imagined she was afraid of getting me into any trouble; she was that considerate. I felt so sorry for her, driven away by the most scurrilous, foul lies. I knew that even though Mrs. Ironwood had let her resign, she would find ways to paint Miss Stevens with the stain of immoral behavior and hurt her chances to find another job.

Finally, one afternoon when I returned, I did find a letter, but it was from Louis.

Dear Ruby,

I'm sorry it took so long for me to write to you, but I didn't want to attempt it until I could do it entirely myself. What you are reading now is a letter written solely by me, with me seeing every single letter and word I put down. Finally, I no longer have to depend on anyone to do the simplest of tasks for me. I don't have to trust anyone with my secret thoughts or put aside my embarrassment and ask for the most basic favors. I am whole again, and once again, thanks to you.

The doctors tell me my eyesight has restored itself nearly one hundred percent. I'm doing some eye muscle exercises and wearing corrective lenses for the time being. But I don't spend that much of my day doting on myself anymore. No, I spend most of it at the conservatory, where I am working with the greatest music teachers in the world, I am sure. And they are all impressed with me.

Tonight I will be giving a recital at the school's hall, and besides all the teachers and their wives, there will be dignitaries from the city. I'm trying not to be nervous, and do you know what helps me overcome it? Thinking about you and the wonderful talks we used to have.

And guess what? They are going to let me play some of your symphony. As I play I will think about your laughter and your soft voice encouraging me. I do miss you a great deal and look forward to seeing you again. Or should I say, see you completely for the first time?

I received a letter from my grandmother, and as usual, she included some news about the school. Why did the art teacher, Miss Stevens, resign? Wasn't she your favorite teacher at Greenwood? All Grandmother says about it is that she was quickly replaced.

Write back when you have a chance, and good luck with your school exams.

As always,

Your dearest friend,
Louis

I put his letter aside and tried to compose a reply that wouldn't reveal how depressed and unhappy I was, but every time I begin to explain why Miss Stevens was gone, I broke out in tears and those tears fell on the stationery. Finally I just jotted off a quick note, claiming I was in the middle of exams and would write him in more detail soon.

Meanwhile, it wasn't until the middle of the second week that I heard from Beau. He apologized for not calling me.

"I had to attend a family gathering and was away for the entire weekend," he claimed. Then he added, "You can't imagine how Daphne carried on about New Year's Eve when she met my parents at a restaurant last night. She made it sound as if we were all part of an orgy."

"I can imagine."

"Why do you sound so down? Is it because you miss me, because if you do . . ."

"No, Beau," I said, and I told him about Miss Stevens. "You think it was Gisselle?"

"I'm positive it was Gisselle," I said. "She once threatened to do the exact same thing if I revealed the secret about her not being crippled anymore."

"Did you confront her?"

"Naturally, she denies it," I said. "It doesn't matter now. The damage has been done, and she has won what she wanted: I hate it here."

"Complain to Daphne," he suggested. "Maybe she'll let you come home."

"I doubt it," I said. "It doesn't matter anyway. I just do my work and plod on. I'm not doing much artwork. The new teacher is nice, but he's not Miss Stevens."

"Well, I'll be up there this weekend," Beau promised. "Saturday, late in the morning."

"Okay."

"Ruby, I hate to hear how sad you are. It makes me sad too," he said.

I was crying, but I didn't let him hear. I nodded, caught my breath, and told him I had to go finish up some homework.

He did drive up on Saturday, and the sight of him getting out of his car in front of the dorm put some sunshine in my heart. I had gone into the dorm kitchen and prepared a picnic lunch of po'boy sandwiches and apple juice. When the other girls set their eyes on him, they expressed their approval with cheers and giggles. With a blanket folded under my arm, I rushed out to meet him and go off to another part of the campus.

"Daphne was supposed to send permission for Gisselle and me to leave the campus on weekends, but she didn't," I explained, "so we can't leave the grounds."

"It's all right. It's nice here," he said, looking around.

We walked around the campus and then spread the blanket on the lawn. We both lay back on our hands and looked up at the blue sky with its puffs of creamy white clouds and talked softly. Our talk wasn't of much at all at the start. He rattled on about some of his friends back in New Orleans, the prospects for the upcoming baseball season, and his college plans.

"You've got to get back to your art," he told me. "Miss Stevens would be very upset, I'm sure."

"I know. But right now everything I do is mechanical. I feel like a robot, getting up, getting dressed, going to school, doing my homework, studying, going to sleep. But you're right," I told him. "I do have to get back to what is most important to me."

I sat up. He played with a blade of grass and then tried to tickle me with it. I was very self-conscious about everything we did, however. We were in plain view of everyone. There was no privacy for us at Greenwood, and I could imagine even Mrs. Ironwood gaping out of a window watching us, just waiting for us to do something she considered wrong.

We ate our sandwiches, talked some more, and then went for another walk. I showed him parts of the school itself, the library, the auditorium, and cafeteria. All the while I felt we were being watched, being followed. I didn't want to take him back to my dorm. I was happy we had been able to avoid Gisselle. We ended up walking toward the Clairborne mansion. Beau thought it was an impressive old house, especially because of how it was set back, with woods between the house and the school.

It was getting late, so we started back toward the dorm and his car, but on the way, we spotted a path that went deeper into the woods, and Beau thought we should explore and see where it would take us. I was reluctant at first, still having this sense of being watched. I even looked behind and around us, studying the pockets of shadows created by the late-afternoon sun, but I saw no one nor heard anyone. So I let him pull me along. We went farther and farther into the small wooded area until we heard the distinct sound of water rushing over rocks. When we came around a turn, there it was: a small but vigorous little stream that had created a waterfall.

"It's very pretty here," Beau said. "You've never been here before?"

"No, and no one's mentioned it."

"Let's sit awhile. I'm in no rush to go back to

New Orleans anyway," he said. I didn't like the way he said it.

"Your parents know you've come up here to see me, don't they, Beau?"

"Sorta," he said, smiling.

"What's that mean, 'sorta'?"

"I said I was going for a ride," he replied with a shrug.

"Just a ride? But you drove all the way to Baton Rouge!"

"It's a ride, isn't it?" he said, laughing.

"Oh Beau, you're going to get into trouble with them again, aren't you?"

"It's worth it to see you, Ruby." He stepped up to me to put his hands on my shoulders and bring his lips to mine. Here in the solitude of the woods, he felt free to be more affectionate. I couldn't help but be nervous, however. We were still on Greenwood grounds, and in my dark imagination, I envisioned the Iron Lady hovering behind a tree with a pair of binoculars. Beau sensed my agitation and felt the tension in my body.

"What's wrong? I thought you would be more anxious to see me," he said, with obvious disappointment.

"It's not you, Beau. It's me. I'm not comfortable here, even though you're beside me. I still feel . . . as my grandpere Jack used to say, like I've stepped on the back of a sleeping alligator."

Beau laughed. "There's no one here but us and the birds," he said, kissing me again. "No alligators." He kissed my neck. "Let's put down our

461

blanket and rest awhile," he coaxed.

I let him take the blanket out from under my arm and watched him spread it over a patch of grass. He sprawled out and beckoned to me. I looked around again, and when I hesitated, he reached up to take my hand and pull me down to him.

In his arms I did forget where I was for the moment. Our kisses were long and passionate. He moved his hands smoothly up my arms and over my breasts. Soon the rush of my own blood competed with the rush of the water over the rocks, the sounds from within me becoming as loud as the sounds without. I felt swept away by Beau's caresses, each kiss, each touch moving the dark sadness off my brow and chasing the gloom from my heart, until I was kissing him as hard and as passionately as he was kissing me. I felt his hands under my blouse, my garments moving away so that we would be closer, skin touching skin, heartbeat to heartbeat. I opened myself to him eagerly and he was there, touching me, holding me, chanting his love and his promises. From somewhere in the forest, I heard the sound of a woodpecker. His tap, tap, tap grew faster and louder, until it sounded as if he was tearing down the whole forest. The water rushed on beside us. My moans grew stronger and more frequent, until we both came crushing down on each other's hunger, satisfying one another with the surrender of our very being.

When it was over, I felt tears streaming down my cheeks. My heart was thumping so hard I thought I would faint. Beau was on his back, gasping with surprise.

"And I thought football was strenuous," he joked. Then he grew serious and gazed down into my eyes. "Are you all right?"

"Yes," I said, catching my breath, "but maybe we love each other too much for our bodies to bear."

He laughed. "I can't think of anyone whose arms I would rather die in," he replied, which brought a smile to my face.

We straightened up our clothing, brushed each other off, and started back through the woods. I had to admit I was feeling lighter and happier than I thought possible these past two weeks.

"I'm so glad you came up to see me, Beau. I hope you don't get into too much trouble."

"It was worth it," he said.

We said goodbye at his car, with some of the girls in the dorm watching us from the front window.

"I can't believe Gisselle hasn't planted herself in my face at least once today," Beau said.

"I know. But whatever she's up to, it's something nasty for someone, I'm sure." Beau laughed at my words. We kissed goodbye quickly, and then I stood there watching him drive off. I didn't turn to go into the dorm until his car was completely gone from sight. Then I bowed my head and strolled into the dorm.

"You'd better get a move on," Sarah Peters warned me after I entered the building.

"Why?"

"We just heard: Our dorm's been chosen for an unannounced inspection. The Iron Lady could be here any moment," she explained.

"Inspection? Inspection of what?"

"Anything. Our rooms, our bathrooms, anything. She doesn't need a warrant, you know."

When I arrived at the quad, I found all the girls in a frenzy, even Gisselle. They were cleaning and straightening up. Everyone's room looked well organized and neat. Samantha had done a pretty good job on ours.

"We'll be hit first," Vicki informed me. "She goes in alphabetical order."

"How was your visit with Beau?" Gisselle asked from her doorway.

I glared at her, the anger I felt still quite strong.

"Why, weren't you spying on us?" I asked. She laughed — but nervously, I thought.

"I had much better things to do," she replied, then retreated to her room quickly.

About half an hour later, Mrs. Ironwood did arrive, escorted by Mrs. Penny and Deborah Peck, who carried a clipboard and took down whatever notes and demerits Mrs. Ironwood imposed. The inspection began in Jacki and Kate's room and then went to Gisselle's. I expected to hear complaints, but Mrs. Ironwood emerged with a look of satisfaction on her face. She stepped into my doorway and gazed around the room.

"Good afternoon, girls," she said to Samantha and me. Samantha looked terrified, and she uttered a reply that was barely audible. Mrs. Ironwood went to one of the dressers and ran her fingers over the top. She looked at her fingers.

"Very nice," she said. "I'm glad you keep your rooms clean and consider them your home." She opened the closet door and peered in at our clothing, nodded, and then looked at my dresser. She stepped up to it and pulled open the top drawer, gazing in and nodding. "Well organized," she said. Samantha smiled at me. Then Mrs. Ironwood reached down and pulled open the third drawer. She stood there staring down for a moment and then turned to me.

"This is your dresser?"

"Yes," I said. She nodded, turned back to the drawer, reached in, and pulled out a pint bottle of rum. "Couldn't you hide this a little better?" she asked sarcastically.

My mouth dropped. I looked at Mrs. Penny, who gaped at me with surprise and disappointment. Deborah Peck had a faint smile on her lips.

"That's not mine."

"You just said this was your dresser. Other people put their things in your dresser?"

"No, but . . ."

"Then this is yours," she said. She handed it to Mrs. Penny. "Dispose of this," she ordered. To Deborah she said, "Ten demerits." She glared at me. "Your punishment will be decided, and you will be told before the end of the day. Until then, you are confined to this room."

She turned and marched out. Mrs. Penny held the bottle in her hand as gingerly as she could, treating it like poison. She shook her head at me.

"I'm so ashamed of you, Ruby."

"It's not mine, Mrs. Penny."

"So ashamed," she repeated, then followed Mrs. Ironwood and Deborah out. As soon as they were gone, all the girls from the quad rushed to our door.

"What did she find?" Jacki asked.

"I'm sure you all know," I said dryly.

"Know what?" Gisselle asked, coming from behind.

"About the rum you put in my drawer."

"See? There she goes again. My fault. I'm not the only one here, Ruby. And other girls from other quads could have gotten into your room. You're not the most popular girl on campus. Maybe someone's jealous of you."

"Someone?" I said, smiling.

"Or maybe," she said, her hands on her hips, "that was your bottle."

I laughed and shook my head.

"I wonder what she'll do to you," Samantha said.

"It doesn't matter. I don't care," I told her, and I meant it. I didn't.

Just before dinner Mrs. Penny arrived to inform me that I was to spend the evening scrubbing all the bathrooms at the school. The head custodian would be waiting with soap and water and a brush. I was to do it every Saturday night after dinner for a month.

I accepted my punishment with a quiet resignation that annoyed Gisselle and both surprised and impressed the other girls. They never heard a complaint from me, even when it meant I wouldn't be able to attend movies or go to a dance. I knew the head custodian, Mr. Hull, felt sorry for me, and he even began to do some of my work and have some of it completed before I arrived.

"These bathrooms never looked so good come Monday morning," he told me.

He was right. Once I realized I couldn't get out of the penalty without causing even more of a problem, I decided to attack it with enthusiasm. It made it bearable. I took out stains that were seemingly embedded, and I got the mirrors so shiny that there wasn't the smallest smudge on the glass. On my third Saturday, however, I found that someone had stuffed the toilets in one of the bathrooms and flushed and flushed so the water would run over the floors. It was a disgusting mess and Mr. Hull came in to assist me, mopping up first. Even so, the stench got to me, and I had to get some fresh air to stop from throwing up my supper.

Two days later, I woke up very nauseous and had to run into the bathroom to throw up. I thought I had a terrible stomach virus or had been poisoned by the cleaning fluids I had to dip my hands into to clean the bathrooms properly. When the nausea came over me again that afternoon, I asked to be excused from class and went to the school infirmary.

Mrs. Miller, our school nurse, sat me down and asked me to describe all my symptoms. She looked very concerned.

"I've been more tired than usual," I admitted when she inquired about my energy.

"Have you noticed yourself going to the bathroom more frequently to urinate?"

I thought a moment. "Yes," I said. "I have."

She nodded. "What else?"

"I get dizzy once in a while. I'll just be walking along and things start to spin on me."

"I see. I assume you keep track of your period," she said, "and at least have an approximate idea of when it should arrive."

My heart stopped.

"You've missed one?" she asked quickly when she saw the look on my face.

"Yes, but . . . that's happened to me occasionally before."

"Have you looked at yourself in the mirror lately and noticed any changes in your body, especially your breasts?" she asked.

I had noticed tiny new blood vessels, but I told her I thought that was because I was still developing. She shook her head.

"You're about as developed as you're going to be," she said. "I'm afraid it sounds like you're pregnant, Ruby," she declared. "Only you know if that's a possibility. Is it?"

I felt as if she had dowsed me with a pail of ice water. For a moment my whole body became numb, and the muscles in my face wouldn't work.

I couldn't reply. I didn't think my heart was even beating. It was as if I had turned to stone right before her eyes. "Ruby?" she asked again.

And I just started to cry.

"Oh dear," she said. "You poor dear."

She put her arm around me and led me to one of the cots. She told me to lie down and rest. I remember that as I lay there burying myself with a mountain of self-pity, hating Fate, cursing Destiny, I wondered why love was made to be so wonderful if it could put me in such a state of affairs. It seemed like a cruel joke had been played on me, but of course, I had no one to blame but myself. I didn't even blame Beau, knowing somehow that I had had the power to say no, to turn him away, but had chosen not to do so.

A little while later, after my crying had subsided, Mrs. Miller pulled up a chair beside me and sat down.

"We'll have to inform your family," she said. "This is a very personal problem, and you and your family will have to make some important decisions."

"Please," I said, seizing her hand, "don't tell anyone."

"I won't tell anyone but your family and, of course, Mrs. Ironwood."

"No, please. I don't want anyone to know just yet."

"I can't do that. It's too much of a responsibility, dear. Surely after the initial shock, your family will give you support, and you and your family will make the right decisions."

"Decisions?" There seemed to be only one decision — suicide, or at least running away.

"Whether to have the baby, to have an abortion, to inform the father . . . decisions. So you see, there's too much responsibility for us to keep it a secret. Others have to know. If we didn't tell them, we would be remiss. I would be irresponsible and certainly held to account. The least that would happen is I would be fired."

"Oh, I don't want that, Mrs. Miller. I'm already responsible for one person losing her job here. I don't want another person on my conscience. Of course, do what you have to do and don't worry about me," I said.

"Now, now, dear. We'll still worry about you. Other girls have been in this predicament, you know. It's not the end of the world, although it might seem so to you right now." She smiled. "You'll be all right," she promised, patting my hand. "Just rest. I'll do what has to be done and do it discreetly."

She left and I lay there, hoping the ceiling would fall in on me and cursing the day I had decided to leave the bayou.

Nearly an hour later, Mrs. Ironwood arrived with Mrs. Miller to inform me that Daphne was sending the limousine for me. I could see the glint of self-satisfaction in her eyes as she spoke.

"Get yourself together and go back to the dorm. Pack your things, all your things. You won't be coming back to Greenwood," she commanded.

"At least there's one good thing to come of this," I said.

She turned bright crimson and hoisted her shoulders. "I'm not surprised. It was only a matter of time before you destroyed yourself. Your sort always does," she snapped, then left before I could reply.

I didn't care anymore anyway. Ironically, Gisselle had been right: Greenwood was a horrible place as long as that woman ran and administered it. I left the building and returned to the dorm to complete my packing. I had most of it done by midday, when Gisselle came running over during the lunch hour. She burst into the quad screaming my name. When she saw my suitcases packed, my closet and dresser drawers emptied, her mouth dropped.

"What's going on?" she demanded, and I told her. For once, she was speechless. She sat on my bed.

"What are you going to do?"

"What can I do? I'm going home. The limousine should be here shortly."

"But that's not fair. I'll be left here all alone."

"All alone? You have the other girls, and you never wanted to do things with me anyway, Gisselle. We're sisters, but up here we were strangers most of the time."

"I'm not staying here. I won't," she insisted.

"That's between you and Daphne," I said.

She went fuming out of my room to make her phone call, but she didn't return to pack her things, so I imagined Daphne had denied her request. At least for now.

Half an hour later Mrs. Penny, her face sallow, came to inform me that the limousine had arrived. She was sincerely sad for me, and she helped me carry some of my things out to the car.

"I'm very disappointed in you," she said. "And so is Mrs. Ironwood."

"Mrs. Ironwood is not disappointed, Mrs. Penny. You work for an ogre. Someday you'll admit that to yourself and then you'll leave too."

"Leave?" She looked like she would laugh. "But where would I go?"

"Anyplace where people aren't hypocritical and mean to each other, where you're not judged on the basis of your bank account, where nice and talented people like Miss Stevens aren't persecuted for being honest and caring."

She stared at me a moment, and then with her face as serious as I had ever seen it, she said, "There isn't any such place, but if you find it, send me a postcard and tell me how to get there."

She left me and walked back to the dorm to return to her duties as the surrogate mother for all of these girls. I got into the limousine and we drove away.

And I never looked back.

Edgar came out and helped the driver carry all my things up to my room when I arrived. He informed me that Daphne wasn't home.

"But madame asked that you remain in the house and speak to no one until she returns," he said. I wondered if he knew why I had come back. He knew it was something terrible, but he didn't reveal whether he knew any details. Nina was another story. She took one look at me when I entered the kitchen to greet her and said, "You be with child, girl."

"Daphne told you."

"She be ranting and raving so loud, even the dead in ovens over at St. Louis Cemetery musta heard her. Then she come in here and told me herself."

"It's my fault, Nina."

"It takes two to make baby magic," she said. "It ain't be your only fault."

"Oh Nina, what am I going to do? I not only make mistakes that ruin my own life, I make the kind that ruin other people's lives too."

"Someone powerful put a fix on you. None of Nina's good gris-gris stop it," she said thoughtfully. "You best go to church and ask St. Michael for help. He be the one who help you conquer your enemies," she advised.

We heard the front door open and close and then the sound of Daphne's heels clicking down the corridor sharply. This was followed by Edgar's arrival.

"Madame Dumas is here, mademoiselle. She wants to see you in the office," he told me.

"I'd rather see the devil," I muttered.

Nina's eyes widened with fear.

"You say that no more, hear? Papa La Bas, he got big ears."

I went to the office. Daphne was behind the desk on the telephone. She raised her eyebrows when I appeared and nodded toward the chair in front of the desk while she kept talking.

"She's home now, John. I can send her up immediately. I am relying on your discretion. Of course. I appreciate that. Thank you."

She cradled the phone slowly and sat back. To my surprise, she shook her head slowly and smiled.

"I must be honest," she began. "I always expected I would be sitting here confronting Gisselle in this situation, not you. Despite your background, you gave both me and your father the impression that you were the more sensible one, wiser, certainly more intelligent.

"But," she continued, "as you now know, being more book smart doesn't make you a better person, does it?"

I tried to swallow but couldn't.

"How ironic. I, who had every right to bear a child, who could provide the best for him or her, was unable to conceive, and you, like some rabbit, just go and make a baby with your boyfriend as nonchalantly as you would eat a meal or take a walk. You're always talking about how unfair this is and unfair that is. Well, how do you like the hand I've been dealt? And then, like salt on a wound, I have to have you enter this house, become part of this family, and confront you with child when you have no right to be pregnant."

"I didn't mean it to happen," I said.

She threw her head back and laughed.

"How many times since Eve conceived Cain and Abel have women uttered that stupid sentence?" Her eyes became dark slits. "What did you think would happen? You thought you could be as hot as a goat or a monkey and make your boyfriend that hot and not ever pay the consequences? Did you think you were me?"

"No, but . . ."

"Forget the buts," she said. "The damage, as they say, has been done. And now, like always, it's left to me to right the wrong, correct and fix things. It was the same when your father was alive, believe me.

"The limousine is outside," she continued. "The driver has his instructions. You don't need anything. Just go out and get into the car," she commanded.

"Where am I going?"

She stared a moment.

"A friend of mine who's a doctor is at a clinic outside the city. He's expecting you. He will perform an abortion and, barring any unforeseen complications, send you directly home. You'll spend a few days recuperating upstairs and then you'll return to public school here. I've already begun to concoct a cover story. The death of your father has left you so depressed you can't continue away from home. Lately you've been walking around here with a long face all the time. People will accept it."

"But . . ."

"I told you — there are no buts. Now don't keep the doctor waiting. He's doing me a very delicate favor."

I stood up.

"One other thing," she added. "Don't bother to call Beau Andreas. I've just come from his home. His parents are about as upset with him as I am with you and have decided to send him away for the remainder of the school year."

"Away? Where?"

"Far away," she said. "To live with relatives and go to school in France."

"France!"

"That's correct. I think he's grateful that's the only punishment he's to endure. If he should ever speak to you or write to you and his parents find out, he will be disinherited. So if you want to destroy him too, try to contact him.

"Now go," she added with a tired voice. "This is the first and the last time I will cover up your faux pas. From here on in, you alone will suffer for whatever indiscretions you commit. Go!" she ordered, pointing her arm toward the door, her long forefinger jabbing the air. It felt as if she had jabbed it into my heart.

I turned and walked out. Without pausing, I left the house and got into the limousine. I never felt more confused or more lost. Events seemed to be carrying me along on their own. I was like someone who had lost all choice. It was as if a strong current had come streaming down the bayou canal, whisking me away in my pirogue, and no matter how I tried to pole myself in another direction, I couldn't. I could only sit back and let the water carry me to the predetermined end.

I closed my eyes and didn't open them again until the driver said, "We're here, mademoiselle."

We must have driven for at least half an hour or so and now we were in some small town in which all the stores were closed. Knowing Daphne, I had expected to be brought to an expensive-looking modern hospital, but the limousine pulled up behind a dark, dilapidated building. It didn't look like a clinic, or even a doctor's office.

"Are we at the right place?" I asked.

"It's where I was told to bring you," the driver said. He got out and opened the rear door. I stepped out slowly. The back door of the building squeaked open and a heavy woman with hair the color and texture of a kitchen scrubpad looked out.

"This way," she commanded. "Quickly."

As I drew closer, I saw she wore a nurse's uniform. She had roller-pin forearms and very wide hips that made it look like her upper body had been added as an afterthought. There was a mole on her chin with some hairs curling up around it. Her thick lips tightened with impatience.

"Hurry up," she snapped.

"Where am I?" I asked.

"Where do you think you are?" she replied, stepping back for me to enter. I did so cautiously.

The rear entryway opened to a long, dimly lit corridor with walls of faded yellow. The floor looked scuffed and dirty.

"This is a . . . clinic?" I asked.

"It's the doctor's office," she said. "Go in the first door on the right. The doctor will be right with you."

She marched ahead of me and disappeared into another room on the left. I opened the door of the first room on the right and saw an examination table with stirrups. There was a sheet of tissue paper over the table. On the right was a metal table, and on that was a tray of instruments. There was a sink against the far wall with what looked like previously used instruments soaking in a pan of water. The walls of the room were the same dull yellow as the corridor walls. There were no pictures, no plaques, not even a window. But there was another door, which opened, and a tall, thin man with bushy eyebrows and thin coal-black hair flattened over the top of his head and cut short at the sides stepped in. He wore a light blue surgical gown.

He looked at me and nodded, but he didn't say hello. Instead he walked to the sink and began to scrub his hands.

"Just sit up on the table," he ordered with his back to me. The heavy woman came in and began to organize the surgical tools. The doctor turned around to look at me. He raised his eyebrows inquisitively.

"The table," he said again, nodding at it.

"I thought . . . I would be brought to a hospital," I said.

"Hospital?" He looked at the nurse, who shook her head without speaking. She didn't look up, nor did she look at me. "This is your first time, right?" he asked.

"Yes," I said, my voice cracking. My heart was pounding, and I felt the beads of sweat forming on my neck and brow.

"Well, it won't take long," he said. His nurse picked up an instrument that looked like Grandpere Jack's hand drill. I felt my stomach do a flip-flop.

"This is a mistake," I said. "I'm supposed to go to a clinic."

I backed away, shaking my head. Neither the doctor nor the nurse had even introduced themselves.

"This can't be right," I said.

"Now look here, young lady. I'm doing your mother a favor. I left my house, rushed my dinner to come down here. There's no time for foolishness."

"Foolishness is what got you here," the heavy woman said, scowling. "You play, you pay," she added. "Get on the table."

I shook my head.

"No. This isn't right. No," I said again. I backed myself to the door and found the knob. "No."

"I have no time for this," the doctor warned.

"I don't care. This isn't right." I turned around to pull open the door. In an instant I was down the dingy corridor and out the rear entrance. My driver was still sitting in the car behind the wheel, his cap over his eyes, his head back, sleeping. I rapped on the window and he jumped.

"Take me home!" I screamed.

He got out quickly and opened the rear door.

"Madame told me it would be awhile," he said, confused.

"Just drive," I screamed. He shrugged but got back into the car and pulled away. Moments later we were back on the highway. I looked back at the dark, murky town. It was as if I had gone in and out of a nightmare.

But when I turned and looked ahead, the reality of what awaited me hit me like a gust of hurricane wind. Daphne would be furious; she would make my life even more miserable. We approached a fork in the road. The arrow on the sign pointed left to indicate the direction of New Orleans, but it also had an arrow pointing right, toward Houma.

"Stop!" I ordered.

"What?" The driver pressed his foot down on the brake and turned around. "What now, mademoiselle?" he asked.

I hesitated. My whole life seemed to flash by me: Grandmere Catherine waiting for me when I returned from school, running up to her with my pigtails flying, embracing her and trying to tell her as fast as I could about all the things that I had learned and done at school. Paul in a pirogue coming out from a bend and waving to me, and me rushing down to the shore to join him, a picnic lunch under my arms. Grandmere Catherine's last words, my promises, walking off to get on the bus to New Orleans. Arriving at the mansion in the Garden District. Daddy's soft, loving eyes, the excitement in his face when he realized who I was . . . All of it rushed by in moments.

I opened the car door.

"Mademoiselle?"

"Just go back to New Orleans, Charles," I told him.

"What?" he said in disbelief.

"Tell Madame Dumas . . . tell her she is finally rid of me," I said, and started walking toward Houma.

Charles waited, confused. But when I disappeared in the darkness, he pulled away and the sleek limousine went on without me, its rear lights growing smaller and smaller until it was completely gone, and I was alone on the highway.

A year before I had left Houma thinking I was going home.

The truth was that right now I was returning to the only home I had ever known.

18

Why Me?

The tears streamed down my face faster and harder as I continued walking through the darkness. Cars and trucks rushed by me, some honking their horns, but I walked on and on until I came to a gas station. It was closed, but there was a telephone booth beside it. I dialed Beau's number and prayed with all my heart that Beau had talked his family into permitting him to stay in New Orleans. As the phone rang, I wiped the tears from my cheeks and caught my breath. Garton, the Andreas family butler, answered.

"May I speak with Beau, please, Garton?" I said quickly.

"I'm sorry, mademoiselle, but Monsieur Beau is not here," he said.

"Do you know where he is or when he will return?" I asked with desperation in my voice.

"He's on his way to the airport, mademoiselle."

"Tonight? He's going away tonight?"

"*Oui*, mademoiselle. I am sorry. Is there a message, mademoiselle?"

"No," I said weakly. "No message. *Merci beaucoup*, Garton."

I cradled the receiver slowly and let my head fall against the phone. Beau was leaving before we had even had a chance to say goodbye. Why didn't he just run away and come to me? I asked myself but then realized how unreasonable and foolish such an act would have been. What good would it have done for him to give up his family and his future?

I sighed deeply and sat back. The dark clouds that had covered the moon slipped off and the pale white light illuminated the road, making it look like a trail of bones that led into yet deeper darkness. I had made a decision back there, I thought. There was nothing to do now but carry it out. I started to walk again.

The sound of a truck horn blaring behind me spun me around just as the driver of a tractor-trailer slowed it down to a stop. He leaned out the passenger-side window and gazed down at me.

"What in all tarnation are you doin' walking along this highway in the dead of night?" he demanded. "Don't you know how dangerous that is?"

"I'm going home," I said.

"And where's that?"

"Houma."

He roared. "You're planning on walking to Houma?"

"Yes sir," I said in a sorrowful voice. The realization of just how many miles I had to go set in when he laughed at me.

"Well, you're in luck. I'm passing through Houma," he said, and swung the door open. "Git yourself up and in here. Come on," he added, when I hesitated, " 'fore I change my mind."

I stepped up and into the truck and closed the door. "Now how is it a girl your age is walkin' all by herself on this highway?" he asked, without taking his eyes off the road. He looked like a man in his fifties and had some gray hair mixed in with his dark brown.

"I just decided to go home," I said.

He turned and looked at me, then nodded with understanding. "I got a daughter about your age. She run off once. Got about five miles away before she realized people want money for food and lodging, and strangers don't usually give a tinker's damn about you. She high-tailed it back as fast as she could when a skunk of a man made her a nasty offer. Git my meaning?"

"Yes sir."

"Same could have happened to you tonight, walking this lonely road all by yerself. Your parents are probably out of their mind with worry too. Now don't you feel foolish?"

"Yes sir, I do."

"Good. Well, fortunately, no harm come of it, but before you go runnin' off to what you think are greener pastures next time, you better sit yourself down and count the blessings you have," he advised.

I smiled. "I certainly will do that," I said.

"Well, no harm done," he said. "Truth is, when I was about your age . . . no," he added, looking at me again, "I guess younger . . . I done run off myself." He laughed at the memory and then began to tell me his story. I realized that driving a truck for long distances was a lonely life, and this kind man had picked me up for the company as much as to do a good deed.

By the time we'd pulled into Houma, I had learned how he and his family had left Texas, where he had gone to school, why he'd married his childhood sweetheart, how he'd built his own home, and how he'd become a truck driver. He wasn't aware of how much he had been talking until he brought the truck to a stop.

"Tarnation! We're here already and I didn't even ask you your name, did I?"

"It's Ruby," I said. And then, as if to symbolically emphasize my return, I added, "Ruby Landry," for I was a Landry again as far as the people of Houma were concerned. "Thank you," I said.

"All right. You think twice 'fore you go running off to be a big-city girl, hear?"

"I will." I got out of the truck. After I had watched him pull away and disappear around a turn, I started to walk home. As I ambled down the familiar streets, I recalled the many times Grandmere Catherine and I came into town together or went visiting one of her friends together. I recalled the times she took me with her on one of her *traiteur* missions, and I remembered how much the people loved and respected her. Suddenly the thought of returning to that toothpick-legged shack of ours without her being there seemed terrifying, and then there was the prospect of confronting Grandpere Jack. Paul had told me so many sad stories about him.

I paused at another pay phone and dug some more change out of my purse, this time to call Paul. His sister Jeanne answered.

"Ruby?" she said. "My gosh! It's been so long since I've spoken to you. Are you calling from New Orleans?"

"No," I said.

"Where are you?"

"I'm . . . here," I said.

"Here? Oh, that's wonderful. Paul!" she screamed. "Come to the phone. It's Ruby, and she's here!"

A moment later I heard his warm and loving voice, a voice that I needed so desperately to give me comfort and hope.

"Ruby? You're here?"

"Yes, Paul. I've come home. It's too long a story to tell you on the phone, but I wanted you to know."

"You're returning to the shack?" he asked incredulously.

"Yes." I explained where I was and he told me not to take another step.

"I'll be there before you can blink your eyes," he promised. It did seem like only a few minutes later that he pulled up in his car and hopped out excitedly. We embraced each other, me holding onto him as tightly as he held onto me.

"Something terrible has happened, hasn't it? What has Daphne done now? Or is it Gisselle? What could either of them do that would send you back here?" he asked, then noticed I had no luggage. "What did you do, run off?"

"Yes, Paul," I said, bursting into tears. He got me into his car and held me until I could speak. It must have sounded like crazy babble to him, for I burst forth with the whole story, inserting almost everything and anything that had been done to me, including Gisselle's planting a bottle of rum in my dorm room. But when I described my pregnancy and the butcher doctor in the dirty office, Paul's face turned pale white and then flashed red with anger.

"She would do that to you? You were right to run away. I'm glad you've returned."

"I don't know what I'm going to do yet," I said, wiping away my tears and taking a deep breath. "I just want to go back to the shack for now."

"Your grandpere . . ."

"What about him?"

"He's been on a real tear lately. Yesterday when I drove by, he was digging up the front and shouting into the wind, his arms waving. My father says he's run out of money for rotgut whiskey and he's got the DTs. He thinks it's almost the end for him. Most everyone is surprised he's gone on this long, Ruby. I don't know as I should take you back there."

"I've got to go back there, Paul. It's my only

home now," I said, determined.

"I know, but . . . you're going to find it a terrible mess, I'm sure. It'll break your heart. My father says your grandmere must be spinning in her grave something terrible."

"Take me home, Paul. Please," I begged.

He nodded. "Okay, for now," he said. "But I'm going to look after you, Ruby. I swear I will."

"I know you will, Paul, but I don't want to be a burden to you, to anyone. I'll get back to doing the work Grandmere Catherine and I did, so I can keep myself."

"Nonsense," he said. He started the engine. "I got way more than I'm ever going to need. I told you, I'm a manager now. I've already approved the plans for my own home. Ruby . . ."

"Don't talk about the future, Paul. Please. I don't believe in the future anymore."

"All right," he said "But you're going to be fine as long as I'm around. That's a promise you can take to the bank," he bragged.

I smiled. He did look much older. He had always been more mature and responsible than other boys his age, and his father had not hesitated to give him important work.

"Thank you, Paul."

I don't think there was a way I could have prepared myself for what the shack and the grounds around it would look like when I set eyes on it again. I was lucky I was arriving at night when so much of it wasn't visible, but I saw the deep holes dug in the front, and when I set eyes on the galerie and saw the way it leaned, the railings cracked and broken, the floorboards torn up in places, my heart sank. One of the front windows was broken wide open. Grandmere Catherine would have been in tears.

"You sure you want to go in there?" Paul asked when we came to a stop.

"Yes, Paul. I'm sure. No matter what it looks like now. It was once my home and my grand-mere's home."

"Okay. I'll go in with you and see what he's up to. He might not even remember you, the way he is," Paul declared.

"Careful," Paul said when we stepped up to the galerie. The boards complained loudly; the front door squeaked on its rusted hinges and threatened to fall right off when we opened it, and the house itself smelled like every swamp creature had made some part of it its home.

There was only a single lantern lit on the old kitchen table. Its tiny flame flickered precariously as the breeze flowed unabated through the shack from the opened rear windows.

"All the bugs in the bayou have come in here, I'm sure," Paul said.

The kitchen was a filthy mess. There were empty whiskey bottles on the floor, under the tables and chairs, and on the counters. The sink was filled with dishes caked with old food and the floor had food drippings decomposing on it, some of it looking like it had been there for weeks, if not months. I took the lantern and walked through the downstairs.

The living room was in no better condition. The table was turned over, as well as the chair in which Grandmere used to sit and fall asleep every night. There were empty bottles in here too. The floor was plastered with mud, grime, and swamp grass. We heard something scurry along the wall.

"Probably rats," Paul said. "Or at least field mice. Maybe even a raccoon."

"Grandpere!" I cried.

We went to the rear and searched and then walked up the stairs. I think the effort it took for Grandpere to climb those steps saved the upper part of the house from the same abuse and deterioration the downstairs suffered. The loom room was not very changed, nor was my old bedroom and Grandmere Catherine's, save everything that could have been opened and searched had been. Grandpere had even pulled off some wallboards.

"Where could he be?" I wondered.

Paul shrugged. "Down at one of the zydeco bars, begging for a drink maybe," he said, but when we descended the stairs again, we heard Grandpere Jack's shrill screams coming from the rear of the house. We hurried around back and saw him, naked but caked with mud, swinging a burlap sack over his head and yelping like a hound dog after game.

"Stay back," Paul advised. "Jack," he called. "Jack Landry!"

Grandpere stopped swinging the sack and stared

through the darkness. "Who's there? Robbers, thieves, git on wit' ya!"

"No thieves. It's Paul Tate."

"Tate? You stay away, hear? I ain't giving you nothin' back. Stay away. This is my fortune. I earned it. I found it. I dug and dug until I found it, hear? Back, back or I'll heave a rock at yer. Back!" he screamed again, but he backed up himself.

"Grandpere!" I cried. "It's me, Ruby. I've come home."

"Who? Who's that?"

"It's Ruby," I said, stepping forward.

"Ruby? No. I ain't takin' the blame for that. No. We needed the money. Don't blame me. Don't go blaming me. Catherine, don't you blame me!" he screamed. Then, clutching his burlap sack to his chest, he went running toward the canal.

"Grandpere!"

"Let him go, Ruby. He's gone mad from the rotgut whiskey."

We heard him scream again, and then we heard the splash of water.

"Paul, he'll drown."

Paul thought a moment. "Give me the lantern," he said, then went after Grandpere. I heard more splashing, more screaming.

"Jack!" Paul cried.

"No, it's mine! Mine!" Grandpere replied. There was more splashing, and then it grew quiet.

"Paul?" I waited and then charged through the darkness, my feet sinking into the soft swamp grass. I ran toward the light and found Paul gazing over the water.

"Where is he?" I asked in a loud whisper.

"I don't know, I . . ." He squinted and then he pointed.

"Grandpere!" I screamed.

Grandpere Jack's body looked like a thick log floating along. It bounced against some rocks and then got caught in the current and continued on until it became entangled in some brush that stuck up out of the water.

"We'd better get some help," Paul suggested. "Come on."

Less than an hour later, the firemen hoisted Grandpere Jack's body out of the water. He was still clutching his burlap sack, only instead of buried treasure, it was filled with rusted old tin cans.

How could I have a more horrible homecoming? Despite the terrible things Grandpere Jack had done and the pathetic creature he had become, I couldn't help but remember him when I was a little girl. He had his soft moments. I would go out to his swamp shack and he would talk about the bayou as if it were his dearest friend. At one time he was a legend. There wasn't a better trapper. He knew how to read the swamp, knew when the waters would be rising and falling, knew when the bream would be running, and knew where the 'gators slept and the snakes curled.

He liked to talk about his ancestors then, about the scoundrels who raised hell on the Mississippi, the famous gamblers and flatboat polers. Grand-mere Catherine said he spun most of it out of his own imagination, but it didn't matter to me whether it was wholly true or not. I just liked the way he told his tales, staring out at the Spanish moss and puffing on his corncob pipe as he rattled on and on, pausing only occasionally in those days to take a swig from his jug. He always had an excuse for it. He had to clear his throat of the grime that floats through the air in the swamp or he had to chase a cold away. Sometimes he just had to keep his gizzards warm.

Despite the break between Grandmere Cather-ine and Grandpere Jack after he had contracted to sell Gisselle to the Dumas family, I sensed that once, a long time ago, they were true sweethearts. Even Grandmere, during one of her calmer mo-ments, would admit that he had been a strikingly handsome, virile young man, dazzling her with his emerald-green eyes and his sun-darkened skin. He was quite a dancer too, who could cut up the floor better than anyone at a fais dodo.

But time has a way of drawing the poisons in us to the surface. The evil that nestled under Grandpere Jack's heart seeped out and changed him — or, as Grandmere was fond of saying, "turned him into what he was: a no-account rogue who belongs with the things that slither and crawl."

Perhaps he had turned to his rotgut whiskey as a way of denying what he was or what he saw reflecting back at him when he leaned over his pirogue and gazed into the water. Whatever it was, the demons inside him got their way, and finally they dragged him down into the waters he had once loved and cherished and even worshiped. The bayou out of which he'd made his life had claimed his life.

I cried for the man he was when Grandmere Catherine first fell in love with him, just as I imagined she had cried for him when he had stopped being that man.

Despite Paul's pleading, I insisted on staying in the shack. If I didn't force myself to do it the first night, I would find reason not to the next and the next after that, I thought. I made my old bed as comfortable as I could and, after everyone had gone and I had said good night to Paul and promised to be waiting for him in the morning, I went to sleep and passed out quickly from total exhaustion.

It didn't take an hour or so after sunrise for all of Grandmere Catherine's old friends to learn of my return. They thought I had come back intending to look after Grandpere Jack. I rose early and began to clean the shack, working on the kitchen first. There was little to eat, but before an hour had passed, Grandmere's old friends began arriving, each bringing me something. Everyone was shocked at the condition of the shack, of course. None had been inside since Grandmere's death and my departure. Cajun women throw themselves at someone else's chores as if they are all of one family when that person is in need. By the time I turned around, they were all scrubbing down the floors and walls, shaking out the rugs, dusting the furniture, washing windows. It brought tears of joy to my eyes. No one had cross-examined me as to where I had been and what I had been doing, I was back, I needed their help, and that was all that mattered. Finally, I felt I really had come home.

Paul came by with armloads of things his parents had sent over and things he knew I would need. He went around the shack with a hammer and nails and tacked down as many loose boards as he could find. Then he took a shovel and began to fill in the dozens and dozens of holes Grandpere had dug, searching for the treasure he imagined Grandmere Catherine had buried. I saw how the women watched him work and whispered to themselves, smiling and glancing my way. If they only knew the truth, I thought, if they only knew. But there were still secrets to be kept locked up in our own hearts; there were still people we loved and had to protect.

Grandpere Jack's funeral was a quick and simple one. Father Rush advised me to have it conducted as soon as possible.

"You don't want to attract Jack Landry's sort to your home, Ruby. You know that kind only looks for an excuse to imbibe and cause a ruckus. Best leave him at peace and pray for him on your own."

"Will you say a mass for him, Father?" I asked.

"That we will. The good Lord has compassion

495

enough to forgive even a man as lowdown as Jack Landry, and it is not for us to judge anyway," he said.

After the burial, Grandmere Catherine's friends returned to the house and only then began to ask some questions about my whereabouts since Grandmere Catherine's passing. I told them I had been with relatives in New Orleans but that I'd missed the bayou. It wasn't untrue, and it was enough to satisfy their curiosity.

Paul went about the grounds and the shack, continuing to do handyman's work, while the women sat and talked into the evening hours. He lingered until they all bid me good night, all still smiling and chattering about him.

"You know what they think," he said when we were finally alone. "That you returned to be with me."

"I know."

"What are you going to do when you start to show?"

"I don't know yet," I said.

"The easiest thing to do is marry me," he said firmly, his blue eyes full of hope.

"Oh Paul, you know why that can never be."

"Why not? The only thing we can't do is have children of our own, but we don't have to now. You've got our baby in your oven," he said.

"Paul, it wouldn't be right to even think of such a thing. And your father . . ."

"My father wouldn't say a word," Paul snapped, and I couldn't remember when I last saw him so dark and angry. "If he did, he'd have to confess to the world what sins he committed. I'll make a good life for you, Ruby. Honest I will. I'm going to be a rich man, and I've got a prime piece of land on which to build my house. Maybe it won't be as fancy as the house you lived in in New Orleans, but . . ."

"Oh, it's not fancy houses or riches that I want, Paul. I told you once before that you should look to find yourself a wife with whom you can build your own family. You deserve your own family."

"You're my family, Ruby. You've always been my family."

I looked away so he wouldn't see the tears in my eyes. I didn't want to hurt him.

"Can't you love me without having children with me?" he asked. It sounded more like pleading.

"Paul, it's not only that . . ."

"You do love me, don't you?"

"I love you, Paul, but I haven't thought of you the way you want me to since . . . since we learned the truth about ourselves."

"But you might start again if you think about us in a different way," he said hopefully. "You're back here and . . ."

I shook my head.

"It's more than that then, isn't it?"

I nodded.

"You still love that Beau Andreas, even though he's made you pregnant and left you, don't you? Don't you?" he demanded.

"Yes, Paul, I guess I do."

He stared a moment and then sighed. "Well, it doesn't change things. I'll still be here for you all the time," he said firmly.

"Paul, don't make me feel sorry I came back."

"Of course I won't," he said. "Well, I'd better get home," he said and walked to the doorway. He paused and looked back at me. "You know what they're going to think anyway, don't you, Ruby?"

"What?"

"That the baby's mine," he said.

"I'll tell the truth when I have to," I said.

"They won't believe you," he insisted. "And as Rhett Butler said in *Gone With the Wind*, 'Frankly, my dear, I don't give a damn.' "

He laughed and walked out, leaving me more confused than ever, and more frightened than ever of what the future had in store.

I made myself at home again faster than I had thought possible. Within the week I was upstairs in the loom room, weaving cotton jaune into blankets to sell at the roadside stand. I wove palmetto leaves into palmetto hats and made split-oak baskets. I wasn't as good at cooking gumbo as Grandmere Catherine used to be, but I tried and made a passably good one to sell for lunches. I would work evenings and be out setting up the stand in the morning. Once in a while I thought about doing some painting, but for the time being I didn't have a spare moment. Paul was the first to point that out.

"You're working so hard at making what you need to eat and get by that you have no time to develop your talent, Ruby, and that's a sin," he said.

I didn't answer because I knew what he meant.

"We could have a good life together, Ruby. You would be a woman of means again, able to do the things you want to do. We'll have a nanny for the baby and —"

"Paul, don't," I begged. My lips trembled, and he changed the subject quickly, for if there was one thing Paul would never do it was make me cry, make me sad.

The weeks turned into months, and soon it felt like I had never left. Nights I would sit on the galerie and watch the occasional passing vehicles or look up at the moon and stars until Paul arrived. Sometimes he brought his harmonica and played a tune or two. If something sounded too mournful, he jumped up and played a lively number, dancing and making me laugh as he puffed out the notes.

Often I took walks along the canal, just the way I used to when I was growing up here. On moonlit nights the swamp's Golden Lady spider webs would glisten, the owls would hoot, and the 'gators would slip gracefully through the silky waters. Occasionally I would come across one sleeping on the shore and go cautiously around him. I knew he sensed my presence but barely opened his eyes.

It wasn't until the beginning of my fifth month that I began to show. No one said anything, but everyone's eyes lingered a long moment on my belly and I knew I had begun to be the topic of afternoon conversations everywhere. Finally I was visited by a delegation of women led by Grandmere Catherine's old friends Mrs. Thirbodeaux and Mrs. Livaudis. Mrs. Livaudis was apparently chosen to be their spokeswoman.

"Now Ruby, we've come here because you haven't got anyone to speak for you anymore," she began.

"I can speak for myself when I have to, Mrs. Livaudis."

"Maybe you can. Being Catherine Landry's granddaughter, I'm sure you can, but it don't hurt to have some of us old biddies squawking alongside you," she continued, and she nodded at the others, who nodded back, all of one determined face.

"Who are we to be speaking to, Mrs. Livaudis?"

"We'll be speaking to the man who's responsible," she said, nodding at me, "that's who. We all think we know who that young man is, too, and he comes from a family of substantial means in these here parts."

"I'm sorry, everyone," I said, "but the young man you're thinking about is not the father of my child."

Mouths dropped, eyes widened.

"Well, who is then?" Mrs. Livaudis asked. "Or can't you say?"

"It's someone who doesn't live here, Mrs. Livaudis. It's someone from New Orleans."

The women eyed each other, their faces now skeptical.

"You're not doing yourself or your baby any good to protect the father from his responsibilities, Ruby," Mrs. Thirbodeaux said. "Your grandmere wouldn't let you do such a thing, I assure you."

"I know she wouldn't," I said, smiling as I imagined Grandmere Catherine giving me a similar lecture.

"Then let us go with you and help you make the young man bear his share," Mrs. Livaudis said quickly. "If there is an ounce of decency in him, he'll do the right thing."

"I'm telling you the truth. He doesn't live here," I said as sincerely as I could, but they shook their heads and looked at me with pity in their eyes.

"We just want you to know, Ruby, that when it comes time to do what's right, we'll be with you," Mrs. Thirbodeaux said. "Do you want a doctor or a *traiteur?* There is a *traiteur* living just outside Morgan City who will come to see you."

The thought of going to some other *traiteur* besides Grandmere Catherine bothered me.

"I'll see the doctor," I told them.

"The bills should be paid by you know who," Mrs. Livaudis commented, shifting her eyes toward the others, who all nodded in firm agreement.

"I'll be all right," I promised them.

They left convinced that what they believed was the truth. Paul had been right, of course. He knew

501

our people better than I did. But this was my burden now, something I would have to live with and deal with on my own. Of course, I thought about Beau and wondered what, if anything, he had heard about me.

As if she heard my thoughts, Gisselle sent me a letter through Paul.

"This came this afternoon," he said, bringing the letter over. I was in the kitchen preparing a shrimp gumbo. I wiped my hands and sat down.

"My sister wrote to me?" I smiled with surprise and opened the envelope. Paul stood in the doorway, watching me read.

Dear Ruby,

Bet you never dreamed you'd receive a letter from me. The longest thing I ever wrote was that dumb English report on the old English poets, and even that was half written for me by Vicki.

Anyway, I found Paul's old letters in your closet when Daphne told me to go into your room and take anything I wanted before she gave the rest away to the needy. She had Martha Wood strip down your room and shut it up. She said as far as she was concerned, you never existed. Of course, she still has the problem of the will to face. I overheard her and Bruce talking about it one night and he told her to get you out of the will. It would take a lot of legal maneuvering and might upset their own apple cart, so for the time being, you're still a Dumas.

I know you're probably wondering why I'm writing from New Orleans. Well, guess what? Daphne gave in and let me come home and return to school here. Know why? Word of your pregnancy spread around the school. I wonder how? Anyway, it became disgraceful and Daphne couldn't stand that, especially when I started calling her night and day to tell her what the girls were saying, how the teachers were looking at me, what Mrs. Iron-wood thought. So she gave in and let me come home, where your secret is well kept.

Daphne's told everyone you just ran off to the bayou to live with your Cajuns because you missed them so much. Of course, people wonder about Beau.

"I bet you're wondering about him, huh?" she wrote at the bottom of the page, making it seem as if she wouldn't tell me anymore.

Just like Gisselle, I thought, teasing me even in a letter. I turned the paper over and found the rest.

Beau is still in France, where he is doing very well. Monsieur and Madame Andreas are telling everyone about his accomplishments and how he will be going to college there too. And it seems he is seeing a very wealthy French girl, someone whose family lineage goes back to Louis Napoleon.

I got a letter from him last month in which he begged me to tell him anything at all about you. I just wrote today and told him I don't know where you are. I told him I'm trying to find you by writing to one of our Cajun relatives, but I heard you might have gotten married in one of those ceremonies on a raft in the swamp with snakes and spiders at your feet.

Oh, I forgot. Before I left Greenwood, I had a visitor at the dorm. I bet you know who: Louis. He was very nice and very handsome. He was heartbroken to hear you had a baby coming and you had run off to live in the swamps with your Cajuns. He had a sheet of music he had hoped to send you, so I promised him if I ever find out where he should mail it, I would let him know.

But promises are made to be broken, aren't they?

Just joking. I don't know if I will ever hear from you again or if this letter will get to you. I hope it does and I hope you write back. It's sort of nice to have a notorious sister. I'm having loads of fun making up different stories about you.

Why didn't you just do what Daphne wanted and get rid of the baby? Look at what you gave up.

Your darling twin sister,
Gisselle

"Bad news?" Paul asked when I lay down the letter and sat back. Tears filled my eyes, but I smiled.

"You know how my sister is always trying to hurt me," I said through my tears.

"Ruby . . ."

"She makes things up; she just sits around and thinks . . . What would hurt Ruby the most? And then she writes it in the letter. That's all. That's what she's doing. That's all."

My tears flowed faster. Paul rushed to me and embraced me.

"Oh Ruby, my Ruby, don't cry. Please."

"It's all right," I said, catching my breath. "I'll be all right."

"She wrote something about him, didn't she?" Paul asked perceptively. I nodded. "It may not be a lie, Ruby."

"I know."

"I'm still here for you."

I looked up at him and saw that his face was full of love and sympathy for me. I probably wouldn't ever find anyone as devoted, but I couldn't agree to the arrangement he was proposing. It wouldn't be fair to him.

"I'll be fine. Thanks, Paul," I said, wiping away my tears.

"A young woman like you, alone here and pregnant," he muttered. "It worries me."

"You know everything's been fine," I said. He had taken me to see the doctor twice, which only added to the rumor that my child was his. In our small community, it didn't take long for people to find out the news, but he didn't care, even after I had told him what Grandmere Catherine's friends believed.

During the last half of my seventh month and the first half of my eighth, Paul was at my house every day, sometimes appearing more than once. It wasn't really until the eighth month that I started to grow real big and carry low. I never complained to him, but a couple of mornings he came upon me without my realizing he was present and he caught me moaning and groaning, my hands on my lower back. By this time I felt like a duck, because I waddled when I walked.

When the doctor told me he couldn't be exactly sure when I would give birth but that it would be sometime within the next week or so, Paul decided he would spend every night with me. I could always reach him or someone else during the day, but he was afraid of what could happen at night.

Early one afternoon at the beginning of my ninth month, Paul arrived, his face flushed with excitement.

"Everyone's saying we're going to be hit with a hurricane," he declared. "I want you to come to my house."

"Oh no, Paul. I can't do that."

"It's not safe here," he declared. "Look at the sky." He pointed to the dull red sunset caused by a thin haze of clouds. "You can practically smell it," he added. The air had become hot and sticky, and the little breeze we had had all day had all but died.

But I couldn't go to his house and be with his family. I was too ashamed and afraid of his father's and his mother's eyes. Surely they resented me for returning and creating all these rumors.

"I'll be all right here," I said. "We've been here for storms before."

"You're as stubborn as your grandpere," Paul said. He was angry with me, but I wouldn't budge. Instead, I went in and prepared some dinner for us. Paul went into his car to listen to the radio. The weathermen were making dire predictions. He came into the house and started to button down whatever he could. I set out two bowls of gumbo, but the moment we sat down, the wind began to howl something fierce. Paul looked out the rear of the house toward the canals and groaned. A dark storm cloud had appeared quickly, and the torrential rains could be seen approaching.

"Here she comes," he announced. After what seemed like only seconds later, the rain and the wind hit. Water poured down the roof and found every crack in the building. The wind lashed at the loose boards. We heard things lifted and thrown, some of them bashing against the house, slamming so hard into the walls we thought they would come clear through. I screamed and retreated to the living room, where I cowered on the sofa. Paul rushed about, closing up and tying down whatever openings he could, but the wind threaded itself right through the house, blowing things off shelves and counters and even turning over a chair. I thought the tin roof would lift away and in moments we would be exposed to the jaws of this raging storm.

"We should have left!" Paul cried. I was sobbing and holding myself. Paul gave up trying to tie anything down and came over to embrace me. We sat beside each other, holding each other and listening to the howling, thundering wind tear trees from their roots.

Suddenly, just as quickly as it had started, the storm stopped. A deadly calm fell over the bayou. The darkness lifted. I caught my breath and Paul got up to survey the damage. We both gazed out the window and shook our heads in shock at the sight of the trees that had been split. The world looked topsy-turvy.

And then Paul's eyes widened when the little patch of blue above us started to disappear.

"It was the eye of the storm," he declared. "Back, back . . ."

The tail of the storm reached us, ripping and howling like an angry giant creature. This time the house shook, walls cracked, and windows came splintering out, their shards of glass flying everywhere.

"Ruby, we've got to get under the house!" Paul screamed. The thought of going out terrified me. I pulled out of his arms and retreated toward the kitchen. But I stepped into a puddle that had formed under a leak in the roof and slipped. I fell face forward, just catching myself in time to prevent the floor from smashing into my nose. However, I did fall sharply on my stomach. The pain was excruciating. I turned over on my back and screamed and screamed. Paul was beside me quickly, trying to get me up.

"I can't, Paul. I can't . . ." I protested. My legs felt like lead, too heavy to bend or lift. He tried to pick me up, but I was a deadweight, I was too much for him, and he too had begun to slip and slide on the wet floor. And then I felt the sharpest pain of my life. It was as if someone had taken a knife and started to cut from my belly button down. I squeezed Paul's shoulder.

"Paul! The baby!"

His face was filled with abject terror. He turned toward the door as if he were considering going for help, realized how impossible that was, and turned back to me, just as my water broke.

"The baby's coming!"

The wind continued to twist the building. The tin roof groaned, and some of it loosened and slammed against the bracing.

"You've got to help me, Paul! It's too late!"

I was positive I would pass out and maybe even die on the floor of the shack. How could anyone endure such agony and live? I wondered. It came in waves of pain and tightness, the waves occurring closer and closer in time until I actually felt the baby moving. Paul knelt before me, his eyes so wide I thought they would burst. He shook his head in disbelief.

It got so I didn't even hear the storm or realize

it was still around us. I seemed to drift in and out of conscious, until finally I gave this great push and Paul exclaimed with delight. The baby was in his hands.

"It's a girl!" he cried. "A girl!"

The doctor had explained about the umbilical cord. I instructed Paul, and he cut and tied it. Then my baby started to wail. He placed her in my arms. I was still on the floor, and the storm, although diminished, remained around us, the rain pounding the house.

Paul brought me some pillows and I sat up to gaze down at the little face that was turned toward me, already searching for comfort and security and love.

"She's beautiful," Paul said.

The rain became a shower, the shower a sprinkle, and then the weak rays of the falling sun broke through the clouds and came through a window to drop the warm illumination over my baby and me. I covered her face with my kisses.

We had survived. We would go on together.

Epilogue

Remarkably, Grandmere Catherine's toothpick-legged shack had survived what everyone in the bayou was calling the worst storm in decades. Many others were not as lucky and had their homes swept away in the torrential rains and winds. The roads were strewn with broken tree limbs and branches. It looked like it would take days, if not weeks, to get things back to some semblance of normalcy.

But as soon as word of my baby's birth had spread, I was visited by Grandmere Catherine's friends, all bringing something I would need.

"What's her name?" Mrs. Livaudis asked.

"Pearl," I told them. And then I told them that I had once had a dream about my baby, and in the dream she had a complexion the color of a pearl. They all nodded, their eyes on the baby, their faces filled with understanding. After all, I was Catherine Landry's granddaughter. Mystical things were bound to happen to me.

Paul was at the house constantly, each day arriving with his arms full of things for the baby, as well as for me. He brought some of his employees from the factory with him the day after the storm and they went about repairing what they could. He was there tinkering about the building and grounds when the women were there.

"It's nice that he does all these things for you," Mrs. Thirbodeaux said, "but he should acknowledge his bigger responsibilities," she whispered. It did no good to protest and explain anymore, although I did feel sorry for Paul and his family. No matter how it looked, he refused to stay away.

In the evenings after dinner, I would sit in Grandmere Catherine's old rocker with Pearl in my arms and rock her to sleep. Paul would lay back on the floor of the galerie, his hands behind his head, a blade of grass in his mouth, and compliment me on how well I was taking care of the baby and cooking wonderful meals. I knew what he was up to, but I pretended I didn't.

One afternoon, a few weeks after Pearl's birth, Paul arrived with another letter from Gisselle. This one was much shorter but much more painful.

Dear Ruby,
    You haven't written back, but Paul has. I told Daphne where you are and that you had a baby now. She didn't want to hear a word. I was going to tell Beau as soon as I saw him, but I just learned that he is not coming back from Europe. He's staying there and going to college there to become a doctor.

And like I wrote before, he is in love with some daughter of some duke or count who lives in a real castle.

Daphne and Bruce have announced their wedding date. Wouldn't it be wild if you showed up with your baby in your arms! I'll keep you up on all the details. I know you're just dying to know about everything that happens here, even though you're pretending you don't care.

Why don't you write me back? I'll read your letter to Daphne. I just thought of something funny: Not only am I an aunt, but she's technically a grandmother. I'll remind her whenever she's unpleasant to me. Thanks. You finally did something I can appreciate.

Just kidding.

I wonder if we will ever see each other again.

> Your darling twin sister,
> Gisselle

"Why did you write to her, Paul?" I asked him.

"I thought your family should know about you and . . ."

"And you wanted Beau to know, didn't you?" I pursued. He shrugged. "It doesn't matter anymore," I said in a defeated voice.

"Then you're really home for good? You're going to stay?"

"Where else would I go? Would Pearl and I go?"

"Then let me make you a home here," he pleaded.

"I don't know, Paul," I said. "Let me think hard about it."

"Fine," he said, encouraged by the fact that I didn't say no immediately.

After he left me that night, I sat on the galerie and listened to the owl. Pearl was asleep inside, content and safe for now. But I had come a long way to make a full circle, and I knew that the world was not a soft place in which to cuddle forever. It was hard and cold, cruel and filled with tragic possibilities. It was good to have someone to look after you, to protect you, to keep you warm and safe. How could it be a sin to want that and have it, if not for myself, then for my baby? I thought.

Grandmere, I whispered. Give me a sign. Help me make the right choices, go down the right roads now.

The owl stopped its hooting when a marsh hawk swooped down and landed in front of the house. It strutted about for a moment and then turned toward me. In the moonlight I could see its yellow-circled eyes fixed on me. It lifted its wings as if to greet me, and then as quickly as it had come, it flew off into the darkness where, I knew, it perched itself on a branch and continued to watch the house, watch me and watch my baby.

And I knew in my heart that Grandmere Catherine was here with me, whispering in the breeze, filling me with hope. I would make the right decisions.

We hope you have enjoyed this Large Print book. Other G.K. Hall & Co. or Chivers Press Large Print books are available at your library or directly from the publishers. For more information about current and upcoming titles, please call or write, without obligation, to:

G.K. Hall & Co.
P.O. Box 159
Thorndike, Maine 04986
USA
Tel. (800) 223-6121 (U.S. & Canada)
In Maine call collect: (207) 948-2962

OR

Chivers Press Limited
Windsor Bridge Road
Bath BA2 3AX
England
Tel. (0225) 335336

All our Large Print titles are designed for easy reading, and all our books are made to last.